Theodore Vogel

A Century of Discovery

biographical sketches of the Portuguese and Spanish navigators from Prince Henry

to Pizarro

Theodore Vogel

A Century of Discovery
biographical sketches of the Portuguese and Spanish navigators from Prince Henry to Pizarro

ISBN/EAN: 9783337294946

Printed in Europe, USA, Canada, Australia, Japan

Cover: Foto ©Andreas Hilbeck / pixelio.de

More available books at **www.hansebooks.com**

CONTENTS.

PART I.—THE PORTUGUESE.

PART II.—THE SPANIARDS.

BIOGRAPHICAL SKETCHES

OF THE PORTUGUESE AND SPANISH NAVIGATORS
FROM PRINCE HENRY TO PIZARRO.

TRANSLATED FROM THE GERMAN

OF

THEODORE VOGEL

D. APPLET[...]AY.

A

CENTURY OF DISCOVERY.

PART I.—THE PORTUGUESE.

CHAPTER I.

INTRODUCTORY.

IN the rugged mountain tract which separates the arid table-land of central Spain from the humid coast of the Bay of Biscay we trace the origin of the modern states of the Pyrenean peninsula. Into this wild and scarcely accessible region, which occupies the whole north-west corner of the peninsula, and lies among the Cantabrian Mountains,.a thousand Christian families fled before the wild storm of Arabs which in 711 destroyed at Xeres de la Frontera the kingdom of the West Goths, and forthwith inundated the whole peninsula. Thus was formed the Christian state of Asturias, which still enjoys peculiar rights among the Spanish provinces. From it the Crown Princes of Spain have been used to take their title, and its inhabitants boast with genuine Spanish arrogance that they, whose soil the foot of the Moslem has never trodden, are the noblest of all the Spaniards.

From mere defence the Asturians soon proceeded to direct attacks upon the invaders, and during the following centuries the neighbouring states, by dint of never-ceasing struggles, were gradually recovered by the Christians. It was usual in

I

those days for a territory to be divided on the death of a prince, and out of repeated divisions and reunions two kingdoms at length arose at the beginning of the eleventh century. In the east was Arragon, with its capital, Saragossa, first wrested from the Arabs in 1130, comprising also Catalonia, and later on Navarre; and in the west, Castile, to which belonged Gallicia, Asturias, and Leon.

King Alfonso VI. of Castile, in the year 1094, gave the land between the Douro and the Minho as a fief to Count Henry of Burgundy, a prince of the Capetian dynasty, who came over the Pyrenees at the head of a large train of followers in order to stand by his brethren in the faith in their struggle with the infidel. With the territory the King also bestowed the hand of his daughter upon the young prince, in the hope of thus binding him closely to the cause of the Spanish Christians. The territory received the name of Portugal from its most important harbour, Porto Cale, now called Oporto, and the young state devoted itself most zealously to the national task—the driving of the Arabs from the Spanish soil. The accomplishment of this task was specially looked for from the spiritual orders of knighthood, and, in imitation of the Castilian Orders of St. Jago of Compostella, Calatrava, and Alcantara, there arose in Portugal the Order of Aviz. Gloriously did the Portuguese kings henceforth share in the struggle against the Moors. But as time went on they sought more and more to direct the attention of their people to the neighbouring coast of Africa, and so to make the enthusiasm of the Portuguese for a religious war serviceable for the extension of their territory. Though with no great result, the expeditions against Ceuta and Tangier scarcely ceased from the beginning of the fourteenth century, and they had a favourable effect upon the Castilian and Arragonese conquests, inasmuch as they occupied the Moslems of Morocco in their own land and hindered them from supporting their brethren in Spain.

But more important than all was the fact that Portugal gradually awoke to a consciousness of the value of its position on the main ocean. The ancient highway of commerce from the Mediterranean to the North Sea had never been completely forgotten since those times when bold Punic seamen first discovered it. But in the night which settled over these shores during the irruption of the northern nations the intercourse ceased, and its timid recommencement at the time of the Carlovingians was suppressed by the piracies of the Normans and Danes. At last these wild forces raged themselves out, and a more orderly state of things together with a certain culture took the place of confusion. During the Crusades many a ship, full of warlike Netherlanders, who had devoted their arms to the service of the Holy Sepulchre, took the old road to the Mediterranean. The Portuguese too many times found valuable allies against the Arabs in these brave and enthusiastic northern crusaders. But this route was not made use of as a highway for commerce until a new centre of industry and of trade sprang up in the Flemish towns of Antwerp, Bruges, and, above all, Ghent. Between them and the great Italian republics that traded in the productions of the east the commerce was soon so important that the thrifty Genoese and Venetians exchanged the troublesome and expensive land route over the Alps and down the Rhine for the comfortable and far cheaper way by sea through the Straits of Gibraltar. As early as the year 1318 the Venetians sent five ships to the fair at Antwerp, and from year to year the number of the ships increased. This commerce was of the greatest use to Portugal. All voyages were then made by creeping round the coast, and this continued to be the case until the middle of the fifteenth century, when the astrolabe was introduced, which enabled ships on the open sea to make something like a correct calculation with regard to latitude and longitude. In the voyage between Flanders and Italy, as long as it was the custom to keep close to the shore, the harbour of Lisbon, which lay about half way, formed a welcome resting-place into which ships seldom failed to run. In fact, this harbour was so much frequented that in the time of King Ferdinand, who ruled from 1367 to 1383, four hundred and fifty merchant-ships might often be counted in it. In shipbuilding too the Portuguese soon acquired such skill that they outdid their teachers, and the Portuguese quick-sailing vessels, called caravels, acquired a fame which they well deserved. A caravel was a particularly round ship with a square stern. It had two masts and carried four three-cornered sails, and was armed like a galley; and the persevering efforts of the Portuguese kings to construct a caravel that should carry cannon, without sacrifice of speed, were at length successful.

The rapid growth of this little state soon secured it a great name, and gave rise to many fables about the riches of the Portuguese. It is certain that at the accession of King Ferdinand the treasury of Lisbon contained, besides other coins and things of value, 800,000 gold pieces and 400,000 marks of silver—an enormous sum for those days.

King Ferdinand, whose weak and disorderly government swallowed up the treasure, was the last of his house. His early death in 1383 called up many claimants for the crown, above all the King of Castile, who coveted the possession of a land so rich, lying on the borders of his own. But the half-brother of the late King, John the Bastard, gained a glorious victory over the foreigner at Aljubarrota, four miles from Lisbon, where he afterwards founded the splendid Abbey of · Batalha, the fine ruins of which are still standing. It was a burdensome inheritance on which the young Prince entered, and it cost him long years and much pains before the prosperity of the land, ruined by the misrule of Ferdinand, was restored. However, the prudence and energy of the young

Prince succeeded at last in healing the wounds of the land. But his predecessor had left behind another inheritance in which the glorious future of Portugal was bound up, and upon which John and his whole family entered with hope and zeal —Africa and the Ocean.

CHAPTER II.

KING JOHN I., the Bastard, had by his marriage with Philippa
of Lancaster five noble sons, all of whom deserved well of
their country. Henry, the third of these brothers, born on
the 4th of March, 1394, became grand master of the Order
of Christ, which King Dionysius had founded after the suppression of the Templars and endowed with their great wealth
—wealth which, according to the rules of the new foundation,
was to be employed for the extension of Christendom. It
may have been this stipulation which first turned the attention
of the young Prince to the wide field which Africa presented
to his desire to spread the faith that he professed. When, on
investigating the matter, he found how exceedingly contradictory and full of fable was all the geographical knowledge then
possessed of that quarter of the world, it awoke in him an
ardent desire to lift the veil and win for his country the great
prize which this enterprise offered. The year 1415 was decisive
in this matter. In this year King John, accompanied by his
three eldest sons, proceeded with a fleet to the fortified town
of Ceuta, which lies on the north coast of Africa, opposite to
Gibraltar. After a gallant defence, Ceuta was taken by storm
and plundered : and of the three Princes who won their spurs
that day, Henry especially exhibited extraordinary bravery.
Ceuta remained in the hands of the Portuguese, and became
the key to Africa. From that day forward Henry decided to
make the investigation of that as yet unknown portion of the

world the task of his life, and for this the newly-conquered town offered a good starting-point. In order to be as near as possible to his field of labour, he afterwards removed his residence to the Castle of Terçanabal in Algarve, which he had built for himself on the Bay of Sagres. Here he spent nearly half a century in retirement, far from the splendour of the court, poring over nautical charts and books of travel, and with the most intense earnestness following every step that was made in the investigation of Africa by the Portuguese expeditions, which were all either undertaken at his expense, or at any rate greatly assisted by him. Admirable, indeed, is the quiet patience which he opposed to the mocking scepticism of his contemporaries and the want of success which fell to his lot for many years, until at the end of his life he saw his efforts crowned with the highest success, and a path of glory opened to his native land.

The current opinion of learned men about Africa was that only the north coast of that continent was habitable, and that farther south the land that lay under the tropics was burnt up by the vertical rays of the sun, and was unsuitable for all animal and vegetable life. This theory, which the great Alexandrian geographer Ptolemy, following a suggestion of Aristotle, had put forth, was held by all Arabian and European savants of the Middle Ages as incontrovertible, and found confirmation, as it appeared, in the band of desert land which begins a few miles south of the shores of the Mediterranean Sea, and which was regarded as a passage to the completely desolate region of the tropics. South of that fearful desert it was thought there might be a tract covered with vegetation and providing man and beast with the means of subsistence. This was the opinion of the Roman poet Ovid, who, in his account of the Creation, says, "The middle one of the five zones is uninhabitable on account of its heat, the two extreme ones are covered with deep snow, but to the two zones which God has placed between these He has given an endurable climate by means of a mixture of heat and cold.

In the southern temperate zones was supposed to be the dwelling-place of our antipodes, the existence of which, however, orthodox savants, following the opinion of St. Augustine, denied.

But how penetrate to these happy regions? Only in East Africa did it appear possible, where the sacred Nile, breaking through the desert, rendered the passage practicable, which, farther west, was barred by the impenetrable waste. Following the Nile upwards, according to the opinion of the time, a glorious land was reached which formed the junction between the two temperate zones, and therefore was specially favoured by Nature, and appeared destined to rule the world. No wonder that the passion for strange stories and the love of the marvellous, which characterised the Middle Ages, should have made the most of such inviting materials. Wonderful things were related of this land, the inhabitants of which belonged to the Christian religion, and under the rule of a priestly King, Prester John, enjoyed an eternal peace and almost supernatural happiness. This marvellous tradition, which pointed to the highlands of Abyssinia, whose inhabitants had already become Christians in the fourth century, long possessed the minds even of educated men, and for centuries there were not wanting people who recognised in every newly-discovered land of the East the fabulous kingdom of Prester John, even if it only bore in some slight degree a resemblance to that land of marvels.

Even Prince Henry had fallen into the popular delusion that the region of the tropics was uninhabitable, until the investigations which he made personally in Ceuta, and by agents in Tunis, awoke doubt in his mind. He learnt that in Morocco, as well as in Tunis, a regular commerce was carried on with lands which lay on the other side of the great desert.

He learnt that caravans traversed that uninhabited region in thirty-seven days, and that they brought to the shores of the Mediterranean gold, ivory, and slaves. Lastly, he learnt that south of that belt of sand there were races that differed from the northern Africans, in that they had black skins and woolly hair; that there were large towns in these territories, such as Timbuctoo, Ghagho, and Kantor, and powerful kingdoms, among which those of Melli and Gana are most frequently mentioned. The latter, which the Portuguese miscalled Guinea, was, according to the report of the traders, the most western of all the central African kingdoms, and extended to the ocean.

These reports had, indeed, before this reached the Italian republics, and had called forth isolated attempts on the part of the Genoese and Venetians to reach by sea the land of the blacks; but the small success of these expeditions had soon discouraged them. It is the distinguishing merit of Prince Henry that he resumed these attempts with fresh vigour, and made use of the singularly favourable position of Portugal for this purpose. That the received opinion about the great distance between the two temperate zones was founded on gross exaggeration, he decided from certain information which he obtained about the length of a caravan journey from Morocco to the Soudan. He considered that the journey might be made from Portugal in the same time by sea, if the west coast of Africa were followed towards the south. This, therefore, was the next task which Prince Henry set himself, and he took it up with a fiery zeal.

But here hindrances met him which appeared almost insurmountable. Uncomfortable reports were current about the nature of the coast and sea, reports which had first been set afloat by the Phenician and Carthaginian merchants. These crafty traders had sought to monopolise the source of their most important commodities, tin, amber, ivory, gum, &c.,

by spreading the most exaggerated and very often most absurd tales about the dangers which awaited the foolhardy navigator outside the Pillars of Hercules, if he sailed either northward towards the tin-producing islands, or southward to the hot lands where the black men dwelt. For a long time all the Carthaginian stories about the northern seas had been recognised as fables, for, with the fall of the Roman empire, the centre of the civilised world had moved northwards; but the faith in the horrible stories which had been related about the coast of Africa was in no wise shaken. On the contrary, they were received even by the learned as of undoubted authority. On the coast of what is now called Morocco, the boldest seamen did not venture farther south than Cape Non, for the proverb said, "He who sails around Cape Non (Not) either will return or not." At that point was supposed to begin the sea of horrors, full of dangerous rocks and shallows. The heat of the sun was said to evaporate the water, so that the sea became more and more salt the farther south you advanced, until at last it became such a dense mass that no ship could cut through it. A constant calm prevented any escape, and the evaporated water lay like a thick mist over the sea.

The restless popular fancy had also erected here magnetic mountains which attracted every particle of iron, and thus caused any ships which came into their neighbourhood to fall to pieces. Of course there was no lack of horrible monsters in the sea and giants on the land, who both lay wait for the poor castaway seaman. And such fables were not mere popular superstitions, but were treated of seriously in scientific works.

It was therefore an important result when, in the first expedition which Prince Henry fitted out in order to reach Guinea, a part of these superstitious fears were found to be groundless. In the year 1415—the year of the taking of Ceuta—he sent out two more caravels, under the command of resolute Portuguese captains, with the express order to double Cape Non, and to penetrate as far as possible towards the south. The promontory which had been so much dreaded was discovered to be perfectly safe, and the voyage along the barren and uninhabited shore was prosperously made until, about sixty miles beyond Cape Non, an obstacle was encountered which put an end to the farther progress of the vessels. This consisted of a rocky peninsula, which stretched far into the sea, and from which a reef extended for six miles. The ocean here dashed with such boisterous violence against the shore that the courage of the sailors sank, and they declared it utterly impossible to sail round the cape, which was called Cape Bojador, from "bojar," to jut out.

Prince Henry would not for a moment entertain the idea of abandoning his design, and the next year sent out many ships, with orders to sail round this point; but not one could fulfil the task. So low was nautical science still in Portugal that none of the captains would venture to steer the few miles out into the open sea which were necessary in order to overcome the obstacle. They each clung in a craven manner to the coast. A mere accident gave for a time another direction to Prince Henry's energy.

A caravel, which he had sent out in the year 1419 to sail round Cape Bojador, was caught by a storm before it reached its goal, and driven far out into the open sea towards the west. When the storm abated, the sailors found themselves on the coast of an uninhabited island, which they christened Porto Santo. It was one of the Madeira Islands which they had hit upon, an island that had some years previously been discovered by some Italian sailors, but which had been almost forgotten again.

The next year the larger sister island was discovered, and taken possession of. Its Portuguese discoverers called it St. Lawrence, as they discovered it on St. Lawrence's day ; but after a time it received the name which it now bears of Madeira, which means the woody island. The whole island was covered with thick forests, which, if we may believe the statements of the Portuguese, consisted principally of cedars.

As soon as the Prince was informed of these discoveries— the importance of which he could well appreciate—he made preparations to people the newly-acquired lands, and to render their productions useful. With the consent of the King, he placed the islands under three governors, and called upon his countrymen to emigrate to those fruitful lands whose virgin soil promised a rich reward to the cultivator.

At the foundation of the little town of Funchal, on the south coast of Madeira—which is still the capital of the group—a part of the primeval forest was set on fire. The fire spread, and burnt, according to some, for seven, according to others, for nine years, and consumed all the timber of the island. Now the island is poor in timber. The richness of soil, so lavishly manured by the ashes of the conflagration, was inconceivable. The corn bore at first sixtyfold ; the sugar-cane, transplanted thither from Sicily, brought forth a rich harvest ; and the vine, which, by the Prince's care, was brought from Cyprus, produced that wine to which the island owes so much of its fame.

The zealous care which the Prince devoted to the newly-discovered Archipelago was richly repaid to him, for as he had fitted out and despatched the expedition, he received the fifth part of all the revenues of the islands, and with the sums which in this way flowed into the treasury of the Order of Christ he could defray the expenses of new undertakings. Afterwards the islands of Madeira, Porto Santo, and Diserta were made over to the Prince by his brother, King Edward, as his own possession, with all their revenues, and with the penal and civil jurisdiction. All the spiritualities were presented to the Order of Christ.

Under Henry's government the population rapidly increased, and it now numbers about 100,000 inhabitants, principally of Portuguese descent. The once flourishing wine trade has been almost ruined by the grape disease, which first made its appearance some years ago, and spread rapidly. In its palmiest days the island produced 15,000 pipes of wine, on which the Portuguese state laid heavy duties. Now the plains are covered with sugar-canes, which form the most important article of export; and very recently attempts have been made to re-introduce the cultivation of the vine. The splendid climate of Madeira has caused it to be chosen as a winter residence for people suffering from pulmonary diseases.

The promising development of the young colony caused the Prince to turn his attention to the neighbouring group of the Canary Islands, and excited in him the wish to gain them also for Portugal. These islands, which had never been quite forgotten, lie not far from the African coast, opposite Cape Non. It was here the old Greeks and Romans placed the happy islands of the Hesperides; it was here that a venerable tradition of the Middle Ages pointed out the island of the holy Brandon; and it was in this direction, at the beginning of the fourteenth century, that the first Venetian and Genoese fleets that ventured into the open sea directed their course. Portuguese ships had in 1335 brought to Lisbon men and goods stolen from these islands, and the name—which is said to mean "the rediscovered islands"—clearly points out that an earlier knowledge of them had existed.

In the bull issued from Avignon on the 15th of November, 1344, the Pope, in virtue of his assumed supremacy over all lands, granted the island to the Spanish Prince Louis de la Cerda, who, however, was prevented by death from entering on his lordship. In the second half of the fourteenth century the islands were now and again visited, partly for the purposes of gain, that is, to carry off slaves and to procure dragon's blood and orchil (a dye) from the inhabitants, and partly with the object of converting them to Christianity.

Of all the islands on the coast of Africa, the Canaries were the only ones that were peopled. From the scanty descriptions and vocabularies which the discoverers have handed down to us, we may conclude that there was some relationship between the Guanches—so the inhabitants were called—and the people of the Atlas Mountains. How the migration from Africa took place is a riddle, for it is certain that when the Europeans arrived ships were unknown to the inhabitants, and from want of boats the intercourse between island and island was so small that the language of one island was not always understood by the people of another. The Guanches are said to have had tall athletic frames, were bright coloured, and had long fair hair; and this description has been confirmed by the numerous mummies found in the sepulchres of the islands.

Their clothing was very scanty, and their dwellings were either rude stone huts or the caves which had been formed in great numbers by the upheaving of the basalt. Herbs, roots, meal, and the milk and flesh of their flocks served for their food. The use of fermented liquors was unknown to them. Their tools also were clumsy; and since they had no iron, they were forced to be content with wood and stone, both for implements of industry and for arms. Cattle and goats appear to have been numerous in all the islands; but the cultivation of corn was only carried on in those most favoured by Nature—Teneriffe and Canary. On these the number of the inhabitants was relatively great (Teneriffe is represented as having 6000 fighting men, and Canary still more), and the people too showed a great superiority over those of the other islands in civil and social development.

Canary was divided into two kingdoms, and each of the Kings had to assist him a council of 190 men, chosen from the noblest families. The people of Teneriffe were divided into many tribes, each with its chief at its head. The division into the nobility, the common people, and a despised class, to whom fell the unclean occupation of slaughtering cattle and goats, appears to have been common to all. Side by side with the civil nobility, there was a priestly class, which possessed considerable political influence. The position of the high-priest of Canary is compared by the Spanish chronicler to that of a Christian bishop, and he possessed the power of examining into the claims of warriors who aspired to be made nobles. Besides priests, priestesses are mentioned.

With regard to the religion of this remarkable people, there are but few indications, which, however, tend to the conclusion that the faith in a Creator of all things, who rewards the good and punishes the wicked, was universal; but that in particular islands special divinities were also honoured. The dead—at least, the illustrious dead—were embalmed, and, wrapped in skins, were placed in holes and caves. Great praise is bestowed on the manners and customs of these Guanches, and many incidents of their short history place them in a bright light, to which the faithless cruelty of the Europeans forms a very ugly contrast. They came confidingly to meet the strangers, and the treaties concluded with them they never broke. To shed blood needlessly appeared to them a most shameful crime. Captives taken by them in war they never killed, but included them in the lowest class. They were passionately devoted to song and dance; but their favourite occupation was the exercise of arms, which they practised in great tournaments. Even the European conquerors feared their obstinate gallantry, although to the muskets and lances of the Spaniards they could only oppose wooden clubs, slings, and spears with points made of horn. Thus the Guanches appear like the remains of a favoured race, once acquainted with a higher civilisation, but, from long isolation, gradually degraded to the condition of savages, though still retaining certain

social regulations and elevated tastes, like noble ruins in the
midst of a deserted plain.

It was the hope of conquering these islands, and bringing
their inhabitants over to the faith, which caused the Norman
nobleman Jean de Béthencourt, of the castle Grainville la
Teinturière, in the Pays de Caux, to embark from La Rochelle,
on the 1st of May, 1402, in a very good vessel, well provisioned and manned. Such is the story of the Franciscan
Boutier and the secular Le Verrier, who accompanied the
adventure-loving nobleman as attendants, and have written a
full account of the whole undertaking. The knight Gadifer
de la Salle, an adventurer, joined him. On the way, in
Corunna and Seville, where they lay to, they had to overcome difficulties raised by the rebellious spirit of the Gascon
and Norman seamen. After a short voyage from Seville,
they reached the Canary Islands, and the two knights took
possession of those which lay most to the north-west. On
the most northerly—Lanceroto, which took its name from a
Genoese, Lancelot Maloysel, its first discoverer, they built a
fortress, to which they gave the significant name of Rubicon.
But the small number of their forces made the subjugation of
the inhabitants impossible ; and so Béthencourt returned, in
order to procure assistance from Europe. Gadifer remained
behind to take his place, but was soon reduced to the utmost
extremity by a conspiracy, which was formed by his subordinate, Berthin de Berneval.

This traitor embarked on board a Spanish ship with twenty
of the inhabitants, whom he had kidnapped and thought to
sell as slaves, and left Gadifer and his men behind in the utmost
need, as he carried off with him all their provisions. From this
unpleasant situation, which was made worse by the hostility
of the embittered Guanches, Gadifer was extricated at last
by the return of Béthencourt, who had paid homage to King
Henry II. of Castile, as his feudal lord, hoping thus to secure

a generous support. The subjugation of the island was then speedily accomplished, and the inhabitants constrained to receive Christianity, the King himself being baptised by the chaplain, Le Verrier, and receiving the name of Louis. More difficult was the subjugation of the neighbouring island, Erbania, or Fuerteventura, the capital of which still bears the name of Bethencuria. It was only accomplished after a year's hard struggle, with the support of the baptised Guanches of Lancerote, and by a sagacious use of the discord between the two races which inhabited the island—a discord so bitter that the weaker race had built a wall for their defence right across the island.

After the arrival of new colonists from Normandy, Béthencourt proceeded with the exploration and conquest of the rest of the Canary Islands. But here he was not fortunate. He suffered seriously in his conflicts with the gallant Guanches, and could only establish a firm footing in the island of Ferro. During these various expeditions he touched on the coast of Africa south of Cape Bojador, and his biographers have much to relate of the plans that he had formed for further discoveries in this part of the world. Promising soon to return, and making his nephew, Maciot, governor, he left the islands and set sail for Rome, in order to make arrangements for the spiritual welfare of his newly-converted subjects. At his request, Pope Innocent VII. created a new bishopric for the Canary Islands, and made Albert de Maison the first bishop. He took up his residence in Rubicon, being under the Archbishop of Seville. From Rome Béthencourt turned towards his home, and there, in the year 1425, he died, without accomplishing his promised return to the Canary Islands.

Even before the death of this worthy knight, whose religious zeal had been considerably influenced by selfishness and love of adventure, his nephew had found it impossible to retain his hold over the islands. He had not sufficient authority to control the community, and the irregularity of the supplies which he received from his uncle caused considerable suffering to the colonists, and endangered the existence of the settlement. Added to this, he had to encounter the opposition of the Guanches and the raids of the Spanish corsairs.

These were sufficient reasons to make Maciot de Béthencourt tired of such an unprofitable undertaking, and he entered into a negotiation with Prince Henry, and gave him the Canary Islands in exchange for territories in Madeira. Greatly pleased at the important acquisition, Henry in 1424 sent out a strong force to receive the islands from Maciot. He could not, however, conquer the larger islands of Canary, Teneriffe, and Palma, all attempts being frustrated by the gallant defence of the natives; and before the Prince could send reinforcements, the King of Castile stepped in with a claim upon the whole Archipelago in virtue of the homage rendered to him by the elder Béthencourt. Considering the expense and difficulty which the conquest of the islands would cost, Prince Henry relinquished them on the payment of a considerable sum of money.

The Castilians contented themselves at that time with the possession of the islands Langerote, Fuerteventura, and Ferro, which had already been conquered and colonised. It was not until the middle of the century that they began the conquest of the other island, and it took them about fifty years fully to accomplish it. Unfortunately, only imperfect and one-sided accounts of this tedious struggle have come down to us, but it is clear even from them that it was a desperate war, the Guanches defending their liberty to the utmost against a better armed enemy, and the Castilians giving proofs of that gloomy, though chivalrous, fanaticism and that utter want of feeling which were afterwards so terribly shown by their conduct in the New World. Many times, even in this unequal struggle, they encountered serious defeats. For instance, the celebrated Alonso de Sago, who finally conquered the island, and who is known to us by the name of Adelantado, was often unfortunate in his contests with them. Thus, in the year 1493, he was allured into an ambush in the mountains by King Benchomo, and lost eight hundred of the one thousand men whom he commanded. In the middle of the battle, say the Spanish historians, Benchomo came into the field and saw his brother, who was wounded by a lance, sitting on one side of the ravine. "What!" said the King, "resting while your soldiers are fighting?" "I have conquered," was the answer, "and have fulfilled my duty as commander. Now my 'soldiers are doing theirs : they are slaying." But this victory at Acentejo was the last day of glory for a people worthy of a better fate. Unheard-of misfortunes followed. Returning in 1496 with new forces, the Adelantado overthrew the Guanches of Tene-riffe, on whom fortune had turned her back. The treaty then sworn to by the Spaniards was not kept, Benchomo was lured on to a ship and taken as a rare animal to Spain, thence to Rome and Venice in order to show him to the Pope and the Doge. In Venice he died. The unhappy islanders were pursued into their most inaccessible hiding-places. Many threw themselves down from the rocks, and died martyrs to a cause they could no longer defend ; others fell with weapons in their hands ; many were sold as slaves ; and the survivors, mingling with new colonists who streamed into the fruitful land, adopted their religion and language. In the whole island there has been nobody for a hundred years who could boast of a pure descent from the Guanches. But if as a people they have passed away, the remembrance of their deeds is lovingly cherished in the land, and the attention of the traveller who climbs the peak of Teneriffe is drawn by the guide to many spots rendered famous by the death-struggles of the Guanches.

After the failure of the attempt to gain the Canary Islands

for Portugal, Prince Henry turned his attention principally to the government of Madeira, which quickly began to flourish. But he did not relinquish his plans to penetrate into the kingdom of Guinea and the land of the blacks. The next thing to be done was to induce the Portuguese to give up the custom of sailing close to the coast, and to inspire them with the courage and knowledge which a voyage in the open sea demanded. With this object he summoned from Majorca the learned Master Jacob, who was celebrated not only for his skill in seamanship, but also in drawing maps and constructing astronomical intruments. Probably Henry himself did something in the way of preparing charts, hence called Portulano ; at any rate he strove by example to inspire the Portuguese with a desire for geographical and nautical knowledge. Just at this time occurred the return of his elder brother, Pedro, a prince whom in later years all the great services which he had rendered to his country were powerless to protect from shameful calumny and a miserable end. His thirst for knowledge had driven him into distant lands. Knowing and sharing his brother's tastes, he brought him from Venice a valuable gift, a manuscript account of the travels of Marco Polo, that bold Venetian who, in the latter part of the thirteenth century, had experienced the most strange adventures in Central and East Asia, and had drawn up a map in which the supposed form of Africa was depicted, together with all the known or imagined islands of the world. This gave a higher flight to the plans and designs of Prince Henry. Guinea, which had hitherto been the end and aim of his hopes, now was looked upon by him merely as a midway station, and behind, in the bright distance, there arose a vision of the earthly Paradise—the Indies.

The products of the Indies—that region so singularly favoured by Nature—had always found a ready market in Europe, and at every period when the intercourse between the East and the West had been reopened the demand for Indian wares had increased ; when, for instance, Alexander the Great, on the wings of victory, entered and Hellenised the East ; when the Romans made conquests on the banks of the Euphrates and Tigris ; and when the Arabs arose to subdue lands and found kingdoms. At the time this intercourse seemed likely to be limited, or indeed entirely interrupted by the advances of the Turks—who understood only too well how to crush the civilisation which they found, but were utterly unable to substitute another—the crusades began and brought about so close a connection between the East and the West that the trade in Indian wares received a powerful impulse. Stuffs, such as silk and cotton ; spices, such as pepper, cinnamon, ginger, and cloves ; precious things, such as gold, ivory, gems, and pearls, soon became indispensable to the luxury of Northern and Western Europe. The commerce between Europe and the East lay in the hands of some of the commercial republics of Italy. Instinctively had Venice, the city of the lagoons, expended her strength in the crusades, and found a rich reward in the trading privileges which were conferred on her citizens in Syria and the Byzantine empire.

An envious rival to Venice was Genoa, which, after the suppression of Pisa, assumed a ruling position in the western portion of the Mediterranean, continually seeking by a greater activity and a more cunning diplomacy to surpass her. For centuries did these two mighty states contend, and the scene of their conflict was the coasts of the Black and Ægean Seas, the imperial palace of Constantinople, and the seraglios of Turkish and Arabian potentates. The renewed advances of the Turks in the fifteenth century closed the harbours of the Black Sea and Asia Minor to the Venetians and Genoese, and henceforth the Indian traffic was carried on with a more complete exclusiveness through Egypt and Syria. With the Mameluke sultans who ruled these lands from Cairo, the two naval states had been from the earliest times on the most friendly terms. The frequent prohibitions which the Pope had issued against all intercourse with the infidel rulers of Egypt had remained without effect, doubtless because they were opposed to the singular advantages to be reaped from intercourse with the East, and even the chair of St. Peter had not been altogether insensible to the golden benefits to be derived from the flourishing Egyptian traffic.

The extraordinary commerce which was carried on in the beautiful valley of the Nile brought new life to that ancient land. The trade itself was considerable, consisting principally in Indian wares brought by Arab sailors from India to Suez, or other harbours of the Red Sea, and from thence to Alexandria, the centre of the Levant commerce. The yearly value of the trade of the Venetians in Alexandria alone was, according to certain information, at least 600,000 ducats. But its real worth was far greater than this. The Italian traders took advantage of their monopoly, and gained a profit of 100 per cent. on the Indian wares. Upper Italy and the Venetian territory alone, according to an official report made by the Doge, Thomas Mocenizo, to the Signoria (the great council of Venice) in the year 1420, yearly received 50,000 cwt. of cotton, worth 250,000 ducats; 520 bales of cinnamon, at 160 ducats a bale ; 3400 loads of pepper, at 100 ducats a load ; 3000 cwt. of ginger; more than 1000 cwt. of sugar, at an average of 15 ducats for 100 lbs. And still greater was the sale of these Indian wares in Germany, whither the Venetians sent their great trading expeditions. Indeed, this traffic, like a magic wand, spread life and prosperity wherever it touched. Trieste, Bozen, Sterzing, Mittenwald, flourished as intermediate stations of the Venetian and Genoese trade, while Augsburg was its centre, and through it attained that high point of power and authority which rendered it such a happy example of German city life in its richest and noblest development. In a similar manner London flourished in England, and Ghent and Antwerp in Flanders, though none of all these towns could rival the splendour of Venice. /

On the Grand Canal stood those costly palaces whose fairy-like splendour is yet reflected in the desolate waters. The churches, filled with the trophies of eastern victories, were adorned by Titian and Paul Veronese. The market-place and the Riva dei Schiavoni were full of life, and picturesque with bright costumes. Like Paris now, Venice was then the oracle of fashion ; it was the goal to which pleasure-seekers most frequently turned their steps, and it was the best school for grace of manner, and for learning the most refined method of enjoying life. Around its venerable Doges, who ruled not only Venice itself, but the kingdoms of Cyprus, Morea, Candia, and a great part of Dalmatia and the valley of the Po, stood the most experienced diplomatists of all the states of Europe, who indeed looked upon this central point of the world's industry, where the threads of eastern and western life were twined together, as their highest school. And all this glory stood upon the foundation of the trade with India.

But whilst this flood of prosperity was filling the city in the lagoons, far in the west by the waves of the ocean a solitary man was brooding over a scheme which was to put an end to all this glory, destroy the foundation on which it rested, and turn to his own land the current of fortune which had been exclusively hers. The plans of the Prince soared ever higher and higher. The representation of Africa given him by the Venetian chart may not have resembled very closely the real form of that continent ; but, at any rate, it convinced the Prince that it was possible to sail round Africa, and arrive directly at the source of the Indian trade. Happy the people who should reach this goal ! To them must flow all the riches of the earth, as from an inexhaustible spring. And for what other people could this future be intended--

what other people had more reason and right to strive after this object than the Portuguese? It seemed only to need an earnest will and a patient constancy, and the tempting fruit would be theirs. But how long a time was to elapse before the Prince's noble dreams were realised. Nearly seventy years passed away before Vasco de Gama landed in Calcutta, and a hundred years before the discoveries of the Portuguese, and the almost contemporaneous conquest of Egypt by the Turks, for ever stopped the source whence had flowed the prosperity and wealth of Venice.

The Prince first determined to assure himself of the trustworthiness of the chart, by sending out an expedition (1430) to look for the islands which were marked somewhere in the middle of the Atlantic Ocean, about 100 miles west of Cape St. Vincent. This journey in the open ocean would also be a test whether the instructions of Master Jacob had borne good fruit. The Commander Gonsalo Velho Cabral ventured on the bold enterprise, and came back without accident; but instead of the expected islands, he had only discovered certain rocks, which, from the surging tumult of the waves around them, he named Formigas, that is, "the Ants." Henry, however, was not discouraged. The next year the commander set sail again for another attempt, and this time with better success. He landed, on the 15th August, 1431, on the island of Santa Maria, and thus became the discoverer, or rediscoverer, of the Azores or Hawks' Islands, which, almost a hundred years before, had been touched by some distressed Venetian or Genoese ships. The discovery caused great joy in Portugal. The most illustrious families took part in the colonisation of the island, and to them Prince Henry gave large territories as hereditary fiefs. Strange to say, the complete exploration and conquest of the island required almost thirty years, and it was not until 1460, the year of the Prince's death, that the most distant islands, Corvo and Flores, were discovered. The rush of colonists was very great, for the climate of the islands was mild and healthy, though damp. The fertile soil was so completely cleared of its forests that the islands now are poor in wood, with the exception of an evergreen laurel forest in San Miguel. But still, thanks to the dampness of the atmosphere, there has been no want of water from this reckless destruction. Some Flemish nobles, who received large possessions from the Prince, brought into the land many colonists from the Netherlands and North Germany. The island of Fayal was specially the one to which these strangers flocked, and hence for a long time it was called Ilha del Framengos, or the Island of the Flemings. Terceira, which the Prince gave (1450) to the Flemish knight Jacob von Brügge, was soon rich and flourishing from the careful cultivation bestowed upon it by the Netherlanders. But it was Jobst van Hürter, of Moerkerke, who had the chief merit of the Flemish emigration, being sent to the Azores by the Duchess Isabella of Burgundy, to whom the islands of Fayal and Piro had been presented. In 1486, when he married his daughter to the German geographer Martin Behaim, he was still in high repute as governor.

The favourable results of Cabral's expeditions increased the confidence of the Prince in the Venetian chart, and strengthened his determination to proceed along the west coast of Africa, hoping at last to arrive in the Indian Ocean by sailing round the continent. One of the gentlemen of his court, Gil Eannes (Gilianes), undertook to sail round the formidable Cape Bojador, which was still the limit of the West African discoveries, and set sail in 1433 with this object. But with him, as with Cabral, the first attempt was not successful, all his efforts were frustrated, and obliged to return, he sought to indemnify himself for the fruitless enterprise by kidnapping some of the inhabitants of the Canary Isles. But this breach of the treaty which Prince Henry had concluded with the crown of Castile, touching the Canaries, only made Gil Eannes's crime blacker in the eyes of his master, and he could only soften his anger by a solemn oath to solve the difficult problem the following year.   He kept his word, and sailed round Cape Bojador, beyond which he found an uninhabited coast, whence he brought home, as his only spoil, some strange plants— Santa Maria roses.   Notwithstanding, he met with a gracious reception from the Prince, who looked upon these flowers as satisfactory proofs of the erroneousness of the popular idea that all vegetable life was impossible in the tropics.

The success of Gil Eannes attracted attention beyond Portugal, and in his own land the rounding of the formidable promontory was looked upon as an heroic deed which deserved the highest honour. "Though," says the historian, Joâs de Barros, "it is no longer considered difficult, it was then looked upon as a mighty achievement, and there were people who lauded it as worthy of Hercules."   It refuted the false opinion prevalent throughout Spain, and gave courage to many who had not hitherto ventured to pursue these discoveries.   Excited by the popular ardour, the Prince sent out his cupbearer, Alfonso Gonsalves Baldaya, with a larger ship, accompanied by Gil Eannes, as guide.   But their discoveries were unimportant, and a second expedition, which was sent out in 1436, only added a few miles of sea to their previous knowledge.   The land was desolate.   Only a few scattered inhabitants were met with, and these offered so determined an opposition to the Portuguese that their wish to bring a prisoner to the Prince, who might give him information about the country, could not be carried out.   To the great bay which they then reached, and from which the Portuguese brought a cargo of sealskins, they afterwards gave the incongruous name of Rio do Ouro (Golden River) in order to gild a fruitless undertaking with a fine name, and to give the idea that the problem, part of which was the discovery of this fabulous river, was solved. But in this case, as so often afterwards, the name preceded the discovery.

Although he was very far from being discouraged by these failures, Prince Henry was unable for the next few years to do anything towards the accomplishment of his plans. First, he was occupied with a great war against Tangier, which he himself had urged upon the King his brother, and to the command of which he was himself appointed in conjunction with his younger brother, Ferdinand. With an army of 6000 men the Princes sat down before the hostile town (1437), but were soon reduced to the direst extremity by a powerful Moorish army which threatened them in the rear. From this situation they were only able to extricate themselves by a disgraceful treaty, which allowed them to depart on the promise of giving up Ceuta. Prince Ferdinand remained as hostage in the hands of the victors, by whom he was brought to the capital, Fez, where he died after a captivity of six years from ill treatment on the part of the Mussulmans. The unfortunate Ferdinand, who well knew that the honour of Portugal did not allow of his being released by the surrender of Ceuta, bore his hopeless fate with a Christian patience which has earned for him the name of the Constant Prince. Under this name he still lives in the noble tragedy of the great Spanish poet Calderon. Great was the grief and dismay of Portugal at this disaster.

King Edward died of grief in 1438, leaving behind him an infant heir. A bitter quarrel arose about the regency between the widowed queen and Prince Pedro, which was decided after a year in favour of the latter. Distracted by these events, and drawn into the war of factions, being called on both sides to act as mediator, Prince Henry was obliged to postpone the execution of his plans until a more favourable time, and it was not until peace had been restored under his brother Pedro's rule that he could resume his work of discovery. In the year 1441 he fitted out two ships, of which one, under the command of Antonio Gonsalves, the Prince's master of the robes, was to explore the coasts already discovered ; whilst the other, under the bold Nuno Tristam, was to proceed as far as possible along the coast. Both were successful. The united crews in a sharp night contest obtained possession of twelve Moorish prisoners, from whom the Prince obtained information about their home and trade with the south. So important did the Prince consider this intelligence, and the new discoveries made by Tristam, who had sailed along the desolate coast as far as Cape Blanco, that in 1442 he sent an embassy to Rome, to give an account to the Pope of the recently-discovered islands and coasts, and to request that, as compensation for the expense and trouble, Portugal might be granted the investiture of all the land still to be discovered between Cape Bojador and the Indies. By granting this request, the Pope shut out all other nations from any concurrence in these explorations, and removed the fears of the Prince, that others might come before him and reap the harvest where he had sown with so much pains.

The Pope, who, according to the spirit of the times, looked upon the opening up of new countries chiefly as a means to extend Christianity, rewarded the efforts of the Prince by granting him the tithes and the spiritual jurisdiction in all the lands hitherto discovered or yet to be discovered by the Portuguese, and forbade any one, whoever he might be, under heavy spiritual penalties, to go exploring without permission of the Prince. This gift was rendered more important by a decree of the Regent Pedro, which granted the monopoly of the trade to the discovered lands to his brother Henry, and so filled the Prince's exhausted coffers. Outside Portugal attention was aroused, and not only learned and able men, who took a scientific interest in the Prince's undertakings, but many adventurers and fortune-seekers began to stream into the country. Thus a German nobleman, named Balthasar (unfortunately his family name is not preserved), who had taken part in the capture of Ceuta, accompanied Gonsalves when the latter took back the Moorish prisoners into their own country, where they were exchanged for gold dust and negroes. Balthasar's wish to experience a good storm was gratified, but it did not deter the bold and adventurous man from taking a share in greater enterprises.

The people of Portugal were not at all eager—in fact, they were unwilling—to pursue the African discoveries. The great contrast between the fruitful islands which had been so quickly peopled with industrious agriculturists, and the rocky and barren lands which had been opened up on the west coast of Africa, did not act upon the mind of the people as a stimulus to push on more vigorously towards the south until that coast of Guinea should be found which promised the adventurer such a rich reward, but rather as a warning to expend no more money or men on the discovery of lands which became more and more barren the farther south you went, and which appeared thoroughly to confirm the popular opinion that the tropical regions were uninhabitable.

But Henry was not only convinced of the complete incorrectness of this idea, he also felt sure that a single piece of success would change the murmurs of the people into enthusiastic rejoicing, and the general indifference into general zeal. Therefore he remained unmoved, and in the year 1443 his patience was rewarded.

Nuno Tristam sailed round Cape Blanco, which he had discovered two years before, and found, farther south, a bay containing several islands, and with rich and fertile shores. The bay is now called the Bay of Arguim. Around it lived a strong Moorish people, called the Azeneghi, who supported themselves by fishing, and were said to be next-door neighbours to the blacks. The news of this discovery awoke in the Portuguese

the spirit of enterprise.   As early as 1444 there set sail from
Lagos, a town of Algarve, which, on account of its nearness,
had been made use of by the Prince for the fitting out of his
expeditions, a fleet of six caravels equipped by a merchant
company which had been formed in the town for the purpose
of turning the newly-discovered lands to good account.   The
Prince had given his consent with joy, and had placed
Lançarote, one of his household, in chief command of the
fleet.   Among the leading men also was Gil Eannes.   It
was made a condition that a fifth part of the gain should go
to the Prince, who had contributed to the expense of the expedition.   The articles to which their attention was particularly directed were gold dust, the musk of the civet cat, and
slaves.   Nobody considered the kidnapping of these heathen
people as either illegal or wrong.   On the contrary, the
cunning and courage necessary in the struggle with these unhappy savages were considered so honourable that very many
Portuguese noblemen were knighted for such heroic deeds on
the shores of Africa.   How lucrative this slave trade was is
shown, not only by the price of the living wares—a strong
slave was on an average, according to the present value of
money, worth £60,—but also by the large number of ships
engaged in this traffic, fourteen being sent out in the year 1445
from Lagos alone, and twelve from other Portuguese harbours.
In accordance with the spirit of the times, the Prince also
thoughtlessly demanded the fifth of the slaves from every
returning ship.   Indeed, in the course of time, the great
profit of this trade led to new agreements with the companies,
by which the Prince was to receive the fourth share if he did
not contribute to the expenses, and the half if he did.   Though
it cannot be denied that the slave trade contributed to encourage the African discoveries because the men-stealers
found themselves continually obliged to turn up new untouched ground, yet the cruelties which they allowed them-

selves to commit upon the savage tribes did much harm to the Portuguese themselves. Suspicion was excited, and an ever-increasing bitterness towards foreigners, to which many of them fell victims, Gonsalvo de Cintia, who was slain with seven companions in the Bight of Alguim, in 1445, by the Azeneghi, was but the first of many. After him one of the most lamented was Nuno Tristam, the discoverer of Arguim, who, with his followers, in the year 1446, was surrounded by the negroes in thirteen large boats on the Rio Grande. When the Portuguese discovered that the enemies' arrows were poisoned it was unfortunately too late. Almost the whole crew, Tristam included, died immediately, and the five men who alone remained alive, although completely ignorant of navigation, brought the ship into the harbour of Lagos after a two months' voyage. But all these losses were outweighed by the extraordinary advantages of the Guinea traffic, and new expeditions were continually being arranged. Prince Henry, whose permission it was necessary to obtain, made this trade subservient to higher objects. From every ship that returned he required an exact report of the voyage, and by the scientific expeditions, which he still continued to send out yearly, he not only tested the correctness of these accounts, but also opened up new territories, into which the traders soon followed. A proof of the anxious desire which Henry manifested to obtain as correct information as possible is found in the story of Joas Fernandez, one of the gentlemen of his court. He consented to be landed on the coast of Africa, and passed seven months among the Azeneghi in order to obtain correct information about their manners and customs, and about the neighbouring land, with which they were acquainted. The Prince sent to fetch him off the next year, and, out of gratitude for his self-sacrifice, named him a commander of the Order of Christ. A similar purpose was answered by the fortified factory which was built in the year

1445 on the islands in the Bay of Arguim, and by the inter-course which was thus established with the Central African traders. To information thus obtained he owed an exact acquaintance with the coasts, even before they were reached by the Portuguese sailors, to whom he was able to give many important hints and suggestions about their journey. Diniz Fernandez, a rich citizen of Lisbon, or as some say, Diniz Dias, once a page of the Prince, was the first to reach (1445) the coasts of the black tribes, which were called Jaloffs. He extended his voyage as far as a cape to which he gave the significant name of Cape Verde.

In the same eventful year Lançarote, following the precise descriptions of the Prince, discovered the mouth of the river Senegal. It was thought to be a branch of the Nile, a mistake which was repeated later about the great river which flows into the Gulf of Guinea, and which still bears the name of the Black Nile (Nilus Niger), which was then given to it. In the next few years the boundary of the Portuguese possessions was carried forward to the mouths of the rivers Gambia and Rio Grande; but there for a long time it remained—a fact which is explained by the necessity under which Prince Henry found himself of directing his exclusive attention to the internal affairs of his country.

A bitter quarrel had broken out between the young King, Alfonso (Affonso in Portuguese), and his uncle and foster-father, Pedro, who up to this time had been regent. Prince Henry naturally played the part of a mediator, and his efforts were successful in preventing the breaking out of an open quarrel for two years; but at last the ceaseless irritation kept up by the courtiers, who understood how to excite the young King's jealousy, made civil war unavoidable. Pedro, with his adherents, fell fighting valiantly, on the banks of the little river Alfarrobeira, against the overwhelming army opposed to him. Although his heart was on the side of his much-loved brother, yet, when recourse was had to arms, Prince Henry remained loyal to the King, and thus disarmed calumny and intrigue. But his spirit was broken, and if the news of newly-discovered lands still awoke his interest, he never again took an active share in any expedition. Indeed, his time was pretty fully occupied in the defence of Ceuta and the other Portuguese possessions in Africa against the Moors—a task which had been committed to him.

One spot of light in this dark period is the appearance of the Venetian Luigi Casa da Mosto, or Cadamosto, born in 1422, who, accidentally finding himself in the neighbourhood of the Prince, was impelled by a strong desire to have an interview with him, on account of the wonderful things which he had heard about the new lands. Whether his motive was a thirst for knowledge, or a wish to grow rapidly rich, or perhaps a patriotic dread of a danger threatening his native city—whatever it was, Prince Henry was more ready to meet him because he hoped to receive from one acquainted with the spice trade authentic information about the spices of Guinea. On a promise of half the profits, he placed at the disposal of the Venetian a caravel under the command of Vincent Dias, the freight of which was to be provided by Cadamosto. On March 22nd, 1455, it sailed from the harbour of Lagos. The account which Cadamosto wrote of this and his next journey fortunately has been preserved, and is rich in information about the condition of the newly-discovered lands. Porto Santo and Madeira, at which places he touched, he found in great prosperity; indeed, the latter he describes as an earthly paradise. Of the Canary Islands, he visited Gomera and Ferro, and has given us an exceedingly interesting account of the Guanches, who still held independent of Spanish control Canary, Teneriffe, and Palma. The Bay of Arguim, whither he next turned, was the seat of a lively trade with the Moorish merchants, who brought from the south all kinds of wares, chiefly black slaves, of whom at that time from Arguim alone between 700 and 800 were annually shipped to Portugal. The most interesting intelligence which he received here about Central Africa concerned a powerful negro state, the kingdom of Melli. A very extensive traffic was carried on between Timbuctoo and Melli in rock salt, which, he was told, was not only eaten in large quantities by the inhabitants to correct the impurity of the blood occasioned by the extreme heat, but was also used to exchange for gold with the inhabitants of some mysterious islands on the coast of a far distant sea. The next place where the Venetian stopped was the Senegal, where the green woody banks, with the fine native race, appeared very pleasing after the desolate landscape and the Moorish Azeneghi of Arguim. Here trade was not so profitable as in earlier days from the great competition, so Cadamosto, after sufficiently satisfying his curiosity about the inhabitants of Senegambia the Jaloffs, continued his journey south to a piece of land which is now held by the French, under the name of Cayor. Here he found a negro King, named Budomel, whose uprightness and friendliness were already famed in Portugal, and deservedly, as Cadamosto himself found. He spent fully four weeks at the residence of Budomel, which was a hut surrounded by seven courts, and situated at a distance of twenty-five miles from the coast, and thus had sufficient opportunity of becoming acquainted with the land and the people. The fruitfulness of the land is so great that the necessaries of life—maize, millet, and pulse—flourish in superabundance, although the lazy negroes take scarcely any pains in their cultivation, and for nine months in the year not a drop of rain falls. Wild animals are very numerous ; the most important domestic ones are goats and a small species of oxen. Cadamosto's traffic in this place went on very smoothly and satisfactorily, and brought him in a valuable cargo of slaves, which he bought for horses, cloth, and silk. The rest of his goods he hoped to dispose of farther south. After having, with this object in view, passed Cape Verde, he was joined by two Portuguese caravels which Prince Henry had meanwhile equipped and sent out, under the command of the Genoese nobleman Antonio Usodimare, for traffic and exploration. They entered the Gambia together, but the negroes, embittered by previous Portuguese kidnapping raids, attacked them fiercely, and utterly refused to enter into friendly correspondence with them. The intention of the two captains to penetrate farther into the country was frustrated by the cowardice of their men, and so the return voyage was begun. After a rapid and prosperous passage they reached Lagos, where Prince Henry received the account of their adventures, and the due share of the profits.

The attempt which Cadamosto had made in vain to enter the interior up the great river was repeated more successfully the next year by the Portuguese, Diogo Gomez, who passed up the Gambia in a caravel as far as Cantor. Here he not only disposed of his wares advantageously, but also received valuable information about the kingdom of Melli, caravans passing between it and Cantor. He was the first to bring an account to Europe of a mighty river called Emin (the middle course of the Niger), which ran through Melli, and a report of violent wars and revolutions, which were laying waste the Soudan, and rendering the communications with it difficult.

But this year 1456 was to be distinguished by an important discovery. The two Italians—the Venetian, Cadamosto, and the Genoese, Usodimare—who had met accidentally the year before, proceeded together on an expedition, each providing a caravel. The Prince added a third. They left Lagos in May, and had sailed prosperously as far as Cape Blanco, when a violent storm drove them out into the open sea. On the third day, to their surprise, they discovered land ; it proved to be the Cape Verde Islands, which had until then been left to the west by the Guinea explorers. From Buonavista—as they named the first island—they saw to the north a second, Sal,. and sailing on towards the south, they touched a third and fourth, Santiago and Mago. All the islands were uninhabited, but the soil seemed good, and water was abundant. Pigeons were very numerous, and so tame that they could be taken with the hand ; and there were large turtles, the flesh of which was a great delicacy. The Italians sailed on without troubling themselves to explore all the islands of the group. They were not thoroughly investigated until six years later, when Diogo Gomez and the Genoese Antonio de Noli visited them. They found that the islands lay in two groups, and although they were mountainous and partly of volcanic origin, yet were well adapted for cultivation. The immigration of Portuguese agriculturists immediately began, but unfortunately their descendants—who now number little more than 100,000 over eighty square miles—live in a miserable condition, from the mismanagement of the Portuguese Government. The state takes no care of them beyond requiring the customary dues, and yet if irrigation were undertaken with the support of the state, and the valuable productions of the islands—salt, coffee, palm-oil, &c.—fostered, this group might be restored to an equally favourable condition with Madeira and the Azores.

On their farther journey the two Italians again entered the Gambia, where this time they were received more amicably. Sixty miles from the coast, at the residence of the negro Prince Battimansa, to which they were conducted, they began a traffic with the blacks, which was carried on very briskly. The heat becoming unendurable, they returned to the ships, and sailed still farther south. They touched at the mouth of the river Casamansa, so called after a negro prince of that name, then at Rio Grande, and lastly at the Bissagos Islands, which were inhabited by negroes, and where they would gladly have stayed longer. The flotilla arrived safely at Lagos in the year 1456. Their new discoveries, and the satisfactory results.

of their trading speculations, ensured them an honourable reception with the Prince. Cadamosto undertook no more expeditions, and, after some years spent in Portugal, returned, a wealthy man, to his native city. But although not himself visiting the coast of Africa, he certainly, as long as he remained in Portugal, took part in the profitable trade with Guinea; and his interest in the land and people of the tropics, which makes his account so valuable, certainly did not flag. We owe to him a very exact report of an expedition made by the Captain Pero de Cintra, the materials for which he received from an old secretary of his who took part in it. This voyage of Pero de Cintra took place in the year 1461. It extended beyond the Bissagos Islands, along a mountainous and beautifully-wooded shore, rising towards the south-east to a considerable range of mountains. On account of the thunder, which resounded ceaselessly from the clouds hanging round these mountains, they named them Sierra Leone, the Lion Mountains—a name which a great part of the coast still bears. The voyage extended a short distance beyond Cape Mesurado, as far as six degrees north latitude, where the shore was covered by a splendid forest—the Bosque de Santa Maria.

Prince Henry had not been able to take any share in the equipment of this expedition—a year before he was laid to rest in the quiet cloister of Batalha. The last years of his life had been troubled by the African campaigns of his adventurous nephew, Alfonso V. The attack on Alcaçar el Seguir, a harbour between Cintra and Tangier, which the King made in the year 1458, was brought to a prosperous issue chiefly by the wise counsel and energy of the Prince. In the land which had witnessed the glorious deeds of his youth the Prince found a fitting theatre for the achievements of his old age. He led the storming party, to him the town surrendered, and it was he who protected from deeds of violence the Moorish garrison as it marched out. But the exertions which he had made seriously affected his health, and, after a tedious illness, death released him from his sufferings, November 10th, 1460, aged sixty-six.

In him the world lost no common man. Indeed, if a man's title to greatness in any way depends upon important results following earnest strivings, he may well be called Prince Henry the Great; for he was the originator of that great work of discovery which finally opened the way to India and gave to us a New World. And if the halo of brilliant success which surrounds the names of Vasco de Gama and Christopher Columbus is wanting to him, yet surely there was truer grandeur in the patience which struggled for ten years against superstition and ill-will, and in the perseverance with which he pursued the object which he had set before him. Certainly he was far from attaining this object, and it was many years before the men appeared who grasped the costly prize; but he was the first who saw it—who saw it in the distance—and prepared the way for its attainment. Our knowledge of the west coast of Africa was by him extended twenty degrees; the discovery of fruitful islands and the profitable trade with the blacks considerably increased the prosperity of his country; the Portuguese seamanship, previously so rude that Cape Bojador for many years prevented any farther advance, was, by his fostering care, so improved that Cadamosta pronounced the Portuguese the best sailors in the world; and, what was the most important of all, he inspired the people of Portugal, who at first watched his proceedings with indifference, with an ardent thirst for discovery. And he succeeded in effecting all this without possessing attractive personal qualities or winning eloquence. On the contrary, the hermit of Sagre was of a stern exterior, taciturn, and unsociable.

Unmarried, with no fancy for women's society, surrounded only by grave men, to whom he was bound by common scientific aspirations, Prince Henry spent a long life, striving after one object which made him indifferent to all the pleasures of the world. How he shared in the details of the work, how he helped Master Jacob in the preparation of his charts, is well known. Apparently he wrote with his own hand the work, " The History of the Discoveries of Prince Henry," the loss of which is much to be deplored. His contemporaries were far from being just to him, and it is therefore all the more the duty of posterity to recognise his merits. A man, high in rank, thus earnestly and unselfishly devoting his whole life to the realisation of a great idea, becomes the benefactor of his country, of Europe, of the human race, and has, in a much higher degree than he himself ever imagined, carried out the beautiful and modest motto which he assumed at his knighthood on the taking of Ceuta—" Talent de bien faire."

CHAPTER III.

THE Prince's heir, Alfonso V., unfortunately had no desire to tread in the footsteps of his uncle. Plans of conquest occupied his active mind. Repeated incursions into North Africa put him in possession of the Moorish towns of Arzilla and Tangier, and justified his adoption of the proud title, " King of the Algarves on both sides of the sea." He was less successful in his long struggle with his Castilian neighbours. After the death of King Henry IV. of Castile, Alfonso was betrothed to his young daughter, and laid claim to the Castilian throne in virtue of this alliance. But the bloody and costly war which the defence of this claim involved ended in his total overthrow, in spite of heroic deeds of arms. His opponents, Isabella, the sister of the late King, and her husband, the heir to Arragon, so fiercely inflamed the warlike pride and national hatred of the Castilians against Portugal, that Alfonso was forced to retreat into his own kingdom, and, after a vain attempt to interest Louis XI. of France in his behalf, was compelled to make peace. In order to obtain this he had to sacrifice his bride, the unhappy Princess Joanna, who was forced to take the veil in a Portuguese convent. This peace, which was made in 1479, was of long duration, and had a beneficial effect upon the foreign possessions of the two states. The sovereignty of the Portuguese King over all lands from Cape Non to the Indies, together with all the adjoining seas and islands, over the Madeiras, the Azores, and the Cape

Verde Islands, and over the conquests in the kingdom of Fez, was solemnly recognised. Without the permission of the King of Portugal, the Castilians were not allowed to trade in those lands and islands; while, on the other hand, the Kings of Castile retained the Canary Islands, and reserved to themselves the conquest of Granada.

A very considerable sum had already flowed into the Portuguese treasury from the lands discovered by Prince Henry the Navigator, especially from the sugar plantations of Madeira. The revenues of the Cape Verde Islands and the tolls paid by traders in Arguim were farmed at a high rate; and the ivory trade, of which the Crown retained the monopoly, steadily increased in value. Also from the trade on the Guinea coast King Alfonso wished to draw something, and for this purpose he entered into a negotiation with the rich merchant Ferdinand Gomez, in Lisbon. From the year 1469 Gomez agreed to pay yearly the sum of 500 cruzados for the trade from the mouth of the Senegal to Sierra Leone, and he promised to explore a hundred leagues of the coast every year from the Bosque de Santa Maria. In order to carry out this last article of the agreement, unquestionably the hardest, Gomez made friends with the most experienced Portuguese sailors. Unfortunately no record whatever has been kept of these expeditions, a negligence which is the more striking when compared with the care shown by Prince Henry in preserving accounts of those undertaken under his auspices. From later sources we learn that, in 1470, Joas de Santarem discovered the Gold Coast, now called Ashantee, north of the Gulf of Guinea. This gulf the Portuguese ships boldly crossed in a south-westerly direction, and thus discovered Prince's Island, St. Thomas's Island, and Annabon—of course, crossing the equator. These achievements, and the accounts brought by the sailors of the luxuriant vegetation and dense population of these coasts, destroyed the last remains of the delusion with regard to the impossibility of supporting either animal or vegetable life in these tropical lands, and of the dangers certain to be incurred by ships in those latitudes. Thus Gomez honestly and unobtrusively carried out his contract, and was rewarded for his services by being raised to the rank of a noble. On the death of Alfonso, in 1481, Cape St. Catherine had been attained, a point 2 deg. 30 min. south latitude.

The death of the King brought about a great reaction. The young King, Joas II., to whom Portugal was indebted for the peace with Castile, earnestly encouraged everything which tended to the welfare of his kingdom ; but the African discoveries he took up with the zeal of an enthusiast. This may perhaps be partly accounted for by the fact that he was the author of works both on geography and astronomy.

Immediately on his accession he sent out a large squadron, under the command of one of his most trusted servants, Diego d'Azambuja, in order to found a port which should not only give a greater impulse to the trade with the blacks, but should also render assistance to expeditions sailing farther south. Azambuja chose for this purpose a point on the Gold Coast, where he landed, on the 19th of January, 1482, 500 soldiers and 100 artisans.

The ruler of the country, Caramansa, with whom they had requested an interview, appeared with a numerous retinue. The weapons of the negroes consisted of spears and shields, or bows and arrows. The chiefs were adorned with gold rings, and were followed by servants carrying their shields, and also seats, lest their masters should at any time feel fatigued. Surrounded by all the splendour of his court, Caramansa appeared, striding proudly forward, his arms and legs adorned with gold rings, and wearing round his neck a band, from which hung a number of little bells, and his beard being ornamented by little sprigs of gold. After a ceremonious greeting, Azambuja made a speech, in which he expressed the wish of the King of Portugal that his brother Caramansa would accept Christianity, conclude a treaty of commerce with him, and allow the Portuguese merchants to build a fort. This last demand appeared to the black King not only unnecessary, but even likely to be hurtful. He said he feared that constant intercourse between the blacks and whites would lead to inevitable quarrels. As an illustration, he pointed out the hostility between the sea and the land, each one trying to rule the other. "On this account," he said, "it would be better to remain as they were before, and he would very gladly trade as of old with the 'ragged' ships." It was not until after a long discussion, and much persuasion, that consent was wrung from the wise negro. The building of the fort, which received the name of San Jorge dá Mena—now called Elmina—was immediately begun; and here Azambuja remained with sixty men, having sent the rest of the fleet back to Portugal.

Around the fort a settlement was quickly formed, which, as early as the year 1486, could claim the name and privileges of a town. This rapid growth was principally in consequence of the gold trade, which was carried on from this place with the interior, and which gave its name to the whole coast. Azambuja himself afterwards returned to Portugal, and rose high in the favour of his King, by whose side he was ever found in the most critical moments. For the next few years Joas II. had hard work to hold down the rebellious barons of Portugal. He ventured on the execution of the first peer, the Duke of Braganza, and did not shrink from murdering, with his own hand, his cousin and brother-in-law, the Duke of Viseu; but, notwithstanding, his interest in the Guinea trade did not abate. He obtained (1484) from Pope Innocent VIII. the ratification of his claim to all the African coasts and islands as far as the Indies; indeed, the Pope added a clause by which all discoveries made by other nations in this direction were to fall to the Portuguese. On the strength of this the King added to his titles that of Lord of Guinea. At the same time he ordered that every ship should carry on board some stone pillars (*padram*), on which should be written, in Latin and Portuguese, the name of the King and the captain, with the date of the year. These pillars were to be erected on the newly-discovered coasts, as a sign of their being taken possession of by Portugal.

The first man who sailed under these new orders was Diogo Cam, who in 1484 passed Cape St. Catherine, and reached the mouth of a mighty stream, now called the Congo, which the natives called Zaïre, but to which Cam gave the name of Rio do Padrão, the Pillar River, because there he set up the first pillar. He sailed some miles up the stream and found the banks thickly peopled. Taking four natives on board as hostages for some of his men who ventured to remain in the country for the purpose of exploring it, he set sail, promising to return. He proceeded prosperously along the coast as far as Cape Serra, near Whale Bay, in twenty-two degrees south latitude.

On his return voyage he entered the Zaire, and exchanged the natives for his own people, who spoke very highly of the treatment they had received from the natives. A very lively intercourse was begun between them, and Cam understood how to manage the negroes so well that the chief gave him ivory and garments curiously made of palm leaves as presents for King John, and sent a request that he would give him priests to baptise him and his people. This response was most readily responded to, and thus the Portuguese laid the foundation of their dominion on those coasts, where they still possess the so-called kingdoms of Angola and Benguela.

These states consist of about seventeen thousand square miles, with about five hundred thousand inhabitants, who acknowledge the Portuguese supremacy, paying tribute and providing troops when called upon. Congo itself has passed out of the hands of the Portuguese, and the Christianity which they planted there—at the end of the seventeenth century there were about one hundred Christian churches—has been rooted out. What kind of Christianity it was may be guessed from the fact that one priest baptised on one day five thousand heathen, and that most of those who had the charge of souls there not only tolerated the slave trade, but themselves took part in it, and grew rich by it. Even in Angola and Benguela the activity of the Government was exerted in the slave trade. The capital, San Paul de Loanda, among all the places on the coast, was most constantly and for the longest period engaged in it, and so enormous was the number of victims that the effect was felt to the very centre of Africa. Since the philanthropic zeal of England has put an end to the slave trade on the west coast of Africa, the whole commerce of the Portuguese dominions there has been stopped, and it appears unlikely that the wretched administration will succeed in developing the resources of the rich lands.

Diogo Cam was accompanied on this voyage by Martin Behaim, the celebrated German geographer. He was born in 1459 in the town of Nuremberg, and was descended from the illustrious family of Schwarzbach. After the early death of his father the gifted youth was taken care of by his uncle, Leonard Behaim, who gave him a good education. Like most youths of good family, he devoted himself to trade, and during his journeys in the Netherlands learnt early to know the world. In the Netherlands he determined in 1480 to visit the Azores, to which islands at that time numbers of emigrants from Flanders were flocking. Here he entered into intimate relations with the principal families, and in 1486 married the daughter of Jobst van Heurter, governor of Fayal. But at the same time he had acquired great influence in Lisbon, and made himself a name. In the circle of famous mathematicians and astronomers, who assembled there to turn to scientific advantage the discoveries of the Portuguese sailors, and by calculations and conjectures to plan new ones, Behaim met with a deferential reception, because he could boast that in his early days he had enjoyed the acquaintance of the greatest astronomer of those times, Johann Müller, of Königsberg in Franconia, also called Regiomontanus.

This great scholar had resided between 1471 and 1475 at Nuremberg, before he was called as cardinal to Rome, and it is probable that young Behaim, inquiring and eager for knowledge, may have been his pupil. At any rate the astronomical knowledge of the latter produced an impression on the learned society in Portugal, and his reputation, which spread rapidly, drew upon him the attention of King John. He was made member of the scientific commission which consisted of the president, Bishop Diego Ortiz, and the two Jewish physicians to the King, Josef and Rodrigo. It was at that time engaged in drawing up tables of the sun's altitude for use on the other side of the equator. In consequence of the want of acquaintance with the southern stars, the altitude of the sun was the only means of reckoning the geographical latitude when the polar star was lost sight of by passing the equator. This nautical commission, as it appears, completed its task by recommending to the sailors the use of the astrolabe, an instrument which had hitherto only been used on land, and which calculated the latitude by the culmination of the most important stars. The instrument itself they improved, made it of metal, and so arranged it that it could be hung up. They also furnished it with tables in which they laid down the course of the constellations in the southern hemisphere. This work brought Behaim into close intercourse with the King, and the clever and accomplished German won so high a place in his confidence that he employed him on many occasions in difficult private affairs. In 1484 Behaim, impelled by the wish to make himself acquainted with the wonders of Africa, accompanied Cam as cosmographer, and received equal honours with Cam on his return. He was made a knight of the Order of Christ, and at the ceremony the King himself girded him with his sword, and the Crown Prince Emanuel put on his spurs. Overwhelmed with gifts, he returned to the Azores, where he settled down and spent the next few years in quiet domestic happiness. But home-sickness seized upon him, and he undertook the long journey to Nuremberg, and spent almost two years (1491, 1492) in his old home, admired by his fellow-citizens, who hung on the lips of their travelled countryman, and would only let him go when he had carried out their wish and made a globe showing all the known lands.

This globe, made of wood covered with parchment, 1 foot 8 inches in diameter, is still in the possession of the Behaims in Nuremberg, and is specially curious as furnishing a faithful representation of the state of geographical knowledge in the very year in which the discovery of a new world was to bring about so mighty a revolution.

The west coast of Africa is exactly and faithfully delineated as far as the Cape of Good Hope, which had already been discovered by Bartholomew Diaz, and the places where, according to the orders of the King, stone pillars had been erected are marked by Portuguese flags. But the east of Africa and the coasts and islands of the Indian Ocean are represented in a fanciful manner. The remarks and descriptions also contain, mixed up with what is correct, a number of absurd statements, and the authority quoted with regard to South Asia and East Africa is Marco Polo, the Venetian, who, in the years 1270 — 1295, made his astounding journey through Asia to Mongolia and China. The most curious part of the globe is the expanse of sea between the west coast of Europe and the east coast of Asia. Of the existence of the New World, which was discovered that very year, Behaim had no notion. On the contrary, he filled the space with innumerable islands, among which was Cipang (Japan), and farther east he marked two great lonely islands, St. Brandon's Land and Antilha, to which he attached as remarks the absurd old fables.

In the year 1493 he returned to Fayal, which, however, he must have left again in the same year, to execute a secret commission of the King's in Flanders. On this journey he was very unfortunate ; twice he fell into the hands of pirates, and in England he became so dangerously ill that he thought his last hour was come. Notwithstanding, he succeeded in accomplishing the King's commission to his satisfaction, and then he could allow himself to think of domestic bliss in Fayal, which had become to him a second home. We know nothing of him from 1494 to 1507 ; but some remarks of the great Magalhaens make it not improbable that he took part in one of the expeditions to South America, perhaps that of Christian Jaquez in 1503, and attained a point so far south that he was able to establish the existence of the important highway which Magalhaens a few years later discovered.

In 1507 death overtook him in Lisbon, where he was then residing. Apparently he was in bad circumstances, for after the death of King John, 1495, the salary which he had received as envoy was withdrawn. He died in a German hospital, and was buried in a Dominican church. His only son, Martin, resided from 1519—1520 among his relations in Nuremberg, who, in vain, tried to make him worthy of his father. After that he disappeared ; but there is still living in Nuremberg a family of his name which was ennobled in 1681.

CHAPTER IV.

BARTHOLOMEW DIAZ AND PEDRO DE COVILHAM.

SHORTLY after the departure of Cam, Joâs Alfonso de Aveiro had been despatched by King John for the special purpose of exploring the Bight of Benin. Previous expeditions had crossed it in a south-easterly direction, but its north coast had not been visited. Aveiro found it inhabited by a population of strong healthy negroes. Their chief came to meet the Portuguese, and sent an ambassador with them on their return to request that the King would give them Christian priests, and would establish a factory there. The desire was willingly responded to, but when it was discovered that the cunning chief had merely designed to enrich himself by the slave trade, and that neither he nor his people showed any intention of being baptised, the factory was abandoned ; and this was done the more readily because many of the whites had fallen victims to the fatal climate.

From another point of view the exploration of Benin promised important results. Every ship engaged in the work of discovery was, by command of the King, bound to carry samples of all the Indian spices, in order to make clear to the natives what they were looking for. Now it was from Benin that the first African pepper was brought, and this aroused in the King the hope that his people would be able to compete with the Venetians. But the pepper proved to be inferior to the Indian, and therefore was of less value in the spice market. The King at first comforted himself with the hope that this

arose from a mistake in the treatment of the fruit ; but experience has proved him wrong and shown that the African
pepper is a different and inferior kind.

Encouraged by Cam's discoveries, King John sent out a new
squadron in July or August, 1486, consisting of two caravels
and a small ship laden with provisions. It was commanded
by Bartholomew Diaz de Novaes, a distinguished seaman, of
whose antecedents we know nothing, except that he was in
the service of the court and belonged to a family which had
already produced many daring sailors, among whom probably
was Diniz Diaz, who had discovered Cape Verde in 1445.
Joas Infante, a nobleman, commanded under him : they took
with them some negroes and negresses whom Cam had brought
home, and who now, having mastered the Portuguese language,
were to be returned to their homes. They had been very
kindly treated, and before they were set on shore were decked
out in bright garments and dazzling ornaments, in order to
fill their countrymen with astonishment at the power and
riches of the King of Portugal. They were also made to
promise to penetrate as far as possible into the interior, and
to inquire everywhere for the country of Prester John. A
large reward was to be given to any one who should bring
information. So closely was the kingdom of this Christian
Priest-king connected in people's minds with the land of
spice !

Having accomplished this commission, the little fleet sailed
on towards the south, and had soon left behind Cam's utmost
limit. In the neighbourhood of Walvisch Bay the first pillar
was set up, and from the contrary winds which obliged him to
keep constantly tacking, Diaz gave the name of Angra das
Voltas, or the Bay of Tacks, to the bay now called St. Helena's
Bay. In order to escape the dangers which threatened him in
such unfavourable weather on an unknown coast, Diaz made
for the open sea. Here, however, the ship was overtaken by a

tremendous storm. For fourteen days it was driven wildly hither
and thither ; tremendous waves broke over it ; and the cold,
which by this time was sensibly greater, took such hold upon
the wearied crew that, when at length the sky cleared, they
were scarcely in a condition to prepare for the homeward
voyage. They tried to reach the coast of Africa, but they had
been driven so far towards the east that their efforts were
fruitless. This at least was their first idea, but in a little while
the suspicion came across them that perhaps they had passed
the extreme south of Africa, and thus accomplished an important part of Prince Henry's plan. They steered therefore to
the north, and the coast was soon reached.

They came to anchor in a large bay near a small rocky
island, which they baptised Santa Cruz, and there they erected
a stone pillar. This island is situated in the north-west corner
of what is now called Algoa Bay. From the numerous woolly-
headed natives who were pasturing their flocks on the shore,
Diaz called this bay Angra dos Vaqueiros, or the Cowherds'
Bay. The joy which Diaz would have felt at this prosperous
issue to his voyage was damped in a most vexatious manner.
His crew began to murmur and demand to return home, com-
plaining of the hardships they had endured, and of the loss of
the ship which contained the greater part of their provisions.
Diaz called a council of his officers, and they also were unanimous for a return. He was therefore obliged to yield, but
made it a condition that the ships should hold on their present
course for three days, in order that they might discover whether
the coast turned towards the north. The three days expired,
and the coast still continuing to lie west and east, they turned
round at the mouth of a river which they named Rio do Infante, from the second commander. It was a very great sorrow
to Diaz to be obliged to relinquish the wish to be the first to
carry the Portuguese flag into the Indian Sea. He clung to
the pillar which he had erected on Santa Cruz, and took leave

of it with as much grief, says the historian Barros, as if it had been a child whom he was leaving for ever.

On the return voyage he soon found the spot where the west and south coasts of Africa meet, and on this important point set up a third pillar. In remembrance of the fearful tempest by which the ship had been overtaken near this spot, Diaz called it the Cape of Storms (Cabo Tormentoso). On the coast of Congo the lost vessel was recovered, and after visiting San Jorge da Mina to take on board a quantity of gold-dust, Diaz directed his course homewards.

In December, 1487, the fleet entered the Tagus, after a voyage of sixteen months and seventeen days. The joy of the King was extreme ; not only a strip of coast 375 miles long had been explored, but, what was much more important, it had been proved that it was possible to sail round Africa, and the Indian Ocean was open to the Portuguese. In the height of his exultation, and to show to the world the importance of the discovery, he altered the name of the Stormy Cape to the Cape of Good Hope, which the south point of Africa still bears.

Diaz was richly rewarded and highly honoured. King John might perhaps have sent him out again had he not been prevented by troubles which came upon him. His successor, Emanuel, immediately after his accession, charged him with the preparation of a squadron. This squadron he accompanied only as far as the Cape Verde Islands, leaving it then with his ship for San Jorge da Mina, according to orders which he had received, for it was the sagacious but ingenious principle of the Portuguese crown never to reward a discoverer with the conduct of the next expedition. This method of proceeding relieved the King of the burden of gratitude, for when a number of persons took part in a discovery there was no one person in particular to whom he felt indebted. Once more we hear of the noble Diaz in an expedition under the command of

BARTHOLOMEW DIAZ TAKING LEAVE OF SANTA CRUZ.

Cabral. Near the Cape of Good Hope a violent storm overtook the fleet, and on the 23rd of May, 1500, he found a watery grave beneath the waves of the Atlantic Ocean.

The year 1487—rendered such an auspicious one for Portugal by the discovery of the Cape of Good Hope—was made further noteworthy by tidings received from the East.

From the negro ambassador of the King of Benin it had been learnt that about twenty months' journey from Benin there was a powerful Prince named Ogane. The sound of the name and certain striking peculiarities made the King quite certain that this Ogane was no other than Prester John, the ruler of the Christian kingdom of Abyssinia. It appeared to him most desirable to enter into communication with this mighty Prince and to make sure of his friendship, as it would be very valuable to the Portuguese in their advance towards India. For this purpose he sent out two men who were good Arabic scholars and thoroughly acquainted with African affairs—Pedro de Covilham and Alfonso de Payva. They left Lisbon in May, 1487, and in the character of merchants reached Alexandria safely. Here they discovered that though Prester John, or, in other words, the King of Abyssinia, was undoubtedly a Christian, he did not possess the slightest influence in Indian trade. Hereupon they separated. While Payva went direct to Abyssinia—where he very shortly died—Covilham, still in disguise, pursued his way to India. There he visited the places most important for trade, collected valuable information about the price of Indian wares and Arabian commerce, and returned by Ormuz, from which place he took advantage of a favourable opportunity to visit the east coast of Africa in an Arabian ship. He went to Sofala and Madagascar, and after a prosperous journey arrived safely in Cairo, where, instead of finding his companion, whom he had arranged to meet there, he received the news of his death. But there were awaiting him two messengers from the King of Portugal, Jews, one a learned

Rabbin, the other a poor shoemaker from Lamego, who brought him orders to proceed, instead of Payva, to Prester John in Abyssinia. Before Covilham set out he wrote an account of his journey, and of the impressions to which they had given rise, and sent it back by the two Jews to Portugal. He was very well received in Abyssinia, whose King, Escander (Alexander), felt himself very much flattered by such an attention from a European sovereign. He was at first in hopes of being able very soon to return to Portugal, but the sudden death of Escander rendered this impossible. The new Prince held firmly to the old principle of Abyssinia: " Let strangers into your country, but never let them out." In vain were all the attempts of the Portuguese to procure his release.

Rodriga de Lima, whom King Emanuel sent to Abyssinia in 1520—a time when the Portuguese power was ruling the whole of the Indian Ocean, and was dominant even in the Red Sea—received for answer that they had given the stranger a wife and property, and that he could live at ease with his family, and altogether had nothing to wish for.

Pedro de Covilham died in Abyssinia without seeing his home again, but the history which he drew up in Cairo reached the King, and disclosed to him many important matters. It informed him that of all the harbours on the coast of India, Calicut was the most important, its ruler, Zamorin, possessing authority over all the other Princes of Malabar, the west coast of India. It was chiefly from this place that Arabian ships fetched the precious spices, pepper and ginger being produced in the land itself, and cinnamon and cloves being brought there by ships from countries in the far east. The profit of a direct intercourse with the Indian harbours would necessarily be very important, for from Covilham's account it appeared the price of spices in Calicut was less by three times, or even five times, than in Alexandria, so that they might reckon safely on annihilating the Venetian trade, if Portuguese ships could fetch the wares from Malabar itself.

Of the east coast of Africa also Covilham gave most important information. He had been assured in Sofala that a voyage along the coast towards the south-west was obstructed by no danger or difficulty. Between East Africa and India, as he could testify from what he had himself seen, lay an open sea, constantly traversed by Arabian ships. So he concluded his account—of which, unfortunately, we possess only an abstract—by earnestly pressing the King to continue, untiringly, the expeditions to the coast of Africa. "When once the south point of that continent is found"—that it had already been discovered by Bartholomew Diaz, he could not know—"it will be easy to reach Sofala and Zanzibar." There a pilot must be taken on board, a native pilot, and the long desired Indian paradise will soon be reached. Information so certain and assurances so confident naturally inflamed the ardour of the King. Only one link was wanting to complete the chain between India and Portugal. He began immediately to prepare an imposing fleet which should sail round the Cape of Good Hope and find its way, by Covilham's directions, India. But a terrible event occurred which ruined the ambitious plans of the King. His only son, Prince Alfonso, a handsome accomplished youth, whom his father idolised, was killed by a fall from his horse only a few months after his marriage with Isabella, the probable heiress of Castile and Arragon.

The unhappy father was utterly shattered by this terrible blow. When, after a long sorrowful retirement, he again appeared in public, not only did his altered countenance testify to the deepest anguish, but his character seemed to have entirely lost the energy and ardour which had been its distinguishing mark. The departure of the fleet, whose commander had been already named, was constantly delayed ;

and when, in 1493, Columbus, on his return from his first journey, entered Lisbon, it was with bitter jealousy that King John found that the prize for which once he had striven so hard had fallen to the Castilians. But even jealousy could not overcome the dejection into which he had fallen, and he concluded that it was now too late to enter the lists with his more fortunate rivals. Until his death, which occurred on October 25th, 1495, there was a complete cessation of all expeditions.

Thus was Portugal, when it had almost reached the goal again, hindered by a freak of fortune, and obliged to share with a neighbouring people the prize which otherwise would have been hers alone. For there is no doubt that the journey of Columbus would never have taken place had the Portuguese previously landed in India, the country which he continually hoped to reach. Certain it is that it would have been much longer before the New World was discovered, and it would be impossible to divine what the next century would have been, had not the treasures of America made the Kings of Spain the masters of Europe. Thus the sudden death of a youth became in the hand of Providence the cause of the most complete revolution in the whole history of Europe.

CHAPTER V.

VASCO DA GAMA.

KING EMANUEL, to whom history has given the honourable surname of Great, at once brought new life into the languishing plans of discovery and reaped the costly harvest sown by his predecessors, Prince Henry and King John II. At his command the preparation of a squadron of four vessels by Bartholomew Diaz was urged on with great zeal and with such success that the expedition set sail from Restello, a port in the immediate neighbourhood of Lisbon, on the 8th of June, 1497.

The King appointed Vasco da Gama commander, and in this choice, which really only confirmed an arrangement already made by John II., had selected the right man for the great undertaking. Vasco, who sprang from a distinguished family, was born at Sinis, a Portuguese seaport, not far from Lisbon, apparently earlier than 1469, which is generally given as the year of his birth. The seaman's life to which, following the example of his father, he devoted himself led him into the African Seas, and soon gave him an opportunity of displaying his striking qualities. His name is first mentioned when, in the service of the King, he took possession of all the French ships found in the harbours of the kingdom. It was intended by this means to avenge the capture by French pirates of a caravel laden with gold coming from San Juan da Mina. But since King Charles VIII. hastened to make good the injury and to punish the offender, the affair had no further consequences.

It is unknown how Vasca da Gama succeeded in attracting to himself the notice of the King to such a degree that he was named commander of the fleet which, following in the steps of Bartholomew Diaz and Pedro de Covilham, was to penetrate to India.

He was at this time in the prime of life. While small in person, and in later years very corpulent, he pleased every one by his dignified bearing and pleasant manners. But affable and agreeable as he could be, he was yet fearful in his wrath. Then his eye flashed, so that the bravest quailed before his glance. Then he knew no sympathy and no mercy, and in these bursts of passion was sometimes guilty of deeds of wild cruelty such as not even the merciless policy of Portugal towards the Moors could justify or excuse. But he possessed exactly the qualities necessary for the great undertaking : an eye which nothing escaped, calm presence of mind, firmness, and thorough control over the crew, whose affection, however, he knew how to gain by courtesy and a zealous care for the welfare of the individual members. All these qualities were united in Gama in such a high degree that it would have been difficult to find in Portugal an equally suitable person, and the choice reflects high honour on the King who made it.

The want of an account of Gama's expedition from the pen of an eye-witness, which has been so much deplored, has been supplied since 1858 by the discovery and publication of a manuscript written by a sailor named Alvaro Velhes—a manuscript which has special worth from its childlike descriptions, and at the same time from the keen power of observation evidently possessed by its uncultivated author. It bears the unpretending title " An Account of a Journey."

But the deeds of " the great Gama " have been more worthily

celebrated by the classical Portuguese poet Camoens, whose "Lusiade" (the deeds of Lus, the fabulous ancestor of the Lusitanians or Portuguese) treats Vasco da Gama in the same way as the "Odyssey" and the "Æneid" treat the heroes whose names they bear.

The squadron, which left Restello on June 8th, 1497, consisted of four ships: the *St. Gabriel* of 120 tons, the *St. Raphael* of 100 tons, the *Berrio* of 50 tons, and a provision ship of 200 tons, which was only to go part of the way. Under Vasco da Gama commanded his brother Paul da Gama, the experienced sailor Nicholas Coëlho, and Gonzalo Nuñes, who had the charge of the provision ship.

The fleet was provisioned for three years, with crews numbering one hundred and seventy men, and every ship had as pilot a man already proved in the squadron of Bartholomew Diaz. Before their departure the King himself received the sailors and exhorted them to patience and obedience to their commander. To Da Gama he presented a silk flag adorned with the cross of the Order of Christ and credentials for the African and Indian Kings, and exact instructions following the reports of Diaz and Covilham. Then Vasco and all his men, having confessed, marched to the ships and weighed anchor amidst the good wishes of the crowd of spectators.

Passing the Canaries, they touched at the Cape Verde Islands, to take in meat, wood, and water, and repair the damage which some of the ships had incurred in a storm. Here Bartholomew Diaz separated from them, to go to his post at San Jorge da Mina. Gama himself left on August 3rd, and held his course in the open sea far to the west of the African shore. It was not till the 4th of November that they touched the coast, and found a wide bay which received from Gama the name of St. Helena's Bay. Stopping here some days, they had much intercourse with the natives, sometimes friendly and sometimes hostile. On November 22nd they sailed round the Cape of Good Hope, but an unfavourable wind for several days prevented them from running into the Bay of San Bras, now called Mossel Bay, where the provision ship was unladed, and the stores being divided among the three ships, it was sent home.

They found here a large population of a race similar to that around St. Helena's Bay. They were Hottentots, of the tribe of the Gonaqua, which has since ceased to exist. They had large herds of cattle—beautiful fat beasts, mostly of a black colour, and so fine that our informant speaks of them as bearing a comparison with those of his native province, Alemtajo. He also praises the musical taste of the savages. "They began to play on four or five pipes, one playing loud and the others softly, and the harmony was very good for negroes, from whom no one expects music. They also began to dance in negro fashion, and our captain commanded the trumpets to blow, and we danced in our ships, and the captain also danced after he had come back to us from the land. After the end of the feast we landed at the usual place, and bought a black ox for three bracelets, which we ate the next Sunday. It was very fat and the meat was good, tasting just like Portuguese beef."

Unfortunately this concord did not last. Gama, without sufficient cause, grew suspicious and made some hostile demonstrations, firing four discharges of powder only to frighten the natives. The unwonted noise caused such a panic that the whole troop fled to the mountains, and were never seen again. Besides intercourse with the natives, the sailors amused themselves by shooting the penguins, which were here first seen, and hunting seals. Before they finally returned to the ships they erected a pillar and a cross on the shore. These, however, they saw thrown down by the natives, as they sailed away.

As they pursued their course towards the east their fleet touched some islands, which they called Ilheos Chaos, or the

Flat Islands, but which the English call the Bird Islands. The wind changing, they tried to reach the coast, but the current was so strong that they were driven in one night to Santa Cruz. Gama's confident bearing reassured the dispirited crew. By renewed efforts they succeeded in mastering the stream and making an advance along the coast, which now bent more decidedly to the north-east and north. Just at Christmas-time they sighted a pleasant land, which still bears the name of Christmas Land, or Natal. The favourable wind, however, forbade any pause here, and they contented themselves with viewing the land from a distance. As long as the wind lasted it was necessary to use it for their onward progress, and the men were now in such spirits that even when obliged, from the want of water, to use salt water for cooking, they bore it without a murmur. However, they found themselves at last forced to run into the shore.

On the 10th January, 1498, they landed at the mouth of a small river, the Rio do Cobre. Here they found the land thickly peopled. From the sailor's description, the people appear to have been Kaffirs, as is evident from the fact that he was surprised at their size, so superior to that of the Hottentots. In the Kaffirs the Portuguese became acquainted with a comparatively civilised people, with whom it was easy to hold intercourse. One of the chiefs was soon won over to the strangers by the gift of a red jacket and pair of trousers, a cap, and a bracelet. Dressed in his new attire, he showed himself to his subjects, who testified their admiration by repeated clapping of hands. He received very hospitably into his hut a sailor, named Martin Alfonso, who, having lived some time in Congo, understood several negro languages, and acted as interpreter. He sent him back the next morning to the ships, with a present of poultry. Then a very brisk traffic was begun between them, and the water-casks were speedily filled, with the help of the blacks. We are told the natives wore much copper—the rings on their arms and legs, and the ornaments in their hair, were all of copper. Besides the azagays and the lances, six feet long, the Portuguese noticed particularly the daggers with iron points and ivory hilts. The natives also understood how to manufacture salt, by dipping up the sea-water, and leaving it to evaporate in large flat trenches.

When the Portuguese, after many days, again set sail, they named the country the Land of Good People, in memory of their pleasant intercourse. The exact spot where they made this landing was probably north of Delagoa Bay, at the mouth of the river now called Inhambane, south of Cape Corrientes. Sailing onward, a flat coast on the left hand was discovered; and as they wanted to make investigations, and also to repair the ships, they again anchored at the mouth of a great river, now called the Zambesi. The natives of this region were negroes, and manifested a most friendly disposition. Both men and women were well formed, but the latter had the strange custom of piercing the upper lip in three places, and inserting bent pieces of tin as ornaments. They lived on corn and vegetables, which they cultivated in the extremely fertile soil, and with which they willingly supplied the Portuguese.

The sailors here learnt with extreme joy that they were approaching civilised parts, and therefore near attaining the object of their voyage. "After we had been two or three days at that place," says Alvaro Velhes, "two of the principal men came to visit us. One wore a silk turban, with bright-coloured stripes, and the other a cap of green satin. They brought with them a young man, who, as far as we could understand by their signs, came from a country a long way off, and had seen ships as large as ours. We were exceedingly rejoiced at this account, because it seemed as if we were approaching the lands we were seeking."

VASCO DA GAMA AND THE KAFFIR CHIEF.

Before their departure they erected a pillar, and named the stream the River of Good Tidings. But the long visit to the flat marshy coasts had unpleasant consequences. A great number of the sailors were attacked by a violent sickness. From the symptoms—swellings of the hands and feet, and festering soreness of the gums, which made it painful and difficult to eat—they called it scorbutus, or scurvy, a disease until then unknown. The medical knowledge of Paul da Gama, and the extreme care which the commander took of the sick, checked the disease before it had got a hold, and a supply of fresh meat put a stop to it altogether.

Vasco da Gama set sail again on February 24th, and the next day three little islands appeared; but he continued his course towards the north without stopping, and did not come to anchor again until March 2nd, when they reached an island separated from the coast by a narrow strait, the entrance to which was much impeded by shallows. On this Island of Mozambique they became perfectly assured of their approach to the civilised East. The copper-coloured inhabitants were Mohammedans, and understood the Arabic language. Their clothing was very rich—bright-striped robes of linen or cotton, turbans of glistening silks interwoven with gold thread, and Moorish swords and daggers. In the harbour lay Moorish merchant-ships, very large, but without decks, and the planks being held together without nails, by means of bast, which was prepared from the shell of the cocoa-nut; the sails consisted of matting made of palm-leaves, and the whole rigging was very scanty. Yet these miserable vessels made long voyages, and, to the astonishment of the Admiral, were well provided with compasses, quadrants, and charts. They were laden with gold and silver, cloth, cloves, pepper, pearls, and precious stones; and the natives stated that all these valuable commodities were to be found in a country not far distant. "These precious stones, pearls, and spice so abounded that there was no need to buy them; they could be picked up by the basketful. The way thither was rendered dangerous by shallows, but all along the coast there were towns. We should also pass a very rich island, the inhabitants of which were half Christian and half Mohammedan." The reports about Prester John also were very numerous. Vasco was told that his kingdom was quite near; that he possessed towns by the sea inhabited by rich merchants; but that he himself lived in the interior, and could only be visited by undertaking a long journey on camels. Vasco became acquainted with some of the subjects of this mysterious prince. With the Moors came on board two Abyssinian slaves, who proved themselves to be Christians by immediately prostrating themselves before an image of St. Gabriel. This caused a firm conviction in the fleet that, as they advanced towards India, the population would become more Christian. The sailors grew hopeful and excited on receiving this news. "We were so glad that we wept for joy, and prayed God that He would keep us in health, that we might at last feast our eyes with that which we had so ardently longed for."

The Prince of Mozambique came many times on board and exchanged presents with Gama. He also granted him two pilots, whose pay was to be thirty ducats and two cloaks. But the condition which Gama insisted on, that from the time of the conclusion of the treaty one of the pilots should be constantly on board, caused a disturbance of the friendly relations. In fact, the Arabs, who were the chief people of the island, were impelled by hostile feelings towards the strangers, since they had discovered that they were not Turks, as they had at first supposed them to be, but infidels. Besides religious hatred, anxiety was aroused lest the monopoly of the Indian trade should pass out of the hands of the Arabs. On the other side, the Portuguese were unnecessarily suspicious, and often discovered some crafty treason in a perfectly innocent transaction.

From fear of a surprise, the Portuguese fleet left the harbour, and anchored off a little island which they called St. George. The boats which were sent to fetch back one of the runaway pilots met with resistance, and a skirmish began which was only put an end to by the arrival of the caravel *Berrio*. Reserving the punishment of the Moors for a later period, Gama set sail with his squadron, which was well stocked with goats, poultry, and pigeons. But a dead calm detained him for many days; the stream which runs southward along the east coast of Africa carried him, against his will, back to Mozambique. While taking in water an affray began, and in consequence of a formal challenge, the Portuguese vessels placed themselves before the palisade fortification with which the Moors had tried to protect their little town, and opened a fire, which did much damage, and caused such a panic that during a pause in the firing the whole population passed over to the mainland. Gama pursued their canoes; some were taken, and their contents given as plunder to the sailors, and their crews taken prisoners.

After this revenge, which was made use of as a precedent for an endless series of acts of violence, by means of which the Portuguese put an end to the Arab trade in the Indian Seas, a favourable wind permitted their departure on May 29th; but they were still in fear of treason. The Mozambique pilot was suspiciously watched, and it was not without reason that the worst designs were attributed to him. The little group of the Querimba Isles long bore the name of Ilhas do Acoutado, Whipping Islands, from the punishment inflicted on him for declaring that these islands were a part of the mainland.

The most important town on the east coast of Africa at that time was Kiloa or Quiloa, 9° south latitude, which was the seat of a brisk trade. The pilots wished to bring the fleet into this place, which was ruled by a Prince who also possessed authority over many other towns; but a strong south-west wind prevented this, and the Portuguese escaped what they afterwards discovered to have been a plot for their destruction. With the help of two Moors, whom they captured in a boat on the open sea, they reached on April 7th the harbour of Mombaza, 4° south latitude.

This town was on an island separated from the mainland by a canal, and being situated on hilly ground would have attracted the Portuguese, had it not been for the numerous merchant ships lying at anchor. On this account they thought it safest to remain outside the harbour, and to receive there the messengers of the King of Mombaza, who brought them presents of fruit and a sheep, and invited them to visit the place. Four Moors of rank remained as hostages for the envoys whom Gama sent into the town. These latter were struck by the regularity of the streets, by the stone houses, and by the ceremonious etiquette with which the King received them, and signified his acceptance of Gama's gift, some valuable coral.

The large Christian population of which the pilots from Mozambique had spoken were reduced to two Abyssinian merchants, to whom the Portuguese paid visits. Then they returned to their ships with many specimens of the spices which were to be bought in the town. This decided Gama to enter the harbour; but the conduct of the Moors upon a slight accident which happened to the Admiral's ship again aroused his suspicion. The Moors who were on board were tortured with boiling oil until they confessed that the destruction of the Portuguese had been determined on as a revenge for the cruelties they had practised in Mozambique. The fleet therefore remained in its position outside the harbour, but it was not safe there, and the night-watch often had to chase away men who were found swimming round the ships, trying to cut the ropes of the anchors.

In consequence of the treachery both real and imaginary,

great discontent arose among the seamen, who were also suffering much from sickness. All the Moors who were on board, even the closely-watched pilots from Mozambique, succeeded in throwing themselves into the water and swimming away, otherwise they would certainly have fallen victims to the sailors' ill-humour. "These dogs," says Alvaro Velhes, "planned these atrocities and many others, but the Lord would not let them succeed, because they did not believe in Him." Probably we may put down to their embittered fancy the unlikely story that the little fortress which protected the harbour of Mombaza was full of Christian slaves in chains.

On leaving the inhospitable Mombaza, Gama found himself in great embarrassment. He dared not venture on the voyage across the Indian Ocean without pilots, but, from the hostility of the Moors, he saw no way of providing himself with these indispensable guides. Fortune, however, favoured him, and compensated him for his earlier difficulties by unexpectedly fulfilling his wishes.

A few miles from Mombaza he captured a Moorish boat containing seventeen men, besides a valuable cargo. From these he learnt that the little town of Melinda—which they reached the first evening—was governed by a Prince whose peace-loving disposition promised to the Portuguese the fulfilment of their wish. Gama determined to try and open communication with him, and therefore, while the fleet anchored far from the town, he sent on shore an old Moor—the most trustworthy of the prisoners—to negotiate with the Prince of Melinda. The same day—Easter Monday—a ship came out bringing a high dignitary with presents, a civility which Gama immediately reciprocated. The result of the intercourse thus auspiciously begun was that the day after the fleet entered the harbour. After a few days a personal interview between the Admiral and the Moorish Prince took place, each in his boat ;

they met in the middle of the harbour, and held a long friendly conversation.

The report of the cruelties of the Portuguese had reached Melinda, but, notwithstanding, the Prince showed himself unprejudiced and friendly. He came near the ships to examine them, and was pleased at the salute which the Portuguese fired in his honour; and when he returned to the town left his son and chief minister as hostages in the ships, while some of the Portuguese accompanied him to his palace.

The next day a second interview on land was proposed, but Gama's prudence forbade his landing. He excused himself on the ground of an express prohibition of his King, and would not yield to the earnest request of the Prince, who wished to show the strangers to his lame father. So the meeting took place on the beach. Well-armed boats rowed along the shore, which was covered with an enormous crowd. The town—which contained many white stone buildings, and was surrounded by a majestic forest of palms—presented a very pleasant appearance. For the convenience of trade there was a high stone pier, from which steps led up to the palace of the Prince. Here the Portuguese stopped and awaited the Prince, who appeared borne in a palanquin, dressed in magnificent attire, and surrounded by his chief men. Again assurances of friendship and presents were exchanged, and Gama received the promise that an experienced Christian pilot—who knew the way to India—should be given him. But when two days had passed away, and yet the pilot did not appear, Gama seized a man of rank, and said he should keep him prisoner until the promise was redeemed. The pilot immediately appeared, a certain Malemo, surnamed Canaca, born at Gujerat, who was experienced in nautical matters, and at the same time trustworthy.

The Portuguese were pleasantly surprised to find in the harbour of Melinda four ships manned by Indian Christian members of the ancient Church said to have been founded by St. Thomas. With these brethren in the faith a hearty intercourse sprang up. They came daily on board the Portuguese ships and performed their devotions before the crucifix and the image of the Virgin. They were people of a brown complexion with long hair and beard, but their clothing was scanty. They lived very simply and did not eat meat. With Melinda, where a whole colony of Indians had settled, they carried on a brisk trade, bringing Indian wares into the land and exchanging them for gold, amber, tar, wax, and ivory. Their friendship for the Portuguese became so hearty that they gave them a great feast on their ships.

This meeting gave the discoverers the idea that India was a Christian country, and at first they looked upon the Buddhists also as co-religionists. The mistrust which Gama felt towards the Moors was increased by these Indian Christians, but with regard to the Prince of Melinda it was never justified. On the contrary, he merited the fullest confidence, not only by his conduct on this occasion, but also by his ready help and assistance on subsequent visits of Portuguese fleets.

The anchor was weighed on the 24th of April, and once fairly on the open sea the ships struck boldly across the Indian Ocean in order thus to reach the coast of Malabar. A strong south-west wind swelled the sails, and it remained true to the Portuguese until they had reached their goal. It was the monsoon, a periodical wind which regulates the trade in the Indian Ocean.

In the unusually short time of twenty-three days the Portuguese ships traversed the 750 miles which separated them from India, and by the 17th of May they saw the coast of Malabar before them. That name is still given to the 220 miles of coast which lie between Cape Comorin and the mouth of the river Nerbudda. Along the whole coast lies the chain of the Western Ghauts which forms a boundary to the Deccan.

Upon an average these mountains have a height of 3000 feet, but some points attain an altitude of 8000 feet. The sea washes their base, and only in the extreme south is there, between it and the mountains, a narrow swampy plain. A number of excellent harbours distinguishes this west coast from Coromandel, the flat eastern coast, and even in old times made it very important. Not only were the productions of the interior exported from these harbours—such as indigo, pepper, and cotton—but the Arab ships also found stored up here the productions of the countries still farther east—cinnamon from Ceylon, nutmegs and cloves from the Sunda Islands. Thus the Portuguese had discovered the very source whence the Arabs drew the Indian wares in which they trafficked, and it was therefore evident that the Arabs would do all they could to prevent the Portuguese settling there. But it was doubtful how the Indians would act, and to gain them, and particularly their Princes, was of the utmost importance to Portugal.

The whole of India was broken up at that time into innumerable little kingdoms ; but whilst the north had had to suffer the attacks of foreign conquerors, by which the people and their religion had been very much affected, the whole south of the peninsula, and particularly the coasts, were inhabited by an unmixed Hindoo race who remained true to their religion.

Almost every town on the west coast, where the Portuguese first landed, was the seat of a little Prince. Most of them, however, were subject to a mighty King who had his residence at Calicut, the most populous and thriving town of Malabar. To this King the Portuguese gave the title of Zamorin, which was their version either of Tamutiri Rajah, that is, lord of the hills and waves, or of Samoudri Rajah, that is, lord of the ocean.

The Portuguese cast anchor in the open road before Calicut on the 20th of May, a time of year in which there were

not many ships in the harbour, it being much more frequented
in the early autumn, as the autumn monsoon was useful for
the return voyage to Arabia.

Some boats came out to greet the newcomers, and on one
of them was a Moor from Tunis, so that the Portuguese were
most agreeably surprised by receiving a welcome in their own
language: "Good luck! Good luck! lots of rubies, lots of
emeralds. You may thank God that He has led you into a
land where there is so much riches." This Moor, whose name
was Monçaide, was of most important service to the Portuguese
during their stay in India, and accompanied Gama to Portugal,
where he was baptised into the Christian faith and finally
settled down.

From him the Admiral learnt that the Zamorin was not at
that moment in Calicut, but fifteen miles up the country. It
appeared necessary to salute him, and therefore two men were
despatched to announce the arrival of the squadron to the
Prince, and to beg an audience for their leader. Although
the population of Calicut must have been considerable, the
town made no great impression on the Europeans. With the
exception of the stone houses which the Moors settled there
had built, it only consisted of wooden houses with roofs of
palm-leaves. The palace of the Zamorin, together with the
houses of the principal men, was situated in a palm wood, half
a mile from the town. The brown inhabitants were mistaken
by the Portuguese for Christians simply because they were not
Mohammedans; some of them wore long hair and beards, and
some had their heads shaven with the exception of the crown.
They wore fine cotton clothes, but were naked from the waist
upwards. Both men and women, but especially the women,
were covered with ornaments—in their ears, on their arms,
breasts, and even toes were decorations of gold; and in many
cases beautiful diamonds were to be seen. The people too
appeared to be sensible, good-tempered, and sociable.

The Zamorin gave Gama's ambassadors a very friendly reception, offering many presents and assurances of goodwill. He promised to go himself at once to Calicut, and begged the Admiral, with the help of a pilot whom he sent to him, to leave the insecure road and cast anchor at a neighbouring place called Pangaray, the usual landing-place of foreign ships, and a spot which offered perfect security against storms. After a little consideration, this counsel was followed, but feeling a little mistrust, Gama would not allow the ships to approach as near to the land as the pilot wished. Gama now received a visit from one of the principal officers of the Zamorin, a man who appears to have been the commander of the town, and who had to watch over the intercourse of the people with foreign traders. He brought an invitation from the Zamorin, which he accepted for the 28th of May. The thirteen men who accompanied him put on their best clothes, and with waving banners and with a flourish of trumpets, the Admiral stepped upon the shore of India. The commander awaited him with a great train and an immense crowd of people. Gama took his seat in a litter which was borne by six men. Behind him came the Portuguese, among whom was Alvaro Vilhes, and the native train. After a meal of rice and excellent fish, which was offered to the foreigners in the house of one of the great men, Gama stepped into a boat prepared for the purpose and went up a piece of the river which flows into the sea by Calicut. Numbers of large ships were to be seen, but drawn up to the shore on account of the season. Then the procession resumed its course by land until a second halting-place was reached, this time a temple, which the Portuguese took for a Christian church.

In the spacious building they saw some bronze pillars, several images of different gods, and seven little bells. They were still more strengthened in their mistake when some priests came to meet them and sprinkled them with water and ashes; and when they saw in a little side chapel, to which only the priests had entrance, an image of the beautiful Maha Madja, and on her breast her little son Buddha, they naturally took it for the Virgin and Child, fell down upon their knees, crossed themselves, and, with Gama at their head, piously offered their devotions. They took little account of the hideousness of the crowd of saints whose pictures covered the walls, in spite of the fact that some of them had their tongues an inch out of their mouths, and others had four or five arms. Only John de Saa, a man given to doubt, entertained any misgiving as to the Christianity of the saints. He made the Admiral laugh by exclaiming, in order to render himself perfectly secure in kneeling before the image, " If it is a devil, may my prayer be heard, not by him, but by the true God."

As the train of Portuguese advanced the surrounding crowds increased, so that it was difficult to make way through them. But at length the vicinity of the palace was reached, and from it there issued a procession of people, who came with music to welcome the Portuguese and conduct them to the Zamorin.

The latter awaited his guests in a splendid apartment, reclining on a couch. He was dressed in a very full garment, which reached down to the knees and was made of the finest white cotton, embroidered with golden roses, and on his head he had a cap adorned with gold and jewels. The heavy rings on his arms and legs sparkled and flashed with costly stones. Near him stood a large golden bowl filled with betel, which the inhabitants of India are passionately fond of chewing, in order to lessen by its spicy aroma the depressing effect of the heat. In his hand he held a golden cup, into which every now and then he spat out the chewed betel. All those who were present covered their mouths with their left hands, in order to prevent their breath reaching the Zamorin, a crime which would have been punished as severely as if one had dared to sneeze or spit in the presence of the Prince.

After the salutations had been made in the fashion of the country the Prince desired the strangers to take their places and ordered fruits to be offered them. Then he retired with Gama into another room, where the latter gave him an account of his home and of his King, after which Gama was dismissed with every assurance of goodwill. The Portuguese passed the night in a hall at some distance from the palace, which had been prepared for their reception.

A second audience was arranged for the next day, but a most unpleasant circumstance compelled Gama to postpone it. He had noticed that no one dared approach the Zamorin with empty hands, and therefore had brought presents from the ship. These would have been very suitable for a Hottentot chief, but were not at all fitted for an Indian Prince who was accustomed to every luxury; twelve pieces of cloth, twelve cloaks, six hats, four branches of coral, a small chest with six bottles, a chest of sugar, two casks of oil, and two of honey. The officers who were sent to inspect these presents declared that they were much too common, that they would not dare to offer them to the Zamorin, and asked whether Gama had not brought with him more valuable things—if possible, gold. The Moors also, settled in the country, spoke just as contemptuously of the presents; Gama therefore was very much disconcerted and determined not to offer them.

When he appeared again before the King, a few days later, there was a significant lessening of cordiality. In his conver- . sation the Zamorin made it evident that he expected a suitable present. "What did you want to discover here," he inquired, "stones or men? If men, why did you bring nothing for them?" At last he said that he had heard about a golden statue of the Virgin which Gama had on board; this must be given him. With sailor-like honesty the Admiral replied that the statue was not of gold, and that even if it had been it could not have been given to the Prince. On the other hand, the letter from King Emanuel, which was presented and interpreted by one of the learned Moors, made a favourable impression on the Zamorin, and he granted his permission to the Portuguese to unlade their wares and open a trade.

Thereupon Gama wished to return immediately to the ships, but he and his men were detained on the shore. Many misunderstandings and the suspiciousness of the Portuguese made their case worse. At last the matter became really serious, and it was not until Paul da Gama, at his brother's order, had sent some wares on shore, that they were set free and allowed to return to the ships.

"We thank God," says Alvaro Velhes, "that He has saved us from men who are as deaf to all reason as if they sprang from beasts. We knew well that if the Admiral were once on board, any one of us who might be yet on shore had nothing to fear." The expedition had occupied five days, and during all that time those who had remained with the ships had suffered the greatest anxiety.

Meanwhile the Moors settled in Calicut had thoroughly awoke to a consciousness of the injury that would result to them and their trade if the Portuguese were allowed to come in, and therefore they did their best to increase the disagreement between the Zamorin and Gama. The discontent which the Zamorin and his officers felt at the stinginess of the Portuguese, and the want of reverence which they had shown in their manner of approaching him, offered them a very good handle. They represented the Portuguese as pirates, and by bribery won over to their side the powerful Catwal or commander, whom the Portuguese soon discovered to be their most formidable enemy.

At first, indeed, Gama obtained permission from the Zamorin to carry on trade with the natives, and the people of Calicut showed themselves so friendly that the Portuguese were able to make purchases without any danger, and a kind of factory was established. But the Moors had the ear of the Zamorin, as the Portuguese were not long in finding out. Diego Dias, whom Gama despatched to the Zamorin as his ambassador, was indeed admitted, but the magnificent presents which he carried with him were again rejected as unworthy, and he himself ungraciously dismissed.

By-and-by the Portuguese became suspicious that there was a design to detain them until the Moorish fleet should arrive and could assist in their overthrow. This suspicion was strengthened when the Zamorin laid an arrest upon all the goods still on shore, and placed a guard over those who had the charge of them. At the same time all intercourse was forbidden with the natives. Notwithstanding, the prisoners succeeded in sending news to Gama of their situation, where-upon he enticed nineteen Indians on board, and kept them as hostages for the Portuguese. At the same time he announced his intention of returning to Europe, and of coming back again shortly, fully prepared to take signal vengeance for the injus-tice with which he had been treated. This resolute way of proceeding made an impression.

The Zamorin summoned Diego Dias before him, expressed himself as perfectly unaware of what had been done by his officers, ordered a strict investigation, and restored freedom to the imprisoned Portuguese. At the same time he sent a letter to Gama by Dias for the King of Portugal. It ran thus: "Vasco da Gama, a nobleman of your house, has visited my land, which gave me much pleasure. In my land there is cinnamon, cloves, ginger, pepper, and precious stones in abund-ance. And what I want from your land is gold, silver, coral, and scarlet."

The remarkable shortness and complete want of polite phrases, which the people of the East usually employ so lavishly, show that the Zamorin had little esteem for the King of Portugal and his ambassadors. And this was doubtless owing to the calumnies of the Arabs, and to the unconciliatory conduct of the Portuguese, which was shown even in little things. For example, Gama insisted in placing on the land a pillar with the Portuguese coat-of-arms engraved upon it, in spite of the most violent opposition on the part of the Zamorin, who looked upon it as an attack upon his princely rights, and without considering that it would be knocked down immediately on the departure of the Portuguese.

When the released Portuguese were conducted back to the ships, Gama only set free six of the Indians, and declared that he should retain the others until all the Portuguese wares were restored. But when next day the wares were brought in seven boats, mutual mistrust prevented a peaceful conclusion of the matter. From fear of treachery on the part of the foreigners, only three boats approached, while the remaining four kept at a distance. They made signs to the Portuguese to place the hostages in the boat which hung at the back of the Admiral's ship, from which they would fetch them, and at the same time unlade the wares. This proposal was considered a cunning trick. Alvaro Velhes calls it a trick worthy of a fox, and Gama declared that now he would not receive the wares at all, but should take the hostages to Portugal.

Naturally this was looked upon in Calicut as an open breach of the treaty, and as a horrible piece of kidnapping ; and it served to verify all the evil reports which the Moors had spread with regard to the Portuguese. The next morning seventy strongly-manned boats rowed out to compel the release of the prisoners, but a few cannon-shots sufficed to scatter them. On the same day, August the 9th, Gama set sail and left Calicut, after a stay of 104 days.

During this period Gama had succeeded in almost filling the ships. But it is much to be lamented that the Portuguese left India in a state of irritation, and full of the most hostile feelings. They believed themselves throughout to have been slighted and treated in an underhand way, and the just mistrust which they had at first felt with regard to the behaviour of the Moors at last became a mania. An impartial investigation of the matter leads to the conclusion that the ignorance of the Portuguese with regard to the manners of Eastern lands was the chief cause of the discord. They came with empty hands where every one was accustomed to presents and bribery ; they stood up stiffly and defiantly where people were accustomed to the greatest deference ; and they often showed a mistrust of the most solemn assurances, which did them the greatest injury.

Hitherto the Portuguese had only held intercourse with the rude inhabitants of the coast of Africa, for whom their behaviour was exactly suitable ; they were quite unable to appreciate the peculiar character of Indian civilisation, and would not condescend to hold intercourse with the natives as equals.

Their mistake in the matter of religion had contributed not a little to this estrangement. They had imagined that, together with the coast of Africa, they had left behind the territory of Islam, and had calculated that the Indians, whose Buddha worship they had taken for Christianity, would render them active assistance against the hated Musselmans; and when they discovered the contrary, their vexation was much increased.

Our informant says, "We were the more provoked that such a trick should have been played us by a Christian King, to whom our Admiral had made presents at his own expense, desiring nothing more than that he should listen to reason."

Thus they left Calicut with unpleasant remembrances and desires of revenge, which they hoped it would please God to enable them to accomplish. Rivers of blood and indescribable suffering resulted from this quarrel—a quarrel which induced the Portuguese to depart from their original plan of peaceable commerce, and enter on the path of conquest. Gama, delayed by repeated calms, continued coasting towards the north. On September 19th he cast anchor off a little island 15° 44′ north latitude, named Anchediva. Here they set up their third pillar ; and as repairs were necessary for the ships, this island, on which were found both large forests and excellent water, was chosen for a long rest. With the inhabitants of the neighbouring coasts they had frequent communication, buying from them fruit and wares, particularly cinnamon, and finding them always friendly.

But here also the mistrust of the Portuguese caused much trouble. When eight ships arrived, coming from the open sea, they concluded that they had been sent in pursuit from Calicut, and received them with a discharge of their guns, and drove them from the shore. The same treatment awaited seven other vessels, although their crews were Christians, and they had come adorned with flags to the sound of music, to greet their brethren in the faith.

About this time the Portuguese made acquaintance with a singular individual. A man presented himself, of about forty years of age, fully clothed, wearing turban and sabre. He greeted the strangers, to their great astonishment, in pure Italian. He was, according to his own account, the descendant of a Jewish family from Posen ; he himself had been born and brought up in Alexandria, but had travelled for trade through a great part of Asia, and was now in the service of a powerful Prince, residing in the neighbouring town of Goa. At first the Portuguese received him in a very friendly manner, but, becoming suspicious of him, they flogged him four or five times, and then he confessed that his Prince had sent him to find out the strength of the Portuguese, and to entice them on shore for the purpose of overpowering them. How much belief is due to the confession is a question. That the Prince of Goa wished to seize the Portuguese, in order by the help of such brave men to overcome the neighbouring princes—such was the Jew's story—does not seem very probable; but the Portuguese were pleased at this acknowledgment of their valour, and congratulated themselves on the prudence by which they had escaped the danger. "They had, you see, said Alvares, "reckoned without their host." The destiny of the Jew was curious. He was forced to accompany Gama to Portugal. There he was converted to Christianity, and in baptism took the name of the man who had flogged him, Caspar da Gama.. His knowledge of languages made him a most important man. He accompanied the next Portuguese fleet to India as interpreter, and rendered signal service to his new countrymen. At last he was made, by King Emanuel, "Knight of the Palace," under the name of Caspar da India, and died at Lisbon, looked up to by all, and the intimate friend of learned men.

On the 6th of October they began their return voyage, hoping soon to arrive at home with the news of their great success. But the return voyage was a time of intense suffering to the sorely-tried sailors. From ignorance of the winds and currents of the Indian Ocean, and not having a pilot on board, they left the East Indian coast exactly at the most unfavourable time. A month later the north-east monsoon would have filled their sails and carried them safely and quickly to Africa, where the current would have borne them comfortably along the shore to the Cape. At present the voyage is made between Bombay and the Cape by sailing ships in about thirty days.

But the Portuguese were driven away from the region of the monsoon, which soon began to blow towards the south, and arrived in the region of calms, which—situated exactly north of the equator—divides the territories of the periodical winds from one another. Gama's fleet was here held fast as if by an invisible power, and had to endure the insupportable heat of a tropical summer. No wonder that dire disease soon made its appearance.

"In the midst of all this misfortune the scurvy broke out. The flesh grew over the teeth, so that the sufferers could not eat ; the legs began to swell, and the swelling spread so completely over the whole body that there was nothing to do but die. Thirty people now died of it, without counting the thirty whom it had previously killed. There were left at the most only seven or eight men on each ship to do the necessary work, and even they were not well. Therefore I can declare certainly that if the voyage had lasted a fortnight longer, no one would ever have ventured to follow our example. Things had already got to such a pass that we saw our end approaching, and could do nothing but make vows to the saints, and implore their aid in behalf of our ships. The captains held a council, and determined that if a contrary wind should arise, they would return to India, and wait until their men had recovered. But it pleased God in His mercy to send us a wind which in six days brought us to the coast, at which we were as glad as if we had reached Portugal, for we hoped now soon to be well again."

The sufferings thus described lasted almost three months, for it was the 2nd of February, 1499, when the ships reached the coast of East Africa. Steering southward, they reached a town with stately buildings rising from the sea. When Gama heard that it was Magadoxo (2° 1′ south latitude), which he had been told was a chief seat of the Moors, he determined to give these crafty people a lesson, and sailing straight to the town, fired upon it.

A very favourable wind carried the ships to the south, and after dispersing with their guns some Moorish boats which attacked them near the town of Pate, the Portuguese found themselves on the 9th of February off the friendly Melinda. Here they were well received by the King and the inhabitants, and fresh provisions amply furnished. In order not to lose the favourable wind, Gama weighed anchor after a stay of only five days. As a proof of friendship, the Prince of Melinda allowed a pillar to be erected, and also despatched an ambassador to the Portuguese King. Pursuing its course, the fleet sailed past Mombaza, Zanzibar, and Mozambique.

The condition of one of the larger ships, the *St. Raphael*, rendered some delay necessary. Many times stranded, once damaged by lightning, the ship was no longer in a condition to pursue its course. As the number of the men had so dwindled down that they were insufficient to man three ships, they divided the cargo and crew of the *St. Raphael* between the two other ships, the *Gabriel* and the *Berrio*, and surrendered the proud vessel to the flames.

On the 3rd of March they reached Mossel Bay, near the Cape, where they were constrained by a violent west wind to stay longer than they had intended. On the 20th of March they succeeded in sailing round the Cape of Good Hope, and found themselves in well-known waters. Impatience to see again their native shore now grew strong in every breast. In the neighbourhood of the Cape Verde Islands the ships lost sight of each other, and whilst the *Berrio*, commanded by Nicolas Coëlho, with Alvaro Velhes on board, continued its way home, and ran into Lisbon on the 10th of July, the *Gabriel* anchored off Santiago, one of the Cape Verde Islands.

Near the end of the voyage the Admiral was visited by a bitter grief. His faithful brother Paul had long been ill, and whilst all the other invalids had quickly recovered after passing the Cape of Good Hope, the strength of Paul da Gama visibly declined. The Admiral, who clung to him with tender affection, left the flagship to follow, and with his sick brother went on board a swift caravel that he might arrive more quickly in healthy regions. But in the neighbourhood of the Azores the sick man's state became so alarming that the worst was dreaded. He was carried on shore at Terceira, and there he died in the arms of his afflicted brother, who for many weeks could not tear himself from the grave. Gama did not reach Lisbon till the 29th of August, 1499, his voyage having lasted two years and two months. Here, though still bowed down with grief, he had to take part in the magnificent festivities which King Emanuel had prepared in honour of the great seaman and his glorious achievement.

After spending nine days in prayer at Restello, whence the expedition had started, he entered Lisbon in procession amidst the shouts of a dense multitude, which had gathered from far and near to see the man who had first unfurled the Portuguese flag on the coasts of India. The important news had been communicated by the King immediately after the arrival of Coelho to all the towns and villages of Portugal, and a special messenger had been despatched to inform the court at Rome.

On Gama and his companions—only fifty-five men returned out of one hundred and seventy—the King showered his favours. Vasco da Gama was made Admiral of the Indies, and at the same time raised to the highest rank among the nobility and allowed to adopt the title of Dom and to quarter the royal arms with his own. In addition to these honours, when the King some time later discovered the immense advantage of direct intercourse with India, he made the Admiral Count of Vidigueira, and also bestowed upon him the annual income of 300,000 reals (about £3000), then a very great sum, which was to pass to his descendants. In an equally liberal manner did the King treat Nicolas Coëlho and none of the much-tried seamen went unrewarded.

His pious disposition also made the monarch anxious to show his gratitude to Heaven, and at Restello, on the spot from which Vasco da Gama had embarked and on which he had landed, he laid the foundation of a splendid cloister which he destined to be the last resting-place of the royal family, and named Bethlehem or Belem. This splendid building is still standing, having been spared by the great earthquake of Lisbon, to remind posterity of the enthusiasm to which it owed its origin.

A touching proof of the respect in which he held the memory of his great uncle is afforded by the statue of Prince Henry the Navigator which he erected at the entrance of the cloister and by the weekly mass which he instituted for his soul.

Many years of rest were granted to Vasco da Gama to restore his shattered health, whilst others were commissioned to carry on his work. It was not until the 10th of February, 1502, that he again left Lisbon at the head of a fleet of twenty ships, strongly manned, with the object of securing the influence of Portugal in India, and monopolising for her the whole of the eastern trade.

No doubt Gama enjoyed appearing at the head of such an important force in seas where the weakness of his first fleet had prevented him from adopting decisive measures, and was well pleased to show himself in the full splendour of power to those who had treated him so contemptuously. He visited on his outward journey Sofala, rich in gold, and concluded a treaty with the Prince of Mozambique, who granted leave for the founding of a factory, and promised that Portuguese vessels sailing past should always be supplied with provisions. Then the fleet stopped before Quiloa, where the Portuguese ships had been insulted, and after a violent cannonade the Prince was brought to declare himself a feudatory of the King of Portugal and to promise a yearly tribute.

Gama's irreconcilable antipathy towards the Moors showed itself in still more fearful colours after his arrival in India.

He pursued all Moorish ships with fire and sword.   One large ship, the *Merii,* which was carrying Mohammedan pilgrims to Mecca from all parts of Asia, was attacked by the Portuguese fleet on the 3rd of October and sunk after a whole day's resistance on the part of the pilgrims.   About three hundred men and women fell victims to this act of vengeance.   Twenty children were spared that they might be brought up as Christians.

Even after this deed of cruelty, which is a foul blot on Gama's name, the implacable man did not think he had sufficiently avenged himself on the Moors.   Remembering the treatment which he had received in Calicut, he appeared before the town, and when the Zamorin did not immediately grant his demand to drive all the Moors out of the land, he opened a terrible fire on the unhappy town, and put to death by torture any Moor who fell into his hands.   Then taking in a rich cargo at the ports of Cochin and Cananore, and leaving the full chastisement of the Zamorin for some future time, he set out on his return to Europe.   Five ships were left behind as a defence to the factories erected on the Indian coast, and five more were to cruise at the entrance of the Red Sea in order to capture Arabian merchant-ships.

On the 1st of September, 1503, Vasco da Gama entered the mouth of the Tagus after having encountered many storms on the voyage.   With great ceremony he presented to the King the first tribute of the Prince of Quiloa and the treaties which he had concluded with the Kings of Cochin and Cananore.   He boasted of having completely frightened away the hostile Moors by his severity.

The reception which he met with from King Emanuel was most honourable.   It seems therefore very strange that the King never employed him again.   Year after year powerful fleets sailed to India, and all the important men of Portugal took part in the enterprise.   But Gama's name is connected with none of the great deeds which were accomplished on the ocean discovered by him.

It is not until after Emanuel's death that he reappears on the scene. John III. sent him to India on the 9th of April, 1524, with fourteen ships and three thousand men as his viceroy. On the voyage thither a great earthquake, which made the waves rise mountains high, gave occasion to the lofty words with which he sought to encourage his trembling companions: "Why should we fear? Do you not see that the ocean is trembling before us?"

He busied himself on his arrival in India in great plans which he was not destined to accomplish. For the sickness which attacked him on his arrival increased from day to day, and on the 24th of December, 1524, he died at Cochin.

It was some time before his ashes found rest. Interred first in Cochin, then in Travancore, his body was in 1538, by command of King John III., brought to Portugal and buried in a chapel not far from Vidigueira, from which place he took his title, and where two of his descendants also rest. The inscription on the grave-stone runs thus: "Here lies the great Argonaut, Dom Vasco da Gama, first Count of Vidigueira, Admiral of the East Indies, the famous discoverer." The tomb was broken into in the year 1840, and has been restored at the expense of the State; but the proposition which has so often been made to prepare a worthy resting-place for the ashes of the great sailor in the cloister of Belem has never been carried into execution.

CHAPTER VI.

PEDRO ALVAREZ CABRAL AND JUAN DE NOVA.

THE return of the first Portuguese ships, laden with the products of India, had aroused in Portugal a storm of national enthusiasm, and presented to the imagination of all such an alluring picture of endless riches that they watched with impatience for further steps on the part of the King.

To this disposition of the people, which was indeed most agreeable to his wishes, Emanuel willingly responded, and hastened the preparation of a new fleet, which he intended to sail by the beginning of March ; for, according to the experience of Vasco da Gama with regard to the winds and currents, that appeared the most favourable time for a rapid voyage to India. If everything prospered, the adventurers would land on the Indian coast in autumn, could lade the ship there at their ease, and then, in the spring of the next year, begin their return. The correctness of this calculation, which experience has verified, is a proof that Gama's observations were carefully made and his conclusions trustworthy.

To the command of the fleet, which consisted of thirteen sail, and carried 1500 men on board, the King appointed Pedro Alvarez Cabral, of whose earlier life nothing more is known than that he belonged to one of the chief families of Portugal, and had distinguished himself as a well-informed and gallant man. It is possible that he was related to Gonsalvo Velhes Cabral, who had been sent out by Prince Henry, in 1430, to discover the Azores.

Under him commanded Bartholomew Dias and Nicolas Coelho, who had accompanied Gama. The strength of the crews shows that they reckoned on hostilities with the Moors. Yet the instructions which Cabral received from King Emanuel directed him to strive for peaceful intercourse, and to conclude treaties of commerce. Besides, an attempt was to be made, by the wish of the pious King, to convert the heathen ; and for this purpose the fleet carried on board eight Franciscan monks and eight seculars, together with a vicar, who were intended to take the spiritual charge in the fort to be founded. Earthly weapons were not to be employed unless these peaceful and pious efforts had no result. Even in that case, Cabral was limited by precise directions from the King, who was informed on all points and had foreseen all emergencies.

On the 9th of March, 1500, the fleet set sail and steered for the open sea, with the good wishes of all. At the Cape Verde Islands a pause was made, that some of the ships which had become scattered by a storm might join company again. According to the advice of Gama, they ought now to follow a southerly course, until the latitude of the Cape of Good Hope had been reached. This is still considered the shortest passage through the two regions of the trade winds, pursued already by Vasco da Gama.

Following closely these directions of Gama's, Cabral, after crossing the line, entered the equatorial current, which carried him imperceptibly towards the west. To the surprise of all, on April 24th, a coast was perceived, which, according to Cabral's reckoning, was 10 deg. south latitude, and quite 450 miles distant from Guinea. At first he thought the land he had discovered was an island; but when he had sailed along it for a whole day, he was convinced that it was the coast of a continent. Although his instructions forbade him to make any stay, the importance of the discovery compelled the Admiral to spend some days in examining the coast, along which he steered as far as 18 deg. south latitude. He found, at 16 deg. 16 min. south latitude, an excellent harbour, which offered a safe refuge for more than 200 ships, and which therefore received the name of Porto Seguro. This name still remains attached to a town situated on this harbour. On the shore, which was adorned with most luxuriant vegetation, there were seen fine copper-coloured people, who came up most confidingly to exchange bright-coloured parrots for the toys offered by the Portuguese.

Cabral well discerned of what importance this coast would be as a station for ships on their way to India, and took possession of it for his native land by erecting a pillar. From this it received the name of Tierra da Santa Cruz, which, however, afterwards gave place to that of Brazil. This name arose from the large quantity of the red dye-wood, which was compared to the colour of red-hot coals, and thence named brasil.

A ship was despatched to bear the news of the discovery to Portugal, and the King, early in 1501, sent out three sail to investigate the important place. Yet several years passed away before the immigration of the Portuguese and the building of forts began. Had not Columbus already, in 1492, discovered the New World, it would thus, eight years later, have been found through an accident.

On the 2nd of May Cabral again set sail, intending to reach the Cape of Good Hope by crossing the Atlantic Ocean. But this passage was not made without painful experience. The superstitious minds of the sailors were much agitated by a large comet, which showed itself at night in the eastern sky. A high sea and stormy weather left no one in repose. Then, on May 23rd, was seen, for the first time, a waterspout; and, while they were curiously watching it, a fearful storm suddenly arose, and sank four ships, with all their crews. Among these unfortunate sailors was Bartholomew Diaz. No one was in a condition to render assistance, for the remaining ships were half full of water, and would probably have perished had not the wind torn away their sails. For twenty days and nights did this tempest rage, while the exhausted sailors struggled for their lives. And when the storm subsided, and the fleet, which had passed the Cape of Good Hope, was stopped by dangerous shallows and contrary winds, it found itself reduced to four much-damaged vessels.

It was only by earnest remonstrances that Cabral persuaded the sailors to renounce their wish to return at once to Portugal, and to declare themselves ready to continue their voyage. They passed Sofala without touching, and proceeded to Mozambique, where they could without danger repair the ships and take in water—so strong still was the recollection of the chastisement inflicted on the Moors by Gama. Here too they obtained a pilot, who conducted them safely to Quiloa, which they reached on July 26th.

The Island of Quiloa, lying 9 deg. south latitude, and surpassing all the other East African islands in fruitfulness, had not been hitherto visited by the Portuguese. Yet, as it was the seat of a Prince who ruled a large portion of the coast and many much-frequented ports, it was worthy of special attention ; and Cabral had therefore received express directions from King Emanuel, if possible, to conclude a treaty with the Prince of Quiloa. However, the interview with this powerful ruler, which took place on the water, remained without result ; and, hearing a report that troops were assembling on the mainland, Cabral considered himself justified in leaving . the place with his six ships—two which he had thought lost had rejoined him—and deferring the negotiation to a more favourable opportunity.

At Melinda he was welcomed with much rejoicing, and many costly presents, and a letter written by King Emanuel's own hand, bound the Prince closely to the Portuguese interest.

He left this place on August 7th, and, being accompanied by two Indian pilots, reached the coast of India in sixteen days.

After a fortnight's stay at Anchediva, the fleet appeared on the 13th September off Calicut. At first all went well. The Zamorin condescended to meet the Admiral on the coast and promised to do all in his power to assist the Portuguese in their mercantile projects. A capacious building was immediately granted them for a magazine, and Ayres Correa, the factor, soon filled it with wares. When the treacherous whisperings of the Moors began again to produce an effect on the Zamorin, Cabral brought about a second meeting, and by means of his firm and dignified behaviour induced the Prince to make a formal treaty, establishing the conditions of the spice trade, and granting the Portuguese equal advantages with the Moors.

Still it was not possible to maintain this peaceful state of things unbroken. The obtrusive missionary zeal of the clergy may have increased the growing bitterness, and Correa's haughty behaviour gave great offence, so that the Portuguese trade progressed but slowly. The natives preferred to offer their wares to the Moors, who had long understood all the peculiarities of the Indian market, and who traded accordingly, rather than to the imperious Portuguese, who treated them in such an unconciliatory manner.

Thus it came to pass that after three months hardly two ships were fully freighted in spite of great efforts. Instead of seeing their mistake and trying to rival the Moors by greater concessions to the Indian method of trading, the Portuguese complained of the favour shown to the latter and considered themselves injured. At last they began to make use of violence, took possession of the goods which were intended for the Moors, and tried to compel the native traders to be satisfied with the prices which they settled as being proper once for all.

While the Portuguese showed such arrogance it was easy for the Moors to stir up the people. A disturbance, caused by some tyrannical act on the part of Correa, became a complete uproar; an enraged mob stormed the Portuguese factory; Correa and his men were beaten, and fifty Portuguese were either killed or taken prisoners. Cabral was, on account of the small force which he had at his command, not in a condition to rescue his people, or at any rate demand full satisfaction. Still he avenged himself by setting fire to fifteen Moorish vessels which lay in the harbour, and by bombarding the town of Calicut for two days, thus killing some hundreds of perfectly innocent persons. But all peaceful intercourse was of course for the present quite at an end. The calumnies of the Moors, who had represented the Portuguese as pirates, appeared of course more than ever credible to the Indians, and especially to the Indian Princes.

In vain did Cabral await an embassy from the Zamorin offering an apology and begging for a resumption of trade. So he determined to depart. But he could not think of returning to Portugal until his ships were fully freighted. He considered it therefore most opportune when the Rajah of Cochin, a port situated about thirty miles to the south, sent him word that great stores of pepper were laid up in that town, which the Portuguese might have for a moderate price. Cochin was at that time a small town dependent on the mighty Zamorin, but one which bore its dependence with impatience. It was particularly vexatious to the Rajah that Calicut had gradually raised itself to be the chief emporium of all Indian wares, while the neighbouring harbours were ruined. He had long viewed with envy the large tolls received by the mighty Zamorin, and it appeared to him worth while to make an attempt to draw into his territory the strangers who had done so much injury to the Moorish commerce, and who had quarrelled with the Zamorin, in order, by means of traffic with them, to raise Cochin at the the expense of Calicut.

His scheme succeeded. He was obliged, indeed, in the great struggle which shortly took place, unreservedly to take the part of the Portuguese, and many times to see his whole power endangered; but when the matter was finally decided Cochin took the place of the desolated Calicut, and became the most important port of Malabar, while the revenues of the Rajah were proportionately increased. In a short time Cabral's ships were laden with pepper.

The example of the Rajah was followed. The Princes of Cananore and Coulam, two towns to the north of Calicut, and also under the supremacy of the Zamorin, begged the Portuguese to visit them. But Cabral could not spare the time, and only promised the Prince of Cananore to fetch a certain quantity of ginger, which the latter agreed to have ready for him.

Just as he was on the point of leaving Cochin there appeared a fleet of 70 sail, among which were 25 large ships, with 1500 warriors on board, sent by the Zamorin to drive the Portuguese out of the Indian Seas. But they did not dare to attack him, and contented themselves with watching the dreaded foreigners. Cabral was not in the least disturbed. He quietly steered out of the harbour of Cochin, sailed past Calicut, in full view of the town, in order to show his utter fearlessness, and took the ginger on board at Cananore.

Here the Portuguese were offered more wares than their ships would hold, and were obliged to refuse much. The Rajah of Cananore thought that this was from want of money, and offered Cabral a loan; but Cabral showed the royal messengers the many chests full of gold which he still had on board, thanked the Rajah for his goodwill, and promised to report his friendliness to the King of Portugal. He then set out with his richly-laden fleet on his return voyage, accompanied by ambassadors from Cochin and Cananore.

But the voyage was not without disaster. In the neighbourhood of Melinda one of the largest ships ran upon a rock, and sank with all its cargo. Its guns afterwards were turned against the Portuguese by the King of Mombaza, who recovered them by means of divers. When the Cape was once rounded all went well, and on the 31st of July, 1501, Cabral cast anchor before Lisbon. But of the thirteen ships that had gone out, six lay at the bottom of the ocean, and only half of the men returned. On account of these disasters the Admiral met with a cold reception from the King. Although he could be charged with no fault, he was never again employed in any of the future undertakings, and the rest of the life of this deserving and ill-used man is veiled in complete obscurity.

The King was particularly vexed that, in spite of the liberal and costly fitting out of the fleet committed to him, Cabral had not been able to establish a firm footing in any part of India, and that he had not succeeded in erecting a fortress and in taking possession in the name of Portugal of some favourable point on the coast. He had so completely reckoned upon this being done that, during Cabral's absence, he had despatched a little fleet of four ships and eighty men simply for the purposes of trade, in order at once to make use of the military advantage which he assumed Cabral to have gained.

His intention was that henceforward a similar little merchant fleet should sail every year in March, the most favourable time. But after the return of Cabral, King Emanuel was filled with anxiety for the little squadron, which was not fitted either for defence or attack.

He had appointed commander of this squadron Juan de Nova, a noble Galician, who had distinguished himself in different expeditions in the Portuguese service as a skilful and brave seaman. On this occasion he justified the confidence of the King, and showed himself well suited for his very difficult position. Under him Vinetti, a Florentine, commanded a caravel, which his countryman, the rich merchant, Bartholomew Marchioni, had fitted out, making use of the permission of the King, who for a certain share in the profit had thrown open the trade to India.

This permission is another proof of the firm conviction on the part of the King that Cabral's imposing squadron must certainly have removed all the hindrances to trade which the hostility of the Moors and the reluctance of the Zamorin could have caused.

On his outward voyage Nova discovered in the Atlantic Ocean (7° 56′ south latitude) a rocky island, which from the day on which it was first seen he called Conception. This was afterwards changed into Ascension, and is now a station of the English ships employed in the suppression of the slave trade. It has a small population. The squadron sped prosperously on, though delayed for a time in the Mozambique Channel by contrary winds. Going round Calicut, it made directly for Cochin, but before it could run into the harbour it had to sustain a sharp conflict with an attacking fleet of the Zamorin, which, however, it succeeded in driving back.

Here and in Cananore the ships were quickly laded with pepper, ginger, and cinnamon, the Princes of both towns showing themselves most friendly, and then Nova, with much haste, left the coast, and cruised about in the open sea until the north-east monsoon arose and quickly bore the ships towards the west.

Nova's return voyage was rendered remarkable by a discovery. On the 22nd of May, 1502 (15° 55′ south latitude, and 5° 44′ west longitude), an island arose before them, which, in honour of the saint whose day it happened to be, received the name of St. Helena. On closer inspection it was discovered that the island possessed an excellent harbour, and abundance of good water, and therefore was well suited for a harbour of refuge, and for a watering station. This small island has now a population of 7000 people. Since 1688 it has been in the possession of the British, and is constantly visited by ships going to and from the East Indies, which stop here to take in water and provisions. But the great interest of the island consists in its having been the place to which the fallen Emperor Napoleon I. was banished, and where he died. It was in the farmhouse, Longwood, in the most dreary part of the island, that he fretted away the last six years of his life. Under the historic willow-tree, which stands near the farmhouse, his ashes rested until 1841, when Louis Philippe and his Minister Thiers caused them to be disinterred, and brought to France, where they found a more fitting tomb in the Hôtel des Invalides.

On the 11th of September, 1502, Nova ran into the harbour at Lisbon, and met with a most gracious reception from the King, and a rich reward, which was due no doubt to the rich cargoes of the ships, and to his circumspect conduct. He had not suffered the least loss, either in ships or men.

King Emanuel now added to the titles which he had hitherto borne—King of Portugal and of the Algarves, and Lord of Guinea—the new one of Lord of the navigation, conquest, and trade of Ethiopia, Arabia, Persia, and India, by which he showed what was the goal he aimed at, rather than what he really possessed.

It was important first of all to get the trade of those lands entirely into the hands of the Portuguese. Since the result of the three expeditions which had already been made to India had shown clearly the superiority of the Moorish merchants and the preference of the natives for them, it was now determined to have recourse to force and to render their Moorish rivals afraid of vying with the Portuguese, and thus to gain a free field.

To carry out this policy of terror, no one seemed more suitable than Vasco da Gama, in whose mind still rankled the bitterest feelings towards the Moors, to whose artifices he had fallen a victim. The command, therefore, of the fleet was committed to him, and he received full powers to use force towards the Moors and any Indian Prince who might oppose him. In what a bloody manner he made use of this power has already been related.

CHAPTER VII.

FRANCISCO DE ALMEIDA.

WHEN Vasco da Gama, in 1503, returned from his second voyage to India, he left at two places in Malabar—Cochin and Cananore—a small number of Portuguese for the protection of the factories established there—in the first harbour thirty, and in the latter twenty men—and a fleet which, besides serving as a protection to the men, was intended to watch the Moorish merchant-ships.

But its commander, Vincente Sodre, allowed himself, in spite of all warnings, to be persuaded to make an attack upon the Moorish ships in the Red Sea, at the most unfavourable time of year, and paid for his folly by his own death and the destruction of almost the whole fleet before it reached the Red Sea.

This appeared to the Zamorin a favourable opportunity to strike a blow at the Portuguese in the factories, and to teach the Indian Princes who protected them that it was vain to make use of the arms of foreigners in order to escape from the rule of their rightful superior. His army was too powerful for them to oppose it in the open field, and therefore the Rajah of Cochin evacuated the town, and withdrew to the Island of Waiping, taking the Portuguese with him. Even here he was hard pressed, until the arrival of a Portuguese fleet put an end to his difficulty, and made the Zamorin's army retreat.

This was a squadron which King Emanuel had prepared

before the return of Gama in 1503. It was principally composed of merchant-ships, which were to return as soon as possible to Portugal with rich cargoes. At the head of this squadron were two brothers, Francisco and Alfonso de Albuquerque; and a small part of the fleet, under Antonio de Saldanha, was directed to cruise about near the Red Sea. With the help of 600 Portuguese, the Rajah of Cochin soon drove the Zamorin out of his territory; and, out of gratitude to his protectors, he consented to the building of a fort on his territory. Immediately—September 27th, 1503—the work was begun, and, close by the town of Cochin, arose a strong building, which would at least serve as a defence in the case of hostile attack. It was called Santiago, and became the foundation of the Portuguese power in India. It had a garrison of 150, commanded by the brave Duarte Pacheco Pereira.

The factories in Cananore and Coulam were then visited, and there the ships were laded; for in Cochin it had been impossible to collect wares, owing to the war that had been raging. Then the two brothers returned home. But only Alfonso arrived safely in Portugal. Francisco, who left Cochin on the 31st of January, 1504, perished, with all his ships, no one knows how or where.

The fear of the Rajah of Cochin, that the Zamorin would renew his attacks as soon as the Portuguese fleet had departed, was only too well founded. The Zamorin had indeed, without the knowledge of the Arabian merchants, negotiated with the brothers Albuquerque, and had even condescended to give compensation for the destruction of the factory; but they soon began to suspect him, and, without waiting for any explanation, attempted to seize the ships of Calicut. Such treatment convinced him that friendly intercourse with the Portuguese would only be possible if he yielded to all their demands unconditionally, and surrendered all his rights

as a prince.   He preferred to try the fortune of war, hoping
that a severe defeat might render a settlement in India odious
to the Portuguese, while it would at the same time inspire with
new courage those whom the imperious conduct of the strangers
had dismayed, and deter the subject princes from following
the dangerous example of revolt.

With a mighty host, consisting of 70,000 men, 160 ships,
200 musketeers, and 300 pieces of ordnance, he entered the
territory of Cochin.   It required the courage of a Pacheco
Pereira even to think of opposition to such a host.   But this
extraordinary man, the first example of that incredible heroism
which was afterwards so frequently displayed, and which surrounded the Portuguese arms with the glamour of magic,
marched straight to meet the enemy's host, and did not return to the island town of Cochin until he had first inflicted
severe losses upon it.   The siege lasted from March until the
end of July, with varying fortune, the besieged suffering much,
but at the same time doing many glorious deeds.   The ap-
proaches to the island had every day to be defended by bloody
contests with the enemy, whose valour was animated by the
personal presence of the Zamorin.   Against the harbour of
Cochin fire-ships were let loose, which with difficulty were
diverted; and eight floating-towers, supported by the whole
fleet of the enemy, attempted to make a landing, but were
driven back by the Portuguese guns.

The exhausted garrison, which was aided by only a few
thousand native soldiers in the service of the Rajah, found a
more powerful ally in a pestilence which broke out in the
enemy's camp, and carried off so many victims that the Zamorin
broke up the siege, after having lost 18,000 men.   This melancholy result so decreased his importance that some of the
subject princes immediately fell away from him, and made
offers to the Portuguese.   Pacheco's fame was great in all
India ; and when he returned to Portugal the King rewarded

him with a significant coat of arms and the governorship of
the African Gold Coast; but, becoming the victim of some
atrocious calumnies, the gallant leader eventually died in
chains, and his family fell into the deepest poverty.

In September, 1504, there appeared in the harbour of the
relieved city of Cochin a Portuguese fleet of thirteen well-
armed ships, having on board 1200 men, among whom were
many noblemen eager to gain fame and wealth in India. The
commander of this fleet, which Emanuel had fitted out because Gama represented that war was absolutely necessary,
was Lopo Soares. He bombarded Calicut for two days, burnt
the Zamorin's town, Kranganor, with all the ships that lay in
the harbour; and at last, at the end of December, made a bold
attack on the well-manned Moorish merchant fleet which,
composed of seventeen ships, lay in the harbour of Ponani,
waiting for cargo, feeling perfectly secure under the shelter of
the batteries which the Zamorin had erected on the shore.
The audacious attack was perfectly successful, and ended in
the utter destruction of the Moorish fleet.

It was the severest punishment which could have been inflicted upon the Zamorin, for such a terrible loss frightened
the Moors away from his ports, and consequently made a
considerable difference in his revenue. At the same time
Soares showed the greatest possible honour to the faithful
Rajah of Cochin, and when he sailed away with his well-
laden fleet, left behind him four ships and a strong garrison
as a protection.

King Emanuel saw with much rejoicing the growing influence of his people on those distant shores, and the constantly increasing wealth which accrued to Portugal.

In the course of a few years Lisbon had become the great
spice market of Europe, and could supply nearly the whole
continent, since from twelve to fifteen well-laden ships came
into her harbour every year. Portugal was able to lower the

prices, and thus monopolised the whole trade, which had once been the wealth of Venice. Of course the use of spice increased as the price diminished, and thus larger sums were spent in Indian wares. The advantage which accrued to Portugal from this impetus to trade was something quite remarkable.

Besides the gigantic sums which flowed into the royal coffers and gave the King means to prepare new fleets, a number of large merchant houses sprang up, and a fresh life came into trade. Moreover the varied undertakings and the presence of many foreigners in the land were of great advantage both to the citizens and peasants, and exercised a beneficial influence even in the most distant corners of the land.

The more evident all this general prosperity became, the more zealous did the King grow to render it permanent. It did not escape him that in the long run it would not be enough to send large fleets to India just to procure cargo and then return. During their absence the impressions made upon the enemies of Portugal by their brilliant deeds of arms were quickly effaced, so that as a rule each fleet had to repeat the work done by the preceding one.

This unsatisfactory state of things was only to be prevented by maintaining constantly a considerable force in India. Emanuel determined to do this. Indeed, to give more uniformity to the conduct of Indian affairs and more permanence to the relations with the Indian princes, he determined that a representative of the King should take up his residence in India with the title of viceroy. The term of office was fixed at three years; for which period also all persons engaged in the service, whether holding civil or military appointments, were to be pledged.

The first man whom Emanuel invested with the dignity of viceroy was Francisco de Almeida, Count of Abrantes, one of those remarkable men who, without any thought of self or their own advantage, know no other glory than that of their country, and seek no other advantage than that of the people to whom they belong. He sprang from one of the most illustrious families of Portugal, and had, since he first distinguished himself in the siege of Granada, added glory to his name by many feats of arms both at sea and against the Moors in North Africa.

He cannot have been a young man when he was appointed by the King to the governorship in India, for he took with him a son old enough to bear arms, who was to earn his first laurels under his father's eyes. His bearing in his new office was dignified without being haughty. He himself submitted to the greatest deprivations and fatigues in the interests of his office, and he demanded from those under him, when necessary, the utmost exertion of their powers. But whilst he displayed an almost incredible unselfishness, and continually gave up spoil which was justly his, he was so generous in praising and rewarding those who faithfully fulfilled their duty or who performed great deeds that he sometimes drew down upon himself the displeasure of the King. This is proved by one sentence of the great man's which has come down to us. " I shall return to Portugal," he said, when he laid down his office, " and place before the King my master the instructions which he gave me, and if he finds that I have exceeded my commands in distributing his wealth, here is my own ; and if that is not sufficient to repair the damage, I shall tell him that another time he must not put the sword into the hand of a fool."

This liberality won for him the hearts of his subordinates, while his heroic greatness, his blameless life, and his strict sense of justice gained him the admiration of India.

He was next employed by the King in East Africa. Emanuel wished that the Portuguese should establish a firm footing on this coast, which was so important when considered

in connection with the Indian trade. He had also cast an
eye upon the province of Sofala, rich in gold but yet scarcely
touched. Almeida, according to the King's orders, sailed
with part of his fleet to Quiloa, the most powerful of the East
African mercantile cities. Disputes, which arose between
him and the Prince of Quiloa, ended in an assault on the town,
which the Portuguese took and plundered. With the new
Prince, whom Almeida established in place of the dethroned
one, he concluded a highly-advantageous treaty, which was
wrung from him no doubt in great measure by fear of the
Portuguese arms. Almeida was allowed to build the fort
Santiago on the harbour of Quiloa, and to furnish it with a
sufficient garrison. Much the same occurred at Mombas,
only that this town was able to make a greater resistance,
by means of the Portuguese guns which had been recovered
by means of divers from the bottom of the sea, as has been
already related, and therefore its defenders thus met with
more severe treatment after the capture. In both places the
spoil was great.

Much more peaceful and friendly was Almeida's entrance
into Melinda. The native Prince was loaded with presents and
reaped the fruits of his wise and pacific behaviour in the increased prosperity of his harbour—a prosperity due doubtless
to the destruction of the more powerful neighbouring cities.

The Viceroy did not go himself to Sofala, the exploration
of that land of gold and the establishing of a settlement there
being committed to a special fleet of six ships which sailed
away from Portugal under the command of Pedro de Anhaya
shortly after Almeida. Permission was obtained for the
Portuguese to land from the Moorish Prince who ruled in
Sofala, and the building of a fort began. It was made of
wood, from the difficulty of procuring stone.

But, in consequence of the murderous climate, all the Portuguese were soon laid low with fever, and the Moorish Prince had

waited just for this to make more sure, as he thought, of their destruction. Stirred up by him, the surrounding Kaffir tribes stormed the fort, but were driven back by one discharge of the guns. The Portuguese revenged themselves for this treachery by murdering the Moorish Prince, and setting up in his place one of his sons, who acknowledged himself a vassal of King Emanuel.

Portugal has maintained its dominion on that unhealthy coast to this day, and countless numbers have fallen victims to the fatal fever, in the pursuit of trade. The gold district itself is fifty miles inland from Sofala, and forms a table-land, which has frequently been visited of late by European travellers, and may perhaps yet be the scene of a future immigration of gold-diggers.

The fact that these mines have undoubtedly been worked from very early times has given rise to the opinion that this was the Ophir of the Bible; but others, as appears, with more justice, have placed that land of gold in India, at the mouth of the Indus.

Whilst Pedro de Anhaya was superintending the settlement of the Portuguese in Sofala, Francisco de Almeida arrived at Malabar. According to his instructions, he began first to build a fort on the island of Anchediva, which King Emanuel considered specially fitted to be the starting-point for future undertakings. But when, after some time, it appeared that the neighbourhood of the great commercial city of Goa, which was under the rule of the Prince of Bujapoor, would be too dangerous for the new fortress, it was given up; but the Portuguese remained on good terms with the chief of the Indian pirates, who had been accustomed to use the island as a haunt. The Viceroy then visited the factories in Cananore and Cochin and found everything in a prosperous state. He sought, by many marks of honour, to bind the Prince of Cochin, the oldest and most faithful ally of Portugal, still closer to her interests; and then, when he had freighted the merchant-ships and despatched them to Portugal, he set himself to execute the task which had been appointed him.

His plan was to gain for Portugal the uncontrolled dominion of the Indian Seas, but entirely to abstain from all conquest on the mainland, which might involve her in incalculable perplexity. He trusted for the necessary support on the coast partly to certain factories, but more to the adherence of the Indian princes who should be brought to serve the cause of Portugal, either by fear or by the hope of a rich reward.

Whilst with this view he distinguished in every possible way the Rajah of Cochin, he punished severely the town of Coulam, the inhabitants of which, stirred up by the Moors, had burnt down the factory with all the goods stored up in it, and had killed all the Portuguese. A similar chastisement had shortly before been the lot of Onor, a town in the immediate neighbourhood of Anchediva. From Cananore the Viceroy superintended the freighting of the ships so successfully that they were ready in a few months to return to Portugal.

Three of these ships, which sailed from Cochin on the 26th of November, 1505, were driven out of their usual course by a violent north wind, and constrained to sail more directly south for the Cape of Good Hope. This mishap caused the discovery of Madagascar, or, as the Portuguese called it, San Lourenço. They sailed round its south point, however, without stopping to explore it. On this new course, which greatly shortened the journey, they have been followed by most ships returning from India.

The next year's fleet did not arrive as soon as it was expected. The delay was caused by the fact that its commander, Tristam da Cunha, whose name is still borne by a group of islands which he discovered (12° 2′ west longitude, and 37° 6′ south latitude), had, at the command of the King, assisted Alfonso de Albuquerque to establish the influence of Portugal on the east coast of Africa, even north of Melinda. Some coast towns on the peninsula Somali were razed to the ground, Cape Guardafui was doubled, and a fort built on the island of Socotra.

This mountainous but most unhealthy island, which lies opposite Cape Guardafui, was designed by Emanuel to serve as a station for the Portuguese fleet, and to enable it completely to close the Red Sea against all Moorish vessels. After a few years, however, it was found that the island could not be held, and it was given up. The two commanders employed a full year in carrying out this commission of their King.

Then while Tristam da Cunha pursued his way to India, Albuquerque sailed to Ormuz. This town lies 56° 29′ east longitude, and 27° 5′ north latitude, and commands the straits between the Indian Ocean and the Persian Gulf. Although the island on which it is situated is small and perfectly barren—for the salt soil will produce nothing, and all the necessaries of life, even water, have to be brought from the mainland—yet on account of its position it was then thickly peopled, and Ormuz itself, next to Malacca and Aden, was considered the most important town of Asia. In its markets were to be found the wares of India, together with the produce of Persia, Armenia, Tartary, and other northern countries.

"The world," says a native proverb, "is a ring, and Ormuz is the gem which it contains." If the title, Lord of the Trade of the Indies and Ethiopia, which Emanuel had adopted, was to be anything more than a title, it was necessary that it should be asserted in the capital of that trade.

So Albuquerque, September, 1507, with seven ships, carrying 460 men, appeared before the splendid city, which had a garrison of 30,000 men, among whom were 4000 Persian archers, and in whose harbours lay 400 ships. With such a disproportionate force, it was yet just like the audacity of Albuquerque, and the recklessness of the Portuguese, who looked upon all the East as their rightful prey, to call upon the King of Ormuz to do homage, and to pay a yearly tribute.

The Vizier Atar, who held the reins of government for the infant Prince over the town and kingdom, which extended along the coasts of Arabia and Persia, did not venture at once to try the fortune of arms, but entered upon negotiations with these terrible strangers, in order to keep them amused. However, the very next morning the Portuguese fell upon the merchant fleet which lay in the harbour, sank a great many ships, and burnt the rest. The fire was so fearful that it placed the town in danger. The Vizier, frightened by the spectacle, agreed to a treaty by which he recognised the King of Portugal as the feudal lord of Ormuz. He also agreed to pay a tribute of 15,000 ducats, and to allow a fort to be erected for the security of the Portuguese influence.

But this treaty, extracted by terror, was never carried out. After a few days new disputes arose, and the Vizier, who felt himself encouraged by the large army which stood at his command, and the hatred of the Portuguese entertained by the people at large, put continual hindrances in the way of the building of the fortress, so that, giving up the vain attempt, they withdrew to Socotra.

However, convinced of the great importance of Ormuz, he appeared again the next year, and spent the whole autumn in spreading terror and dismay in the city. But, as on the first occasion, he had been able to accomplish nothing, so now this attempt, in which he had only three ships and about 300 men, was perfectly fruitless, and he was at last obliged to make up his mind to leave Ormuz, fully intending to attempt the execution of his plan at some future time, and when circumstances should be more favourable.

Meantime Tristam da Cunha had reached Malabar with the merchant fleet, and had taken on board the stores which Almeida had prepared. This, thought the Viceroy, was the time to strike a blow against the Zamorin, whose fleet had many times shown itself on the high seas, but had continually been driven back by the Portuguese, under the leadership of a brave youth, Lourenço de Almeida. He, however, had not been able to hinder a number of merchant-ships from entering the harbours of the Zamorin, where they had procured rich cargoes. Just then—October, 1507—there lay a large number of them in the harbour of Ponani, a few miles south of Calicut, where they appeared to be protected against every surprise by the Zamorin's fleet and the fortifications, which were manned by 4000 soldiers. ·

But even there the Portuguese sought them under the leadership of Almeida and of Tristam da Cunha. The two young sons of the general commanded the vanguard of the fleet; they forced a landing under the fire of the enemy's batteries, and defeated the natives in a most murderous fight, in which indeed almost all of them were slain. Threatened on shore, the Moors now left their ships in the lurch and saved themselves. The conquerors only took the guns from the ships, setting fire to everything else, even to the town with its rich stores.

The effect produced by this deed of arms was very great, and increased in the whole of India the dread felt of the Portuguese. The Moorish ships found it wise to avoid the dangerous harbours of the Zamorin, and preferred to take the long voyage to Ceylon and the Trade Isles, in order to procure the costly productions from the lands where they were indigenous. But even this was soon put a stop to by the Portuguese. Not content with capturing and destroying numbers of the ships on their return voyage, the Portuguese soon supplanted the Moors even in their trade with these distant lands.

Thus a strongly-fortified factory was established by Lourenço de Almeida on the Maldives, not only for the sake of the excellent coir—rope made from cocoa-nut fibres—which these islands produced, but also to lay wait here for the Moorish merchant-ships. It was the same youthful hero who first displayed the Portuguese flag in Ceylon. He landed in Galle, in the south of the island, and entered into friendly intercourse with the ruler of Ceylon.

The dominion of Portugal over the Indian Seas appeared more and more firmly established. The great merchant fleets, which had in earlier times carried the productions of India to Arabia, were either destroyed or no longer ventured into the Indian Seas, where they found themselves treated with the most relentless severity, just as if they had made an inroad into an enemy's land. With an iron foot the Portuguese trampled upon their flourishing trade, in order upon its ruins to establish their own mercantile power. This change was accompanied by great revolutions. Mighty princes lost their influence, insignificant harbours became in a night important places of trade; whilst at the places which had hitherto been centres of commerce trade came to a standstill, and poverty speedily ensued.

Thus it was at Alexandria, the old emporium for the Mediterranean, which quickly lost its importance. The decrease in the customs was highly disagreeable to the Mameluke Sultan of Egypt, and moved him to an attempt to drive the Portuguese out of India, in order to assist the Moors, whose trade had been of such service to Egypt. Venice, which felt its very life imperilled by the commercial prosperity of Portugal, did not fail to give both encouragement and active support. The Sultan, Kansu Ghwari, therefore caused a large fleet to be fitted out in the Red Sea, which put to sea, in 1507, under the command of the Emir Hossein, a native of Kurdistan. It was calculated that allies would be found in India; above all, that the Zamorin of Calicut and the Mussulman King of Cambaya, whose revenues had been seriously injured by the progress of the Portuguese, would certainly assist him.

The near approach of this hostile fleet was reported to the Viceroy; but he did not consider the report worthy of credit. So the Emir Hossein succeeded, in January, 1508, in surprising the young Almeida, as the latter, with a fleet of twelve men-of-war, was conducting the Malabar ships of the Kings of Cochin and Cananore to Choul, a little harbour north of Goa. In spite of the overwhelming force of the enemy, Lourenço attacked the Egyptian fleet, but without doing it much damage; and when the fleet of Cambay, under the command of Mel-ek As, the governor of Din, came to the support of the enemy, he recognised the necessity of retreat.

But in order to avoid the appearance of flight, the Portuguese squadron left the harbour by day—the merchant-ships in front, and then, one behind the other, the men-of-war. Lourenço himself covered the rear. At first every attack of the hostile fleet was repulsed, until, by an unlucky accident, the battle took an unexpected turn.

At the entrance of the harbour were several rows of movable piles—thin poles fixed into stones sunk in the water —which the fishermen used to fasten their nets to. They in no way hindered ships sailing out, since they bent under them. But a hole had been made in Lourenço's vessel under the water by a shell from one of the enemy's guns, and into this hole one of the poles got fixed. Thus the ship became entangled in the other piles, and was kept back, while the others sailed prosperously out into the open sea.

The enemy immediately rushed from all sides upon the vessel, to the assistance of which the others could not come. A boat which the nearest Portuguese ship despatched to rescue the crew Lourenço sent back, and he and his men prepared for a death struggle. The ship and the crew seemed in the very jaws of destruction, but Lourenço showed no signs of surrendering. Soon a ball carried away half his thigh. He was then compelled to allow himself to be placed on a chair near the mainmast, and thus he continued to cheer on his men until a second ball carried away half his ribs, and he fell. The death of this heroic youth increased the fury of the Portuguese crew, and strengthened them in their determination to sell their lives as dearly as possible. Three times was the enemy driven back; and when at length they succeeded in boarding the ship, they found, among the heaps of slain, only nineteen men, all severely wounded, whom they took prisoners.

Although this glorious defeat only increased the reputation for superhuman bravery which the Portuguese had gained in India, it yet showed that the dreaded enemy was not altogether invincible, and made the Indian princes inclined to enter into negotiations with the Emir.

This determined the Viceroy, who had his son's death to avenge, to make a great attack on the Mohammedan fleet, which had retired to the peninsula of Gijerat.

During the summer the men-of-war were refitted, and when in the autumn the merchant fleet came from Portugal it also was equipped for war. Just as they were preparing to start from Cananore Alfonso de Albuquerque arrived, having, while at Ormuz, been appointed successor to Almeida in the viceroyalty. He demanded immediate installation in his office, reminding Almeida that his three years had expired. The latter, however, decidedly refused to lay down his power until he had executed his scheme of revenge. "I have already," he said, "drawn the sword, and am not accustomed to surrender it to another in order that he may avenge wrongs done to me."

This refusal led to a serious quarrel between the two great men. It even went so far that Albuquerque was arrested by Almeida, but finally ended in a complete reconciliation. Whilst Albuquerque went to Cochin and undertook the government of the factories, Almeida, on the 12th December, 1508, went towards the north with a fleet of 19 sail, on which

LOURENÇO DE ALMEIDA'S LAST ENGAGEMENT.

there were 1200 Portuguese soldiers and sailors and 400 Malabar auxiliaries from Cochin and Cananore. Among the Indian Princes who, after Lorenzo's death at Choul, had negotiated with Emir Hossein, the most important was a Persian, named Sabayo. In his best harbour, Dabul, which was strongly fortified and garrisoned with 6000 men, there was stored up for the Moorish merchants, to whom Sabayo was allied by a common faith, a large quantity of Indian wares ready for lading.

Almeida ordered this harbour to be stormed. It was taken after a hard struggle and given over to the troops to plunder. But a fire broke out, and the town, with all its treasures, was reduced to a heap of ashes.

The Portuguese fleet then proceeded to Diu. This town, which is situated on a little island south of the peninsula of Gujerat, was the most important harbour of the kingdom of Cambay, and, on account of its position, peculiarly well fitted as a station for a fleet intended to rule the Indian Ocean. For this reason, the Emir Hossein had gone thither, and had found in Melech As, the Governor of Diu, a warm ally. More than 200 ships prepared for war lay in the harbour, among which were about 100 small ones which the Zamorin had sent to their aid.

Undismayed, the Portuguese pressed into the harbour; a frightful battle ensued, which ended with the flight of the Zamorin's ships, and the utter destruction of the Egyptian fleet. The victors had thirty killed and 300 wounded; the enemy lost 1500 men, among whom were 440 Mamelukes, who had defended themselves to the last. Of the captured ships, Almeida only retained six; the rest he set fire to. The booty was very considerable, and two Egyptian standards were sent as trophies to Portugal.

This battle put an end for ever to the attempts of the Egyptians to destroy, or, at any rate, to injure the Portuguese trade in India. A short time after (1518) the kingdom of the Mamelukes fell into the hands of the Turks, who, in 1538, made a single vain attempt to establish themselves in India.

In the pride of conquest, Almeida returned to Cochin. Very unwillingly did he surrender his dignity to Albuquerque. He would much have liked to have carried out the great undertaking he had planned. Before he could embark on board the fleet, which every year returned to Portugal, and leave behind what had been the scene of his labours for so many years, he was obliged to witness the honours which had hitherto been his pass to his successor.

Much displeased at the ingratitude which he fancied he had experienced, he set sail, on November 19th, 1509, for his home, where he might be sure of an honourable reception and a rich reward. But no such happy fate was in store for the hero; a premature and inglorious death awaited him.

In Saldanha Bay, not far from the Cape of Good Hope, the squadron cast anchor to take in water. While Almeida and the crew—consisting of 150 men—were thus engaged, they became involved in a quarrel with the negroes, who fell upon the Portuguese, and drove them back to their boats. Unfortunately, the boats had drifted along the shore, and so they had to make their retreat over a long stretch of burning sand. Stones and spears meanwhile were hurled at the exhausted men, and many a noble Portuguese was stretched upon the earth.

Among them was Almeida, pierced through the breast with a spear.

His body was buried at the spot where he fell. The sad news plunged all Portugal into deep mourning. King Emanuel honoured his memory by rich presents to his

DEATH OF FRANCISCO DE ALMEIDA IN SALDANHA BAY.

family; and King Ferdinand of Aragon, on the receipt of the melancholy tidings, retired into solitude (as was the custom on the death of a person of royal blood), in honour of the man who had performed such heroic deeds before the walls of Granada.

CHAPTER VIII.

ALFONSO DE ALBUQUERQUE.

THE new Viceroy, who, in the prime of life—he was born in 1453 —entered upon his office, was no novice in Indian affairs. He had, as we have seen, defended the fort of Cochin against the attacks of the Zamorin ; and lately, the enterprises with which the King had entrusted him on the coasts of East Africa and Arabia, had given him full opportunity to display his heroism, his powers as a general, and his force of character. Entering on his office in the autumn of 1509, he immediately commenced a course of policy completely different to that of his predecessor. Almeida had made it his object to maintain the Portuguese supremacy on the sea, and to secure the Indian trade, which, in the few years since Vasco da Gama's landing at Calicut, had made Portugal the richest country in Europe. In his opinion, it was well to be satisfied with a few strong factories on the mainland of India, because the distance of the mother country made it difficult to supply forces sufficient either for making conquests or for retaining conquests when made.

Albuquerque considered such limits unworthy. He did not wish to work merely for the present, but to do something which should last for all time. The employment of providing as much pepper and cinnamon as possible for the market of Lisbon did not satisfy him ; but to lay the foundations of a new empire seemed to him a worthy object. And it was just the distance of the mother country which in his eyes rendered it necessary to create a power in India sufficient to support the Portuguese dominion on the sea without having to wait for months for help from home. With these views, which the event justified, Albuquerque undertook to found the Portuguese Empire in India, and this self-imposed task he nobly accomplished.

At first he felt himself in some degree obstructed by the presence of the Marshal Fernando Coutinho, who had arrived shortly before Almeida's departure, and held a joint command with him. Against his better judgment, he was obliged to join in a war which Coutinho had planned against Calicut. Together they appeared with a considerable force before the town, on which already signal chastisement had often been inflicted, and on January 2nd, 1510, began to storm it. They succeeded in making themselves masters of the town ; but in the somewhat distant castle of the Zamorin the native soldiers defended themselves most obstinately. The Portuguese who had penetrated so far were cut off from the main force, and surrounded in their retreat in the thick woods which environed the town. The Marshal himself and eighty men lost their lives. Albuquerque avenged their death by burning down the whole town and all the ships found in the harbour ; then he forsook the untenable spot.

In the very same month he sailed again out of Cochin at the head of a fleet of twenty-one sail, bearing 1600 armed men. His object originally was Ormuz, which he intended to punish for resisting him twice ; but on the way he suddenly changed his mind, and determined upon a *coup de main* against Goa. This town, which had flourished for many years on the Moorish trade, lay on a little island named Tissuari, which, three miles long from east to west, and a mile from north to south, is situated in 15° 30′ north latitude, on the west coast of India, from which it is only separated by a narrow arm of the sea. It had a secure harbour, difficult of access, however,

during the summer monsoon. Next to Dabul, which lay more
to the north, and which Almeida had burnt, it was the chief
trading-place for the kingdom of Beejapoor and the other
states which had separated from the great empire of the
Deccan. This island, which lies about half-way down the
coast of Malabar, Albuquerque destined to be the future
centre of the Portuguese dominions which he intended to
found.

The moment was well chosen. Sabayo was just dead, and
his son Ismael Adil Khan, whose name the Portuguese turned
into Hidalkano, was expecting an attack from the neighbouring princes, who had unwillingly submitted to the usurpation
of Sabayo, having been specially provoked by his marriage
with the daughter of the lawful King of the Deccan, and by
the claims to the supremacy which he founded upon it. It
was not therefore to be expected that Hidalkan would be
able to defend Goa. This good news, brought by Timoja,.
who was the captain of the Anchediva pirates, and since
Gama's time had been a faithful ally of Portugal's, decided
the Viceroy to make an immediate attack upon the important
town, which, after a short resistance on the 25th of February,
1510, fell into his hands. They immediately began to build
a church, to appoint magistrates, and to take all the measures
necessary for defence, for they felt pretty certain that Hidalkan would use his utmost efforts to recover his most important port.

 And so it happened. A vanguard of 10,000 men forced a
passage over the narrow strait which separates the island from
the mainland, and sat down before the town. Then Hidalkan
himself approached with 60,000 men, among whom were 5000
horse-soldiers. Opposed to such an overwhelming force were
the Spaniards, behind unfinished ramparts, and surrounded
by the native inhabitants of the place, and by Moors whose
sympathies were all on the side of the besiegers. Albuquerque

therefore determined for the present to give up his conquest
and withdraw to his fleet. The monsoon, however, began to
blow, and hindered the ships from sailing away, and three
months of the greatest suffering ensued. Besides continual
conflicts with the enemy—for "three drops of Portuguese
blood flowed for every drop of water" that they procured—
a fearful pestilence broke out in the army, and carried off
numbers of brave men. Still they held out courageously,
and at last, in August, 1510, were able to get away from the
fatal spot.

But Albuquerque was far from being deterred from the
execution of his plans by this first calamity. Scarcely allowing
himself any time for rest, he again left Cochin—much to the
vexation of the Prince, who disliked the idea of the Portuguese
head-quarters being removed to Goa, since it would considerably
diminish both his revenue and importance—and sailed with
twenty-three ships, having on board 1500 Portuguese and 300
natives of Malabar, against Goa. The town was defended by
a garrison of 9000 men, Hidalkan being engaged in the field
against some of the neighbouring princes.

On the 25th of November, 1510, the Portuguese, whose
courage despised all obstacles, again entered the town. Indeed, taking advantage of a panic which spread among the
enemy, they took possession not only of the whole island, but
also of a strip of the mainland opposite. The treacherous
Moors were tried, and either put to death or driven out of the
town. But full security, both of life and property, was granted
to the Indian inhabitants, and when they had offered their
submission and pledged themselves to pay the usual taxes,
Albuquerque gave them a native chief, in the Prince of Onor,
Melreu, whose duty it should be to judge them and to collect
and deliver up the taxes. By such lenient treatment he sought
to reconcile the great body of the people with the new order
of things. And with the same object he encouraged the

marriages of the Portuguese with Indian women. To such young couples he gave the houses, fields, and gardens of the exiled Moors, and in this way created a burgher class, on whom he could depend, and to whom he gave the offices of greatest trust in the town.

Changing thus what had hitherto been a mere system of pillage and oppression into a regular and well-ordered government, he naturally made many enemies among the Portuguese, who looked upon themselves as defrauded, and sent prejudicial reports to the King.

No one, however, ventured openly to oppose the great man, who soon succeeded in giving Goa an importance greater than that it had hitherto possessed. New buildings sprang up, numbers of ships were fitted out in the harbour, and in the mint, which Albuquerque set up, gold, silver, and copper coins were struck off that soon found their way into all the Indian harbours.

A particular importance was given to Goa by an enactment of the Viceroy, which prohibited to all the other East Indian ports the traffic in Arab horses. Since the climate of a great part of India makes the breeding of good horses impossible, the Indian princes were obliged to import Arab horses, in order to maintain their cavalry, the flower of their army, in a fit condition for war. All this important traffic was now turned to Goa, and brought in a considerable revenue. At last Albuquerque, in order to render the trade secure, erected a great fort, which he called Manuel, in honour of the King. In it he placed a garrison of 400 men, 80 of whom were horse-soldiers, while Melreu commanded a body of 5000 Indians. To such forces could be trusted the defence of Goa against any attempt which Hidalkan might make to recover it, and in March, 1510, Albuquerque quitted it for new enterprises.

Of course Hidalkan immediately attempted another siege, but the garrison held out bravely until help arrived and then made a sally. This was repeated many times until, in the autumn of 1512, Albuquerque himself stormed the enemy's fortress Benestarin, which covered the passage from the mainland to the island, and so alarmed Hidalkan that he begged for peace. Henceforth the possession of Goa was secured, and the town rapidly rose to an importance which was much increased by its being made the seat of government.

The great change which now took place in Portuguese politics did not fail to produce a deep impression on the Indian princes, who up to this point had esteemed it beneath their princely dignity to enter into negotiations with the Portuguese, whom they looked upon as pirates. Ambassadors came to Goa from all the great kingdoms of South India, in order to enter into alliance with the new power. The hostile Kings of Calicut and Cambay begged for peace, and consented to allow the building of forts in Calicut and Diu.

With every spice fleet which returned to Portugal went ambassadors from Indian princes with presents to King Emanuel and assurances of friendship. Thus the bold capture and brave maintenance of Goa secured to the Portuguese power a firm hold over the whole west coast of India. The trade also was regulated by treaties. All ships that were not Portuguese were excluded from traffic in the harbours of the allied princes, unless they could show Portuguese passes.

After these great successes the restless Albuquerque turned himself to new tasks in the far east. When the Portuguese had taken possession of the land whence ginger, pepper, and cinnamon are brought into the European market, their attention had been directed to the coasts which produce camphor, the nutmeg, and the clove; that is to say, the Sunda Islands and the Moluccas.

Mysterious and dark as is the early history of these distant lands, it is yet certain that they have for a long period played an important part in the commerce of Asia. The merchant

fleets of civilised nations, which sought their valuable productions, and the lively intercourse maintained by them with
Chinese, Arabs, and Indians, had aroused the gifted Malay
inhabitants of these islands and coasts.   There, too, the re-
ligions of other countries had found a ready reception.   As
Buddhism had conquered Brahminism, so it, in turn, had given
way before the Islamism spread by the Arabs, which shortly before the arrival of the Portuguese had become the general faith.

Of the native races, two showed themselves peculiarly re-
ceptive of external influences; the Javanese and the Ourang-
lout, or men of the sea, who, having their origin in Sumatra, have
established themselves on the various coasts, and distinguish
themselves by their remarkable skill as sailors and traders,
and also by their inveterate inclination for piracy.

In very early times there were regular social institutions;
and the splendid ruins on the island are a proof of the advance
even then made by the Javanese.   When the Portuguese
appeared on their coasts there existed several Mahometan
principalities which, with much mistrust, entered into trade
with the foreigners, and a century later were swallowed up in
one kingdom.   The Ourang-lout had, in 1160, built on a little
island at the south of the Malay peninsula the town of Singa-
pore, which had quickly become the centre of trade in that
neighbourhood.   But, oppressed by the jealous King of Siam,
they had deserted this city, and, in 1253, had built, farther
west and in a singularly fine position, the town of Malacca,
which soon had risen to importance, and had diverted the
stream of commerce from its old course round Sumatra and
through the Straits of Sunda, into the Straits of Malacca and
between Nicobar and Andaman.   The princes and people of
the Ourang-lout had soon afterwards embraced Islamism, and
were continually engaged in war with the Buddhist Emperor
of Siam.   From the Portuguese accounts we gain but a slight
impression of the uncommon prosperity of this commercial

town; but we learn from them that between 30,000 and 40,000 houses were scattered for a mile along the coast, so we may calculate the population at about 150,000. Besides the Ourang-lout, who were the governing race, numerous foreign traders had settled there. These were divided into four quarters — that of the Javanese, Moors, Bengalees, and Chinese, each with its own chief. Among the merchant families there was such wealth that they reckoned their property by tons of gold.

To this great emporium of trade Almeida had sent, as early as 1509, Diego Lopez de Segueira with five ships, and orders to conclude a treaty with the Sultan of Malacca. The genuine Portuguese recklessness, with which on the way Segueira seized some ships and burnt them because they had not Portuguese passes, did not prevent his being well received by the Sultan. But this act caused so many delays, intrigues, and secret plots against the Portuguese, that at last he lost patience and returned without finishing his business. Indeed, he left several of his countrymen prisoners in the hand of the Sultan, but threatened due revenge if they were badly treated. To fulfil this threat Albuquerque appeared in the Malacca roads on the 1st of July, 1511, with nineteen ships, carrying 800 Portuguese and 600 armed natives of Malabar.

All negotiations for peace having been put an end to by the exorbitant demands of the Portuguese and the contemptuous refusal of the Sultan, hostilities began. In a military point of view, the most important feature of the town was a bridge over the little river that divided the town into two halves— the north and foreigners' quarter; and the south, containing the palaces of the Sultan and native nobility.

The first attack on this bridge failed, with heavy loss to the assailants; but a second attempt, on the 10th of August, succeeded; and from the strong position thus won, piece by piece, the whole town was conquered in a few days, while the

Sultan fled.   Of all the inhabitants, only the Ourang-lout and Moors were treated as enemies; all the Javanese, Chinese, and Hindus were spared.   The booty was immense, and is said to have exceeded a million ducats.

With his accustomed energy, Albuquerque began the building of a Christian church, and of a strong fortress, in which he placed a garrison of 300 men.   He made the same civil arrangement as in Goa.   He appointed a native governor of the city, and native judges for the Mahometans and Buddhists, from whose judgment, however, there was to be an appeal to the Portuguese tribunal.   The tolls for exported and imported goods were fixed, and produced a considerable revenue.   A mint was also set up.

Edouard Fernandez and Ruy da Cunha were sent as ambassadors to the neighbouring Emperors of Siam and Pegu. They succeeded in forming alliances with these courts, and on their return gave the most astonishing accounts of their Oriental magnificence.   Antonio de Abreu was despatched with three ships and 120 men, in order to visit the Banda and Molucca Islands, the home of the most important spices.

Without waiting for the return of all these ambassadors, Albuquerque left Malacca in the spring of 1512, leaving Fernam Peres de Anrade behind as governor.   But the return voyage to India was very disastrous, owing to unfavourable weather.

On the coast of Sumatra, the flag-ship and several others were wrecked on a sand-bank, and the crews only saved with great difficulty, while "the richest booty ever seen since the discovery of India" was buried beneath the waves.   Quick and successful as had been the undertaking against Malacca, the maintenance of that important place was very difficult, and called for many sacrifices.   Many enemies from the outside came to the support of the inhabitants, who felt themselves ill-used by misrule, often by injustice and utter want of consideration. Javanese pirates threatened the town, and the exiled Sultan several times established himself in the neighbourhood, and pressed upon the Portuguese fortress both by land and water. The little garrison was often hard beset; but it held out until, with the monsoon, a fleet came to its relief from India.

Driven out of his haunts, the old Sultan drew back to the neighbouring island, Bintang, while on the peninsula itself his son founded a new kingdom, which still stands. This struggle for the existence of the Portuguese rule in Malacca lasted for years. In 1526, the island, Bintang, was taken, and then the possession of Malacca could be reckoned secure.

For a long time after his return from Malacca, the Viceroy was occupied with the ordering of the Portuguese possessions in Malabar; yet at the same he made preparations for another great undertaking. This time he wished to pay the Arabs a visit in the Red Sea itself, and, if possible, to prevent them coming into the Indian Seas at all.

At last a fleet of twenty ships of war was ready, manned by 1700 Portuguese and 800 allied natives of Malabar. On the 18th of February, 1513, they set sail, and on the 24th of March they appeared before Aden, a very strong town, with an excellent harbour, situated on the south coast of Arabia (45° 5′ east longitude). The possession of this harbour would have made the Portuguese masters of the Red Sea, just as now, in the hands of the English, it is the key to that sea. The importance of the place decided Albuquerque to make an attack, which, however, was repulsed, in spite of the great bravery displayed by the Portuguese in a struggle which lasted four hours. The strong position and good defences of the town rendered it useless to attempt another assault; so the fleet sailed away through the Straits of Babelmandeb (the Gate of Sorrow) into the Red Sea.

These straits are six miles broad, but there are seven islands in them, which render their navigation in stormy weather dangerous even for sailors who have a knowledge of the place. But the Red Sea is even worse. The Arabs call it the Closed Sea, and it is only in the middle that there is just a narrow channel of deep water. In this channel there is not much danger to be feared; but it is subject to frequent calms, which render a voyage along it very tedious. But along both the African and Arabian coasts are many rocks and islands with shallow straits between them. The coasts are, indeed, only accessible by the help of experienced pilots, and even these always observe the precaution of casting anchor every night.

Under such circumstances, the Portuguese fleet made but slow progress, and at last was obliged to lie to for two months off the island of Kamarang, near the Arabian coast. But with the first favourable wind, Albuquerque left this unhealthy spot, which had brought sickness and death among his men, and hastened to quit the treacherous sea, in which he could find no place suitable for a fortress. The undertaking had failed, but the Arabs were frightened by Albuquerque's boldness, he being the first of all Christian sailors to penetrate into the Red Sea.

On the return voyage several Arab ships were captured, and then the fleet sailed to Diu, whose cunning Governor, Melek As, had not yet consented to the building of a Portuguese fortress. Having returned again to Goa, the Viceroy devoted the whole year, 1514, to the affairs of government, which demanded a close attention.

Numerous and very often just complaints were brought to him of the covetousness and tyranny of the officials, and these complaints demanded from him a stern interference. His impartiality and high sense of justice were now fully seen; but it was only to be expected that many of the men who suffered at his hands should express themselves as dissatisfied, and even assume a hostile attitude towards the Viceroy.

He knew his enemies quite well, but continued to act towards them in a most generous manner, and contented himself with sending those to Portugal for punishment whom he could prove to be guilty of treason. But the men thus sent hastened to spread all sorts of calumnies with regard to Albuquerque, making capital, of course, of the disastrous expedition to the Red Sea, which had cost so much money and so many human lives. They succeeded only too well in destroying King Emanuel's confidence in him. He was rendered more ready to listen to their reports by the fact that his self-love had been wounded by Albuquerque's decided refusal to carry out some of his orders; for instance, to evacuate Goa. Thus the fall of Albuquerque was preparing in Portugal while he, in the full consciousness of his faithfulness and receiving tokens of royal favour, believed himself to be secure.

Just at that time Albuquerque was occupied with active preparations against Ormuz. To be sure, the tribute to which the King had pledged himself had been, at least in part, paid, but no exhortation with regard to the fort which he had promised to build produced any effect. And the place seemed to Albuquerque so important that he swore he would not shave or cut his beard until he had enforced performance of the promise.

At last all the preparations were complete, and Albuquerque was able, with a fleet consisting of fourteen large men-of-war, seven caravels, and six galleys, and having on board 1500 Portuguese and 700 Indians, to proceed from Goa against the town which had so long occupied his care and attention.

On the 26th of March the fleet arrived at Ormuz, where immediately the greatest alarm ensued. The leading persons in the town were no longer the same as the Portuguese had found eight years before; and a new King was on the throne; but, like his predecessors, completely in the power of his First

Minister. This man, a Persian of the name of Ahmed, intended to play into the hands of the Persian Shah Ismael, and had therefore provided a strong garrison of Persian archers. Still he did not dare to bid defiance to the great power of Albuquerque, and entered into negotiations which ended in a complete ratification of the previous treaty. As a sign of the Portuguese supremacy, the Portuguese standard was unfurled on the royal castle, which was greeted by a salute from the fleet. In a short time the fortress was erected on the most favourable place and armed by the King of Ormuz with all his guns, which, however, he was unwilling to give up.

When Albuquerque saw that the discontent of the King was nourished by his minister, he freed himself in an oriental manner of the dangerous man, having him struck down by some Portuguese noblemen while on a visit. The King, whom this murder relieved from a most disagreeable subjection, henceforth honoured and loved Albuquerque as his deliverer, and the latter strove, by a dignified conciliatoriness, to render the relation between them firm and lasting.

A disease which attacked Albuquerque in August grew worse day by day, and at last made him think of returning to Goa. He placed as governor in the fortress at Ormuz his nephew, Pedro de Albuquerque, whom he named as his successor in case of his death. Then he set sail on the 8th of November in the hope of yet recovering his health on the salubrious Indian coast. He was met by a Moorish ship, which brought him news from India that utterly crushed him. King Emanuel had recalled him to Portugal, and his successor, Lopo Soarez, a personal enemy of Albuquerque's, had already arrived in Cochin, bringing with him, in offices of high trust, others of his opponents, some even of those very men whom he had sent to Portugal for punishment. At the same time he learnt that the commands with regard to the government which

DEATH OF ALBUQUERQUE OFF GOA.

King Emanuel had laid on the new official were diametrically opposed to his own plans and principles.

Such ungrateful treatment he had not expected. He was deeply pained and broke out into the words, " Now it is time to turn to the Church, for I have ruined myself with the King out of love to the people, and with the people out of love to the King." Henceforth he had done with earthly cares, and rejected all nourishment. Only after much persuasion was he induced to allow his secretary to write the following letters to the King :

" SIR,—This is the final letter which now, at my last gasp, I write to your Royal Highness. Many letters have I written to you with a lighter heart on occasions when I had succeeded in rendering you some service. I leave behind in this land a son, Bras de Albuquerque, and I beg your Highness to allow him to reap the reward of his father's services. As regards Indian affairs, they will speak for themselves and for me."

The signing of this letter exhausted all his remaining strength. When the ship reached Goa they did not venture to carry him on shore. A priest was summoned to offer him the last consolations of religion, and on the morning of the 16th of December, 1515, he breathed his last in sight of the town which he had made the queen of India. His body was buried at first in Goa. Hidalgos carried it on their shoulders into the church which he had founded, and the whole population of the town, Christians, heathens, and Moors, followed with loud and sincere lamentation.

His wish to be buried with his ancestors in Portugal was not fulfilled for a considerable time, the inhabitants of Goa being unwilling to part with his remains, for which they erected a costly shrine. Indeed, soon after Albuquerque's death it became the custom among the heathen and Moors, when they suffered any injustice from the Governor, to repair to his grave, bringing oil for the lamp and adorn-

9

ing the tomb with flowers, while they implored his departed spirit to procure justice for them. It needed a bull from the Pope, threatening the inhabitants of Goa with excommunication if they any longer opposed the removal of the body, before the accomplishment of the great man's last wishes could be effected.

The interment in the family vault in Lisbon, which took place on the 6th of April, 1566, was accompanied with much pomp and magnificence.

Alfonso de Albuquerque was of middle height and well-proportioned ; his features were pleasant and attractive, but no one could stand against the wrathful glance of his eye. A long snow-white beard fell down to his girdle. In society he was agreeable, lively, and full of wit. He had received an excellent education for his time, and was well able to express his thoughts in writing. Having a keen insight into character, he knew how to treat every one according to his peculiarities, and had even shown himself a match for the cunning Moors. The greatness and precision of his plans, the care employed in their preparation, and the speed and power of their execution are worthy of all admiration. But still higher honour is due to his noble nature, his highmindedness and detestation of everything base. It is just this which makes his image stand out bright and shining from the background formed by the low passions of his countrymen.

The general grief which his death caused, even in the hearts of those who had been hostile to him in life, speaks in the clearest manner possible for the noble character of this great man. What he did in India, the result has shown. He was the founder of the colonial power of the Portuguese in that country.

CHAPTER IX.

THE LAST DISCOVERIES OF THE PORTUGUESE.

STARTING from their new possessions, the Portuguese soon made themselves acquainted with all the neighbouring countries, beginning with those which were most important to their rising trade. The Bay of Bengal had been visited by Portuguese ships under Almeida, and a few years later commercial treaties were concluded with the Indian Princes who ruled its coasts. There was, however, a peculiar charm in penetrating farther into the mysterious East, and thus a special interest was excited by the settlements of the Portuguese in the Moluccas and their intercourse with the early civilised states of China and Japan.

The Moluccas are five little islands lying very close together under the equator in 128° east longitude, near the curiously-shaped island Gilolo. Their names are, beginning from the north, Ternate, Tidor, Motir, Makjan, and the larger Batchang.

They are of only a few miles' circumference, and in each island the centre is occupied by a volcano, so that only the narrow coast is fit for habitation and cultivation. But they are the home of the nutmeg tree, which is found nowhere else, except in the little Banda Islands (4° 33′ south latitude, 130° 3′ east longitude), and of which the blossom, as mace, and the fruit, the nutmeg, are such valuable articles of trade.

The trade in these spices, carried on by the Javanese, the Chinese, and even the Arabs, had created considerable prosperity among the simple inhabitants of these islands, and produced an ample revenue for their Princes.   When the appearance of the Portuguese in the Sunda Islands, and their forcible settlement in Malacca, caused an entire revolution in the East Asiatic trade, the Princes of the Moluccas perceived that it would be for their interest to make a friendly alliance with the new rulers of the sea, who on their side were aiming at extending their influence to the very centre of the spice trade. With such desires on either side it was easy to come to an understanding.

Antonio de Abreu, whom Albuquerque had sent, in 1511, to search for the Moluccas, only reached the Banda Islands. There lading his three ships with nutmegs he began his return.   But one of these ships, commanded by Francisco Serrao, foundered in a storm.   Upon this the bold Portuguese attacked and captured after a hard struggle a pirate vessel, on board of which they returned to the Island of Amboyna, which lies midway between the Banda Islands and the Moluccas.   They were fetched off from this island by the Prince of Ternate, and Serrao, the first European who had set foot on the Moluccas, was overwhelmed by him with tokens of friendship.

About the same time ambassadors were sent by the Princes of Ternate and Tidor to Malacca, requesting the foundation of a Portuguese factory in their islands.   The jealousy of the two Princes, each vying with the other for the friendship of the Portuguese, and each hoping to have the factory built on his island, made the game a very easy one for the Portuguese. Nevertheless, a delay of many years took place, and nothing was done, until a report arose that the King of Spain was preparing to form a settlement in the important group from the other side.

Then they hastened to make up for the delay.   The building of a fort on Ternate was begun on June 24th, 1522, but shortly before some Spaniards from Magalhaens's fleet had touched on the islands, and a vehement dispute, which was only composed after much trouble, arose between the two crowns for their possession.

A commission of Spanish and Portuguese astronomers met on a bridge between Badajoz and Elvas, in 1524, to settle the question whether, according to the papal bull of 1494, the Moluccas belonged to Spain or Portugal. As at that period they were not thoroughly conversant with the method of fixing the longitude of a place, and there were even different opinions about the number of miles in a geographical degree, it was found impossible to come to an agreement. And it was not until 1529 that the matter was settled by a treaty between the two kingdoms. The islands became the property of Portugal, but had to pass through ten wretched years of oppression and violence, until the noble Antonio Galvao, made governor in 1536, by his wise and just rule persuaded the natives to submit to the Portuguese supremacy, and converted many of them to Christianity.

In the meantime most of the islands of the Sunda group had been visited by the Portuguese. On some factories had been established and forts built, as, for example, on Java and Amboyna. Other places they had been obliged to abandon through the violent opposition offered by the natives. Thus the Portuguese had not succeeded in establishing themselves in Acheen, the north-west part of Sumatra ; indeed, in 1522, they were obliged to evacuate a fort they had founded in Padang.

Farther to the east the Portuguese had not extended their discoveries, but ships which had been driven by bad weather into the region beyond the Moluccas brought back reports of great countries. Thus, in 1526, Jorge de Menezes became, against his will, the discoverer of New Guinea, which he named Papua ; and, in 1601, Emanuel Godinho de Eredia found in the south-east a long piece of coast, which proved to be a part of the west coast of Australia.

The Portuguese had opened communication with China very early. By their settlement at Malacca they had been brought so near this old empire, that intercourse between them could not be avoided. There were also in Malacca multitudes of Chinese settlers, and great numbers of Chinese trading vessels or junks were constantly engaged between the harbours of the Sunda Islands and China.

It therefore appeared advisable to form an official connection, and Fernam Peres de Andrade was sent by the Viceroy, Lopez Soares, with eight ships, to open negotiations with China. On the 15th of August, 1517, he reached the island of Tamang, which lies at the entrance of the Bocca Tigris, the mouth of the river Se Kiang. Here all foreign ships which wished to sail up the river to the harbour of Canton were obliged to cast anchor and get permission to do so from the harbour officials.

The Portuguese at once began to experience that evasive smoothness and suspicious courtesy with which the Chinese, even to this day, seek to keep at a distance everything and everybody that is foreign to them. The requests of the strangers were passed from one official to another, and were only granted after numberless ceremonies had been gone through.

At the end of September the Portuguese fleet, accompanied by a pilot, who conducted it through the dangerous passage, arrived in the harbour of Canton. But here they found themselves surrounded by the most injurious mistrust, and hindered from anything like free action. It was only owing to the great conciliatoriness of Andrade that a good understanding was maintained, and it was by means of all kinds of concessions to Chinese arrogance that permission was obtained to despatch a Portuguese ambassador to the court of the great Emperor, who just at that time was engaged in a war with the Tartars in the north of his enormous empire.

Thomas Pires, a man of low birth, for he was an apothecary, but remarkable for his knowledge and his dexterity, was chosen for this office.   He was put on shore with several companions, and was treated by the Chinese magistrate with all the consideration due to his office.   The Portuguese wares, principally Indian spices, were eagerly bought, while the Portuguese in their turn made purchases in silk and rice.   In this way they became acquainted with what seemed to them the very strange manners and customs of the great commercial city, while, thanks to Andrade's judicious management, they contrived to keep on good terms with the inhabitants.

The sickness which broke out among his men made him set sail sooner than he had intended to do.   Before his departure he had notice of it proclaimed in all the markets, in order that any one who had any claim upon the Portuguese might come and be satisfied.   This method of proceeding had a very good effect, and when Andrade, in September, 1517, left the Chinese Seas, there existed very friendly relations between the two nations, to both of whom Andrade's expedition had been of great profit.

But soon the Portuguese had occasion to notice that the unfavourable reports spread by the different nations whom they had ill-treated had reached China, and injured their position.   Pires had to wait for a year in Canton before he procured permission from Pekin to proceed to the Emperor's court.   When at last he was admitted, in 1521, the Emperor treated the Portuguese proposals with considerable suspicion, and said openly that he had been informed that the Portuguese, under the pretence of trading, reconnoitred lands in order to conquer them.

Then a change took place on the throne, and the new Emperor sent Pires back to Canton, where he was kept in prison, all friendly intercourse with the Portuguese being broken off. The breach was made irremediable by the arrogant and haughty behaviour of the commander of the Portuguese squadron, Simon de Andrade, the brother of his predecessor. A battle ensued before the harbour of Canton, during which, fortunately for the Portuguese, a storm arose which scattered the enemy's ships and favoured the retreat of the Portuguese. In 1524 Pires died in chains, his companions were dragged away as prisoners into the interior, and all peaceful intercourse between the Chinese and Portuguese appeared for ever at an end.

But after some years matters improved. As a reward for the important services rendered by the Portuguese in the suppression of piracy in the Chinese and Indian Seas, the Emperor Kang-hi granted them leave, in 1556, to establish a factory in the harbour of Canton.

The peninsula Macao was chosen for the purpose; a brick wall was built across the narrow sandy peninsula which unites it to the mainland; and with well-founded mistrust the Portuguese were forbidden to build a fort or to cross this wall on any pretext whatever. But they knew how to manage: they built a cloister with portholes, and a bishop's palace, which they provided with cannon; and they placed in the new town a strong garrison under the name of trading officials. Under such protection Macao soon began to flourish. On the sandy coast magazines sprang up, and on the naked rock beautiful houses; while the fleets of Malacca, Goa, and Lisbon anchored in its harbour. This prosperity lasted till the eighteenth century. Then the place rapidly sank, partly in consequence of the new commercial treaties which China formed with the Dutch and English, and partly on account of the deterioration of its inhabitants, in which the worst elements of the Chinese character had become evident. The corrupt descendants of the Portuguese settlers were indeed barely tolerated; the Chinese had become the real masters, and the Mandarins of Canton had more influence in the Portuguese colony of Macao than the King of Portugal and his officers.

Before the resumption of friendly relations with China, the Portuguese had visited the group of islands which lie near Japan, and in 1542 had reached that remarkable archipelago. In all the harbours of that empire they met with a friendly reception, and were able to carry on a profitable trade. At the same time a most rich and fruitful field was opened here for Christian missions. After the arrival of the celebrated Jesuit, Francis Xavier, the number of conversions increased year by year, until, in 1589, a terrible persecution of the Christians began, which lasted for fifty years, and at length completely rooted out Christianity.

At the same time that this persecution occurred, all the Japanese harbours were closed against the Portuguese, and indeed against all Christian nations, with the exception of the Dutch, who, under a surveillance that was scarcely bearable, and on the most humiliating terms, were allowed to maintain a factory on the little artificial Island of Desima.

CHAPTER X.

As early as the year 1508 the great extent of the Portuguese possessions in India had compelled King Emanuel to divide their rule. He appointed two governors—the one, with his seat of office on the Island of Socotra, was to rule over the coasts of East Africa and of Asia as far as the peninsula of Gujerat; and to the other, who was to reside at Cochin, was given the control of Malabar.

But like so many appointments which are settled in royal cabinets without a correct knowledge of the true state of matters, this arrangement was soon seen to be perfectly impracticable. The Island of Socotra was perfectly unsuitable for a settlement, and the management of all affairs in the Arabian and Persian Seas needed henceforth to be under the control of the Indian Viceroy. So it was finally arranged that all the East African settlements should be placed under a government of their own, while all the other possessions on the coasts of Arabia, Persia, India, and the Sunda Islands should be handed over to the Viceroy, who should reside at Goa.

But in later years even this arrangement proved insufficient. The Viceroy's territory was too large to be governed from one spot. Under King Sebastian, therefore, in 1571, all the possessions east of Cape Comorin were placed under a new governor, who had his headquarters in Malacca.

Goa, however, was still considered the capital of Portuguese India, and it displayed all the magnificence suited to such a position. Its population was 200,000, principally Indians, though a good number of Portuguese settlers and a mongrel race, the offspring of the mixed marriages between Europeans and Indians, were to be seen in the magnificent streets, remarkable for their handsome stone buildings. The public squares were adorned with fountains, triumphal arches, and statues, whilst among the eighty churches might be seen, towering above them all, the gigantic dome of the cathedral. In 1559, the Bishop of Goa had been raised to the dignity of Archbishop and Patriarch of all India, and the Bishops of Cochin and Malacca were placed under him. The Viceroy's palace, which lay near the harbour, was a very imposing building.

Among the Viceroys who resided here, Nomo da Cunha, 1528—38; Juan de Castro, 1545—48; and Louis de Ataide, 1568—71, distinguished themselves by their abilities and governing powers, as well as by great deeds of arms. As with the decline of the Portuguese power the number of inhabitants began to diminish, so also the climate of Goa, which had hitherto been very favourable, began to change, and became so fatal that in the beginning of the eighteenth century New Goa was built, some miles from the old city, and thither both the Government and population removed. Since that time Old Goa has become a heap of ruins, and only a few hundred people live in it.

The dominions of Portugal in Asia were very scattered. On the coast of Malabar it possessed fortresses in Cochin and Cananore, etc. To each of these fortresses was attached a small piece of territory, which was the property of the Portuguese crown, while the principal revenue was drawn from the tolls and from all sorts of privileges which they possessed. But it was different with Goa. Here not only the island, but a large piece of territory on the neighbouring coast was the immediate property of the Portuguese ; and it was carefully cultivated by a hardy population. Farther north the Portuguese possessed the island of Salsette, the harbours of Choul, Bassim, and Daman, and the important Diu. In this latter place they had first established a firm footing as somewhat obtrusive allies of the Sultan of Cambay, who had been attacked by the Mongols. They had then established a fort ; but the next year, on the murder of Badur, who, returning from a visit to the Viceroy, became, in some mysterious manner, involved in a quarrel with the Portuguese, the whole island of Diu, with its excellent harbour, fell into their hands. A few years later it was defended with heroic bravery against a powerful Turkish fleet. From that time forward it was, after Goa, the most important harbour which Portugal possessed in India.

One rich source of revenue was the money paid in tolls at Ormuz, whose King sank more and more into a dependent condition. But the advances of the Turks, who had taken possession of Aden and the land at the mouth of the Tigris and Euphrates, gradually lessened the importance of the place.

On Ceylon the Portuguese had fortresses in Galle and Colombo. In the treaties which, taking advantage of their mutual discord, they concluded with the different native princes, they exacted a yearly tribute in the productions of the island.

In the extreme east, Malacca, whose harbour tolls steadily increased in value, was the centre for the numerous possessions of the Portuguese on the Sunda Islands and of their trade with China and Japan.

The history of these possessions is that of one continual struggle against the hostile powers which laboured for their destruction. It was necessary to be ever on the watch against the attacks of the Turks, as well as against the designs of the native princes, who were continually seeking to shake off the yoke of the Portuguese. The Zamorin of Calicut especially was continually making attempts to recover the position of influence and importance which he had held before the arrival of the Portuguese. It was not until 1540 that he was brought to conclude a peace which lasted for thirty years—the happiest years of Portuguese rule in India. At the conclusion of that period the great alliance of Indian princes was formed which, in 1571, began the war against Portugal. At one and the same time Choul was besieged by the Nizam Orhan, the successor of the Nizam Maluk; Goa by Hidalkan, and Shalle by the Zamorin, while smaller princes threatened the harbours of Cananore, Culet, and Cochin ; and the Sultan of Acheen reduced Malacca to the greatest distress.

But the great Viceroy, Louis de Ataide, by straining to the utmost all the powers of the Portuguese, who displayed the most heroic courage, succeeded in driving back the monstrous armies of the enemy, and only Shalle, which the guns of the Zamorin turned into a mere heap of ruins, was lost.

Peace was soon restored ; but the Portuguese were not able to overcome the dislike which their behaviour from the very beginning had called forth in the Indian princes. This was seen when other Europeans—the Dutch and English—appeared in India, and were received with much goodwill, because they were looked upon as valuable allies against the Portuguese. The unwise and often unjust measures of government contributed not a little to foster this feeling of hostility, and it was further increased by the covetousness and arrogance displayed in its administration. Since the great thing was to bring as much money as possible into the royal treasury, oppression and robbery were resorted to to procure it. Thus the tribute demanded from the Prince of Ormuz was in a few years raised from the 15,000 ducats, which he had agreed to, to 20,000, 25,000, 60,000, and 100,000.

These sums were more than the King could pay, and therefore, in the year 1543, he was a debtor to the Portuguese trea-sury for no less than 518,537 ducats. In order to collect this the royal household was remodelled in the most economical manner. At last a claim was laid by the Portuguese upon the duties which the King raised on palm wine ; and it was with much difficulty that they were induced to withdraw it, although the poor King declared that he did not know what he should have left to live upon.

The King of Colombo, a faithful ally of the Portuguese, was treated in much the same way. The Viceroy, Alfonso de Noronha, in 1550, caused the palace of the late King to be searched, just as if all in it belonged to him by right, and finally had it plundered ; while at the same time he defrauded the new King in the most shameless manner, and, by the threat of taking him prisoner, wrested from him all he pos-sessed.

Thus the Portuguese rule was little calculated to gain the favour of the Indians. A few of the Viceroys acted in an honourable manner, and did their best to protect the natives from oppression, and procure justice for them ; but these were only exceptions, and, as a rule, the Indian peasant or citizen was utterly defenceless against the tyranny of his Portuguese neighbours, who considered it the lawful right of the conqueror to satisfy all his desires at the expense of the subject race.

Religion also gave an edge to the ill-feeling between the two 'nations. Except a small number of Thomas Christians, the Indians were all either believers in Mahometanism or Brahminism. From the beginning the former stood in an attitude of hostility to the Christian conquerors, and repaid in full measure the fanatic intolerance which the Portuguese felt towards them. The latter suffered from their misguided missionary zeal, a zeal which did not shrink from violence, and which evidently tended to the political subjugation of the people.

Especially calculated to embitter the Indians against them was the desecration and destruction of the ancient temples. The Archbishop of Goa, for instance, carried on the forced conversion of the people of Salsette in such a manner that in 1564 he had all the temples of the island, 200 in number, and most of them ancient places of worship, broken into by his troops and turned into the ruins which still excite the admiration of numberless visitors.

Very often it was not religious zeal at all, but mere greed, which led to these attacks upon the temples ; for in long ages immense treasures had been heaped up in these sacred places by the presents of pious pilgrims. Thus in 1544 the Viceroy Alfonso de Sousa received a command from John III. of Portugal, to take possession of the pagoda of Tremel, and place its treasures in the royal chests. Nobody even hesitated because the pagoda was in the land of the Sultan of Narsinga, a Prince who was an ally of the Portuguese ; and when a storm dispersed the fleet, on board of which was the Viceroy himself, he was still unwilling to return without having at any rate in some measure fulfilled the royal commands. So he and his men fell upon the pagoda of Tebilicare and plundered it instead. On their return the robbers were attacked by troops of irritated natives in a narrow pass. It was not until they had suffered the loss of thirty men killed and 150 wounded, among whom was the Viceroy, that they succeeded in reaching the ships with their booty.

The Viceroys during their term of office occupied a princely position. In warlike affairs, in matters of administration and of justice, they were absolute masters. In the most important towns royal palaces were built for them, and their emoluments were great. Their most important privilege was, that during their term of office no court could receive a complaint against them.

Yet the position of the Viceroys was not so influential and

independent as appears at first sight. They were often obliged to carry out measures of which they did not approve, but which had been settled in the royal cabinet in Lisbon. Their Portuguese officers and subordinates were constantly guilty of disobedience. Even an Albuquerque considered it advisable, before any great undertaking, to take counsel with his higher officers and hidalgos, and to have minutes taken of the meeting, so that he might be provided against accusations in the case of disaster.

In later times the rancorous disputes between two rival candidates for the Viceroyalty contributed not a little to undermine the authority of the Viceroy. As instances, we may cite the cases of Vaz de Sampayo and Pedro Mascarenhas in 1526, or that of Moritz Bareto, who supplanted Antonio de Maronha in 1573.

The Portuguese nobility required from the Viceroy special respect, and if they thought themselves injured, immediately brought their grievances and calumnies to the King, whose ear was usually open to them. The officials shamelessly defrauded the treasury. They sold too, at a high price, wares which they had extorted from the Indians; and when out of sight of their superiors, took a most shameful advantage of their official position. Thus it happened at last, incredible as it may appear, that in the year 1570 the rich Portuguese possessions in India did not produce a sufficient revenue to pay the expenses of the government.

If, in the interests of the royal treasury or of the Indians, an attempt was made to restrain the robberies and oppressions of the Portuguese officials, not seldom they broke out in open rebellion, and the state itself often suffered serious damage. A royal decree had declared the trade in cloves with the Moluccas to be a privilege of the crown, but the Portuguese on the islands, with the governors, Vincenzio da Fonseca and Tristam de Tayde, at their head, formed a conspiracy to oppose both secret and open resistance to this measure, in order to retain the profitable trade in their own hands, and Antonio Galvao was the first who succeeded in enforcing obedience to the King's command. The Viceroy himself was frequently constrained to make sacrifices from his own income. Money came in irregularly. Nothing could be obtained from Portugal, unexpected dangers produced unforeseen expenses; the Viceroy must pay out of his own purse, or if he wished to persuade the Portuguese who lived in India to make a sacrifice, he must set them an example. It was common to procure loans from the town of Goa, but often this could only be accomplished by the Viceroy himself becoming security. And when the term of this laborious and ungrateful office had expired, even the well-deserving Governor would see himself put on one side as useless, while his successor, to whose rising sun even those whom he had overwhelmed with favours paid homage, overthrew all he had done, and most usually adopted a policy entirely opposed to his own. He might think himself happy if at the close of his office there did not arrive a royal order to arrest him and bring him to trial on charges laid against him by his enemies and calumniators in Lisbon.

Besides, it was the custom to throw into prison at Lisbon returning Viceroys, and only to release them on the payment of a large sum, they being looked upon as sponges who had filled themselves in India, and must be squeezed in Portugal. The heart of many a deserving man was broken by such ungrateful and ungracious treatment from the Princes in whose service they had borne so many troubles and deprivations.

The gallantry of the Portuguese, which they manifested from the first in the Indian waters, and the heroic fearlessness which caused them to begin and carry through successfully a struggle against such odds, must not make us blind to the hateful characteristics which made themselves more evident year by year. The riches of India developed in them an unbridled luxury, and allured them to the most dissolute course of life. Their own historians accuse them of hatred of work, godlessness, cruelty, and faithlessness, and this reproach is supported by a long series of terrible examples.

Georg Pock, the Nuremberg merchant, writing on January 1st, 1522, from Cochin to his countryman, Michael Behaim, draws an ugly picture of the Portuguese character. He writes of them plainly : "The Portuguese, who are born Portuguese, poison the air with their pride. Should one of them possess ten ducats, he must have a velvet coat, a silver dagger, polished boots, and a violin with which to steal about the streets at nights and serenade the ladies. The Moors see that one Portuguese never wishes well to another, but that they deceive one another and oppress the poor, so that the common people fall into distress, and are forced to go to the Moors and make themselves Moors (that is, deny their faith. Moors here signifies Mohammedans). The officials never keep faith : they will give a Moor a letter when he is going to sea. The letter runs thus : ' Whoever reads this letter signed by me, let him give credit to the Moor and allow him to go where he will.' For such a letter he receives 200 ducats. Then, when the Moor goes to sea, the official sends after him, causes all the cargo to be seized and the ship sunk. In this manner they become rich. When the Moors see that the Portuguese never keep faith, they say that our religion cannot be a good one. You will find people who have lived here fifteen years, have never gone to confession, have 15,000 ducats in the land ; but they never reflect on their ways, being fully occupied with the thought that possibly the Moors may murder them all."

This description, given by a man deserving credit, refers to the early times of Portuguese rule ; but the moral declension was rapid, and at the end of the century the Portuguese and their descendants in India appear an utterly corrupt race, displaying, however, in danger and distress that imperishable inheritance of the nation, heroic courage and contempt of death. But all these evils—the hostility of the Indian princes and of the Indian people, bad government and terrible social depravity—would not have brought about the ruin of the Portuguese rule in India ; the cause of its fall came from Portugal itself. The real reason of it was the change and degeneration of the national character.

Incalculable wealth had been poured into the country. The chronicler Goes tells us that he had often seen merchants appear in the Indian market in Lisbon with sacks full of gold and silver to pay for the goods they had received, and that the officials were obliged to put them off to another day, because the time did not suffice to count the money, the sums being so great that were received every day.

These riches were employed in the pleasures of life and in the gratification of ever-increasing desires. The allurements of easy gain enticed many from labour and created a nation of idlers and revellers, who were unwilling to make any sacrifice for the greatness of their country. The impetus, therefore, which had been given to the nation by the perseverance of Henry the Navigator, and by the great successes of Emanuel, under such circumstances soon began to abate. The strong young men who yearly set sail in thousands for the tropics returned either to their native land cripples or physically and mentally enfeebled, or they perished miserably in Asia. This yearly loss of men, which was increased in 1578 by the disastrous battle at Alcassar in North Africa and the fall of King Sebastian with the flower of the Portuguese youth, necessarily exhausted so small a land.

Emanuel's son and successor, John III., introduced the Inquisition into Portugal in 1536, and allowed the Jesuits to establish themselves in the country immediately after the order was founded. Very soon they had gained a firm foot-

10—2

ing in all classes of society, and exercised a most injurious influence on the measures of the King and of his successors, who were all quite dependent on them.

As was the case everywhere, they introduced into Portugal a bitter struggle against all freedom of thought and any ideal conception of life, and sought to substitute instead an external devoutness, thus destroying the whole counterpoise to moral aberration.

Thus the political catastrophe which overwhelmed Portugal came upon a people that even the bitter smart of national ruin could not shake out of its mental dulness and stupidity. In the year 1580 the House of Burgundy became extinct, and, after a slight resistance, which was soon overcome, Philip II. of Spain ascended the throne. Thus the union of Portugal with its more powerful neighbour—a union which it had so often successfully resisted—was at length effectually accomplished. In India also Philip II. was proclaimed King, and he hoped the riches of the East would prove a mighty assistance in the struggle which he was carrying on against Protestantism and freedom of thought, and in the attempt that he was making to maintain absolute authority both in civil and ecclesiastical affairs, even at the expense of the vast progress made during the last century.

How little he succeeded in attaining his object is well known, but Portugal had the most to suffer from his audacious undertaking. For the Dutch, to whom the Portuguese harbours were closed after the union of Portugal with Spain, boldly sought the wares that they needed in India itself, and indeed soon made their land a general emporium of Indian produce. At first they avoided the Portuguese possessions, and restricted themselves to the remote and unimportant parts of the Indian Sea, but with time their courage grew. In 1603 they bombarded Goa, and even before that time had expelled the Portuguese from the Moluccas, and had established themselves side by side with them in Ceylon, while in 1641 they took Malacca.

Everywhere the Indians received them with open arms, and supported them in their struggles with the Portuguese. And when the latter at last succeeded in freeing themselves from the hated Spanish yoke, and in raising a native prince—the Duke of Braganza—to the throne, the Dutch did not agree to relinquish their Indian possessions, but, on the contrary, took care to secure them in the Peace of Westphalia.

Since that time the rule of Portugal in India has been limited to the towns of Diu, Daman, and Goa, to the eastern half of the Island of Timor, and to the town of Macao in China.

PART II.—THE SPANIARDS.

CHAPTER I.

INTRODUCTORY.

THE kingdom of Spain was formed by the union of the two kingdoms of Aragon and Castile. This union was eventually brought about by the marriage at Valladolid, on the 19th of October, 1469, of Queen Isabella of Castile with the Crown Prince Ferdinand of Aragon. But the mutual jealousy of the kingdoms opposed a resolute resistance and for a long time prevented any blending of them into one ; and the first prince who really united the two crowns on his head was the grandson of Ferdinand and Isabella—Charles V.—who, in 1516, was proclaimed King of Castile and Aragon. He was at once the first and the mightiest Prince of the Spanish nation, which, under him, ruled the fate of Europe. This European Power at the same time gained an immense accession of strength by the discovery and conquest of America, which not only poured an inexhaustible stream of wealth into the state coffers, but also gave Spain a high and well-deserved importance as a naval power.

All the conditions necessary to this rapid rise were to be found in the two states of which Spain was formed. To be sure, Aragon, and particularly Castile, were in the main inland states, and the only power of the people lay in the bold ungovernable knights and the manly burghers of the great towns. But the inhabitants of Catalonia, which had been united with

Aragon since the thirteenth century, had from early times devoted themselves to trade, and were a seafaring nation. Here was the town of Barcelona, which, specially favoured by Aragon, and possessing a constitution which was almost republican, profited by its favourable situation and by the neighbourhood of the mighty forests, which produced wood well adapted for ship-building.

In the kingdom of Castile too there was a promising beginning of a maritime power, which, however, could not develop itself in such a favourable manner as the Catalonian. Its north-western provinces, Galicia and Biscay, had in early time an important fishery in the Atlantic Ocean, and the fleet which, in 1247, they sent against Seville was powerful enough to defy the Moorish fleet, and to keep the town completely shut in on the side of the sea. But with the taking of Seville the Castilians first gained a harbour corresponding to their importance, and their commerce began to be of consequence. The Kings of Castile bestowed great care on their new possession, began the formation of great arsenals, and gave a hearty welcome to any traders possessing nautical experience who chose to settle there. Many Genoese took advantage of this opportunity, and erected great warehouses. It very soon became a lively commercial city, and possessed a large fleet, which was also useful to the Castilian King in his political undertakings. Thus it was employed with much success at the siege of Carthagena and Algeciras, 1263—78 ; and the foundation of a military order for service on the sea must have been a mere whim and piece of kingly ostentation, as was also the appointment of an Admiral of Castile. The ceaseless struggles with the Moorish states exercised the warlike powers of the young fleet, but they hindered it from taking a peaceful share in the great trading movement in the Mediterranean Sea, from which the Castilians were as good as excluded.

Thus in Barcelona and Seville the conditions existed which,

under certain favourable circumstances, promised the development of considerable maritime power. And the favourable circumstances soon occurred ; the marriage of Ferdinand and Isabella bound the powers of the two kingdoms together, and thereby attained the object of struggles which had gone on for 500 years—the destruction of the Moorish Kingdom in the Spanish Peninsula, and the erection of a kingdom which had an important influence on the affairs of Europe. And happy fate led the man to Spain who poured incalculable riches into her lap, and opened a sphere in which all the powers of the nation could develop themselves and find occupation.

CHAPTER II.

TEN places on the north coast of the Ligurian Bay have laid claim to the honour of having produced the great man who discovered the New World; yet it is almost certain that he was a native of the great mercantile city of Genoa. The time of his birth is more doubtful. While some think he was born in 1436, others decide for the year 1446 or 1456. If we follow the indications given by Columbus himself, we shall give the preference to the last date. For in the letter which he addressed to King Ferdinand on the 7th of July, 1503, he says he was twenty-eight years old when he came to Castile, which certainly was in the year 1484. Also all the other indications given in his report agree with the supposition that he was born in the year 1456. The name of the family to which he belonged was Colon or Colombo. It was not noble; for in his letter to Prince Juan's nurse he compares himself to King David, whom God raised to high honour from the rank of a shepherd. Therefore the claims put forth by the ancient family of the Counts of Colombo, in Piacenza, to relationship with the celebrated discoverer are proved to be groundless.

His family was of the burgher class, but not undistinguished. In the letter already mentioned Columbus boasts that he was not the first admiral of his family, and claims as a relative a Colon el Mozo, of Cogoleto, who was Genoese admiral in the middle of the fifteenth century. The father of our hero was Dominico Colombo, an honest weaver in a suburb of Genoa, who afterwards removed to Savona, and who was still alive shortly before the death of his great son. From his marriage with Susanna Fontanarossa sprang three sons—Christopher, Bartholomew, and Jacob—and a daughter, who married a tradesman. The family was well-to-do, and could give the promising boy a moderately good education, traces of which are evident in his later letters and reports. Having chosen a seaman's life as his calling, he was sent at a very early age to the high school of Pavia, where at that time famous scholars taught mathematics, astronomy, and geography. How long he remained under their instruction is uncertain; but at fourteen he went to sea, and on the Genoese merchant-ships in the Mediterranean became a skilful sailor. Most of the harbours of that sea were known to him, and we learn from his own mouth that he visited the island of Chios, and had there watched the collecting of mastic (resin from the pistacia lentiscus). In the course of these voyages, among other places, he visited Portugal apparently about 1475.

There he became acquainted with Dona Felipa Perestrello, the daughter of Bartholomew Perestrello, an excellent seaman, who had been many times employed by Prince Henry. He very shortly married, but his young bride brought him no dowry. Perestrello himself was already dead when Columbus first came to Portugal, and his possessions on the island of Porto Santo, which his grandfather had discovered, were, it appears, quite lost to the family, except one estate in which Columbus spent some time as the guest of his mother-in-law. The happy union only lasted a short time, being put an end to by the death of the wife, apparently at the birth of a son, who was christened Diego. It was not difficult for so clever and striving a seaman to gain his livelihood at that time in Portugal. Columbus drew maps, prepared mathematical works, and, first as pilot and afterwards as captain, entered the service of the great merchant houses.

In this position he found opportunities to become acquainted with the whole of the Atlantic Ocean, as far as it was then known. In his last writings, " The Prophecies," he declares, with justice, " Every part of the ocean which has yet been sailed through, I have sailed through." Of the voyages which he then made we have accounts of two, and they are particularly interesting. In one he visited England, and from Bristol, which at that time was a place of considerable trade, he went to Iceland, and even proceeded more than 100 Spanish miles beyond it. This voyage took place in the year 1477, and led him to the borders of that continent which he afterwards discovered. Some years later (1483) we find him on the Gold Coast of Africa, in the recently-built fortress of San Jorge de Mina. Such extensive voyages in such opposite directions must have given him, in addition to the extraordinary gifts of observation that he possessed, a rich treasure of experience and knowledge, which he increased by diligent study.

The writings and diaries of his late father-in-law had a great influence on the direction of his mental activity. At that time —that is, between the years 1478 and 1484—the conviction became firmly fixed in his mind that the east coast of Asia could be reached from the west coast of Europe, and that this way to India was much to be preferred, on account of its shortness and convenience, to the other, which the navigators of Portugal were then striving to find. This idea Columbus was not the first to put forth, just as he was not the first European who trod the soil of America ; but the enthusiasm with which he defended the idea and proved it to be practicable, the perseverance with which he devoted his whole life to it, combined with the deep obscurity which rests on all the earlier visitors of America, secure to him for all time the fame of being the discoverer of the New World, and make his name one of the most glorious in the history of the world.

About 500 years before Columbus bold sailors had landed on the shores of the New World. They were Normans ; some of those wild sea-robbers who from the ninth century were the terror of all the coasts of France and Germany. From the deep fiords of Norway, on the shores of which their wooden dwellings stood, the ships of the Vikings every year poured out in hundreds and assembled in fleets, over which the bravest and most distinguished had the command under the title of Sea Kings. Woe to the coast which they pitched upon for attack. Mercilessly were the most fruitful regions turned into utter wastes, and there was no obstacle at which they did not mock, no enemy that could withstand them. The struggle with the most unheard-of dangers they looked upon as a mere pastime and a manly enjoyment of life, and these mighty giants in their little fragile barks, which were without decks, and, at the most, only possessed the protection of a tent, ventured out into the unknown ocean, trusting only to their unflinching powers of endurance and the sharpness of their wits. From the Faroe Islands they had, at the end of the ninth century, discovered and colonised Iceland. The civil order which had at that time been established in Norway, from its union under one government by the conquests of Harald Harfagar, impelled the wildest and most untamed of the Normans to emigrate to that distant island, the Thule of the ancient Greeks and Romans, where they preserved their national characteristics and religion for many centuries, un-affected by foreign influence.

From this island, in the year 982, Eric the Red, who on account of his many deeds of violence was obliged to leave his native land, sailed directly to the west, where he suspected there was land, and found, after a few days, a coast which ran north and south, and on whose rocky mountains he observed enormous glaciers stretching even into the sea. It was the east coast of Greenland. He followed it to its most southernly point, Cape Farewell, and found on the other side of that cape deep fiords and a number of little islands which reminded him of the home he had left. He settled there, and the charming descriptions of the delightful climate of the land which reached Iceland soon drew crowds of Norman colonists to it. The west coast far up to the north was speedily covered with settlements. As early as the year 999 as many as 190 dwellings might have been counted, and when Christianity was introduced it became the seat of a bishopric and of several convents. But from the middle of the fourteenth century all knowledge of the colony in the distant Greenland disappeared. In some way, which has never been explained, it was forsaken or died out, and since the coast was taken by the Danes in 1727—though many monuments of the earlier people, such as ruined walls, gravestones, Runic inscriptions have been found—no indication of the fate of the people has been discovered.

Greenland is only part of the Archipelago lying near the American coast, but the mainland itself was apparently discovered by the bold Normans. As early as the year 986 Bjarni, sailing from Iceland to Greenland to seek his father, who had gone thither, was driven by stress of weather towards the south, and saw coasts, the description of which answers to those of Nova Scotia and Newfoundland.

Hearing of this, Leif, the eldest son of Eric the Red, went thither and passed a whole winter in a beautiful woody and grassy land, which, on account of the wild grapes growing, received the name of Winland. With tolerable certainty this has been identified with the coast of Rhode Island, one of the most northerly states of the Union. Leif's brother, Thorwald, went even farther south, and perished in a struggle with the aborigines ; his grave may be seen in what is now the State of Massachusetts. After an attempt on the part of another member of the family to establish a settlement in Winland, which was completely frustrated by the hostile conduct of the savages, all further attempts at discovery appear to have been given up.

The fabulous account of the voyage of an Icelandic merchant, Gudleif Gudlangson, who, in 1027, having been driven from his course by a violent storm, reached a distant shore, and there found a missing countryman in high honour among the natives, deserves small credit. About the same amount is due to the discovery of the shores called Hoitramannaland (the land of the white men), which some people have imagined to be Georgia and Florida.

The news of this discovery of a new world by Iceland and Greenland Normans only reached the civilised states of Europe in a very confused manner. But in Iceland it remained an old tale of the highest interest, and, much altered and improved by passing from mouth to mouth, was finally written down.

Among the learned the possibility of reaching the east coast of Asia from the west coast of Europe, by sailing directly west, had been many times mooted. The conviction of the spherical form of the earth was at this time universally spread, and the question only remained whether the space of water between the two continents was not too great to allow of a passage. The necessity of being prepared with provisions and water for the journey both ways made it a more serious matter. Happily a mistake was made about the distance between the continents, the circumference of the earth being calculated about a fifth (more exactly ·19) less than it really is.

In the works of the French savant, Pierre d'Ailly, which appeared in 1480, and were accessible to Columbus, there is a certain passage in which are collected together all the expressions of Aristotle, Seneca, Strabo, and other learned men, tending to make the distance between Spain and the coast of Asia appear smaller. Still greater was the authority of Paulo

Toscanelli, the famous cosmographer of Florence, 1397—1482, who supported this opinion. Writing in answer to a question proposed to him by an ecclesiastic, Fernando Martinez, in the name of the King, Alfonso I. of Portugal, the Florentine astronomer, in a letter dated June 25, 1474, accompanied by a chart, thus expresses his emphatic opinion : "From the town of Lisbon westward you may count twenty-six distances of 250 miles each to the large and noble city of Cathay (the capital of China at that time)." This distance is about a third of the earth's circumference. He estimated the distance between the two towns to be about ¦120 degrees, though in reality it is nearly as much again. It was known also from Marco Polo's journey that about 10 degrees from the mainland of Asia lay the islands of Cipango (Japan), and thus the space left to be traversed became comparatively small, and the voyage no longer appeared impracticable. They expected, therefore, to find the coast of Japan in the meridian of San Francisco, in California. The space which still remained considerably lost its terrors by the supposed existence of the traditional islands of Antigua and St. Brandon's Land, the first of which, according to Toscanelli, should lie about 50 degrees west of Lisbon.

His residence in Portugal, and his intercourse with the most renowned astronomers and sailors in the land, made Columbus acquainted with these opinions, and the active mind of the young man seized with ardour on the great idea, the accomplishment of which promised him a good position and undying fame. He set himself to collect carefully all evidence which seemed to prove the existence of land to the west. On the shores of Madeira and Porto Santo and the Azores there had often been washed up from the west by the waves foreign trees, pieces of carved wood, according to some reports, even the dead bodies of an unknown race of men. Sailors driven to the west had frequently picked up these strange things ;

there were even stories of land having been seen in the distance.

That Columbus received his first impulse to discovery on his visit to Iceland, from hearing of the Norman voyages to Winland, is certainly erroneous, for the news of the proximity of such large tracts of land would have entirely altered his views respecting the distance of the Asiatic coast, which he aimed at reaching. More likely the great thought first came to him after this journey, which he took in 1477 ; it was after his return from Iceland that he became intimate with the family of Perestrello (to whose papers and journals he had access), and was introduced into the circle of the most illustrious seamen. So it probably was not until 1479 that he addressed to Toscanelli a letter, in which he says, that having heard of the astronomer's opinions, he wished for his counsel, since he had determined to make the great venture. The complaisant Florentine answered readily, sending at the same time a copy of his former letter with the chart. Columbus's hopes were raised to certainty. "You will see," so the letter ran, "that the journey you are intending to undertake is much less difficult than is supposed." Thus encouraged and with his convictions strengthened, Columbus sought for an audience with King John II., who had zealously furthered the Portuguese discoveries. It was granted him, and he tried to gain the interest and active support of the King by a lively and distinct explanation of his plan.

But then began the long series of disappointments to which the great man was destined. The King hesitated to carry into execution such a costly and expensive plan, broached by a still unknown sailor, and referred him to the nautical commission, which was at that time engaged in adapting the astrolabe to sea voyages. After a long careful examination, Martin Behaim, who during his residence in the Azores had himself become well acquainted with the strange objects drifted up, pronounced in favour of attempting the bold expedition to the west, but the other members of the commission, the two Hebrew physicians and the Bishop of Ceuta, considered that many of the premises were unfounded, and the conclusions drawn from them uncertain. They could not therefore advise the King to spend large sums on an undertaking of such doubtful result, while it appeared that, persevering in the African discoveries already begun, they might hope to reach India very speedily. Perhaps the exorbitant demands of Columbus, which afterwards endangered his scheme in Spain, may have been one cause of his want of success. However it was, he failed to obtain a favourable answer from the King. The story that King John dishonestly sent out a Portuguese to make the attempt, and did not give an absolute refusal to the Genoese until the attempt had failed, cannot be proved, and contradicts the known character of the King. The truth probably is that the King balanced the certainty of sailing round Africa against the uncertainty of a voyage to the west.

Much mortified, and still thoroughly convinced of the future success of his plan, Columbus resolved to turn his back on Portugal, and to make to other states who could better appreciate the grandeur of his conceptions the great offer which that country had so short-sightedly refused. While his brother Bartholomew, who had followed him to Portugal, remained in Lisbon, and perhaps accompanied the expedition of Bartholomew Dias in the year 1487, Columbus in 1484 secretly escaped over the border, for the Portuguese, who jealously concealed their African discoveries from strangers' eyes, would certainly have prevented the departure of one so well acquainted with them.

The story goes that he then proceeded to his native city Genoa, passing on to Venice, in which places his plans suffered a double rejection. But no proofs can be produced of his residence in either town, and there is an entire absence of records, which could scarcely be the case had he negotiated with the authorities of those cities.   Apparently he went straight from Portugal to Spain, where he first applied to the Duke of Medina Sidonia, one of the mighty vassals of Castile, lord of great possessions in Andalusia and master of a not inconsiderable naval force.   Won over to the stranger's plan, the Duke had already prepared ships to be placed at his disposal, when he changed his mind, considering that such a great undertaking with all its possible consequences was not an affair for a private man, but rather for a great state.   He therefore sent Columbus with letters of recommendation to Queen Isabella, and on January 20th, 1486, he was taken into her service.   The learned men of the University of Salamanca were formed into a commission, before which Columbus laid his plans, together with the letter of the famous author which supported his ideas.   But except the Dominican, Diego de Deza, who became afterwards Archbishop of Seville, and remained to the end a faithful patron of Columbus, none of these learned men were convinced by the arguments of Columbus. In recent times this commission has been on this account treated with the utmost scorn.   The charge has been brought against it of opposing to the deep thoughts of the Genoese texts of Scripture, and of treating the whole affair in a highly unscientific manner.   But this was not the case, and we are bound in justice to acknowledge that the arguments of Columbus might very easily have been answered out of the very books from which he drew them.   The opponents of Columbus were fighting on the side of truth, the Genoese was only contending for a happy delusion, which ended in the discovery of the New World.   A result which he had not reckoned upon put him in the right, and those who are easily dazzled by success have thought to glorify the deed by heaping contempt on those who with justice opposed him.

The decision of the commission is not known, but the fact that the undertaking was not carried out does not prove its rejection. The final struggle with the Moors of Granada already begun, fears lest Portugal might be irritated, perhaps even provoked to war, were important weights in the scale. Columbus remained in the service of Castile and took up his abode in Cordova, where his small salary and the money he procured by making charts, etc., secured to him a tolerable livelihood. Under these circumstances he determined to wait for happier times, and in the meanwhile secured many lasting friends among influential persons of the court of Ferdinand and Isabella. But this delay became at length unendurable; the Moorish war long remained undecided, and his bitter experience as suitor to haughty patrons appeared humiliating to his over-sensitive nature.

After a residence of five years, he left Cordova in 1491, with his son Diego, who was then about twelve years old, to try his luck at the court of France, where a young and adventurous monarch was holding the reins of government. But he had now reached the crisis of his fate. The traveller knocked at the gate of a Franciscan convent, La Ribida, at the port of Palos, and begged for refreshment for himself and his boy. The Guardian, Juan Peres de Marchena, a brother much looked up to, who bore the honourable title of Confessor to the Queen, took an interest in the gifted man, who related to him his plans and their disappointment in vivid colours. The Guardian's heart was soon entirely won, and he invited him to remain, and promised to use all his influence on his behalf.

A letter which he immediately despatched to the Queen shortly received a very kind answer, in which Columbus was summoned to appear at the court, which was then in the camp of Santa Fé before the walls of Granada. A small sum was also remitted to defray the expenses of the journey.

With warm thanks he took leave of his new friend, leaving little Diego in his care, and hopefully began his journey.

He entered the court at a happy moment (Dec., 1491), just when Granada had made offers to surrender, and the glorious end of the war which had raged for so many years appeared in sight. To the enthusiasm called forth by this great achievement no plan, however great or expensive, appeared impossible; so Columbus met with a most friendly reception. Yet months went by. The entrance of the monarchs into the conquered town took place on the 2nd January, 1492, with extraordinary magnificence, and Columbus received no decided answer.

The unheard-of demands of Columbus caused this delay. He required, in case of the discovery of a western route to India, a patent of nobility rendering the title of Don hereditary in his family. He also required that he should be made Admiral of the Atlantic Ocean, and should rank as high as the Admiral of Castile; that the power and title of Viceroy over all the discovered countries should be conferred upon him; with the right to name three men for all offices in those lands out of whom the Crown should choose; that he should have the tenth of the revenues which should flow to the Crown from the lands to be discovered; and, lastly, the right to an eighth share in all mercantile undertakings which the Crown might engage in in those lands.

These demands met with decided opposition. King Ferdinand and a great number of the most important people at court were irritated by the presumption of the Genoese. Who was Columbus, and what deeds had he to boast of, that he should thus dare to demand control over the most proved and deserving officials—men too who could point proudly to their old nobility? Where were the securities that the results of his undertaking would at all fulfil the hopes on which he founded his demands? How monstrous were these demands when compared with the poor rewards bestowed in Portugal on the most distinguished seamen for the greatest services!

The lands over which Columbus demanded the Viceroyalty, and of whose produce he demanded the tenth part, were not virgin shores with a wild population, but the imperial Japan and China, with millions of civilised and industrious inhabitants. All these important considerations were discussed; but when something less was offered him, he immediately departed with wounded pride, and threatened to go to France or England, whence he had received promises.

What wonderful faith in himself! What bold confidence that the benefits which would result to Spain from his work, must justify the great and really unheard-of demands which he made. And yet it would have been better if he had yielded, and had lowered his demands in those points particularly which caused the most offence—the claim upon the Viceroyalty and the tenth. A little earnest self-examination and a calm glance into the future must have made it clear to him that he was pushing himself into a position for which he could not be fit, and involving himself in embarrassments with the Crown which, as it was at that time the great object of the Crown to render vassals powerless, would be sure to be to his disadvantage. The exorbitancy of his demands bitterly avenged itself on him.

He had hardly quitted the court, when his friends, who meanwhile had increased in numbers, interceded for him with great zeal. Among them Luis de Santangel, the Treasurer of Aragon, distinguished himself by his unwearied persistency. He dwelt particularly on the responsibility which they would incur if, in consequence of their parsimony, other lands should gain the advantages which were now offered to Spain, and added that even supposing the expedition did fail, it was quite worth while to undertake it, in order to be assured of the impracticability of any route to India in that direction.

The resolution of the Queen was somewhat shaken by these representations, and when Santangel went on to remind her that she was denying the knowledge of Christianity to countless multitudes of heathen, he touched the right chord. The pious Queen, whose most earnest desire was the conversion of her Moorish and Jewish subjects, was won by this clever move; and she was filled with such zeal that she said she would pledge the crown jewels to procure the funds necessary for the execution of the undertaking. This offer, however, was not carried into execution, for Santangel, who firmly believed in Columbus, provided from his own estates the 5000 ducats which were required.

Messengers announcing the unconditional granting of his demands recalled Columbus to Santa Fé. The treaty was concluded on the 17th of April; on the 30th of the same month Columbus received the dignities that he had demanded, and immediately set out for Palos, a port between the mouths of Guadiana and Guadalquiver, whence the expedition was to start.

He made use of this harbour because he was bound in the service of the crown within ten days to fit out two caravels. A third ship was also chartered, and in accordance with the treaty Columbus bore an eighth of the expense. Very useful to him was the celebrated maritime family of the Pinzons, out of which three brothers, Martin Alonso, Vincente Yanez, and Francisco Martin, offered to accompany him. With their assistance the fitting out of the ships and the engaging of the crews were speedily accomplished, and all was ready for the start by the 3rd of August, 1492.

The little squadron consisted of three ships: the *Santa Maria*, the *Pinta*, and the little *Nina*. All three, especially the *Pinta*, were very indifferent sailers; and owing to the hasty manner in which they were prepared, were found to have many defects which could with difficulty be remedied on the high seas.

The *Santa Maria* was commanded by Columbus himself, the *Pinta* and the *Nina* by the two eldest of the Pinzons. The crews numbered altogether ninety men, for the most part experienced seamen, who had pledged themselves to follow Columbus whithersoever he should go. Thus with no pomp, and but ill-prepared for the difficulties that might be expected, Columbus set out to discover a new world. Of this voyage he kept a most comprehensive journal, which has been published, abridged by the Bishop Las Casas. It gives us an exact idea of it.

Only a few days after the squadron started, the rudder of the *Pinta* broke, and it could not be repaired until they reached the Canaries. On the Island Gomera, which belongs to that group, and which had already been taken and colonised by the Spaniards, Columbus remained for some months improving the vessels. He also took in provisions for a voyage of such uncertain length. The diary tells us that on the 12th of August a great eruption of the Pik de Teyde on Teneriffe took place, the first of which we know anything. On the 6th of September Columbus left the Island of Gomera, and took his course straight towards the west.

Unconsciously he chose that part of the Atlantic Ocean in which it is the broadest ; but this misfortune was pretty well compensated for by the favouring wind which blew at first most unceasingly, the north-east trade wind. The passage therefore was a comparatively quick one, and only occupied thirty-four days. The temperature was very pleasant. Columbus compares it to the climate of Andalusia, and only deplored that the song of the nightingale was wanting.

On the 13th of September the compass was first noticed to decline towards the north-west, a circumstance which Columbus took care to explain in such a manner that the crew should not be alarmed. The many stories of the terror of the sailors, and of their increasing bitterness against Columbus, which at last became open mutiny, are the inventions of later writers, for whom the course of the remarkable voyage was not sufficiently adventurous. But Columbus himself confesses that he kept a double reckoning, and thus strove to deceive the crew as to the distance that they had come. But the deception was nothing very considerable.

On the 18th of September the difference between the two reckonings was only fifty miles. It must be remembered, however, that all calculations of the speed of vessels rested at that time upon conjectures which could lay no claim to certainty. The only complaint which Columbus makes about the cowardice of his crews we find on the 23rd September: " The sailors began to whisper, when they saw no considerable waves, that there would never be a wind to take them back to Spain."

The monotony of the voyage was enlivened by frequent signs of land being near, though they were over and over again found to be deceptive. Thus on the 25th of September they thought they were near a vast land. Indeed, from the *Pinta* the crew declared they had seen land, and sang the " Gloria in excelsis." But the next morning they discovered that they had been deceived by the clouds. Also the numerous birds which were seen from the ships kept the sailors in constant excitement, for they erroneously thought they could not fly many miles from the shore. Columbus explained to himself all these appearances by the supposition that the ships had passed near the traditionary Island of Antiglia without seeing it ; but he would not stop to seek for it, since he wished first to find the mainland of Asia.

The confusion into which the crews were constantly thrown by the repeatedly mistaken announcements of land induced Columbus to forbid such announcements to be made, except on good grounds; but at the same he promised, as the monarchs had desired, a pension of 10,000 maravedis to the man who should first discover land, and undertook to add at his own expense a silk doublet.

Up to the 7th of October they had maintained a course directly west, but on that day Columbus yielded to the representations of Martin Alonzo Pinzon, and steered W.S.W., chiefly because great flights of birds—Pinzon thought they were parrots—had been seen flying in that direction. Had Columbus persevered in the original direction, he would about the next day have reached the northern islands of the Bahama group, and thence probably the mainland of America in the part now called Florida, whilst by changing his course he was carried to the southern islands of that group, and past the south point of Florida to the West Indies.

After this change of course the signs that land was near multiplied. Carved sticks and branches of trees, etc., were picked up; and on all the ships hope and expectation swelled high in every breast. On the 11th of October, about ten o'clock, Columbus, who was looking out from the poop of his ship, perceived before him the uncertain glimmer of a light, which appeared again several times, and looked like a wavering torchlight. Others whom he called thought they saw it too, although the Admiral himself was very likely deceived. The excitement increased, no eye was closed.

The *Pinta*, commanded by the ambitious Martin Alonso Pinzon, kept in front, and it was from her masthead that at two o'clock in the morning of the 12th of October, 1492, came the long-expected cry of "Land ahead!" It was a sailor named Rodrigo de Triana who first perceived the coast in the uncertain twilight. He, however, never received the promised pension, Columbus claiming it for himself on the ground of the light he had seen; Rodrigo in a rage left Spain, and passing over to Africa abjured his faith. This conduct of

Columbus, which certainly was not amiable, proceeded probably less from mere greed than from the anxious desire to prove that the discovery of Asia from the west was entirely his work, even in the minutest details.

They gazed impatiently into the dim light, until the rising sun dispelled all doubt. At a little distance was stretched out a flat coast, over which rose green hills. The goal was reached, the difficult and dangerous undertaking was accomplished. But where were they? According to Columbus's secret calculations, the ships had traversed after leaving the Canaries, which lie 10° west of Lisbon, 1122 Spanish miles, or 90°. Now according to Toscanelli, the distance between Lisbon and Cipango (Japan) amounted at the most to 110°. So there could be no doubt that they had reached Cipango, or at least one of the group of islands lying near.

As soon as the ships had found anchorage, Columbus entered an armed boat and landed on the coast, accompanied by the eldest of the brothers Pinzon. Then in the presence of notaries with great formality he took possession of the land for the Queen of Castile. He set up a wooden cross, and named the island—for such the land proved to be—San Salvador. It was called by the natives Guanahani. It has no mountains, but is beautifully wooded, with a lake near the centre. It is one of the Bahama or Lucayan group, which lies something in the form of a crab off the coast of Florida to the south-east. There has recently been a violent dispute as to which island was first trodden by Columbus, and it has been settled in favour of Watling Island (latitude 23° 56' north, and longitude 74° 28' west). To the error of Columbus, who thought he had arrived on the coast of Asia, is due the name of West Indies, which he gave to all the islands he discovered in the course of years, as also that of Indians, which was conferred on the natives of America.

The natives looked upon the Spaniards as descended from the sun, and came to meet them with the greatest reverence ; their confidence was secured by little gifts, glass beads, little bells, etc., and they showed themselves thoroughly harmless and friendly. The simplicity and poverty of their condition excited the astonishment of the Spaniards. They went perfectly naked ; they were well proportioned, and of a brown complexion, which Columbus compared to that of the Guanches, and which they themselves sought to beautify by the use of bright paint. Their dwellings were simple reed huts roofed with palm leaves. Their food was principally vegetables, maize, manioc, yams, and potatoes, but they ate also fish, mussels, and the flesh of birds.

In fishing they made use of a little fish called by the Spaniards reverso, whose back was armed with thorns. Fastened to a thin but strong line, the Indians took it to the sea, and as soon as a large fish showed itself let it loose. It at once rushed upon its prey and fastened itself firmly to it by its prickles ; the tortured fish made for the shore, and there was easily caught by means of a rod which was attached to the end of the line. The tools of which the Indians made use were very rough ; they were unacquainted with iron, and employed instead sharpened stones and mussel shells. They so little understood other weapons that they took hold of Columbus's sword by the blade and wounded themselves. Since many of them had fresh wounds the Spaniards inquired the cause and learnt that they had gained them in struggles with neighbouring warlike races, who often visited these shores for kidnapping purposes. This was the first news which the Spaniards received of the more highly-organised but fiercer people of the Carribee Islands, with whom, in later times, they had such serious struggles. But Columbus considered them to be inhabitants of China. "I thought," he said, "and I still think that people come over here from the mainland to make prisoners and slaves. They must be most faithful and docile servants. I am convinced that they would be converted to Christianity without any difficulty, for I believe that they belong to no heathen sect."

But for the present Columbus gave up his plan of converting the Indians, and of erecting a fortress on the island, as he was anxious to reach Cipango as soon as possible. By various accidental resemblances of names, he was strengthened in the delusion that he was near the coast of Asia. Thus he first mistook Cuba and afterwards the district of Cibao in Hayti for Cipango, and the name Caniba, by which the Carribeans called themselves, he thought pointed to their being the subjects of the Khan of Mongolia, whom their ruler sent out to kidnap slaves.

Still labouring under this delusion he left Guanahani on the 14th of October, taking with him seven Indians to show him the way from island to island. In his progress towards the south-west, he touched on a mass of small coral islands. Only on two of the larger ones, Santa Maria de la Concepcion (the present Rum Key) and Fernandina (the present Long Island), did he make any stay. These he took possession of for Castile. They, in every way, resembled Guanahani. The voyage was then continued towards the south-west, "for," he writes in his diary, on the 24th of October, "I am determined to visit Quinsay, and to present your Royal Highnesses' letter to the great Khan."

On the 26th of October the squadron arrived at the north coast of Cuba, with the beauty of which Columbus was charmed. He seems never to weary of telling of the fragrance of the tropical woods, of the charming voices of the birds, of the glorious mountains, and of the tranquil pleasant harbours. In the intoxication of his discovery, he believed he saw mastic in the primeval forests, pearls in the clear sea, gold dust in the rivers, and in the most animated language he praises the earthly paradise which he had won for Castile. The ships pursued their course along the north coast until they were about 60° west of Ferro. Here they made a halt, since Columbus was now convinced that Cuba was not Cipango, but part of the mainland. In order to examine it more closely, he sent two Spaniards, one of whom was a converted Jew, on an embassy into the interior, and gave them, as interpreter, an Indian, who had been captured in Guanahani. If possible they were to penetrate into the chief city of the Khan, which they, misled by the ill-understood directions of the Indians, thought to be close to the coast.

After three days the embassy returned. They had found, twelve miles inland, an encampment of the natives, consisting of fifty huts, containing a population of about 1000 persons, by whom they had been received with great honour and curiosity; but about the great Khan and the lands in which gold and spices were to be found, they had been able to discover nothing. They mentioned, as a peculiar custom of the natives, that they carried about with them "a glowing coal and a certain herb, wrapped in a leaf like a cartridge, in order to light one end and suck in the smoke from the other. These cartridges they called tobacco."

According to the account of a later writer, it was not the rolls of leaves that were so called, but the reed through which the smoke was sucked up. These reeds were of a peculiar form. While one end was intended to hold the glowing roll of leaves, the other end was divided into two little reeds, which the Indians placed in the nostrils, for they smoked with their noses, not their mouths.

Undeceived by the report of the ambassadors, the Admiral determined to give up any further voyage towards the west. The new direction taken by the ships was decided by Columbus's wish to seek for the land of gold he believed to be near, and where, by finding larger treasures, he hoped to indemnify himself for not having reached India. At Guanahani and on all the islands he had discovered since he had noticed that the Indians wore thin gold plates as ornaments in their noses. When asked where the gold came from, the Indians had pointed towards the south, and had said that a land lay there which they sometimes called Bohio and sometimes Babeque. There large quantities of this noble metal were to be found. The stories told by the Indians of this wonderful land aroused the covetousness of the Spaniards, and they took such a hold upon Columbus that he made the discovery of this land his goal. Thus even in the first discoveries of the New World was proved the justice of the saying, that the colonisation of America by the Spaniards and the progress of their discoveries was governed, as by a law of nature, by the presence or absence of gold.

On the 12th of November Columbus set sail again. Sad to say, before his departure he had five young men, seven women, and three children captured to take to Spain with him, by which cruel action he inspired the confiding natives with the greatest terror and hatred. The next night a man came swimming up to the ship and begged him to take him with him since his wife and children were among those who were being carried away. Henceforth the shores of Cuba were deserted. Warned of the cruel stranger by messengers and fiery signals, the inhabitants had fled into the woods. The squadron pursued its way along the north coast of Cuba to the east and south-east. So great was the Spaniards' greed for gold that Martin Alonzo Pinzon separated from the other two ships, in order to find the land of gold for himself and to secure the glory of its discovery. In vain were all the signals which Columbus made during the night of the 21-22 November, the fugitive did not return. On the 5th of December the Admiral reached the east point of Cuba, which he named Juana in honour of the Crown Princess, and at the

same time there arose in the east a new land with high mountains which the Indians on board said to be Bohio. But the
people of the island itself called it Quizqueia, that is to say
the world, or Cibao (the stony), or Hayti (the rough land).
The last name has remained to this day and has outlived the
Spanish name, Hispaniola (Little Spain), which Columbus
gave it.

On Hispaniola the Spaniards found a much higher development of social life than on the coast which they had hitherto
touched. The whole island was divided into several kingdoms, governed by hereditary princes called caciques. Of
these kingdoms some were specially important on account of
their extent and of the power of their caciques, such as, on
the north coast, Marien and Maguana, and on the west and
south coasts, Xaraqua and Higuey. The power of the
caciques over their subjects was unlimited, they were the
possessors of the land, and they adjudged the work and the
pay. All the little dainties of the island, the flesh of the rabbit
and the lizard, were reserved for their table, and the people
were kept at a distance from the sacred persons of the princes
by a troublesomely precise etiquette. By the greater convenience of their dwellings, and by some attempts at decoration, the inhabitants of Hispaniola showed themselves superior
to those of Cuba, though they evidently belonged to the same
race. But at the time of the arrival of the Spaniards these
gentle people were threatened with destruction by another
stronger race. These were the Kalina, or Kaniba,* or Kari-
ben, that is heroes, as the natives of the Antilles called them,
a people who originally dwelt on the south coast of South
America. They had already conquered a part of Hispaniola
and Caonabo. The cacique of the kingdom was a Carribean
adventurer. Tall and strongly made, they were superior in

* From this word, in consequence of the imperfect pronunciation of
the Spaniards, we have got our word cannibals, or men-eaters.

courage and warlike qualities to the natives of the Antilles, and were feared even by Spaniards. In war they were frequently accompanied by their wives, who were little inferior to the men in ferocity. Their most terrible weapon was a poisoned arrow. In their piroques, forty feet long and capable of holding fifty men, they went from island to island, and often in perfect fleets made plundering expeditions on to the coasts, where the inhabitants, if they were unable to escape by flight, were carried off prisoners. The men were cooked and eaten, the women made slaves. Against these fearful enemies the natives of the Antilles were defenceless, and there is no doubt that if it had not been for the arrival of the Spaniards they would in a short time have been destroyed by them.

In his first expedition Columbus came but little into personal contact with the Carribeans, and learned most about them from the descriptions of their victims, since he sailed only on the north coast of Hispaniola. Here the farther he approached towards the east the more lively became the trade with the natives, who came in hundreds on to the ships, and exchanged provisions, cotton, and golden ornaments for all sorts of trifles. When they noticed the eagerness of the Spaniards for gold, they gave them to understand that in a land farther to the east, which they called Cibao, gold was found and smelted. This news still more inflamed Columbus's desire to find this land of gold. " May the merciful God," he exclaimed, " help me to find this gold, or rather these mines." Then a great misfortune befell him, and dashed all his hopes. On Christmas night, when all were asleep, even the Admiral himself, who had watched for two nights, the ship, owing to the helm having been committed, contrary to his express orders, to a sailor-boy, ran on a sand-bank. The Admiral was the first on deck, and by ordering an anchor to be cast from the stern, did all he could to prevent the complete destruction of the ship. But the crew, stupefied by the disaster, disobeyed his commands, sprang into the boat, and tried to escape on to the *Nina*, which was about half a mile off. There they were brought to reason, and returned to the *Santa Maria*, which by that time, however, it was hopeless to think of saving.

Fortunately Columbus had for some days been carrying on friendly intercourse with the Cacique of the Haytian kingdom of Marien—Guanacanagari was his name—and on hearing of the disaster he showed the greatest sympathy, and ordered his subjects to give the Spaniards all the help possible in the saving of their goods. This was done in their most zealous and honourable manner; so that in a few days everything was saved. Between Columbus and the Cacique, a stately dignified man, who immediately hastened to the spot, visits and presents were exchanged.

The fear of the Caribs betrayed by Guacanagari was skilfully made use of by Columbus to gain his consent to the building of a fortress, the garrison of which should keep the Caribs at a distance. The building had become necessary, because the *Nina* was too small to bear the crews and freight of two ships. In a few days the little fort was finished, consisting of some buildings and sheds made of reeds, and protected by wooden palisades and a ditch. From the season when it was built, it was called Natividad, and forty men were appointed as a garrison, under the command of Diego de Arana from Cordova. They received instructions to continue the profitable gold trade with the natives, and, if possible, find the mine itself. A wise and friendly behaviour towards the Indians was also specially inculcated. In order to arouse a desirable dread of their arms, Columbus caused his archers to display their skill, and arranged sham fights, with repeated discharges of the cannons, which made a great impression.

He thought himself so secure of the result he desired that as early as the 4th of January, 1493, before the palisades were finished, he set sail in the *Nina*, after having promised to return at the very latest in a year. The cause of this sudden departure was the news, brought by the Indians, that another ship was engaged in the purchase of gold ornaments not far off. It could only be the *Pinta*, and Columbus was very anxious that it should return in his company, and should not arrive a little before him in Spain, which would considerably diminish his glory as a discoverer.

On the 6th of January they met the fugitive, and Martin Alonzo Pinzon immediately came on board the *Nina* to excuse himself and to represent the separation of the ships as unintentional. Columbus pretended to believe him, but was full of mistrust, and gave Pinzon fully to understand that he was under his control and must obey. The names which he had given to the promontories along the coast were immediately changed. From that time the relations between these men, who had been once so intimate, became hostile, and so continued until death separated them. The insubordination of the one and the somewhat petty jealousy of the other prevented any reconciliation.

The *Pinta* had in the meantime visited some little groups of islands off the coast of Hispaniola, and carried on a profitable barter, by which the Spaniard had become possessed of much gold, some pieces being as large as a man's fist. Pinzon himself, with twelve companions, had penetrated into the interior of Hispaniola, and had brought back news of an island rich in gold, called Yamaye (Jamaica), to the south of Cuba, and also of a coast lying to the west, easily attainable, whose inhabitants were always clothed. Columbus paid no attention to this important information, which evidently referred to Yucatan, or perhaps even Mexico, not only because it was brought him by Pinzon, but also because his first intention to visit at any cost the Great Khan of China, and if possible to reach India, had long been given up. Hardly was he sure of having discovered a land of gold than all his bold plans took to flight, his enthusiasm for discovery cooled, and he thought of nothing else but carrying away the discovered treasure.

The two ships set out together on the return voyage. They touched at many points on the coast of Hispaniola, and found the natives everywhere friendly and trustful. In some places they believed they saw gold in the sand of the rivers, but nowhere did they make a stay of any length. At the east end of the islands they first met with the Caribs, who, as they at once perceived from their form and bearing, belonged to quite another stock. After a fight with them, in which the first blood was shed and four Caribs were taken prisoner, the ships, on the 17th of January, left the coast, and sailed north-east into the open sea. Until the 12th of February they allowed the ships to run before the wind, though the steersmen found it impossible to agree as to the longitude in which they were. But on that day a fearful storm arose, in which the frail ships were in the greatest danger. It lasted for three days, and so utterly wearied the crews that every moment they believed death to be at hand. In this distress the pious Admiral proposed to seek the assistance of the Virgin and of the saints by vowing pilgrimages. As many beans as there were men on board were placed in a cap, among which one was marked by a cut. Each drew a bean, and whoever had the marked one was to make the promised pilgrimage. Three times the lot was drawn in this manner, and twice it fell upon the Admiral; the third time it fell upon a sailor from Cadiz, but Columbus promised to pay the expenses of his pilgrimage. In addition to this the whole crew vowed, if they were saved, to make a pilgrimage in their shirts to one of the chapels consecrated to the Virgin.

When everything was thus done to procure the favour of Heaven, Columbus bethought himself how he might get the news of his discovery to Europe in case they were all lost. He wrote down a short account of his voyage with a statement of the lands discovered, and placing it sealed in an airtight vessel, together with a note which begged the finder to take it to the Court of Castile, and promised him a reward of 1000 ducats for so doing, threw it into the sea. Fortunately this was unnecessary. The weather began to improve on February 16th, and the next day land was discovered, which proved to be one of the Azores—Santa Maria.

But in the fearful storm the ships were separated, and the *Pinta* was still on the high sea, while the *Nina* had found a temporary resting-place. The crew returned thanks for their deliverance. For Columbus it was a special triumph, as it proved him to be correct when he reckoned that they would reach the Azores, if they held on in the course they had taken. Full of joy, he writes in his diary, " I have always purposely exaggerated the distance, in order to lead astray the pilots and sailors, and thus keep the key of the western navigation to myself. I have succeeded so perfectly that now nobody can point out with accuracy the way back to India."

The *Nina* was detained at Santa Maria until February 24th, partly from the need of rest after so much fatigue, and partly from the hostility of the Portuguese commander, Joäs de Castanheda. Half the crew was suddenly attacked by him and taken prisoners, as, in fulfilment of their vow, they were travelling in their shirts to a lady chapel near the coast. However, after some days, the good understanding was restored. What was the cause of the quarrel has never been clearly known. Whilst some believe that Castanheda was secretly commissioned by the Portuguese King, Joäs II., to destroy Columbus, others with greater probability declare that he

suspected the Spanish ship of having come from Portuguese
Guinea, and that he suspended hostilities directly he was convinced of the groundlessness of his suspicions. Rested and
refreshed, they began their journey home on February 24th,
hoping in a few days to touch their native coast.

But their trials were not over yet. On March 3rd they
again encountered a storm, which excited the greatest alarm,
and impelled the Admiral anew to solemn vows. The ship
was in extreme peril, being driven by the storm with fearful
force towards the Portuguese coast, and it required all the
skill of the Admiral and the utmost exertions of the crew
before the Tagus was at last successfully entered. On the
evening of March 4th the *Nina* came to anchor at the famous
landing-place Restello, near Lisbon. The news of their arrival
naturally excited great attention in the city, in which Columbus in earlier times had had many acquaintances. With the
congratulations which their great success called forth was
mixed much envy and jealousy at the good fortune which
had fallen to their hated neighbours, and many complaints of
the blindness of the King, who had rejected a man of such
distinction.

The Government was doubtful how to act. On March 5th
Bartholomew Dias appeared on board the *Nina*, and summoned Columbus before a court of inquiry to justify himself
for his secret departure, but was satisfied when Columbus
produced the letter which nominated him Castilian Admiral.
Then followed an invitation to the royal castle at Valparaiso,
situated a short distance from Lisbon, and in which John II.
was at that time residing. On the 9th of March Columbus
went thither, accompanied by some of his companions, and
he took with him, to amuse the King, the captured Indians
and specimens of the plants and animals of Hispaniola. He
met with a better reception than he expected. The King
appeared interested in the detailed account which he gave

him, and succeeded admirably in mastering the vexation and jealousy by which he was consumed. He, however, let slip the words that he should lay claim to the newly-discovered lands in virtue of the grant made to Castile by the Pope, and of the treaty concluded between Portugal and Castile in the year 1479. But he nobly refused the offer of some courtiers to try and engage the hot-blooded Admiral in a dispute and stab him as if in haste, and thus remove out of the way the only man who understood how to find the way to the New World. Indeed, he honourably entertained the great discoverer, and when the latter took his leave on the 11th of March dismissed him in the most gracious manner. Re-embarked on board the *Nina*, Columbus hastened his departure and arrived at Palos on the 15th of March.

Here all hope had quite been given up that the long-looked-for fleet would ever be seen again. The joy therefore was all the greater; indeed, it was little short of ecstasy when the adventurers themselves related the grand results of their expedition, and described the wonders of the distant paradise. The very next day appeared the *Pinta*. It came from Bayonne in Galicia, at which place it had first touched the Portuguese shore, and from whence Pinzon had despatched a letter to Ferdinand and Isabella, in order to communicate to them the happy news, and to beg an audience.

But the monarchs, remembering their agreement with Columbus, had directed him to go to Palos and there await the Admiral, in whose train he might appear at court. This ungracious answer broke the heart of the proud and self-conscious man, who could not bear to be in subjection to a foreigner, whose superior he considered himself to be. An illness with which he had been attacked shortly before his landing quickly grew worse, and carried him off in a few days. But the Pinzons, whose support had been of such service to Columbus's undertaking, now withdrew; and this may have had a good deal to do with the rapid and most unfavourable change of public opinion concerning Columbus.

A glorious triumph awaited the great discoverer on his arrival, and it was the greatest moment of his life. Those who previously had expressed a doubt as to the result of his plan, and, indeed, had laughed at the fanatic, now felt themselves bound to make up for their mistrust by their ostentatious applause; and those who had always taken Columbus's part now proudly joined their friend, a part of whose glory they felt reflected upon themselves.

After he, accompanied by his whole crew, had fulfilled the vow made during the late storm, he went to Seville, where he made his entrance on Palm Sunday, surrounded by a re-joicing crowd, who could not satisfy themselves with gazing at the curiosities he had brought with him. Here he awaited the answer of the monarchs to the report which he had des-patched to them immediately after landing at Palos. When it arrived he could read in the inscription what a gracious re-ception awaited him. It ran thus: "To Don Christopher Columbus, our Admiral on the Seas, and Viceroy and Gover-nor of the islands discovered in the Indies." The letter was full of most flattering congratulations, and invited him to appear at the court, which was then residing at Barcelona, the second great harbour of Spain.

He began the journey immediately, and arrived before Barcelona in the middle of April. His entrance into the city became a great triumphal procession, exceeding the boldest flights of his fancy. A glittering troop of horsemen met him before the town and preceded him as he entered; then fol-lowed six Indians (the rest Columbus had left behind in Seville sick); then came noble pages carrying parrots, stuffed animals, and other curiosities, with open chests full of gold ornaments; and lastly, Columbus on horseback in splendid attire, attended by the chief men of the two kingdoms. With

the festive pealing of the bells and the deafening shouts of
the populace who crowded the streets, the procession reached
the market-place, where, on a balcony erected for the occasion,
the King and Queen awaited the Admiral. On his appearance
King Ferdinand rose, and when Columbus knelt and kissed
the hands of the royal pair the King raised him and invited
him to be seated—the greatest honour a Spanish monarch
can show a subject.

Columbus had frequently in unconstrained intercourse with
the Prince to relate his adventures, and he was often seen
riding by the side of the King. A significant coat-of-arms
was bestowed upon him. In the two upper fields were the
castle of Castile and the lion of Leon, while below to the
right was a sea full of islands, and to the left five anchors.
The globe and cross on the helmet of the coat-of-arms, and
the inscription, "Columbus found a new world for Castile and
Leon," were apparently added later. And this brilliant
reception by the Princes corresponded to the homage which
the proud nobility and all classes of the people offered him.
We may rejoice fervently that the Admiral was thus recom-
pensed for his many years of disappointment and suffering,
and we cannot grudge him the proud pleasure of seeing himself,
though of lowly birth, raised to the highest honours. Still we
cannot help anticipating a reaction after such extraordinary
favour, and feel that at the latest it must ensue as soon as it
was found out that the newly-discovered land was not India,
the way to which might yet be found by the Portuguese. For
all this immoderate rejoicing arose from the delusion that, if it
was not actually India that had been discovered, India could
at any rate be very easily reached from the lands found by
Columbus, and there was a most discreditable pleasure in the
minds of the Spaniards at the thought of the disappointment
of the hated Portuguese.

The enthusiastic descriptions of Columbus of the riches of

ENTRY OF COLUMBUS INTO BARCELONA.

the lands he had discovered aroused the whole people ; the sanguine man reckoned with the greatest confidence how many millions of gold the colonists he had left behind would have collected before his return, and drew such exaggerated and enticing pictures of the ease with which treasures might be collected that a perfect gold fever took possession of the whole nation, and it was not without justice that a charge of deception was subsequently brought against him.

The Government contemplated colonising in a great measure the discovered lands, and consented to all the projects formed by the Admiral with that view, while they appointed Juan Rodriquez de Fonseca, afterwards Bishop of Badajoz, to superintend the necessary supplies and to conclude the contracts.

As early as the 8th of May Columbus left Barcelona and betook himself to Andalusia, where all the preparations were carried forward with energy. Seventeen ships, including three large merchant-ships, were made ready, on which embarked 15,000 men, among whom were many farm labourers and soldiers. Among the adherents of Columbus were now many important personages, especially the great pilot Juan de la Cosa, and the heroic nobleman Alonso de Ojeda. A number of priests were to open the Christian mission among the Indians. All kinds of European animals, and among them horses, were shipped off for the new colony, and every one prophesied a rapid prosperity. These important preparations delayed the departure of the fleet, and it was not until September 25th, 1493, that it sailed from Cadiz, steering first for the Canary Islands, where the cargo of domestic animals was to be completed. On the 13th of October they left the island of Ferro, and crossed the ocean without any adventures worthy of mention.

The Admiral this time steered rather more to the south, in the hope of reaching more directly India itself. Thus he enjoyed the full benefit of the trade wind which brought him in sight of land after a prosperous voyage of twenty-one days. It was the Lesser Antilles, which stretch northward in a half circle from the mouth of Orinoco to the Greater Antilles. The first land, which was seen on Sunday the 3rd of November, was called Dominica. Without touching it, the ship turned towards the north, and the same day a flat island was dis-covered, which was named after the Admiral's ship, Maria Galante. The next day there appeared a larger island with lofty mountains, which received the name of Guadaloupe, after a famous shrine in Spain. Columbus landed there. The inhabitants, Caribs, fled to the woods, but some women and children, who appeared to be prisoners taken by the Caribs in one of their raids, came to implore protection from the Spaniards. The latter examined the forsaken huts, and from their appearance concluded that the inhabitants belonged to a higher grade of civilisation than those of Hispaniola. But to their horror they found in most of the huts human flesh being prepared for eating.

After a delay of some days, caused by some of their crew being lost in the woods, they left the island. Proceeding on their way they met a canoe, with eight men and women, and sent their boats out to seize it; but the Caribs being over-taken offered a desperate resistance and wounded two Spaniards with their poisoned arrows. Even when their boat was sunk they continued to fight, swimming, and took refuge on a rock almost covered by the water, and from which, how-ever, they were dragged one by one and brought on board bound. Even then they were violent and resembled " Lybian lions caught in nets." They were well formed and had long thick hair and no beard. They cut off their front hair and painted circles round their eyes, which increased the wildness of their appearance.

The voyage was continued in a north-westerly direction

through a number of little islands, to which Columbus gave the name of St. Ursula and the Eleven Thousand Virgins. Then they came to a large island, now called Porto Rico. Though the coasts appeared attractive, Columbus could not be induced to make a stay there, as he was impelled forward by a lively anxiety for those left behind in Natividad. Porto Rico being passed, he soon reached the north coast of Hayti, along which he continued his journey with such haste that on the 27th of November the squadron came to anchor off the spot where eleven months before he had built the little fort. But his salute was not responded to. No boat put off from the shore, and a mysterious silence reigned. Then the presentiment of a great misfortune came over Columbus, a presentiment that he found only too true when he landed. The fort lay in ashes, and every here and there were the remains of the unhappy garrison. By degrees the mystery which enveloped their fate was cleared up, chiefly by the account of Guacanagari, who, detained by illness, could not come to visit the Admiral, but was visited by him. Shortly after the departure of Columbus, the Spaniards had given themselves up to all sorts of evil courses, had become disunited, and the greater part of them had been killed during a plundering expedition into the land of Maguana by the cacique of that country, the warlike Caonabo. This chief had then invaded the land of Marien, burnt the fort, destroying the little garrison, whose commander Arana, taking refuge in a boat, had been drowned with all his companions. Guacanagari himself, who related this unhappy story, represented himself as having been wounded in battle with Caonabo, and many of his subjects had fresh wounds, evidently made by Indian weapons. But the Spaniards did not trust the cacique, and accounted him guilty of their countrymen's death. Although this opinion was confirmed by the flight of their Indian prisoners, yet the Admiral could not

persuade himself to bring to account this his first ally.
But the ships soon left this gloomy spot, seeking more to the
east a favourable place for the foundation of a new town. It
rose rapidly, and under the name of Isabella became the
first settlement of the Spaniards in the New World. But
very soon the insidious nature of the climate showed itself,
many of the colonists, including Columbus himself, being
struck down with sickness. As soon as he was tolerably
restored, he sent twelve of the ships home, to request new
supplies of men, animals, and provisions. As he felt that
these demands would excite surprise in Spain, where,
from his former prophecies, they would look rather for the
arrival of great riches, he renewed his glowing descriptions
of the abundance of gold in the island, especially in the interior, where Ojeda had found earth containing gold. He
suggested also that the expenses of the repeated expeditions
might be covered by capturing and selling the Indians for
slaves. "Your Highness," he writes, "should send out every
year caravels with cattle, provisions, and implements for agriculture at a moderate price. The expense might be repaid
by sending back slaves, for which purpose the Caribs, once
tamed, would answer better than the other races, on account
of their strength, agility, and intelligence. With the help of
the boats which I am building here, they may be captured in
great numbers."

After sending off the fleet, Columbus, on March 12th,
started for the interior, taking with him 400 men and a little
troop of horsemen. He penetrated without difficulty to the
mountainous district of Cibao, meeting with a most friendly
reception from the Indians, who were greatly astonished at
the Spaniards' horses. The unmistakable abundance of gold
suggested to the Admiral the idea of securing the possession
of the country by building a fort. The work was begun immediately, and was completed in a few days. It stood on a

height, protected by a river, and received the name of Saint Thomas. It was garrisoned with fifty-two men, under the command of the knight Pedro Margarite. Returning at the end of the month to Isabella, Columbus undertook several measures for the purpose of making the new colony inhabitable. He cut down the forests, cleared the land, began to plant, and to build mills. He strained to the utmost the powers of all in this work, making no exceptions in favour of the nobles, and sparing only the sick, whose number the heat increased every day. Thus in a land where they had expected to gather riches without any trouble, the emigrants saw themselves compelled to hard labour, for worse pay than they would have received in their own country. A dissatisfied rebellious spirit soon showed itself among them, to which, in isolated cases, Columbus opposed a relentless severity. Yet he thought his position sufficiently secure to allow him to resume his voyages of discovery. He appointed a council to manage the government during his absence, in which was the rancorous Benedictine monk Buil, and over which he nominated his youngest brother, the quiet kind-hearted Diego Columbus, president. Then, on April 24th, 1494, he left the harbour of Isabella with three ships and turned towards the west.

He soon reached the east point of Cuba, which he believed to be the most easterly point of the mainland. This time he sailed along the south coast of the island. He found it everywhere well peopled, but when he inquired for the land of gold the natives so invariably pointed to the south that he resolved to go in that direction. After two days he came to land, the island of Jamaica. The inhabitants, who resembled those of Cuba and Hispaniola in appearance and manners, though more warlike in their disposition, swarmed round the ship in their canoes, which were ninety feet long, challenging the Spaniards to an encounter. It was not until they had had a bloody lesson that they could he induced to carry on more peaceful intercourse. Even then Columbus could obtain no more certain knowledge about the wealth of the land, but was again directed to the south. He followed the north coast until he reached the western point of the land, which proved it to be an island, and then he returned to what he imagined to be the mainland, Cuba. But the navigation along the south coast was extremely difficult. Legions of little islands continually compelled the ship to keep close to the shore, and it was frequently endangered by sandbanks and reefs. Not the least sign appeared of any approach to the civilised states of Asia, though a deceitful resemblance of names now and again raised false hopes.

On the 12th of June the patience of the Admiral was exhausted. In order to assure himself against future reproaches, he caused the assembled crews to take an oath, administered by the royal notary, that in Cuba they had discovered the mainland, and not a mere island. If they should ever change this opinion the officers were to be punished by the loss of their tongues and a fine, and the common sailors by flogging. By this singular document Columbus sought to quiet the accusations of his conscience, which told him how wrong it was to return yet to Hispaniola. The voyage had been continued along the south coast of Cuba as far as the Isla de Pinos. If Columbus had only persevered for three days longer, he would have reached the west point of Cuba and would have proved it to be an island. Then news certainly would have reached him of Yucatan and Mexico, and he would probably have been the first to reach the populous highly-civilised states of that coast. The peculiarity of the culture possessed by their natives would have removed the delusion that he had reached the coast of Asia. From mere longing for Hispaniola Columbus forfeited the accomplishment of his great task.

On the return voyage they coasted along the hitherto unvisited south shore of Hispaniola, and were intending to pass over to Porto Rico when the Admiral, who from fear of an accident had not closed his eyes for thirty-two nights, suddenly fell ill. He lay in a deep lethargy without sight or hearing, and the doctor doubted whether he would ever recover. The ship was therefore turned round as quickly as possible, and they steered for Isabella, where they arrived September 29th, 1494. That the sickness, which lasted five months, at length abated Columbus owed to the faithful care of his brothers, Diego and Bartholomew. The latter, himself an experienced seaman, had been negotiating for Columbus at the English court until the news reached him that the discovery of India had fallen to the share of the Castilian crown. Then he hastened to Spain, was well received by the court, raised to the rank of a noble, and at last sent to the New World, having under his command three ships. He arrived during the Admiral's absence in Cuba and Jamaica, but on the return of the latter he found many opportunities of assisting him, and indeed, on account of his manly bearing and keen intelligence, soon became indispensable to him.

Already there appeared the first traces of those troubles which soon rendered the very existence of the colony doubtful. Many Spaniards seized the first opportunity to turn their backs upon the New World. Thus Marguerite and Buil had returned to Spain, where, by their exaggerated accounts of their sufferings and by their complaints of Columbus's rule, they aroused general attention. Others roamed through the island, ill-treating the Indians, and thus exciting the extreme hostility of the harmless people towards their heartless persecutors. Already their cruelty had been revenged by the murder of a few scattered individuals, and the caciques formed a secret alliance against the Spaniards. The soul of this alliance was Caonabo. Already he had besieged the bold Ojeda for thirty days in Saint Thomas, and at last had only been compelled to withdraw from want of supplies. In him the Indians hoped they had found the liberator of their island. Terrible therefore was the fear on the one side, and great the joy on the other, when the dreaded cacique, by a deed of almost incredible heroism on the part of Ojeda, was brought prisoner to Isabella. The bold Spaniard, by means of a cunning trick, induced Caonabo to allow some bright jingling chains to be put on him. He then seized him, placed him on a horse, and by the threat of stabbing him if he made the slightest resistance, succeeded in carrying him off to a Spanish dungeon.

Columbus treated his prisoner with respect on account of his rank and heroism ; he declined to sit in judgment upon him himself, and subsequently took him with him to Spain ; but he died on the voyage of a broken heart. Warned by Guanacanagari, the Spaniards took measures for defence, and Columbus marched out as soon as he was recovered, in the spring of 1495, with 200 men and twenty horsemen to subdue the island. The most formidable allies of the Spaniards were the bloodhounds, who at a word from their masters threw themselves on the naked Indians and tore them to pieces. The poor creatures were perfectly defenceless against these four-footed assistants of the two-legged devils, as they called the Spaniards.

Soon every spark of opposition was extinguished in blood, and even the caciques themselves submitted. Guanonex, one of the most powerful, gave his sister to the interpreter, Diego, to wife, and was obliged, like the rest, to suffer the settlement of the Spaniards in his territory, and to allow the building of forts. All the centre of the island was subdued, and Columbus was able to think of fulfilling, at the expense of the vanquished race, the expectation of great riches that he had excited in Spain. Five hundred prisoners were shipped off in order to be sold in Seville as slaves, though, through the interference of the gentle-hearted Isabella, they were subsequently set free and returned to their native land. The fate also of those who went unpunished was deplorable. The Admiral laid upon every grown person a yearly tax of as much gold dust as was contained in four little bells, in weight from three to four ducats, or 100 pounds of cotton. This was the death-warrant of the poor Indians; they could not work. Their life had hitherto been a peaceful enjoyment of the gifts, which their glorious land yielded to them either of itself or with slight trouble. Hard work, from which they reaped no benefit themselves, took away all enjoyment from their existence. They fled in numbers to the mountains, and there died of hunger. Of those who remained behind, numbers committed suicide, casting away a life which the ill-usage and licentiousness of the Spaniards rendered valueless. Columbus, however, saw with great satisfaction a vast treasure of gold and cotton accumulating.

Then a heavy blow fell upon him, the forerunner of more evil times which were yet to come. In October, 1495, Juan Aguado suddenly appeared from Spain with a royal mandate which, with laconic brevity, directed all the Spaniards then in Hispaniola to refer to him. The monarchs had been moved to send out this embassy by anxiety for Columbus, having heard nothing of him for a long time. Besides, the evil reports spread by Buil and Margarite had aroused in them concern for the distant colony which had been founded at such cost. From Aguado, whom Columbus had himself recommended to them, they hoped to obtain certain information and, at the same time, they proposed to cut down the exorbitant expense caused by the wages and support of so many hundred colonists, by reducing the number to five hundred. Columbus, rendered uneasy by this step, resolved to proceed himself to Spain that he might set himself right in the King's opinion. He appointed his brother Bartholomew his substitute or Adelantado, and arranged that in case of his death this power should go to his younger brother Diego. By these appointments, although indeed ratified by Ferdinand and Isabella, he yet brought upon himself the displeasure of the Princes, for they were calculated to confirm the reports spread by his enemies that he wished, by the neglect of the general Spanish interest, to make the island of Hispaniola a private possession of his own family.

On the 10th of March, 1496, he left the island with 220 men, embarking on two new ships. He stayed for some time among the Lesser Antilles, and arrived in the harbour of Cadiz on the 11th of June, after a voyage of fifty days, which, except for a failure of provisions, was a very prosperous one. He met the King and Queen at Burgos, and succeeded once more in convincing them of the brilliant future which lay before the West India Islands by presenting them with the gold which he had collected in the last few years, and by giving an exaggerated estimate of the revenue which might be expected in the future. Chanca, the doctor and notary who accompanied Columbus on this journey, says in his report: "If the Admiral's people had not been fonder of sleep and idleness than work they would have brought with them gold, amber, and Brazil wood in abundance. But most of them refused to obey his commands, as if they were unjust."

Columbus obtained a number of favourable decrees, by one of which all private persons were forbidden to make any voyages of discovery to the West Indies; for so deluded was the great man that he dreamed of restraining the great impulse of the age by a family monopoly. The most difficult question was that of money. The ceaseless demands which Columbus made in behalf of the colony on the royal purse were constantly met by evasions and refusal on the part of Fonseca, the Minister for Indian Affairs, and his conduct was justified by the complete exhaustion of the treasury. In order to lessen the serious expense of the pay of the colonists, Columbus made the unhappy proposition that Hispaniola should be used as a place of banishment for condemned criminals, whom he hoped to turn into docile and grateful colonists. Unfortunately this proposition was adopted, and Columbus subsequently had to suffer much from the evil elements which were thus let loose among a population already rebellious and indolent.

Still, however, the equipment of the new squadron, which Columbus was to conduct to the New World, was delayed. It was not until January, 1498, that he could despatch two ships to Hispaniola; and the remaining six ships, which the Seville house of Gianotto Berardi from Florence was commissioned to equip, were not ready to sail until May. How impatiently he bore these delays we may see, not only from his conduct to a subordinate of Fonseca's, but also from a passage in the next letter which he despatched to Ferdinand and Isabella from the New World. "I was," he writes, "still suffering from the hardships of my earlier journeys, and I had hoped to have found repose in Spain after my return from the Indies; but, on the contrary, I found only trouble and vexation."

From the Canary Islands he sent on the 21st of June, half the squadron to Hispaniola, in order to announce his arrival, and to satisfy the most urgent needs of the colony. He himself with three ships went to the Cape Verde Islands, and from thence struck out in a south-westerly direction, in order if possible to reach India at some point near the equator. In this design he was strengthened by Jacob Ferrer from Barcelona, the Queen's jeweller, who assured him that the proper home of gold and jewels was only to be found in the tropics. But after a journey of many weeks, the calms and the terrible heat, which threatened to burst the seams of the ship and to

melt the tar, made him give up his design and sail more decidedly to the north and north-west.

In this way, on the 31st of July, Trinidad was discovered,
which lies in 10 degrees north latitude, off the coast of South
America ; and the next day, the 1st of August, South America
itself came in sight, the first part of the mainland which Columbus touched. It was the inhospitable delta of the Orinoco ;
and the desolate appearance of the land, which he took for an
island, prevented him from landing and exploring it, and determined him to sail through the narrow straits which he saw
before him to the west.

In the night the ships were almost swamped by a great
tide-wave which poured through the strait ; and next morning
the passage was effected only after a hard conflict with
the stream. The ships then found themselves in a basin that
was almost enclosed, and which the people on the shore called
Paria. Into it such mighty streams flowed that for some
distance it had no salt taste.

This made Columbus doubtful about his idea of the insular
form of the land. "If it should be a continent," he says in
his diary, "the learned world will be very much astonished
about it." But with this suspicion of the truth he soon
mingles a highly fanciful mistake. He thinks that at this
place he has discovered a wart-like swelling of the earth, so
that the shape of the world is less like that of a ball than of a
pear ; and in this way he explains the force and rapidity of
the streams. He also imagines that the land from which
they come is no other than Paradise, situated in the south-east
of Asia, and by its height saved at the time of the flood.

But instead of either confirming or disproving these ideas
by a longer examination, the Admiral turned his back
upon this land of wonders, and forcing a passage through
the dangerous Dragon's Mouth, hastened by the Island Mar-
guerita to Hispaniola, whither most important interests sum-

moned him. If he found everything in a prosperous condition there, he resolved to send his brother Bartholomew to make a further examination of the new land. Thus he forgot that his object had been to discover China and India, and allured by enjoyment and possession, he abandoned any further glory as a discoverer.

On the 31st of August he entered St. Domingo, the new Spanish town which, at the command of the Admiral, his brother Bartholomew had built in his absence on the south coast of Hispaniola, and from which subsequently the whole island took its name.

Shortly before Columbus had touched the mainland of America, it had been discovered much farther north by a bold adventurer. Sebastian Cabot, the son of a Venetian family who had settled in Bristol, had with his father Giovanni sailed, in 1497, on a voyage of discovery under the royal flag of England, and on the 24th of June, 1497, 402 days before Columbus, had in north latitude 56 found an inhospitable coast, the peninsula of Labrador. On a second voyage, 1498, he succeeded in rediscovering Newfoundland, whose valuable cod-fishery has been from that time to this a source of wealth to both England and France.

He also both in his second and third voyages touched on the coast of North America, and explored it for some distance in a southerly direction ; but by degrees this was almost forgotten, since all eyes were directed to the gold lands which had been discovered by the Spaniards and Portuguese. Yet we can judge of the extent of Cabot's voyages, by the fact that in 1500 the Spaniards found traces of the presence of English ships in the Bahama Islands.

The indefatigable man for a time entered the Spanish service, but quitted it again ; and in 1517 started from Bristol to find the North-west Passage, the conclusion in the meantime having been generally arrived at that the lands hitherto discovered formed part of a continent of their own. It is true that he did not attain his object, being compelled to return by a mutiny among his men; but according to his diaries and maps, he penetrated far into that labyrinthine archipelago of islands lying north of Hudson's Bay, which has been more thoroughly explored only in the present century.

Contemporaneously with Cabot, the Portuguese family Cortereal, in which the governorship of Terceira, one of the Azores, was hereditary, undertook a succession of expeditions to the north-west. In 1500 they discovered the coast of Greenland, and in 1501 the woody shores of a land more to the south, which, from the bodily strength of its inhabitants, whom they thought to make slaves of, they called Labrador, or "the labourers' land." But when in subsequent years a number of ships were lost, and in them the most active members of the family, King Emanuel forbade the dangerous voyages to be continued.

Both Sebastian Cabot and Gaspar Cortereal have been cited by the English and Portuguese to prove that to them and not to the Spaniards belongs the glory of the discovery of America. But Cabot alone did in reality land on the New World before Columbus. And even this discovery, which occurred almost five years after the landing of the great Genoese on Guanahani, had scarcely any effect on the gradual conquest and settlement of the New World. Indeed, the English let nearly seventy years pass away before they made another attempt to visit the lands discovered by Cabot, whose voyages by that time they had almost forgotten. They are therefore not in a position to contest the glory of Columbus, the discoverer of the New World.

When Columbus ran into the harbour of St. Domingo, at the end of August, 1498, he found awaiting him news that were far from cheering with regard to the state of the colony.

The energetic Adelantado had successfully put down a

rising of the natives under the leadership of the cacique Guarionex, and also after a ceaseless pursuit in the mountains for three months had captured the ringleader. But a much more serious danger threatened the colony. A conspiracy among the Spaniards themselves, some of whom had been punished for cruelty to the natives, was formed against Bartholomew, and at its head was the Chief Justice Roldan, a man whom the Admiral had advanced. The conspirators did not indeed succeed in getting possession of the fort, but their ungovernable behaviour caused the greatest anxiety. Some seventy men strong, but with a camp following of 100 Indian women and burden-bearers, they withdrew to the west coast of Hispaniola, which as yet had been little touched by the Spaniards, and where was the kingdom of Xaragua, governed by a family of caciques favourable to the foreigners. Here they established themselves, and behaved like lords of the land, subjecting the natives to all kinds of ill-treatment.

When those three ships which Columbus had sent out from the Canary Islands, by an unlucky accident landed in Xaragua, it was easy for Roldan from among the convicts whom they carried to persuade a considerable number to join the rebels. This he did by drawing a most enticing picture of a life of complete idleness full of unbounded pleasure. Grown confident by this accession to their numbers, on October 17th the rebels solemnly renounced their allegiance to the Admiral, and he found himself powerless against them. Even by those who remained faithful he was little loved, for in his efforts to secure as large a share as possible for the Crown and for himself, he had often run counter to the interests of others, and brought upon himself the charge of being hardhearted and avaricious. He was also most anxious to prevent anything from occurring which might shake still more the confidence of the monarchs in his powers of administration. He therefore entered into negotiation with the

rebels, but a year elapsed before it was brought to a successful conclusion.

By the treaty of September 28, 1499, Roldan was restored to
his office of Chief Justice, his friends were granted assigna-
tions of service from the natives, the payment of their wages
during the whole time of their rebellion, and the right to ex-
tort the fulfilment of these conditions by force of arms.
Though the Admiral showed himself so conciliatory, it was
with the intention, as he informs the monarchs, of breaking
his promises on the first opportunity, an intention which he
tried to justify to his conscience by all kinds of sophistry.
In fact, he took advantage of a renewal of the disturbances to
arrest and execute some of the insurgents, leaving others to
languish in prison.

At last his dreams seemed about to be fulfilled. The
labour of the Indians, who tilled the fields for the Spaniards,
brought in sufficient for the supply of the colony; and the
the mines of Cibao, let out by the Admiral to certain persons,
paid the wages of the colonists, and produced also considerable sums for the Crown and the Admiral. Columbus began
to look forward with hope to the future, but he awoke from
his dreams to a dismal reality.

The rebels had several times found means to send letters to
the monarchs of Spain, in which they made most vehement
accusations against Columbus, representing themselves as
victims of the selfish family policy of the Admiral. These
reports, added to the curses of the hundreds who returned,
disappointed, sick, beggared, from the countries which had
been represented to them as golden lands and paradise, raised
to the highest pitch the mistrust which Columbus's government of the new colony had excited many years before.
Fonseca and the rest of the zealous ministers were irritated
at his arbitrariness and constant demands for money. Ferdinand's suspicious character was alarmed at the great power

which was united in one hand in a country so remote, and
he feared his royal authority would suffer ; and Isabella, who
had till now been the Admiral's protector, was offended by the
actual illtreatment of royal officers, and by the sale of captured
Indians constantly repeated in spite of prohibition. And
lastly the glory which had shone till now round the great
discoverer was suddenly dimmed by the return of Vasco da
Gama from his voyage, bringing proofs that the boasted
discoveries of the Spaniards were not, as they had proclaimed
them to be, the Indies. The latter were forced to confess
their error and with inward bitterness see the relations reversed, and the hated Portuguese, who till now had looked at
Spain with envy, in possession of all the endless treasures of
the East.

Compared to one cargo of Vasco da Gama, all that had
poured into Spain from the New World, since the discovery
of Guanahani, was unimportant and worthless. This change
of feeling naturally altered the public opinion of Columbus :
if he were not a deceiver, he was himself deluded, a fanatic.
Such was the disposition of mind in which the Princes received
the letters of Columbus, describing his journey and arrival in
Hispaniola.. They heard with consternation of the disorder
reigning in the colony, and were particularly concerned at
the determination expressed by Columbus, to extirpate, if
necessary, the rebels to the last man. They feared the
Admiral would be carried away by his passions into hasty and
unjust actions, and they more and more lent an ear to the
accusations of his enemies.

After much consideration it was determined to remove
Columbus for a time from his office, and to appoint a successor, to bring the colony into order. The new Governor
was to be allowed to make fresh appointments to all the
offices and to remove any persons at his pleasure. This was
indeed to be only a temporary measure, and the rights of the

Admiral were to remain untouched. Unfortunately the choice of the monarchs for an office, which certainly ought to have been filled only by a man of the greatest caution and tact, fell upon the hot-headed Francis de Bobadilla.

In June, 1500, the new Governor left Spain, and arrived in St. Domingo on the 23rd of August. He was able to obtain possession of the government without any resistance, for he at once drew all to his side by the promise of the pay which was in arrears. In the most undignified manner he chose to upset everything which Columbus had established. He heaped favours upon Roldan and his adherents, remitted the tenth to the settlers, with a free permission to dig for gold, promising every one an unrestrained golden life. "Scrape together what you can, who knows how long it may last," he is reported to have said to somebody, and he himself set them the example. With the greatest effrontery he took possession of the Admiral's house, and all he found in it. Columbus writes with regard to this in his letter to Ferdinand and Isabella : "The Commendador (Bobadilla) on his arrival seized my house and, to be brief, appropriated its contents. Perhaps, indeed, he wanted it, but no corsair could have treated a merchant worse."

Columbus's brother, and afterwards himself, coming peaceably to St. Domingo, were arrested and thrown into chains. An examination carried on secretly naturally called forth a number of charges against the fallen man, and produced a long accusation, which, with the three prisoners, was sent to Europe. When Columbus was committed a prisoner to Alonso de Valleja, who was to take him to Spain, he thought at first that he was going to be taken to execution, and was only pacified on the repeated assurance of Valleja that such was not the case. As soon as the anchor was weighed Valleja approached the Admiral and offered to relieve him from his chains, but the latter waved him back, saying that the chains

COLUMBUS SENT IN CHAINS TO SPAIN.

with which their majesties had loaded him should only be removed at their command, and that he should then preserve them to remind him of the reward which the Spanish crown had granted him for his faithful service.

At the end of November, 1500, the ships arrived at Cadiz, and quick as lightning spread the news that the Admiral, whom seven years before every one had gone out to meet in triumph, was now brought home in chains at the command of the Princes. The public opinion of Spain was unanimous in condemning the unworthy manner in which they had treated the great benefactor of the nation. Even Ferdinand and Isabella were indignant when they heard of Bobadilla's conduct. They sent immediately a command to Cadiz to set the Admiral at liberty, and treat him with due honour. They sent to himself a present of 2000 ducats and an invitation to come to their court at Granada. There Columbus appeared on the 17th of December, and cast himself with bitter tears before their throne. Greatly moved, the King and Queen raised him up. The generous Isabella could not restrain her tears at the thought of the injustice that had been done in her name to such a faithful subject. The least satisfaction that could be granted to a man so injured was the deposition of Bobadilla, who had far exceeded his commission, and it was immediately determined upon. But when the first impulse had spent itself there was considerable hesitation as to the advisability of restoring Columbus to his command. Would not the impetuous man abuse his power against all who had contributed to his fall, and was there not important testimony to prove that in the government of Hispaniola he had not succeeded in winning the love and trust of the settlers? It appeared better to entrust to an impartial man the adjustment of the vexed questions and the tranquillising of irritated feeling. Such a man the Princes thought they had found in Don Nicolas de Ovando, an unselfish and strictly just man, who, on the 3rd of September, 1501, was appointed governor of Hispaniola. The trustworthy lawyer Maldonado was sent out with him to examine into the conduct of Bobadilla and Roldan.

The invitation to accompany the new governor to the transatlantic settlement, which was now to be reduced to order, met with an extraordinary response from the Spanish people. On the thirty-two ships 2500 persons left Spain, with Ovando, on the 13th of February, 1502. It was with pain that Columbus saw himself thus pushed aside, and even though the monarchs treated him with kindness and assured him that his claims to the tenth part of the produce of the colony should remain undisputed, yet, from the scant intercourse with Hispaniola, it was inevitable that Columbus should sometimes be in want, especially as he had returned to Spain without any money.

This inactive waiting was hard to bear, since it might be years before he were re-installed, and he saw, with bitter vexation, how every year numbers of bold men set out to discover lands which he had reserved for himself. For as early as the year 1499 the crown had taken off the absurd prohibition of all private undertakings which the selfishness of Columbus had procured, and since that time large extents of coast had been discovered on the other side of the Atlantic Ocean. The bold Alonso de Ojeda had, in 1499, discovered the coast of South America as far as the river Amazon, and after that a great part of the north coast. Also, the experienced seaman, Per Alonso Nino, and Vincente Yanez Pinzon, who in 1492 had commanded the *Nina*, had set out on discoveries. While the former brought back a great treasure of gold and pearls from the island Margarita, Pinzon, who sailed S.S.W. from the Canary Islands, was the discoverer of the Brazils, since, on the 26th January, 1500, almost three months before the landing of Cabral, he discovered Cape St.

Augustine, and from that point followed the coast towards the north as far as the Caribean Sea. Lastly, Rodrigo de Bastidas who, accompanied by the great seaman Juan de la Cosa, had sailed from Seville in 1500, completed the investigation of the north coast of South America by steering steadily westward from Venezuela until he reached Darien. He also had brought home great treasures with him.

When now Ojeda prepared for a second voyage, Columbus was afraid that his glory as a discoverer would be still more diminished, and offered himself to the crown for a new expedition into unknown regions. Thus we see the great man by a number of painful circumstances restored to his true vocation, which unfortunately he had forsaken. The monarchs eagerly accepted the proposal of the Admiral. It was arranged that the object of this voyage should be to reach China and India ; for between Cuba, which was still considered part of the Asiatic mainland, and the coast of South America it was the universal idea that there must be, towards the south-west, a passage to India. After the departure of the great fleet which had sailed with Ovando to Hispaniola, it was not easy to provide Columbus with a sufficient squadron, and therefore he was obliged to content himself with four ships and 150 sailors. Besides his brother Bartholomew, he was accompanied by his younger son, Ferdinand, who was born at Cordova on September 27th, 1488, of Donna Beatrice Enriquez d'Arana, and whose coolness in danger during this voyage is warmly praised by his father.

On the 9th of May, 1502, Columbus left Cadiz, touched at the Canary Islands on the 26th of May, and after a voyage of unparalleled prosperity reached Matinono, now called Martinique, which had not been visited by him previously. Instead of proceeding immediately to discover the west passage, he could not resist the temptation of showing himself again free and in authority to his beloved Hispaniola, which had seen him depart in chains, and thus infringed a distinct command of Ferdinand and Isabella. For the monarchs, in their well-founded fears that a visit of Columbus would renew the irritation and disturb Ovando in his work of reconciliation, had exacted a promise from the Admiral not to touch Hispaniola except on his way back from China. A desire to exchange an unseaworthy ship for a better sailer formed his excuse for breaking this promise. But Ovando, who followed scrupulously the orders he himself had received, refused him permission to enter the harbour of St. Domingo, and Columbus experienced the bitter pain of being treated as an enemy and repulsed from a land that he had presented to Spain. The great fleet was lying ready for its return to Europe, but leaving the safe harbour in spite of the warnings of Columbus, it encountered a violent storm and was almost entirely destroyed. In this fearful catastrophe Guarionex, Bobadilla, Roldan, and other enemies of Columbus whom Ovando was sending to Spain for trial, met their deaths. It was not only to the Admiral that this appeared an act of divine retribution upon those who had offended against him.

On the 14th of July the little squadron, which had taken refuge from the violence of the storm in the shelter of a bay, left the island of Hispaniola and steered for the west. Jamaica was only touched at, and on the 30th of July the ships anchored before Guanaja, a coral island in what is now called the Gulf of Honduras, close to the coast of the mainland. While the Spaniards were trying to make themselves understood by the inhabitants, there approached them from the open sea a boat, the workmanship of which struck Columbus with astonishment. It was, indeed, only the trunk of a single tree hollowed out, but in length it equalled a galley, and was eight feet wide. It had an awning, made of reeds and leaves, for the commander and his wives and children. This strange vessel came alongside of the Spanish fleet without fear, and its crew immediately climbed on board.

At the first glance Columbus, now a practised observer, perceived that he had to do with people of a higher cultivation than those he had hitherto met. The men wore a garment round their waists, and the women were carefully concealed in their wide mantles. They represented themselves as merchants coming from a land called Maya, to exchange their wares with less civilised people. Among these wares Columbus mentions cotton-cloth, skilfully woven carpets, and copper axes, knives, pans, vessels of stone, wood, and clay, and, lastly, swords made of hard wood, in the blade of which were placed great pieces of obsidian. They also brought a great quantity of brown seeds, which they valued very highly, and which were unknown to the Spaniards. They were the seeds of the cacao-tree, which were used as money at that time in Mexico and Yucatan.

Although these remarkable Indians, who, at any rate, must have come from Yucatan, extolled to Columbus the abundance of silver in their country, and spoke of its dense population, yet he would not be persuaded to visit the land of Maya, the name of which he immediately connected with the Chinese province of Manchoo. He was rather strengthened in his original plan by the information that they gave him of gold lands to the south-east. Thus for the third time Columbus put off visiting Yucatan and Mexico, the discovery of which would have brought him new glory, and would have saved him the bitter experience of the last years of his life.

Instead of this, the voyage continued to the south. But the coast soon took a bend towards the south-east; then directly towards the east; and it was difficult to make way along it on account of the opposing winds and the stormy water. At last, on the 12th of September, a cape was reached, and beyond that the coast again took a most decidedly southerly direction. At the sight of this a great burden fell from the soul of the Admiral, who for a moment had begun to doubt the possibility of finding a passage to the south-west, and full of joyful thankfulness to God, he named the cape, which now is generally called Cape Honduras, Gracias a Dios.

Still struggling against opposing winds, the squadron sailed in a southerly direction, to the barren coast of what is now called Mosquito Land, until it reached smiling regions thickly peopled. Columbus did not doubt that he was on the eastern coast of the so-called Golden peninsula—that was the name given by Ptolemy to the Malay peninsula in Further India; and in this delusion he was strengthened, not only by the riches of the country, but also by the information which he received from the Indians, that nine days' journey to the west there was another sea. According to Columbus's idea, this could be nothing else but the Bay of Bengal; and so he repeatedly assured himself that he was only ten days' journey from the Ganges. Thus he was mistaken by not less than 180°—half the circumference of the globe. But so certain was he of the justice of his idea, that he believed the south point of the peninsula to be quite close, and eagerly pursued his course, in spite of the stormy weather. But the coast bent round again to the east, and he could scarcely hide from himself any longer that he had reached the coasts discovered by Ojeda and Bastidas.

Fortune did not allow Columbus to correct his mistake. On the 5th of December he was obliged by the violence of the contrary winds to return; he had arrived at the narrowest part of the Isthmus of Panama. Only a few days more, and he would have reached coasts where he must have found clear traces of the recent visit of Spanish ships—coasts the connection of which with Paria, which he himself had discovered, had been proved. But, just as on his second journey to the south coast of Cuba, he turned round at the decisive moment, and so died in the belief that Hispaniola was Japan, Cuba a peninsula of Asia, the Isthmus of Panama the peninsula of

Malacca, and that between the latter and the north coast of South America, which he supposed to be an enormous island, there must be a passage to the Indian Seas, and that this way would prove shorter and less dangerous than the Portuguese way round the Cape of Good Hope.

The ships continued to suffer from rough weather on their return voyage, and in a few days it increased to such violence that destruction was hourly expected. But after some weeks' cruising about, they came to anchor at the mouth of a river on the coast of Veragua, which they had passed some months before. To the general surprise, it appeared that they were in a land of gold, the riches of which, as far as could be discovered from expeditions that Bartholomew made in February, 1503, appeared to be inexhaustible. They proceeded immediately to erect huts, where fifty men, with the Adelantado at their head, determined to remain as the nucleus of a colony. Fortunately the departure of the ships was delayed by a sandbank which the dry weather formed at the mouth of the river; for just when they had intended to depart, the Indians, embittered by a rash attack which the Adelantado had made against the most powerful Prince of the land—Quibia—made so violent an assault on the young settlement that it was evident it could not be held. With considerable loss—thirteen Spaniards were killed, many wounded, and both the boats lost—the colonists succeeded in getting on board, and thereupon, on the 20th of April, the fleet left the inhospitable coast, abandoning the fourth ship, which was no longer seaworthy.

For the same reason they were obliged to forsake and sink another ship on the open sea. The two remaining vessels could scarcely be kept above water; their keels were eaten away by a kind of shell-fish, and there were such serious leaks that the whole crew was continually employed at the pumps. Fortunately the weather was favourable, and the ships were carried without wind by the currents to the north, until, on the 10th of May, they reached the south coast of Cuba.

Only Columbus knew where he was, and apparently he confirmed the mistake of the pilots, who thought they were at Porto Rico, in order to keep to himself the knowledge of the gold land of Veragua. After only a short stay, steering south, he crossed over to Jamaica, and there he allowed the two ships, which were only miserable wrecks, to run on to the sand. He hoped that help would be sent him from the neighbouring island of Hispaniola, where by some fortunate accident they might soon hear of his distress. He also made the experiment of sending two canoes to Hispaniola, to hire a ship at his own expense. For this daring undertaking, which was sometimes ventured upon by the Indians of Jamaica, he chose his faithful secretary, Diego Mendez, and the Genoese Bartholomew Fiesco. To each he gave six Spaniards and ten native oarsmen.

The brave men reached the coast of Hispaniola after a four days' voyage, but did not succeed in doing much for those left behind in Jamaica. The cold prudence of Ovando judged that in the half-pacified state of the island the appearance of the Admiral would be injudicious; so he deferred giving an answer to the envoys, and it was not until after seven long months had elapsed that the faithful Mendez received permission to hire a ship. It was only the open discontent of the Spanish colonists that impelled Ovando at last to despatch a small vessel to inquire about the condition of the Admiral.

Before the departure of Fiesco and Mendez, Columbus had been ill, and even when he was able now and then to leave his bed he was obliged to remain in one of the wrecks, in which he had fixed his dwelling. There the account of the journey for Ferdinand and Isabella was written, which, dated the 7th of July, he committed to the care of Mendez. The style of this remarkable letter is very melancholy. In contrast to his earlier letters, there is a striking want of order in his relation of facts, and only every now and then he launches forth in the lively descriptions of nature and in the exaggerated calculations which occur so often in his other writings. Humboldt has already pointed out that the peculiarities spring from the deep excitement of a proud soul, hurt by a long course of injustice and deceived in its most cherished hopes. In bitter words he holds up before the monarchs the ingratitude which they had shown him, and breaks out in the most piteous complaints. "Where is the man," writes he, "not even excepting Job, unhappier than I? The very harbours which I discovered at the peril of my life refused me a refuge from the death which threatened me, my young son, my brother, and my friends. The service, pains, and dangers of twenty years have brought me no gain. At this present time I possess not a brick in Spain, and inns alone offer me shelter when I need rest or a simple meal, though, alas! I often have not the money wherewith to pay the bill. For the same reason I have left my son Don Diego in Spain, without the means of subsistence and without a father, hoping that he would find in your highnesses just and grateful Princes, who would repay him with interest that of which your service has robbed him." In another place he plainly attacks his opponents, particularly Fonseca. "Let him who has caused these evils come and heal them if he can. . . . . Favour and honour ought to be granted to him who has exposed himself to the dangers of the undertaking; and it is unjust that he who has opposed it should, together with his heir, reap the profits." This disjointed account of his experiences is interrupted by a stubborn defence of his geographical blunders. "The earth is not so large as people think; six parts of its surface are land, and only one-seventh is sea." Then come enthusiastic descriptions of the discovered treasures. Thus he declares Veragua is the Ophir of the Bible, from which Solomon procured gold for the Temple ; and about the riches of traditional lands, Ciambe and Ceguarra, which ought to lie south-west of Veragua, he breaks out in the most exaggerated style.   More frequently too than was the case in his earlier letters the religious fanaticism of his natural character becomes evident, as in the lofty description which he gives of a vision he had had in January.   A voice from Heaven had reproved him for his faintheartedness, and had revealed to him the wisdom of the Divine ways.   But the deepest vexation breaking out in passionate complaints is the great characteristic of the letter.

Approaching events were not calculated to remove this dejection.   The crew, unoccupied and no longer bound together by active service, became most unruly, and neither the sick Admiral nor the stern Adelantado could force them to obedience.   Under the idea that Columbus intended to hinder their return, and would force them to remain as colonists on the unhealthy coast, some fifty men, under the leadership of two brothers, named Porras, combined together and quitted the ship, intending to try and get back to Spain by themselves.   Failing to do this, they wandered about the island illusing the Indians.   Columbus and those who had remained true to him had to suffer for the excesses of these men ; for the Indians, who hitherto had brought them all the necessaries of life in exchange for the most trifling gifts, now kept aloof, and even showed such a hostile disposition that the disabled crews of the stranded ships were in the greatest danger.   An eclipse of the moon, which Columbus had calculated beforehand, made the Indians friendly again ; for when they saw the face of the moon darkened in displeasure at their inhospitality, as Columbus had told them it would be, they sought to avert the anger of the god by rich offerings to the starving strangers.

As the first token of an approaching rescue appeared that

little ship which Ovando had sent out to procure news, under
the command of Diego de Escobar, a rival of Columbus. To
be sure, he only brought letters and a small quantity of provisions, refused to land, and soon departed, without taking any
of the shipwrecked party with him ; but they felt they were
not altogether forgotten, and learned that Mendez was negotiating for the hire of a ship. But before it made its appearance there was a regular fight between the two parties of
Spaniards. With fifty men the dauntless Adelantado went
out against the rebels, who had established themselves in the
neighbourhood of the ship, and forced them to submit, after a
bloody battle.

At last the longed-for ship appeared, and Columbus quitted
Jamaica on the 28th of June, 1504, having endured great
sufferings on the island for more than a year. He was
honourably received in St. Domingo ; but the suspicious
Ovando watched with such anxiety every step of the Admiral
that the latter determined to return as soon as possible to
Spain. On the 12th of September, 1504, he left his beloved
Hispaniola, never to see it again, and, after a stormy passage,
landed at Cadiz in the beginning of November.

Thus ended Columbus's last voyage, in which he had discovered a great part of the coast of Central America, and had
found a new land of gold. But little attention was bestowed
upon these results, because he again had not found the western
passage to China and India. The death of his patroness
Isabella, which took place on the 26th of November, shortly
after Columbus landed, was a severe blow to him. From the
cold Ferdinand, who always behaved in a suspicious and
reserved manner to Columbus, he could not expect a reinstal-
lation. He was, indeed, well received at Court, and in a
manner suited to his rank, but the utmost to which the
King would condescend was to propose that the Vice-royalty
of the West Indies should be exchanged for a Castilian

earldom.   But upon that point Columbus would not give up his right, and so the breach between them became wider and wider.   He cannot at that time have wanted means, for the royal revenues from the West Indies, which were even then considerable, came in regularly, and the tenth of them fell to Columbus.   The property too which he had left behind him in Hispaniola in 1500 was restored in the most honourable manner.   But anxiety about the establishment of his claims to the Viceroyalty, and vexation at the arbitrary enactments of the Indian Council which, under the President Fonseca, managed the affairs of the Spanish colonies in the New World, undermined his already shattered health.   In Valladolid, in the spring of 1506, he had a violent attack of his old complaint. He saw that death was approaching and prepared himself for it by arranging his affairs and by exercises of pious devotion. With the ejaculation, " Lord, into Thy hands I commit my spirit," he expired in the arms of his son on Ascension Day, May 21st, 1506.   According to his wish, he was buried in the Franciscan cloister at Valladolid, but in 1513 Ferdinand caused his remains to be disinterred and gave them a new resting-place in the Carthusian cloister of Santa Maria de las Cuevas in Seville.   But neither there were they destined long to remain.   At the wish of the Spanish settlers in the New World, they were in the year 1536 transferred to the Cathedral of St. Domingo ; and when, in the year 1795, Spain was forced to yield the island of Hispaniola to France, she would not leave to the new possessors the bones of the great discoverer. Once more exhumed they were with great pomp interred in the principal church of Havana, the capital of Cuba, and à splendid monument was raised over them.

Columbus was only fifty years of age, but during his lifetime he was generally supposed to be older, and his appearance justified this idea, for his frame was thoroughly worn out by the superhuman exertions which he had made.   Even in his thirtieth year his hair was quite white. He is described as of middle height, well proportioned, and strongly built. His long face, with an aquiline nose and rather prominent cheek-bones, was fresh-coloured. His light-grey eyes had a friendly look, and were particularly expressive when he spoke, as he usually did in a lively manner, and with many gestures. He liked simple attire, preferring a garment which resembled in colour and cut the garb of the Franciscans.

The great man, even though we do not seek to hide his faults, may well claim not only the grateful reverence of posterity for the discovery of a New World, but also our interest in his personal life. If he was too hasty in his conclusions, yet the strength of his convictions, which led him to scorn all disappointments and vexations, was truly wonderful. His power of observation in apprehending and explaining so many new appearances in land trodden by him for the first time was very great. And though the mistakes which he made in his geographical calculations were preposterous, yet we must remember that they were shared by the greatest scholars of his time.

How rich an imagination is displayed in his vivid descriptions of the splendours of tropical nature, and how varied are the similes and illustrations ever at his command in his descriptions of his voyages, has often been pointed out. In disposition Columbus was gentle and humane, but he required from his subordinates the same unwearied diligence that he imposed upon himself, without considering that they could not possess his enthusiasm. In times of difficulty, when those under him were rebellious and refractory, he never knew the right times for compliance and firmness, so that he constantly failed in authority. On his soft, almost sentimental disposition, which preserved him from injustice towards others, the wrongs and injuries which he himself had to endure made so deep an impression that he could not easily forgive people who had done him harm. The discovery of gold in Hispaniola was disastrous to him; the wish to fulfil the great expectations which he had raised made him blind to his impotence to restrain the wild rapacious colonists, and turned the soft-hearted man into a merciless slave-dealer.

Very singular too is the manner in which, in spite of his great learning, he clung to the superstitions of his time. The grounds of his geographical conjectures he sought in the Prophets and in the mysterious intimations of the writers of the Middle Ages; and his greatest hope was, with the help of the boundless wealth which the New World was certain to produce, to effect the deliverance of the Holy Sepulchre from the rule of the Turks. A short time before his death he was employed upon a work which he never finished, "The Prophecies," in which he calculates that the destruction of the world would take place in the year 1656. It has been already mentioned that his excited fancy led him to believe that he saw visions.

The death of this great man was almost unnoticed in Spain. Even in the year 1520 Spanish writers were in doubt whether he still lived, but later ages have been just to his memory.

The faithful brother of the great discoverer, Bartholomew the Adelantado, was in the year 1511 granted by King Ferdinand the island of Mona, between Hispaniola and Porto Rico, but it reverted to the Crown upon his death in 1514. Diego the younger brother, who in 1503 had received an office at court that brought him a considerable income, must have died shortly before Bartholomew in Seville, also without heirs. Of the two sons of the Admiral, the younger, Ferdinand, the brave companion of his father on his fourth voyage, occupied

an honourable position at the Court of the young King and
Emperor Charles V., in whose company he several times visited
Germany and Flanders.   He was one of the members of that
famous court which at Badajos, in 1524, was appointed to divide
the world between Spain and Portugal.   He was not an ecclesiastic, as some have thought; but being unmarried and childless,
spent his very considerable income in collecting a library of
rare and precious books, which, though much reduced by
dishonest hands, still exists at Seville under the name of
the Columbian Library.   Before his death, which occurred
at Seville in 1539, he composed a memoir of his great
father, of which an Italian translation was printed in Venice
in 1571.

Diego, the eldest son of the Admiral, married, in 1508,
Donna Maria de Toledo, of the family of the Dukes of Alva,
who was herself related to the royal house.   This high alliance
immediately procured for him the appointment of Viceroy of
the Indies, and in 1509 he relieved Ovando in the government
of the Island of Hispaniola.   But in the interests of the Crown,
the influence and authority of the distant Viceroy was gradually reduced, so that at last it became a mere empty dignity.
The successful issue of the lawsuit against the Crown which
his father had instituted was some compensation to him for
this.   The results of other lawsuits by which he hoped to
gain for himself the coasts of Central America, he did not live
to see, being carried off by a sudden death in the year 1526.
For his infant son the widow entered into a compromise,
by which he received the title of the Duke of Veragua, Marquis of Jamaica, Captain-general of Hispaniola, and Admiral
of the Indies, together with an hereditary yearly income of
10,000 ducats.   This title and revenue were only enjoyed for
two generations, the second Don Diego, great-grandson of the
discoverer, dying in 1576 without children.   In a great lawsuit

the relatives struggled for the inheritance of the estate, but it was not until 1608 that a decision was obtained, by which Don Nuno de Braganza, Count of Gelves, a descendant of the great Admiral through his mother, obtained the succession to all the titles, rights, and revenues.

CHAPTER III.

AMERIGO VESPUCCI.

ALTHOUGH a thankful posterity has recognised the merits of
Columbus, and accorded to him boundless honour and glory,
the great reward, to which he had a right, they denied him,
not naming after him the New World, which he first imagined
and discovered beyond the Atlantic Ocean. The injustice
thus inflicted on the great discoverer is certainly not miti-
gated by the honour, through a mere whim of fortune, falling
to a man who, though in every respect honourable and
worthy, could never be placed by the side of Columbus, and
indeed never thought of emulating him.

Amerigo (an Italian form of the German Almerich) Vespucci was born on March 9th, 1451. He was the son of the
rich and esteemed Anastasio Vespucci by his marriage with
Elizabeth Mini. The family to which he belonged was one
of the chief in the flourishing state of Florence, and like most
other important families of that town was devoted to trade.
Even the youthful Amerigo, who had received a careful education from a learned uncle, became a merchant; at the same
time mastering so thoroughly all knowledge accessible to him
that he was afterwards much distinguished for his acquaintance with mathematics and geography.

But about the general course of his youth and early man-
hood we have no certain information. We first hear of him
again in 1490. In that year he left Florence, and went to
Seville, where he became manager in a large house of busi-

ness belonging to his countryman Gianotto Berardi. It had only been established a few years, but had already become the largest firm of the town, and could boast of all kinds of distinctions that had been conferred on it by the royal house of Castile.

Amerigo came to Seville just at the right time, for only a few years later the newly-instituted Indian Council held its sittings in the town, and from it numerous expeditions started for the New World. The house of Berardi took a most active share in this new movement. Indeed, it provisioned in a great part Columbus's second fleet, and the fitting out of the third fleet was entirely owing to Vespucci, who after Berardi's death in 1495 became principal of the firm. Intercourse with great seamen awoke in Vespucci that dormant inclination for discovery which finally induced him to give up his life as a merchant. When, owing to the efforts of Bishop Fonseca, the President of the Indian Council, and in spite of all that Columbus could do, the path of discovery was opened to all, Vespucci was one of the first to enter upon it.

On the 20th of May, 1499, he left Seville in the company of Alonso de Ojeda, who, having distinguished himself during Columbus's second voyage, had through his cousin, the Inquisitor Ojeda, obtained permission from Fonseca to visit Paria and the neighbouring coasts. In what capacity Vespucci accompanied him, whether as merchant or astronomer, or, as he states himself, as a functionary of the King, is not very clear.

The little fleet, consisting of two ships and fifty-seven men, had as pilot the famous Juan de la Cosa, with whom Ojeda had become acquainted in the service of Columbus. On the 18th of May, 1499, they left Cadiz, and the wind constantly favouring them, at the beginning of July they sighted the coasts of the New World, and reckoned they were 200 miles south-east of Paria, and therefore near the country now called Guiana.

Impelled by the desire of reaching the south coast of Asia, the Spaniards steered towards the south ; but their hope that the coast would at last turn towards the west was disappointed. On the contrary, they came to the mouths of two large rivers three or four miles wide, the fresh water of which affected the sea for a great distance. They were the Amazon and the Rio Para. The region appeared to Vespucci an earthly paradise. He was specially struck with the magnificence of the vegetation, and at night he never tired of studying the stars of the southern sky, which were all new to him. He observed and described with great acuteness the manners of the inhabitants, and this part of his travels many readers have studied, and thus the name of the author has become famous. He describes the Indians as a careless race, without any belief in a God, knowing no distinction between right and wrong, and without any sense of shame. He praises their activity, but expresses himself warmly about many of their wicked customs, especially their cannibalism.

The voyage to the south was continued for some time, until contrary winds forced them to return. The little fleet sailed back to the regions already discovered, and reached Trinidad, which Columbus had explored on his third voyage. Following his example, they passed through the Serpent's Mouth into the Gulf of Paria, and after some stay among the friendly natives left it through the Dragon's Mouth. From the Island of Margarita, which Columbus had seen previously, they obtained some pearls, and turning again southwards along the coast, they entered a region untouched by Europeans. They discovered everywhere beautiful lands and friendly natives, and continued their voyage along the coast, landing occasionally ; but nowhere could they find the precious things that they so eagerly sought. However, leaving the coast, some fruitful islands were discovered towards the north, the largest of which, Curaçao, from a story originating in the terror of one of Ojeda's sailors, long had the reputation of being inhabited by giants.

Pressing on towards the west, the bold sailors found a lofty peninsula, which they rounded, and on its west beach came upon an Indian village, the construction of which excited their astonishment. The huts were supported on high pillars, and were connected with one another and with the land by drawbridges. From this circumstance the whole territory received the name of Venezuela, or Little Venice, which it still bears. The Spaniards soon became involved in a quarrel with the warlike 'inhabitants of the town, in which, as might be expected, they were the conquerors. The ships left with a stolen cargo of cotton, and steering southwards, traversed the broad Gulf of Venezuela. They thus discovered the narrow canal which leads into the Sea of Maracaybo, but Ojeda, although he had no difficulty in procuring provisions and met with a friendly reception from the Indians, found neither gold nor pearls, and therefore determined to return. He sailed along the west shore of the Gulf of Venezuela, from which the snowy peaks of the Sierra di Santa Marta were visible, and when the ships reached the open sea a favourable south-west breeze filled their sails and brought them in a few days to the coast of Hispaniola.

Columbus's dispute with the rebels under Roldan had just been brought to a conclusion by the treaty so humiliating to the Admiral. The arrival of Ojeda, who had a good repute among the Spanish settlers, appeared dangerous to both parties, and the Admiral was especially irritated at the infringement of his rights, which he considered Ojeda's voyage to be. Quarrels ensued, amounting even to bloodshed, until Ojeda, at the beginning of January, 1500, determined to quit the island. In order to make up for the lack of gold and pearls, which were so much looked for, Ojeda turned his ships towards the north, and from the the little islands at the south of Florida, and from the Bahama Islands, which had not been visited since 1492, collected a cargo of 200 Indian slaves These, after his return in the middle of June, 1500, he publicly sold in Cadiz. Nevertheless, the profit falling to those who had taken part in the voyage was miserably small.

But love of adventure impelled the fiery Ojeda to new enterprises. As early as July 28th, 1500, he made an agreement with Fonseca by which, undertaking a new voyage, he secured to himself the Governorship of all the Coasts of Maracaybo which he might discover. But the Crown delaying the ratification, Ojeda did not set out until January, 1502. The settlement then formed was very soon abandoned on account of the want of provisions, the hostility of the irritated Indians, and discord among the Spaniards. Thrown into chains by his own men, Ojeda was brought through Hispaniola to Spain, where he had hard work to hold his own in a lawsuit instituted against him. A third voyage to Venezuela in 1505 was also unsuccessful. For some years the brave man lived at Hispaniola in straitened circumstances, until at last he was named Governor of Nueva Andalusia, a province of the north coast of South America, between the Gulf of Venezuela and the mouth of the Atrato, and departed in 1509 for his post. He endeavoured vainly to form settlements at various points, and a series of fierce engagements with the Caribs caused the Spaniards serious loss, the famous pilot Juan de la Cosa being among the killed.

The colony of San Sebastian, which finally he established near the mouth of Atrato, was reduced to such a condition by sickness, famine, and constant battles—in which all the heroism of Ojeda could not break the power of the enemy— that he was obliged himself at last to proceed to Hispaniola to seek for assistance.   During his absence the colony became scattered, and he himself having reached Hispaniola, after going through all kinds of dangers and deprivations, died there in 1515 in the greatest misery, stripped of everything and forgotten by all.

He is perhaps the most interesting figure among the thousands of adventurers who at that time made the New World the scene at once of the most atrocious crimes and of the most heroic deeds.   He united in a striking manner all the most contradictory qualities which those adventurers displayed.   Heroism and a thirst for gold, a keen enjoyment of life and a great capability of enduring hardships, an utter deafness to the dictates of conscience and a fanatical adherence to the commands of the Church.   Whilst Ojeda was constantly impelled by love of adventure to new enterprises Vespucci discovered such a taste for the excitement and varied experiences which travelling offered as rendered it impossible for him to return to his mercantile life.   It is generally assumed that he accompanied Vincente Yanez Pinzon, that distinguished seaman from Palos, who had served under Columbus as commander of the *Nina*, in an expedition to the coast of Brazil, about three months before Cabral's voyage. This opinion is supported by an account of a voyage, published under the name of Amerigo, in which the name of Pinzon is not mentioned, but the principal circumstances of the voyage are described in accordance with the facts.

Pinzon, however, left Palos on the 18th of November, 1499, when Ojeda's squadron, in which was Vespucci, lay on the coast of Hispaniola. Even if one assumes that Vespucci, immediately on his arrival in the island, which at the earliest could not have occurred before the 23rd of September, 1499, separated from Ojeda and returned to Europe, it still does not allow time for the voyage and the preparations unavoidable before Pinzon's departure.   Besides this, his first account, in which he describes the occurrences of Ojeda's voyage, is dated July 18th, 1500, at which time Pinzon, who did not return until September 30th, was still in America. Therefore there is greater probability in the idea that these excellent "Voyages," which are only preserved in a very mangled condition, were not written by Vespucci, or were drawn up by him from the accounts given him by some one who took part in the voyage.

But his participation in Ojeda's expedition drew upon the Florentine the attention of King Emanuel of Portugal, who, from Cabral's report of the discovery of Brazil, at once perceived the importance of that land for connecting Portugal with India, and hastened to take possession of it before the Spanish discoverers should have entered it. Apparently before Pinzon, the real discoverer of Brazil, had returned from his voyage, an offer had been made to Vespucci to enter the Portuguese service and to take part in an exploring expedition along its coast. He gladly consented, and on the 13th of May, 1501, we see him leaving the harbour of Lisbon on board a squadron consisting of three vessels. We do not know who was the commander, but at any rate it was not Vespucci, who did not possess the necessary experience, and who is much more likely to have accompanied the fleet as a cosmographer, as Behaim had once accompanied Bartholomew Diaz. The object of the voyage was not merely to prove the identity of the coasts discovered by Cabral and Ojeda, which Pinzon's voyage had rendered doubtful, but also, if possible, to sail round the newly-discovered coasts in a westerly direction, and thus discover a second route to India, by which might be reached the Moluccas and the rich Sunda Islands, as yet only known by report. Vespucci did his utmost to attain a result that would have brought him the fame that now surrounds the name of Magalhaens. But he did not suspect what the latter knew, that a monstrous ocean separates the New World from the east coast of Asia.

15

After a long delay in the Bissagos Islands off the coast of West Africa and a tedious voyage, the sailors on the 16th of August first sighted a smiling coast at 5 degrees south latitude, and drew near to a peninsula, which, in honour of the saint whose day it happened to be, they called San Roque, the name which the east point of South America still bears. The aborigines here showed themselves very hostile, attacking and devouring some sailors who ventured into the interior. Without stopping to chastise them the ships continued their course towards the south, landing every now and then and carrying on friendly intercourse with the Indians. One can still trace the stations of the discoverers in the names of the principal points, which they always called after the saints' days. Thus, on the 28th of August, they arrived at Cape Agostinho, which had already been discovered though not named by Pinzon. On the 4th of October they found the mouth of the river San Francisco; on the 1st of November the Bay de Todos os Santos, where now is situated the town of Bahia; on the 21st of December the Cape of St. Thomas; and on the 1st of Janauary, 1502, the Bay of Rio Janeiro (the river of St. Januarius), which they took for the mouth of a river. They stayed for some time in the Bay of Cananea, 26 south latitude, erroneously stated by Vespucci to be 32 south latitude. Vespucci describes the natives of this province to be fine people, of a reddish colour, who disfigured themselves by piercing their lips for the purpose of inserting ornaments made of a blue stone or of bone. This most unbecoming custom—Vespucci once saw in the lip of a man a stone of half a hand's breadth, and weighing seven ounces —procured for these Indians in later times the name of Botocuden (cork wearers). They had their goods in common, and lived without religion a thoroughly sensual life, frequently interrupted, however, by wars with the neighbouring races. Those who were conquered were devoured, and Vespucci heard a man boast that he had eaten 300 men. In the huts too the Portuguese often found salted human flesh. The splendid climate, which was rendered clear by almost unvarying east winds, made the Indians so healthy that, according to Vespucci, they often lived to be a hundred and fifty. Finding no precious metals on the whole of this coast, the sailors were eager to return, but were persuaded by Vespucci to make another attempt to find the western passage to India. They again set out on the 15th of February, and steered directly to the south-east, not allowing themselves to be deterred by the increasing cold. On the 3rd of April they encountered a fearful storm, which lasted several days. During this they discovered an inhospitable coast, which the ships followed towards the south for twenty miles. At last the sky cleared, but the storm and the cold had deprived every one of any desire to examine more nearly the coast, which, according to Vespucci's reckoning, lay about 55 south latitude. What this land could have been it is impossible to decide with certainty. Most probably it was the most southerly part of Patagonia, close by the Straits of Magalhaens. Every one on board was glad when they turned round, steering to the north-east for the coast of Africa, but it was not until after much contending with the winds and waves that they reached it on the 10th of May. In Sierra Leone they were obliged to set fire to one of their ships, which had become perfectly useless. The other two entered the harbour of Lisbon on the 7th of September, 1502, after an absence of sixteen months.

King Emanuel, in spite of the empty hands with which the discoverers returned, was well pleased with their perseverance and with the large extent of coast explored by them. He immediately prepared a new squadron to complete the discovery and to seek the passage to the Moluccas, of the existence of which they felt certain. Of the six ships which set sail on the 10th of May, under the orders of Gonzalo

Coelho, one was commanded by Amerigo Vespucci.   But the
great hopes that were aroused by this expedition were lament-
ably disappointed.   Coelho, against the advice of Vespucci,
kept along the coast of Africa as far as Sierra Leone, instead
of sailing to the west, direct from the Cape Verde Islands.
In crossing the ocean he discovered, in 3 degrees south latitude, an island of some size, which afterwards received the
name of Fernando de Moronha, after a captain to whom it
was presented by the King.   The commander's ship having
run upon rocks, Coelho gave Vespucci orders, with a large
boat and a few sailors, to explore the island and see whether
there was a secure harbour for the fleet.   This commission
Vespucci executed, and found on the island, which was well
watered and inhabited by countless birds, a spacious and
well-protected harbour.   But in vain did he wait here for the
squadron.   After a week of painful suspense, he was fetched
off by his ship, which at the same time brought the announce-
ment that Coelho, his own vessel having been sunk, had
sailed with the remaining ships farther towards the west.
Very much hurt, Vespucci followed him to All Saints' Bay,.
the appointed meeting-place, and waited there for two months.
But in vain, so at length he determined to leave.   On his own
responsibility he sailed along the coast until he reached about
18 degrees south latitude, and there on a favourable spot
founded a little fort, in which he left behind twenty-four men
with provisions for six months.   Then he started on the return
voyage and reached Lisbon on the 18th of June, 1504.   The
remaining ships of the fleet came in singly one after another,
without any valuable cargoes and without having discovered
the western passage, or indeed having sought it with anything
like earnestness.   After that the Portuguese many times visited
the Brazils, either to seek for the passage to India, or to procure a cargo of the valuable Brazilian wood.   But the first

colony which they established was Pernambuco, which they built in 1526.

But the displeasure of Emanuel, which fell upon all who took part in the unhappy undertaking, was the cause of Vespucci's emigration. He accepted a call from the Castilian court, which made him great promises, and in the spring of 1505 entered Spain. It was intended to employ him in an expedition which, under the command of Vincent Yanez Pinzon, was to visit the new-found southern continent. Probably the desire to find the western passage was the real cause of the scheme. Vespucci himself from Seville urged on the preparation of the squadron, but for some unknown reason the plan was never carried out, and in 1508 Vespucci was appointed to the newly-created office of royal pilot, with the considerable revenue of 200 ducats. In this new position it was his duty to examine the pilots of the West Indian vessels in their use of the astronomical instruments, and to make a trustworthy map of the New World, in which should be inserted the newly-discovered countries according to the accounts brought back by the discoverers. This very important and honourable position, which made his name known in distant circles, he continued to occupy until his death, which occurred in Seville, on the 22nd of February, 1512. Vespucci left behind him a widow but no children. He died convinced that the New World was a part of Asia, and had no suspicion that it was an independent continent, which by a wonderful whim of fate would immortalise his name.

We can entirely clear him from the design attributed to him of endeavouring to lessen Columbus's glory, or to substitute his own name for that of the great discoverer. On the contrary, he was always on the best terms with Columbus. This is clearly proved by a letter which Columbus, on the 5th of February, 1505, addressed to his son Diego, and in which he tells him that Vespucci, who has just gone to the Castilian court, will labour in his (Columbus's) interest. "Vespucci," he writes, "has always been very friendly to me. Fortune has been unkind to the worthy man, as to so many others. He too has not received the reward due to his services." The sons of the Admiral never showed the least ill-will towards Vespucci, and Ferdinand Columbus, the biographer of his father, never once mentions him. Las Casas is the first person who expresses his displeasure at the adoption of the name America, but even he does not give the least intimation that he considers Vespucci at all to blame.

The reason of the injustice done to Columbus arose from the ignorance that the West Indies and the land discovered in the south had anything to do with each other. The mistake of Columbus, who took the West Indies for Japan and its neighbouring islands, suggested the idea that that southern land, the size of which was more clearly proved by every expedition, was a completely independent country, a gigantic island, separated somewhere from the West Indies and the east coast of Asia by an arm of the sea. As late as the year 1530 the maps of the world show this channel, or at any rate a gap between South and North America. Whilst the name of Columbus is indissolubly connected with Hispaniola, Cuba, and the other West Indian islands, little or nothing was heard of his third and fourth voyages, which carried him to the coast of the mainland, and therefore people were perplexed to find a name for it. Amerigo Vespucci was the first to describe the nature of the country and its inhabitants, which he did in a series of "Voyages," and his name therefore naturally occurred to people.

A letter addressed by him, either at the end of 1502 or the beginning of 1503, to Lorenzo di Pier Francisco de' Medici, a member of a collateral branch of the celebrated princely house, did not reach Florence until after the death of Lorenzo

(Lorenzo died March 10th, 1503), and so fell into other hands. In this letter Vespucci gave his friend a concise account of his adventures from June 4th, 1501 (the time of his stay at Cape Verde), till September 7th, 1502 (the time of his return from the first Portuguese voyage). The interesting nature of this letter, which contained much that was new, led to its publication. This took place in Paris, 1503, in Latin, and it made such a noise that a number of editions and translations in German and Italian followed. This result caused the publication, certainly either against the will or without the knowledge of the author, of a number of other letters of Vespucci, which he had addressed to Pietro Soderini in Florence. They appeared translated into Latin from a French translation, and were collected into a continuous whole under the title of "The Fourth Voyage," in 1507, in St. Dié in Lorraine. The original compilers of this work, whether out of ignorance or with an evil intention, allowed a number of errors, mutilations, and interpolations to creep in, which place Vespucci's voyages in a completely false light.

Among the early voyages with Ojeda, which he describes to Soderini in two long letters, there are two remarkable expeditions, the second of which in many points appears identical with that of Pinzon, and there is the most utter confusion in the dates, so that, resting upon these voyages, it was for a long time declared that Amerigo had reached the mainland before Columbus, and it is still uncertain whether or not he took part in Pinzon's voyage in 1499-1500. The errors have been more clearly manifested by the discovery of two earlier letters, written by him to Lorenzo Medici on July 18th, 1500, and June 4th, 1501. These only mention one voyage in the Castilian service, and are tolerably exact in the dates.

The rapid circulation of Vespucci's letters had closely connected the name of the Florentine with the great con-

tinent in the south with which most men had become acquainted from those writings, and it was natural to name the
land after him which as yet had no other name, and of whose
discovery by Columbus they were ignorant. This was first
done by Martin Hylacomilus (Waldseemüller), a native of
Freiburg in Breisgau, at that time a bookseller and teacher of
geography at St. Dié, where, under the protection of Duke
René the Second of Lorraine, he was engaged in the editing
of the works of Ptolemy.

In 1507 he published an "Introduction to Cosmography,"
which he dedicated to the Emperor Maximilian I., and
to which he added a Latin edition of the "Voyages." In
this work he says: "The fourth continent may very fit-
tingly be called Amerigo—that is, the land of Amerigo,
or America—because Amerigo discovered it." The proposition received support. Little geographical treatises,
which appeared in 1509, 1512, and 1515 in Strasburg and
Nuremburg, repeated it, and in 1520 the name America first
appeared in the maps of the world which the monk Camers
published in Vienna from the drawings of Peter Apianus
(Bienervitz). The name indeed is limited to what is now
Brazil, and by the side of it stands the remark, "This land was
discovered in 1497, with the adjacent islands, by the Genoese
Columbus."

But the new name quickly naturalised itself, and soon was
adopted for the whole south mainland. Indeed, as advancing
discoveries proved that it, together with the West Indies and
the northern mainland, was a great division of the earth, the
well-sounding name America was employed for the whole
continent, and thus the just claim of the name Columbia was
set aside.

While we deplore the injustice done to the memory of the
great discoverer, we need not let it mislead us into attributing
to the fortunate author a wilful appropriation of another's

fame, and thus become guilty of another injustice. Rather let us accord him due honour for his discoveries and explorations in the New World, and do nothing to lessen his reputation as a man of honour, to which Columbus himself bears witness.

CHAPTER IV.

VASCO NUNEZ DE BALBOA.

WHEN Ojeda, in 1510, left the town of St. Sebastian near the mouth of the Atrato in Darien, in order to procure aid from Hispaniola, he placed over those whom he left behind Francisco Pizarro, afterwards so famous, and extracted a promise from them all to remain fifty days in their miserable position, for he hoped in that time to bring them assistance. Pizarro waited in vain for his return; and at last, after the number of those under his command had melted down to about sixty, the largest number which the two shattered ships could hold, he set sail for Hispaniola. Shortly afterwards one of the vessels was wrecked, and sank with all on board before the eyes of those on board the other ship. A few days later they unexpectedly met a stately vessel coming towards them. It was commanded by the Advocate Martin Hernandez de Enciso, who had gained considerable wealth in Hispaniola, and whom Ojeda had enticed to assist in the founding of the colony on the Atrato by appointing him governor.

After long preparations and many hindrances on the part of Don Diego Columbus, who laid claim to Central America, he had at length taken 150 men, a number of animals, and a good stock of provisions and arms to the new colony, which he hoped to find in a prosperous condition. Instead of this, thirty half-starved men came to meet him on a crazy ship, these being all that remained of the colonists. In spite of the miserable accounts which he received from them, he determined to re-establish the forsaken colony, and forced the fugitives to unite with the 150 fresh men whom he was bringing with him from Hispaniola. Among these there was one of the most distinguished of the Spanish discoverers.

Vasco Nunez de Balboa, born 1475, at Xeres, near Badajoz, in the province of Estremadura, sprang from a rich and respectable family, though in his early youth he had squandered his wealth, and by his giddy pranks had forfeited his good name. Like many others, he sought to recover both by joining in the expedition to the New World which promised to courageous fortune-hunters fame and spoil in rich measure. He was a companion of Rodrigo de Bastidas, who in the year 1500 explored a part of the north-west coast of South America, and returned to Spain with a rich spoil of gold and pearls.

As was the case with all who took part in it, this expedition produced for Balboa a little property, which he spent in settling in Hispaniola. But here also his extravagance and love of gambling made him a poor man; and, pressed by many creditors, he soon found himself in the greatest distress, from which he knew not how to escape except by flight. Now for the protection of creditors it had been rendered exceedingly difficult for any one to quit the islands, and Balboa could not find means to carry out his projected retreat.

At last he succeeded in smuggling himself on to the ship which Enciso had fitted out for Darien. He is said to have been carried on board concealed in a cask, and to have remained there for some days. When he at last ventured forth Enciso was very unpleasantly surprised; for, by the laws of the Spanish colony of Hispaniola, the captain who assisted in the flight of a debtor became himself responsible to the creditor. However, he did not carry out his threat of setting Balboa on shore on the first desert island, fearing the bodily strength and the well-known audacity of his unwished-for companion, but tried to comfort himself with the hope that Balboa would prove himself of value in the new settlement.

The arrival at the forsaken San Sebastian was not auspicious. Enciso's ship ran upon the rocks, and with its valuable cargo sank so quickly that it was all the crew could do to save even their lives. Thus the settlers had from the beginning to struggle with hunger, and in the unceasing conflicts with the natives, who made use of poisoned arrows, their numbers rapidly diminished. It was no wonder therefore that despondency seized upon them. Balboa, however, by proposing to cross over to the west coast of the Gulf of Darien, inspired them with new courage.

On his earlier visit in the ship of Bastidas he had found there a rich country, friendly people, and handsome towns. The proposal was carried out, and all Balboa's statements were proved correct. After an easy victory over the Indians, the adventurers took possession of a large village, where they found provisions in abundance and a considerable quantity of gold.

In gratitude for the protection that had been granted to them by the miraculous image at Seville, they named the new town Maria del Antigua. This indeed was not situated in the province of New Andalusia, which Ojeda and Enciso had been charged to colonise, but west of the mouth of the Atrato, in the province of the Knight Diego de Nicuesa, which embraced the whole east coast of Central America, from the Atrato to Cape Gracios a Dios, and bore the pompous name of Castilla del Oro.

This circumstance was made use of by those among the settlers hostile to Nicuesa to deprive him of the command. Vasco Nunez Balboa was chosen in his place until the King's pleasure should be known. It was the first step to fortune made by the bold unscrupulous adventurer. The unexpected

arrival of two well-manned and well-provisioned ships, prepared at Nicuesa's expense at Hispaniola, and now on their
way to him, had put it into the settlers' heads to ask him to
come and take the command.

The messengers found him and his people reduced to a
miserable condition at Nombre de Dios, not far from Aspion-
vall. The band of settlers, diminished by every possible pri-
vation, greeted the invitation to the rapidly rising town of
Santa Maria del Antigua as deliverance from certain destruction, and Nicuesa himself arranged their transmission with
much pleasure.

But among the men whom he sent in advance there were
some whom he had wronged or cruelly punished for disobedience. They excited the people of Santa Maria against the
new ruler, who had aroused general displeasure by errors of
judgment and careless speeches. He allowed himself to be
persuaded by Balboa, who feigned the greatest friendship for
him, to submit his claims to an election. It turned out un-
favourably for Nicuesa. Almost unanimously Balboa was
raised to the head of the settlement, and with the proviso
that the choice should be ratified by the King, he undertook
the government of Castilla del Oro. Although he had promised his protection to the deposed governor, he yet allowed
the rebels to force the hated Nicuesa on board an unseaworthy
ship, with sixteen men who remained faithful to him. Nothing
was ever heard of the unfortunate men. Probably they and
their miserable bark were swallowed up by the waves.

Thus through a series of intrigues and acts of violence Balboa found himself ruler of one of the richest lands of America
hardly a year after he had escaped on board Enciso's ship a
fugitive in the utmost misery. He succeeded, however, in
making men forget the unworthy means through which he
had obtained the government by the power and wisdom with
which he conducted it. All the best features of his great

character now came to the front. His manner of life was simple and devoid of all show ; he was generous and liberal, bold in his schemes ; the valour he displayed in contests with his enemies was almost superhuman, while he was mild and humane to the conquered. The dominion he gained and maintained over the minds of 300 lawless men borders on the wonderful. By the force of his example he carried them from one enterprise to another, where danger and hardship, but not rewards, were alike to all.

The inhabitants of Central America were superior to the harmless Indians of Hispaniola and to the men-eating Caribs. Certainly on account of the warm climate they went completely naked and lived in simple huts, but they were divided into various ranks. They honoured the sun and moon as divinities, and the care with which they embalmed the bodies of the dead makes it probable that they believed in an existence after death. Thus they formed a connecting link between the inhabitants of the Antilles, who were little raised above the animals, and the highly-developed people whom the Spaniards afterwards met on the tablelands of Anahuac and Quito.

All these tribes were fond of gold ornaments, and the nobles among them were served from gold vessels. Therefore it was easy for the Spaniards to collect considerable quantities of the precious metal, and by constant attacks and surprises they soon increased their treasure. On one of these expeditions Balboa received from the son of a Prince, who was astonished at the Spaniards' thirst for gold, the first news of an ocean which lay not far off towards the south-west, beyond a ridge of mountains, and which was visited by ships little inferior in size to those of Spain. The richest gold lands were said to lie on the coasts of this great sea. Balboa immediately divined that this must be the sea that washed the shores of India, but the whole importance of the news he could not appreciate. He burned with the desire to make his name immortal by the discovery of the new ocean, and his followers, whose thirst for gold was whetted by the Prince's descriptions, showed themselves ready to accompany him through all dangers and difficulties. But the plan could not be carried out for a long time. The subjugation of the neighbouring Indians and the suppression of a dangerous conspiracy formed by them, which was discovered and frustrated by the faithfulness of Balboa's Indian wife, took up a considerable time, and until this was accomplished it seemed unadvisable to divide the little company.

It was not until reinforcements had arrived from Hispaniola—whose Governor, Don Diego Columbus, the crafty Balboa acknowledged as his superior—that the expedition to the Western Ocean could be thought of. On September 1st, 1513, they began their march from Maria del Antigua. Balboa himself led the little army, which consisted of 190 Spaniards and 600 Indian bearers, and was accompanied by several of the formidable bloodhounds. The precise point of departure was Careta, a place on the coast a few miles from the settlement, whose Prince was friendly to the Spaniards, and had been baptised, receiving the name of Don Fernando. The distance between the shores of the two oceans measures at this point scarcely thirty miles, and would therefore under ordinary circumstances be accomplished in three or four days' march. But on this narrow strip of land were crowded together the greatest difficulties and obstructions.

The mountain range indeed was not formidable from its height, but its slopes were covered with dense primeval forests and poisonous vapours arose from the swampy ground traversed by numerous sluggish rivers. Added to this there was the necessity of forcing a passage through the territory of various Indian tribes. It was almost three weeks from the time Balboa and his men left Careta (September 6th) before they reached the neighbourhood of the coast.   On the 25th of September his Indian guides informed him that from a neighbouring hill the sea could be seen.   He wished to be the first to enjoy the sight, so he climbed the hill alone.   Arrived at the top he saw close beneath him a bay with many inlets towards the south-west, opening into the boundless ocean.   Overcome with joy Balboa fell upon his knees and praised God, who had favoured him with so great a revelation.

On the 29th of September he reached the shore, and bearing a banner upon which was emblazoned the Virgin and Child, he waded up to his knees into the water and solemnly, in the names of the Kings of Arragon and Castile, took possession "of these southern seas, lands, shores, harbours, and islands, with all that they contained, their kingdoms and their marches, and swore to defend them against any foreign claim, for the monarchs of Castile present and future, to whom belongs the empire and dominion of all these Indies, the islands together with the north and south mainland, with their seas from the north pole to the south pole on both sides of the equator, within and without the tropics of Cancer and Capricorn, all being by right the possession of their majesties and their successors."   Then he made each of the Spaniards convince himself by the salt taste that it was the shore of an ocean, and sign his name to a deed drawn up by the notary, Valderrabano, formally taking possession.

The bay which Balboa then reached still bears the name of San Miguel, from the day on which it was discovered.   Its shores are extraordinarily rich in pearls.   The Spaniards collected a great number, among them some singularly large specimens, but quite dull, because the Indians knew no way of opening the shells but by fire and smoke.   They were mostly found on the shores of some neighbouring islands, later named the Pearl Islands.   Bad weather prevented Balboa from taking possession of them, and after several weeks' sojourn with the chiefs of the country, whom he attached to him partly by show of power and partly by friendly conciliation, he determined on his return. He chose a different way, but encountered equal difficulties. The opposition was so great that he tried to overcome it by accusing some of the chiefs of treason and criminality, and condemning them to be torn to pieces by bloodhounds. This horrible punishment spread terror far and wide, but we should do him injustice if in our detestation of Balboa's bloody cruelty we forgot that he did not act thus wantonly, but in the hope of breaking down all opposition; and that he chose as his victims those who were hated and feared by their countrymen. Compared with those who followed him indeed he appears mild and humane.

On January 19th, 1514, Balboa returned to Santa Maria, where he found everything prospering. In March he sent the great news of his discovery to Spain, together with 20,000 ducats and 200 of the most beautiful pearls, which was the royal share of the booty. By such dazzling proofs of his fitness he hoped to wipe out the stain which rested on his accession to power, and to stifle the complaints of his enemies. And indeed the stir which his news excited was quite remarkable. Learned men recognised the mistake Columbus had made in supposing he had reached the east coast of Asia, while an unknown ocean lay between it and the new continent. Still it was possible that west of Cuba it might be connected with the Atlantic Ocean.

In the Spanish nation there broke out a new and violent attack of the gold fever. To reward the skill and success of Balboa King Ferdinand appointed him Adelantado of the newly-discovered South Sea—the name given to the new ocean, Balboa having crossed the Isthmus of Central America from north to south—and made him Governor of Coiba on the Atlantic Ocean, and Panama on the South Sea, thus compensating him for certain enactments made previous to the arrival of his messenger. Enciso and the friends of the unfortunate Nicuesa had accused Balboa at court of having unjustly seized the governorship, and had excited a strong feeling against the traitor, as they named him. Ferdinand, desirous of securing civil order to the hopeful colony, had appointed Pedrarias de Avila, a man of sixty, its governor, as successor to Nicuesa, thereby setting aside as illegal the rule of Balboa. Pedrarias set sail on April 11th, 1514, with twenty-two ships and 1200 men, and landed on June 30 at Santa Maria.

He was unfit for his post, but no opposition was offered to him, and he obtained possession of the reins of government without difficulty. Almost immediately he began a secret examination of Balboa, in the hope of gaining over to his side the man who had the greatest influence among the colonists and the surrounding Indians. But the cunning of Balboa was too much for him, and the examination ended in his acquittal. The rule of Pedrarias was altogether very un-unfortunate. The colony was visited by intense heat, and the produce of the land was not sufficient to support the increased number of Spaniards. Many died of hunger in the streets of the town; others perished in the plundering raids which want drove them to make upon the Indians, whom of course this kind of treatment turned from friends into enemies.

No wonder that the colonists wished for Balboa's rule back again. This becoming known to Avila filled him with hatred of the great discoverer, which increased when he found that Balboa had been appointed by the King governor of two provinces, which were thus withdrawn from his immediate jurisdiction, although Balboa was to remain his subordinate. However, he kept up an appearance of friendship, and even betrothed to Balboa one of his daughters left behind in Spain, but secretly he was brooding over plans for his destruction. Balboa at last succeeded in obtaining his permission to build some ships on the South Sea, in which to visit the gold lands. With great trouble the ships were conveyed in separate pieces over the isthmus and there put together, and Balboa was just ready to put off, when on some urgent pretext he was summoned by Avila to Santa Maria. There he was thrown into chains, and the accusation brought against him that he was intending to rebel and set up an independent government on the shores of the South Sea. At the same time the old charges of rebelling against Nicuesa and supplanting Enciso were brought up again. The judges being already gained over, pronounced sentence of death on Balboa and four of his adherents in January, 1517, and at Avila's command it was carried out at Acla, a little offshoot from Santa Maria.

Thus the Spaniards robbed themselves of the man most fit to explore the coast of the South Sea just at the moment when he was on the point of accomplishing the task, which afterwards fell to the share of the rough Pizarro. By his unjust death Balboa atoned for the many crimes which had stained his life. And the heroism of his character and the glorious results which his great qualities enabled him to achieve throw an undying charm around his memory.

CHAPTER V.

FERNAM DE MAGALHAENS.

By Balboa's discoveries some of the mistaken ideas were
cleared up which until then had been entertained with regard
to the New World. It was now known that the Antilles were
not Japan, and Darien was not Malacca, and that between
Europe and Asia there lay a great continent, separated from
Europe by the Atlantic and from Asia by Balboa's great
ocean. But to most minds it appeared perfectly incompatible
with the purpose of the world's creation that these two great
oceans should be completely separated from one another by
a large continent stretching from north to south, and that
such an almost insurmountable obstacle should be placed in
the way of communication between the two civilised parts of the
earth. Every one was convinced that there must be a strait,
possibly in a direct line between Spain and India, which united
the two oceans and would be a most convenient path for trade.

To discover this strait was the unceasing object of the
Spanish discoverers. Their zeal stirred up the still open
question concerning the possession of the Moluccas. The
mistaken measurement of the earth assumed, as we have
before mentioned, that the boundary of the territory granted
to the Portuguese by the Pope (180 degrees east of the Canary
Isles) was in the Bay of Bengal, and the Spaniards were angry
that the Portuguese had overstepped it by their conquests in
Further India and in the Sunda Islands. With anxiety and
vexation they saw the Portuguese discoveries extending

steadily towards the east, and approaching nearer and nearer to the Spice Islands, concerning which they were fully convinced that they lay on the Spanish side of the globe. Yet they were not in a condition to resist these encroachments unless they could find a direct western route to these islands, for to pursue the Portuguese by the route round Africa and to seek to pass them in the Indian Ocean would render a desperate struggle certain, the result of which was by no means sure.

Columbus therefore sought this passage in the neighbourhood of Darien; some years later hopes were entertained that it would be discovered in the Gulf of Mexico, and later still Cortes explored the whole east coast of North America from Florida to Labrador with the same object. But in vain. Still more zealously was South America examined for the same purpose, that being for a long time looked upon as an island. All the numerous expeditions along its west coast had the same object, but without the desired result. Still they did not give up hope.

Juan Diaz de Solis, who had accompanied Pinzon on his third voyage in 1509, thought, in 1516, he had discovered the long-sought-for passage, when he found about 35 degrees south latitude the east coast of America suddenly turn towards the west and continue in that direction for miles. But he recognised his mistake when the water lost its saltness; he had run into the great fresh water estuary of the two gigantic rivers Parana and Uruguay, and which afterwards received the name of Rio de la Plata. He landed on the shores of this gulf and was killed and eaten by the wild Indians. His horrified companions at once turned round without accomplishing the task which Solis had set himself.

But a greater man soon followed in his footsteps. Fernam de Magalhaens, better known under the Spanish form of his name, Magellan, was born about the year 1480, in Oporto, of

an old noble Portuguese family. We know nothing of his
youth. Like other young men of his rank, he probably knew
something of struggles with the infidels and of dangerous
voyages. It is certain that in his early life he went to India
in the service of the Portuguese crown, and there distinguished
himself. Though his personal appearance was mean, he soon
brought himself into notice by his boldness and activity. He
served as an officer in the great fleet which, in 1511, Alfonso
de Albuquerque led against Malacca, and took part in the
taking and defence of that important town.

The next year he took part in the war against the infidels
in Africa. At Azamor he received a wound in the thigh from
a lance, which made him lame for the rest of his life. Having
come to court, in order to beg for an appointment in reward
for the services he had rendered, he was at once dismissed because he had presented himself without leave, and sent back
to Africa. Some time afterwards, finding all his endeavours
fruitless, he determined to forsake for ever his native land, in
which he had been publicly disgraced by having a groundless
charge of embezzlement brought against him. He formally
gave up all his rights in Portugal, and on October 20th, 1517,
removed his residence to Seville. A short time afterwards he
married a daughter of a Portuguese named Diego Barbosa,
who had settled in Seville.

Magalhaens was in possession of information which he
thought he could make more use of in his new home than in
his old. Francisco Serrao, the first of all the Portuguese who
reached the Moluccas (1512), and who had spent some years
there, was his greatest friend. From him he had received
letters containing a detailed account of his experiences. The
distances given by Serrao were, according to the fashion of discoverers, exaggerated, and firmly convinced Magalhaens that
the delightful islands which brought forth the costly products
of the east might be fairly claimed by the Spaniards. He con-

sulted about it with an an astronomer named Faleiro, who had also emigrated from Portugal, and he arrived at the same conclusion. Together they applied to the Honourable Council for India, offering their services for the discovery and settlement of the Moluccas.

In February, 1815, they arrived at the royal court of Valladolid, and began their negotiation with Fonseca, the well-known President of the Council. The prudence and caution natural to this man would probably have prevented these plans being adopted had not Magalhaens assured him most confidently that he could find the desired passage. Being questioned more closely, he stated that he had seen it marked on a large map of the world which was kept in the treasury of the King of Portugal, and which had been drawn up by the Nuremberger Martin Behaim.

Now it is not at all impossible that this man, besides the voyage in which he accompanied Cam, 1484, may have taken part in other expeditions, and perhaps have even become acquainted with the coast of South America. But in the year 1492, when he prepared the globe for the Nurembergers, he appears to have had no knowledge of the American coasts, and if we refer to a map of the world added by him to an edition of Ptolemy published in the year 1507, we find the extreme limit of the continent fixed. At the Rio de Cananea, 32 degrees south latitude, and on the other side of a broad gulf is represented a belt of large islands evidently drawn from fancy.

It is most probable that Magalhaens invented the story when he saw that, without pretending to a knowledge of the shorter way to the Moluccas, he should not obtain the appointment he desired. He trusted that he should be able to justify his assertions, if fortune were not adverse. At any rate the careful investigation to which afterwards he subjected every bay along the coast of South America makes him appear quite uncertain of the position of the desired strait. However, he obtained his object, Fonseca was quite won over and seconded most warmly the plans of the sailor who was in possession of such important information.

When Magalhaens had made up his mind to relinquish his claim to the rank of Admiral he succeeded in concluding a very favourable treaty (March 22nd, 1518). The crown promised to fit out five good ships and man them with 234 skilful sailors, whom it undertook to pay for two years. All other seamen were forbidden for ten years to make use of the passage that should be discovered by Magalhaens. To him the command of the fleet was committed, and the rank of Adelantado and the governorship of all lands that he should discover were promised to him. Of the revenues that should flow to the crown the twentieth part was to be paid to the discoverer, upon whom also was conferred the right to import into Spain, yearly, spices to the value of 1000 ducats, and to receive a fifth part of the produce of the voyage. Finally, of the islands discovered after the crown had chosen six, the seventh and eighth were to be allotted to Magalhaens, that he might receive the fifteenth part of their produce.

Full of zeal Magalhaens set to work to prepare his squadron. Soon the five ships lay in the harbour of Seville, ready to sail. They were the *Trinidad*, which Magalhaens himself commanded; the *San Antonio*, under Juan de Cartagena; the *Conception*, under Gaspar de Quesada; the *Victoria*, under Luis de Mendoza; and the *Santiago*, under the Portuguese Juan Serrao, probably a relation of the discoverer of the Moluccas. But the departure was delayed by all sorts of jealousies which sprang up against the foreigner, and which could only be overcome with the greatest difficulty. The Portuguese too put in a protest against the undertaking as infringing their rights, and their consul in Seville sought by promises and threatenings to move his faithless countryman from his purpose. But he remained immovable, and successfully overcame all the difficulties that lay in his way.

On the 20th of September, 1519, the squadron left San Lucan de Barremeda, a harbour at the mouth of the Guadalquiver, and on the 2nd of October it passed the Canary Islands. Then it took a westerly course, until on the 29th of November it reached San Agostinho, and thence went southward along the coast. In January, 1520, they passed the mouth of the Rio de la Plata, after which they were in a perfectly new region. Magalhaens then kept close to the coast, and narrowly examined every bay which offered the least possibility of a passage. On the 24th of March they reached the Gulf of St. Matthias, a few days later St. George's Bay, and at the end of the month a narrow inlet which is now called Port Desire (47° 50′ south latitude), but to which he gave the name of Puerto de los Patos (Goose Harbour), because on its coasts and on the island at its entrance there were an incredible number of penguins.

Meanwhile the southern winter had begun, and it was unwise to continue the voyage. But since there was a want of wood and water in Puerto de los Patos they went on until they found (49 degrees south latitude) a very convenient harbour, which received the name of St. Julian. Here a most dangerous conspiracy broke out. Whilst on the way Magalhaens had been obliged to place Juan de Cartagena, his second in command, in confinement, on account of mutinous conduct. Arrived at Port Julian he was set free by Quesada and Mendoza, and on Easter Monday three ships, the *San Antonio*, the *Conception*, and the *Victoria*, were in open rebellion against Magalhaens. Their captains accused him of having overstepped the royal orders and of having arrogated to himself unlawful powers. Magalhaens saw that all his authority would be at an end if he yielded, and that he should never succeed in accomplishing his dangerous and difficult undertaking with mutinous and untrustworthy crews. He adopted the sternest measures, a course to which his hard nature inclined him. He had Mendoza stabbed, whom he looked upon as the soul of the conspiracy. Edward Barbosa, a brother-in-law of the commander, immediately took possession of the *Victoria*, and Magalhaens himself, who with a wise foresight had placed himself with the two faithful ships at the entrance of the harbour, by a charge of artillery compelled the other two ships to surrender. Stern justice was exercised towards the heads of the conspiracy. Quesada was condemned, Mendoza's body was quartered, Cartagena and a priest who had taken part in the mutiny were landed on a barren shore. The sailors, whose services could not be dispensed with, were pardoned ; but the bloody scenes had greatly terrified them. Henceforth every one trembled before the stern inexorable man, and no one ventured to contradict him, much less oppose him.

Until August the winter detained the little fleet in its harbour of refuge. During that time Magalhaens became acquainted with the uncouth inhabitants of the land. They were very tall, though not giants, as for a long time they were reckoned on account of the exaggerated accounts of travellers. They wore as clothing the skins of some unknown animal sewn together (probably the huanaco, a kind of llama). Even their feet were covered with skins, and this circumstance gave them the name of Patagonians (the flat-footed), which they still bear. At first they were quite confiding, but an attack of the Spaniards, who wanted to carry off some of these strange people, soon made them suspicious and hostile.

The quarrels deprived the Spaniards of the opportunity of a close observation of the manners and customs of these Indians. Yet they noticed that their worship consisted of prayers to the devil.

The Patagonians have no settled dwellings, but wander about at pleasure, carrying with them huts, mere wooden frames covered with skins. They live mostly on raw flesh and a sweet root from which they prepare a kind of meal. Rats and mice, which were caught for them on board the ships, they devoured raw without even skinning them. They appeared insatiable. Six of them emptied a kettle of broth intended for twenty sailors, and of the two whom the Spaniards had captured each daily consumed a basket of biscuits, and could swallow at one draught half a bucket of water.

On the 24th of August they weighed anchor, and the four ships—one of the ships had been wrecked on an exploring excursion—pursued their way to the south. But the weather was so unfavourable that they were obliged to lie to for some weeks in the harbour of Santa Cruz. There Magalhaens informed the crew, to their great consternation, that if necessary he should continue his journey southwards as far as 75° south latitude. Fortunately, however, their patience was not tried so far, for October 21st, only three days after leaving the harbour of Santa Cruz, the ships rounded Cabo dos Virgines, and found the entrance to a broad channel running in a south-westerly direction.

It was the long-desired passage, which ever since has borne the name of its discoverer. It consists of a number of rocky chambers with narrow branching passages. Running to the north there are numerous deep fiords, and to the south narrow outlets into the sea.

Contrary winds hindered the forward progress of the ships. Even to this day a great knowledge of the place is necessary to steer safely through such a labyrinth. Cape Froward, the south point of America, divides the strait into two halves, of which one, the Atlantic, has a north-easterly direction, while the other runs to the north-west. In the former there is a refreshing prospect of green woods, but the latter is a narrow pass through rocks, some of them 7000 feet high, between which glaciers float down to the sea.

Arrived at Cape Froward, Magalhaens called a meeting of his principal sailors, and laid before them the question whether they thought it advisable to continue the voyage, since their provisions would only last three months. All voted to do so, since they knew that such was the decided desire of their chief. Only Stevam Gomez, the helmsman of the *San Antonio*, an experienced sailor, counselled that they should return to Spain, and come back the next year with a new fleet. But he was out-voted ; and Magalhaens angrily interrupted his representations with the words, "Enough of this. Even if we are compelled to eat the leather on the ships' yards, it shall not prevent my keeping my word with the Emperor."

A short time afterwards he sent the *San Antonio* to explore, and when it returned it did not find the rest of the ships at the appointed place. The crew at once demanded that they should be allowed to return home ; Gomez supported them in this demand, the captain was put in chains, and the vessel started on the homeward voyage. It arrived in Spain on the 6th of May, 1521, where the worst possible reports were immediately circulated about the disastrous results of the undertaking.

The desertion of his best ship was a blow to Magalhaens, but it did not shake his resolution. Without hesitation he pursued his way, and on the 27th of November arrived at the end of the strait, and to the great joy of all sailed out into the open sea.

In order to reach a warmer region, Magalhaens steered towards the north for nearly a month, and then sailed in a north-westerly direction. The equator was crossed on the 12th of February, 1521, and a few days later they reached a latitude of 13° north, where they remained. The voyage over the ocean lasted more than three months, and Magalhaens named it the Pacific, on account of the calms from which they suffered. All this time they only came to two inhabited islands, their course carrying them by an unlucky accident beyond the swarm of islands which are scattered over the tropical zone of the great ocean.

Oppressive heat rendered the sufferings of the almost exhausted voyagers very great, for the small supply of water which yet remained had long become bad, and its nauseousness was so great that it could scarcely be drunk. For weeks the only food that remained was biscuit, mouldy, decayed, and defiled by rats. At last they ate the leather with which the yards were covered to protect them from the friction of the ropes; but this was so hard that it had to be soaked for five days in the sea before it was soft enough to cook. And all this suffering was of course accompanied by the horrible scurvy, which caused the gums so to swell that those attacked by it could not take any nourishment.

At last there came an end to the terrible torture. On the 6th of March there appeared before the longing eyes of the starving seamen two green islands, which rose out of the waves like gardens, and the ships were soon surrounded by numerous boats full of natives, who brought them all kinds of fruits, and among others cocoanuts and bananas. These boats were distinguished by three-cornered mat sails and crooked poles sticking out right and left, which served to balance them. The naked natives, of an olive colour, who were distinguished by symmetry of form and had pleasant countenances, came on board the Spanish vessels with perfect fearlessness, and conducted themselves with the utmost ease.

Everything was new to them, and everything that pleased them—and what did not please them?—they immediately tried to appropriate. In vain the Spaniards many times cleared the decks of them. Any attempt at harshness so enraged them that they pelted the ships with stones and burning pieces of wood—bows and arrows they had none. A few cannon shots indeed put them to flight, but they came back at night, and under cover of darkness succeeded in cutting off one of the best boats and carrying it ashore. To recover this the Spaniards landed, gained possession of the boat, burnt down a village, and carrying off all the provisions they could find, weighed anchor. They gave to the group of islands the name of Ladrones or Thieves' Islands, which they still bear. The two islands visited by the Spaniards were probably Guahan and Santa Rosa, the two most southerly ones.

Three days only had their stay lasted. From the 9th to the 16th of March they pursued their way westward, till they reached the coast of an island covered with dark green woods and luxuriant vegetation. They soon discovered that it was one of a group of large and populous islands, to which the Spaniards gave the name of St. Lazarus Islands from the day on which they were found. The year 1542, however, when they were carefully examined by Ruy Lopez de Villalobas, the name was changed to the Philippines.

Magalhaens anchored cautiously in a retired bay on a small uninhabited island, where the sick sailors soon got well. After a week's rest the fleet again set sail, and soon reached the Island of Massana, now called Limasagua, whose inhabitants came out immediately to greet the strangers. Presents were exchanged, and such intimate relations were established that several Spaniards at the invitation of the King passed the night in his palace; and the assembled crews celebrated their Easter with great solemnity on shore. The inhabitants were Malays, for the most part entirely naked, but tattooed all over. The Spaniards were exceedingly disgusted at their habit of betel-chewing. All the islanders, without distinction of age or sex, were provided with pieces of a pear-shaped fruit, the areca nut, which, with the addition of a little lime, they wrap up in the betel leaves and put into their mouths. They never left off this occupation the whole day, and declared that they would die if they gave up the betel, which excites the heart.

Here Magalhaens learned that at no great distance lay the most fruitful and most beautiful island of the whole archipelago. It was named Zebu, and he crossed over to it on the 7th of April, accompanied by the friendly King of Massana. In the harbour of a considerable town lay several merchant-ships, and from one of these, which belonged to Siam, the King of Zebu learned that the new comers belonged to the mighty nation that had conquered Malacca. Impelled by fear, he sought to gain their friendship, treating them with the utmost courtesy. They were supplied with plenty of provisions, and splendidly entertained at the court of the King. So anxious was his brown Majesty to conciliate the Spaniards that he declared himself ready to embrace Christianity, and acknowledge the supremacy of the Spanish crown. On the 14th of April therefore he was baptised, with his wife and many subjects. The hideous idols were burnt, and crosses erected in their place, the whole country being proclaimed Spanish.

But the surprising speed of this revolution, which highly delighted the Spaniards, had yet its great dangers. A number of the inhabitants were very dissatisfied with the change, and particularly irritated at the ill-treatment of their gods. They retired into the little island of Mactan, which lay in the immediate neighbourhood of Zebu, and was the seat of a universal discontent.

When Magalhaens received news of this he determined, in spite of the advice of all judicious persons, to attack the malcontents, who, as he hoped, were not in a condition to hold out against the superior arms of the Europeans. In the night of the 26th and 27th of April he sailed with sixty well-armed people on three boats, on each of which there was a cannon, to Mactan, accompanied by the King of Zebu and a fleet of native boats.

In the first grey of the morning they saw the coast. As the shallowness of the water hindered the boats from approaching, the warlike leader sprang into the water, and with forty-nine of his companions waded to the shore. The overwhelming crowds of the enemy, reckoned at about 1500 men, fell upon the little troop, which were obliged to depend entirely upon their own exertions, as the cannons in the boats could do nothing at so great a distance, and Magalhaens had expressly forbidden the native auxiliaries to take any part in the battle, so sure was he of speedy victory.

But the wooden shields of the natives were some protection against the firearms of the Spaniards, whilst the latter were unable to stand against the furious attacks of their enemies, who swarmed on them from all sides with a perfect hail of arrows. Several of them fell, and Magalhaens himself was severely wounded in the leg by a bamboo spear. He ordered a retreat, which with most of his men became a flight, and by wading they succeeded in reaching the ships. Only seven or eight of the bravest remained with their general, who retired slowly, still fighting, towards the beach. The nearer they came to the water the more inpetuous became the attacks. Twice Magalhaens's helmet was struck off, and at last he was wounded by a lance-thrust in the forehead. He ran his spear through his antagonist, but could not succeed in drawing it out of his body again. He tried to draw his sword, but a severe blow disabled his arm. Almost at the same moment he was struck down by a lance, and once prostrate he was soon overwhelmed by the natives, and expired under countless wounds. Seven Spaniards fell with him, and the rest escaped to the ships. But the battle was continued in the water, and was only brought to an end by a discharge of cannon.

DEATH OF MAGALHAENS IN THE ISLAND OF MACTAN.

Thus the great seaman found a sad end among savages; after having so often braved the rage of the elements, and having been the first to open the mysterious gates of a great ocean, he fell a victim to over-confidence in the irresistible power of European arms and Spanish gallantry. He was not allowed to reap the reward of his great deed. Perhaps a gracious Providence wished to spare him the fate of Columbus.

His death was disastrous to the whole undertaking. Together with the belief in the invincibility of the strangers departed the Christian faith of the new converts; and when the victorious islanders threatened the King of Zebu with war if he remained in alliance with the enemies of their country, he was easily persuaded to betray those whom he had hitherto treated as his guests. He invited them to a feast on the 1st of May, for the purpose of giving them presents for his liege lord the King of Spain. Twenty-two Spaniards, under the lead of Barbosa, who had taken the command, accepted the invitation, and Barbosa's scornful taunt, that whoever feared might stay on board, impelled the gallant Serrao to accompany them. His mistrust was only too well founded. At the feast all the guests were put to the sword, Serrao only being spared. Him they dragged down to the shore bound, and offered to release him for a ransom of two cannons. But the Spaniards did not venture near, and hastily weighed anchor. The unhappy Serrao, whose entreaties for deliverance died away unanswered, was dragged back to the town, and there probably miserably murdered.

Deeply cast down, the sailors continued their way towards the south. The crews being so sorrowfully diminished in numbers, and many of the survivors being wounded, it was no longer possible to manage the three ships, and it was therefore determined to burn the worst of the vessels, the *Conception*, on the open sea. They then sailed west in search of the Moluccas, and touched the island of Palawan, whence they

steered towards the south.   Thus they reached the island of
Borneo, and entered the harbour of that name.

This was the seat of a powerful Sultan, who prepared a very
friendly reception for the exhausted Spaniards, and displayed
the greatest pomp before them.   Beautifully decorated boats
brought them all kinds of presents, especially provisions ;
among other things arrack, a spirit prepared from rice, with
which the Spaniards now for the first time became acquainted.
An embassy which they despatched to the court of the Prince
was conducted to the splendid palace by monstrous elephants
having wooden constructions on their backs.   Here they found
a richly-dressed bodyguard and numerous dignitaries ; but the
Sultan himself sat with his wife in a kind of box with a grat-
ing in front of it, and everything which the strangers wished
to say to him was passed from mouth to mouth up a perfect
staircase of officers until it reached the Prime Minister, who
transmitted it through a speaking-trumpet to the ear of the
Prince.   The reply came back in the same way.   After the
audience the ambassadors were well entertained, and then
conducted back to the ships.

The very active people over whom the Sultan ruled were of
Malay origin, and had recently become Mahometans.   They
are particularly good sailors, and singularly skilful traders,
and they also understand agriculture and the management of
cattle.   The principal articles of commerce produced by their
very fruitful land are cinnamon, ginger, sugar-cane, and camphor, and the brisk trade draws into their land foreign merchants in crowds, especially Chinese.

From the 8th to the 29th of July the Spaniards lay in the
harbour of Borneo, bartering for provisions and other necessaries.   But when, from mutual misunderstandings, they
became engaged in strife with the numerous merchant-ships,
they left the harbour in over-anxious haste, and sought farther
north a solitary bay, in which to carry out the repairs necessary

to their ships.   Here they examined carefully the plants and animals peculiar to the island, and amused themselves with hunting wild boars and turtles.   After some weeks they resumed their voyage in search of the Moluccas.   On their way they captured all the Malay boats that they met, and made those on board act as pilots.   At length, on the 8th of November, 1521, they anchored off the coast of the island of Tidor, more than two years after their departure from Spain.

Almansor, the Sultan of this island, immediately came on board, and made himself exceedingly obliging, even going so far as to take an oath of allegiance to the Emperor Charles V.   In this way he hoped to procure the assistance of the Spaniards against the Portuguese, towards whom he had a strong feeling of hatred.   It is even said, as the Spaniards heard afterwards, that Francisco Serrao, the discoverer of the Moluccas, and a close friend of Magalhaens, had been poisoned by Almansor.   In spite of there being no Portuguese at that time in Tidor, the Spanish sailors yet did not feel themselves secure, and freighted their ships as hastily as possible with cloves.   Fortune favoured them.   Pedro Affonso de Lourousa, the Portuguese factor on the neighbouring island of Ternate, probably influenced by a bribe, delivered over the goods he had stored up by him, and united himself with the Spaniards. He also procured for them alliances with the Sultans of Ternate and Batchang.   In a few weeks the ships were freighted, and they were just on the point of weighing anchor when a great leak was discovered in the *Trinidad*, the largest of the two ships, which made it necessary to delay the start. While the vessel was being repaired, the crew, consisting of fifty men, with their captain, Gomez de Espinosa, took up their dwelling on the island.   At last everything was made right, and they set sail towards the north-east, for they dared not approach the Portuguese possessions in India, where the landing of the Spaniards in the Moluccas was known, and precautionary measures had been taken.

Espinosa preferred to return across the wide ocean, hoping to find the harbour of Panama, in Central America, where for some years a Spanish Governor had ruled. But he waited vainly for a favourable west wind ; he sailed up to 42° north latitude, but all to no purpose. At last he was compelled to turn round ; and, dismasted and almost wrecked by a storm that lasted for five days, the *Trinidad* returned to the Moluccas. Here meanwhile the Portuguese had arrived with a considerable force, and there remained nothing for the unhappy Spaniards but to surrender to their rivals. The hard treatment which they received in prison and the unhealthy climate soon swept them off, and only four of them—three sailors and a chaplain—returned, in 1526, in a Portuguese ship, to their native land.

The *Victoria*, which quitted Tidor on the 18th of December, 1521, had a happier fate. On it there were forty-seven Spaniards and thirteen natives, principally prisoners who had been captured in the Malay boats. The captain was Juan Sebastian Elcano ; the helmsman, Francisco Albo. The pilots, who were taken from Tidor, conducted the ship first towards the south, until it had passed out of the Sunda Sea by the island of Timor into the open Indian Ocean. They then steered directly to the west, and after a prosperous voyage of three months, reached the south point of Africa. Violent contrary winds, however, hindered them from passing the Cape, and even after they had entered the Atlantic Ocean the patience of the crew was severely tried by continued bad weather. Their number was reduced by hunger and sickness to thirty, and these were so enfeebled that they stopped at St. Jago, in the Cape Verde Islands, to recruit.

As they artfully gave out that they had come from America, and were part of a fleet sailing to Hispaniola that had been driven out of its course by a storm, they met with a very friendly reception from the Portuguese colonists. They did not, however, exercise the caution necessary, and the latter soon found out the truth. The Governor of the town immediately acted according to the orders which King Emanuel had issued for all Portuguese colonies in case at any time they should be visited by people circumnavigating the globe. He seized a boat, and took the thirteen men that were in it prisoners, at the same time arming the ships lying in the harbour in order to overpower the *Trinidad.* But the watchful Elcano had carefully observed the movements on the shore, and without troubling himself about the fate of the prisoners, sailed away with all speed.

At last on the 6th of September, 1522, the ship reached the Spanish coast, and ran into the harbour of San Lucar de Barrameda, which it had left almost three years before. Of the sixty that had then manned it only thirteen returned, and they were utterly exhausted both in body and mind. They had long been given up as lost, and their return was looked upon as a miracle. They themselves considered it so, and immediately after their landing, true to the vow which they had made in the day of their distress, went barefooted and bareheaded in a solemn procession to the church Santa Maria del Antigua to offer their thanks to Heaven for their wonderful deliverance. The whole learned world was deeply interested in the successful accomplishment of the great undertaking of circumnavigating the globe. The most important result, with the exception of the discovery of the great ocean, was the curious fact that the voyagers had lost a whole day on their way. Many thought this an oversight, but the astronomer Contarini immediately showed that this was the natural consequence of their circuit from east to west, whereby they had accompanied the sun, and that in the same way the opposite movement from west to east would bring the gain of a day.

It was also thought a great thing that by this first circumnavigation of the globe a palpable proof of the spherical form of the earth was given.

The Emperor Charles summoned the bold sailors to his court at Valladolid, and there heard with the greatest interest their wonderful story. He rewarded each with a pension, and to Elcano he granted also a significant coat of arms, on which were displayed in a field of gold nutmegs and cloves, and a globe with the inscription, "Primus circumdedisti me."

But he had no intention of neglecting the political consequences of the expedition, the discovery of a western route to India and the seizure of the Moluccas. He fitted out a new squadron of seven sail, which left Seville on the 24th of July, 1525, in order to take the new way to the Spice Islands. The commander was Garcia de Loaysa, but under him Elcano again took part in the expedition. In making for the Straits of Magellan, one of the ships strayed to the south point of Tierra del Fuego, which was afterwards called Cape Horn. Of all the ships only the Admiral's, with a crew that had been sadly lessened by sickness, reached Tidor on the 31st of December, 1526, where the Spaniards established themselves and engaged in hot struggles with the Portuguese, who had built a fort at Ternate. A ship despatched to their aid by Cortes from Mexico, and which anchored at Tidor in 1528, was most welcome. But internal discord crippled the undertakings of the Spaniards. In 1529 Tidor was betrayed into the hands of the Portuguese, and the few Spaniards who survived were obliged according to the treaty to retire to another island. Here the struggle continued until the news of the treaty of 1529, by which the Moluccas were conceded to the Portuguese, reached them. There were only seventeen Spaniards who then (1534) returned home.

CHAPTER VI.

HERNANDO CORTES.

WHILE the Spanish ships were traversing the newly-discovered ocean, and striving with the Portuguese for their most
valuable possession in the Indian waters, nothing had been left
undone to increase the value of the Antilles. The wealth of
Hispaniola, though by no means inconsiderable—in 1520,
according to some authorities, 100,000 ducats are said to have
flowed into the royal coffers ; according to others, £300,000
—was yet not important enough to satisfy the expectations
of the adventurers who streamed into the land, and who
were therefore compelled to support themselves as planters.
Bishop Fonseca, the worthy President of the Council for
Indian Affairs in Seville, did all in his power to encourage the
emigration of industrious and steady colonists. Such received
free passages, were exempted from all taxes with the exception
of the tenth, and the piece of land which they pledged themselves to cultivate for four years then became their own
property. Only metals, jewels, and dyes the Crown reserved
to itself, and it made special arrangements with certain distinguished persons for the procuring of these. Upon all other
productions of the island it only placed a moderate duty.
But favourable as everything was to the emigration of an
industrious labouring class, there were few adventurers who
were inclined for a life of quiet work. A spirit of feverish
restlessness had come over the whole of Spain and had
penetrated to the very lowest stratum. With a greed for the
treasures of the New World was united a knightly joy in the

stirring and romantic dangers—a joy which had first been inspired by the wars with the Arabs, and which now could be satisfied in that land of wonders on the other side of the ocean. And, lastly, there was added to this the pious delusion that in fighting with, and indeed destroying, the heathen natives, the Spaniards were executing a work useful to the Church and well pleasing to God. A longing for wealth and the easy enjoyment of life, the desire for unheard-of adventures, and a fanatical missionary zeal are the striking characteristics of the thousands and tens of thousands who in a few years flocked into America. Only a few of them returned with anything like wealth to their native country ; the majority found their death in some foolhardy enterprise ; while many returned home beggars and infirm, having wasted their quickly-gained wealth in play and dissipation. The lives of these fortune-hunters oscillated between the greatest extremes ; to-day they were the possessors of rich plantations, lords of hundreds of brown slaves—all subject to every wish of their masters, and the objects of every kind of inhumanity—drunkards, and gluttons—men are even said at their feasts to have placed on their tables gold-dust instead of salt; to-morrow they were poor, in debt, in jail, threatened with lawsuits. But it was exactly men like these, reduced by misfortune and their own wickedness, that were always ready to engage in the most adventurous undertakings, and to follow the brave leader who could promise them deprivations, struggles, and adventures, and as their reward, riches and unbridled enjoyment. Thus Hispaniola was the starting-point of numerous expeditions which gradually covered the coasts and islands of Central America with Spanish colonies.

Under the governorship of Nicholas de Ovando, Hernan Ponce, who from the place of his birth was called de Leon, had colonised the island of Porto Rico, and after a bloody struggle had subdued the natives. The gold of the island—though it quickly proved to be not very great in quantity—and its fruitful plains, allured many Spanish settlers to it, while the natives rapidly died out. For the same reasons the coasts of Cuba, the insular nature of which was at last firmly established, was quickly covered with Spanish settlements, as soon as the knight Diego Velasquez (1511), with the consent of the Governor, Diego Columbus, had begun the colonisation of the island. Here the opposition of the Indians was but weak, and ended with the capture and execution of their leader, the Cacique Hatuey.

When Diego Columbus had victoriously established his claim to the governorship of Porto Rico, the conqueror, Hernan Ponce de Leon (1513), left the island, in order to procure for himself a new governorship in some of the yet undiscovered lands. The report of a wonderful medicinal spring in the land of Bimini which made the old young again made him direct his course towards the north-west. He discovered on this voyage a country to which he gave the name of Florida, but he did not find the wonderful spring, neither did he succeed in forming a settlement on the peninsula, both coasts of which he visited, because the warlike Indians opposed most vehemently every attempt to land.

On his return the Bahama Islands and the little groups off the coast of Florida were more thoroughly explored, but the whole expedition did not fulfil the hopes of Hernan Ponce. This want of success did not, however, discourage him. In the year 1515, by personally conducting his affairs in Castile, he obtained the appointment of Adelantado of Bimini, and in 1520 he sailed from Porto Rico with a stately squadron to found a settlement in Florida. This time the expedition was even more disastrous. A number of the Spaniards fell in battle with the Indians, and the rest Hernan Ponce was obliged to take back to Porto Rico, himself suffering from a wound which soon afterwards proved fatal.

Just as Porto Rico was the starting-place of expeditions intended for the north, Cuba was the point of departure for the unknown west. The immediate object of these expeditions was the slave trade, and it first led the Spanish sailors to the little islands in Honduras Bay. On the 1st of March, 1517, Hernandez de Cordova found himself opposite an unknown promontory, Cape Catoche (21 degrees north latitude), where the Spaniards first met traces of high civilisation. Populous towns with white houses, above which arose stately towers and mighty temples, with a stirring population, decently clothed and skilled in all kinds of arts and manufactures—this was a sight quite new and entirely unexpected by the Spaniards, who until now had only met with the naked children of nature. As far as Cordova continued his voyage along the coast to the west the same sight met his eyes, and in Compeche he learnt to know the superior gallantry of the natives and their skill in war, being forced by them after considerable loss to return to the ships. He left the coast, called by the natives Maya, but to which, mistaking a reply received from its inhabitants, Cordova gave the name of Yucatan. He returned by Florida to Cuba, where he soon after died. But the surprising information which he brought with him awoke in the Governor, Velasquez, the desire for discovery. Out of his own means he fitted out a squadron of four ships to obtain exact information about the newly-discovered lands, and gave the command to his nephew, the upright Juan de Grijalva.

On the 1st of May, 1518, he discovered south of Cape Catoche the important Island of Cozumel, with a surprisingly large number of temples, and after rounding the cape he proceeded along the whole north coast of Yucatan without entering into friendly intercourse with the natives until he reached the river Tabasco, the boundary of the great kingdom of Mexico, the size and importance of which was not

known to the Spaniards. The coast then turned towards the
north-west, and Grijalva followed it to a group of little islands
which, from their bloody altars, received the name of Isla de
Los Sacrificios.

The coast of the mainland, where the town of Vera Cruz
now stands, was then called Ulua, and was thickly peopled.
Here Grijalva succeeded in opening a friendly communication
with the natives and their rulers, and for some unimportant
trifles obtained great treasures of skilfully worked gold.
Faithful to the directions received from Velasquez, Grijalva
withstood the wish of his sailors to establish a settlement in
Ulao, and contented himself with despatching a ship, under
the subsequently famous Pedro de Alvarado, with the treasures
and important news to Cuba. He himself for a time continued
his voyage along the coast, which bent towards the north,
turning round at last at the mouth of the river Panuco
(22 degrees north latitude). The gap which was still left
between the utmost point of Grijalva's discoveries and the
west coast of Florida, traversed by Ponce de Leon, was filled
up in 1519 by Francisco de Garay, the assistant-governor of
Jamaica. The squadron sent out by him explored the whole
north coast of the Gulf of Mexico, and thus made clear that
the two peninsulas of Florida and Yucatan belonged to one
and the same continent. This was the last link in the long
chain of Central American discoveries.

When Grijalva, on the 30th of September, 1518, landed in
Havannah he was much surprised to receive a cool reception
from the Governor Velasquez. The capricious man blamed
him for having faithfully carried out his orders, and resisted
the proposal to found a colony. Immediately after Alvarado's
arrival he had begun preparations, and passing over Grijalva,
appointed another to the command of the undertaking. This
was a man exceptionally fitted to overcome the unheard-of
difficulties of his task and to carry it through in a brilliant

manner, but one whom Velasquez certainly would never have chosen if he had fully known his aspiring and independent spirit.

Hernando Cortes was born of a good family in the year 1485, at Medellin, in the province of Estremadura. He was designed by his father, a captain of the Spanish army, for a lawyer. He received a good education, and to complete his studies was sent to the University of Salamanca. But after two years, which the fiery youth spent in dissipation and riot, his parents saw that it would be impossible to make a lawyer of him, and let him follow the bent of his adventurous mind. So in 1504 he embarked for the New World, and after a very dangerous voyage landed at Hispaniola, where Ovando granted him a considerable repartimento (piece of land and the compulsory service of some Indians), and appointed him notary of the new town of Azua.

Some years passed away in the pleasant enjoyment of his possession, and the monotony of his life he varied by many affairs of honour and by the share which he took in the struggles with the Indians. In this way he became acquainted with Velasquez, whom he accompanied to Cuba in 1511. At first a favourite of the new Governor, he subsequently became hostile to him and headed a conspiracy to obtain the deposition of Velasquez. But Velasquez was on his guard and got possession of the person of Cortes. He is said even to have intended to have him executed, and was only deterred by the urgent entreaties of some important persons. After a time Cortes gave up his hostile designs against the Governor, and in order to evince his change of mind married the beautiful Catalina Xuarez, from Granada, who was under the protection of Velasquez. The reconciliation was a durable one. Cortes lived almost exclusively on the large estate granted to him near the harbour of St. Jago, in which he was invested with the dignity of Alcalde, and all the restless and ambitious wishes of his soul appeared to slumber. Then came Alvarado's news of the wonderful discoveries of Grijalva, and immediately all Cortes's love of adventure awoke.

By the mediation of good friends he procured from Velasquez the command of the expedition that was projected, and at once became unweariedly active in endeavouring to complete the preparation of his squadron, upon which he spent his whole wealth, and indeed plunged deeply into debt. But his hopes were almost shattered at the last moment. Doubts had arisen in the mind of Velasquez concerning the faithfulness of his former antagonist, and he meditated placing a more reliable person in command. Cortes no sooner suspected the design than with his half-completed squadron he immediately left the harbour of St. Jago (on the 18th November, 1518). In other harbours of the island he made up what was wanting, and in spite of the hurry of the preparations he completed everything with care and exactness, superintending all himself to the minutest detail. In spite of the prohibition of the irritated Governor the best soldiers joined the force of the rebel general, in whose energy and skill all placed the greatest confidence, and when he mustered his forces at the west point of Cuba, Cape St. Antonio, he found himself in command of eleven ships, 110 sailors, 503 soldiers, and 200 Indian servants.

The management of the ships was entrusted to Anton de Alaminos, who had accompanied Columbus, Cordova, and Grijalva. His chief strength lay in artillery, which consisted of ten heavy and four light cannon, and in a cavalry force of sixteen horse, which had been obtained at great expense, but proved afterwards of the greatest service. Full of confidence, Cortes weighed anchor on February 18th, 1519, and proceeded with his little force to the conquest of a powerful empire, which counted its subjects by millions.

In the centre of this kingdom lay the country of Anahuac, consisting of a large portion of the high tableland, which rises 7000 feet above the Atlantic Ocean. This territory had been in early times the seat of a people of high development —the Toltecs—who, from some unexplained cause, had entirely vanished, leaving as the only proofs of their existence the ruins of some venerable temples. New tribes poured into the empty land from the north—the savage Chichemecs, the more developed Acolhuans, and the warlike Aztecs. The second tribe built their capital, Tezcuco, on the east shore of the lake which lies in the middle of the high land, while the Aztecs found a site for their chief town in the lake itself— Tenochtitlan being built on piles in the marshy ground like a second Venice, and being only accessible from the shore by narrow causeways. Soon after the building of the town, which must have taken place about 1325, the two nations concluded an alliance offensive and defensive ; but the warlike Aztecs proceeded from conquest to conquest, and soon ruled both in the tablelands and also on the sultry shores of the two oceans.

The town of Tezcuco remained small, and its citizens sought their glory in peaceful acquisitions, by which their more powerful neighbours and allies profited. Both the states were kingdoms, the King being chosen by four electors from the brothers or nephews of his predecessor. His power was almost unlimited, his person sacred, and he was honoured almost as a god. But next to him was an aristocracy, with great landed possessions and a certain legal influence in the government. The rest of the population was divided into freemen and slaves. The chief occupation of every Aztec was war, to which he was brought up from his youth. A warlike disposition and an exaggerated sense of honour was cherished by the distinctions accorded to the brave ; and even the highly influential priestly order did their utmost to preserve uninjured the warlike tendencies of the national character.

The religious opinions of the Aztecs offer a strange mixture of lofty simplicity and gloomy superstition, of mild worship and bloody sacrifices; possibly the brighter side should be attributed to the old Toltecs, and the gloomy and savage to the natural disposition of the Aztecs. Besides one chief god, creator of the world, they acknowledged several hundred lesser gods, who were represented by ugly images. Amongst these, those who possessed most influence over the nation were the bloodthirsty god of slaughter, Huitzilopotchli—whose name the Spaniards changed into Vitzliputzli—and the god of war, Mexitli, the chief town, and afterwards the whole land, being named after his temple. In fearful contrast to the cheerful feasts, to the processions of women and children in honour of the mild deities, were the horrible human sacrifices offered to the god of slaughter. The unhappy victim was stretched alive upon the altar, and the chief priest, with a skilful hand, opened the breast and tore out the throbbing heart. In every town of the kingdom rose temples to Huitzilopotchli, and the number of human beings offered to him annually in the whole kingdom of the Aztecs is estimated at the lowest calculation as 20,000, while on special occasions, such as an accession or the dedication of a temple, it probably reached twice or three times that number.

Most of these victims were prisoners taken in war; and in order that there might be a sufficient number to offer, the Aztecs, who in battle always strove to make prisoners rather than to slay, annexed to their kingdom certain provinces—as, for example, Tlascala—in order in their ceaseless wars to have undisturbed territories in which to attend to their altars and sacrifices. What rendered the whole matter more revolting and horrible, was the custom of the priests to give back the body of the victim to the warrior who had taken him in battle, in order that he might feast on it with his friends. And this was no savage meal of hungry cannibals, but a banquet in which costly beverages and all kinds of dainty dishes were served up in golden vessels, and at which all the guests conducted themselves according to the rules of good manners. "Surely never," says Prescott, "were refinement and the extreme of barbarism brought so closely in contact with each other."

But this revolting picture must not make us blind to the extraordinary achievements of the Aztecs in almost every department of social life. Their well-cultivated land was covered with numerous towns built of stone. Among the public buildings the most remarkable were the temples, teocalli, consisting of immense flattened pyramids of earth, upon which were high towers. Well-kept roads united the towns, between which there was the liveliest traffic. For money were used quills full of gold-dust, pieces of lead, and cocoa-beans. The knowledge of the Aztecs in astronomy was not inconsiderable, their temples were adorned with sculptures, and, written in hieroglyphics, they possessed songs celebrating the deeds of their heroes, and also a history of their country.

Unfortunately, only a few of these valuable monuments have been saved from the fanatical wrath of the Spanish priests. With consummate skill the Aztecs made entire pictures from the down of humming-birds, and manufactured splendid garments and quilts out of feathers. The administration of the great kingdom was ordered to the minutest detail. The governors of provinces had to send to the capital by runners, who were relieved from station to station, reports of every important event in their jurisdiction, and in a few days received answers and commands by the same means. There were garrisons in most of the important towns, and there were special arrangements by which the militia of the whole kingdom could be drawn together at the shortest notice. For armour the Aztec warriors wore coats of quilted cotton, and the nobles had also breastplates of thin silver and magnificent garments of feathers. Their weapons were, besides slings, arrows and lances, the points of which, however, were not made of iron but of brass.

But the hour of destruction struck for this wonderful and singular civilisation when the Spaniards under Cortes landed on their coast. After its departure from Cape St. Antonio, the fleet steered first for the island of Cozumel, where the pious zeal of the Spaniards displayed itself by destroying the idols and obliging the people to submit to baptism. A more important event, however, was the adhesion of a man who made himself particularly useful as interpreter and adviser. Geronimo de Aguilar was a Spanish priest who had been appointed to the colony in Darien, and through shipwreck had been obliged to spend many years in Yucatan, where he had become perfectly familiar with the customs and speech of Maya. It was only on the payment of a considerable sum that the Cacique, to whose house he belonged, would consent to the departure of Aguilar, who, full of ardent gratitude, attached himself to his deliverer, Cortes. The expedition met with a new interruption in Tabasco. Here, where Grijalva had been received so hospitably, Cortes was treated in a most hostile manner, a change of feeling that was caused by the vehement reproaches with which the Tabascans had been overwhelmed by all their neighbours for their friendly reception of the strangers.

Cortes prepared for hostilities, and twice gave battle to the Indians, capturing and occupying their city. But the courage and pertinacity which the Indians opposed to the superiority of European arms excited the admiration of the Spaniards. Peace was made and an alliance concluded, and presents were exchanged. Among the twenty slaves whom the Cacique of Tabasco presented to Cortes there was one whose influence tended greatly to the successful issue of the enterprise. Marina, as the Spaniards called her, was the daughter of one of the principal Caciques in Anahuac, and had been sold by her heartless mother into slavery in Yucatan. She was therefore able to translate the language of the Aztecs into the Maya tongue, from which Aguilar could translate it into Spanish. Her beauty and rare gifts of mind enchained Cortes, and the Indian, through passionate love to the great adventurer, espoused his cause against her fatherland. She was soon able to speak Spanish, and rendered essential service to the Spaniards, who escaped many serious dangers by following her counsel. Thus her name is closely united to that of Cortes, and is still mentioned with honour in the land of Mexico.

On the 20th of April, 1519, the little fleet anchored opposite the island of San Juan de Ulua, where now Vera Cruz stands. With the friendly assistance of the inhabitants, they soon encamped, and learned that they were in the kingdom of the mighty Montezuma, and that Teotlili, the Governor of the province, dwelt near. He soon made his appearance with a great train, greeted the strangers with much courtesy, offered them presents, and inquired the reason of their visit. Cortes declared himself the ambassador of a mighty Prince on the other side of the sea, and asked for a personal audience of the Emperor Montezuma, at the same time offering presents. Teotlili promised to present the request, and accordingly sent it immediately to Tenochtitlan, together with pictures of the wonderful strangers.

Montezuma had been King of Anahuac since 1502. Belonging to the priestly class, he had given before his election many proofs of his bravery and warlike skill, and the altars of the god of slaughter had never bled with more numerous offerings than during his reign. But, in spite of many beneficent institutions, he had not been able to retain the love of his subjects; his ostentatious manner of living and his arrogance had estranged from him the minds of the people in his capital, while those in the provinces were embittered by the increasing pressure of an excessive taxation. The news of the landing of the Europeans made the deepest impression upon him. It reminded him of an old saying, according to which Quetzalcoatl, the god of the air, and the great benefactor of Anahuac, exiled by the hatred of the other gods, had embarked from the shores of the Atlantic, promising to return, with his descendants, after the lapse of centuries, when a good time would begin for the whole of Anahuac. The Aztecs faithfully looked for the return of this benevolent god, and had exactly at that period discovered different appearances in the heavens which they took for signs of the approach of the happy event. Just then landed on the Atlantic shores from a great ship men who, from the white colour of their skins, from their curly hair and long flowing beards, resembled the pictures of the expected god ; and they bore thunder and lightning with them. Were they the promised descendants of Quetzalcoatl ? Was he himself among them ? These questions occupied the minds not only of the lower people, but also of the pious Emperor ; and they gave to his intercourse with the perplexing strangers a character of indecision which Cortes well knew how to take advantage of. So the remarkable tradition contributed much to the Spanish conquest.

After long consideration Montezuma chose the most ill-judged course. He offered the Spaniards presents of immense worth, but at the same time forbade them to come to the capital, and bade them leave the kingdom. Of course, the more the boundless wealth of the land was displayed before the greedy eyes of the Spaniards the less was it to be expected that they would do this, and therefore Cortes replied that he could not think of returning to his own land until he had delivered the messages of his King personally to Montezuma. Then there followed a new report to Tenochtitlan, and then came more presents and an answer like the first. But when the Spaniards made no preparations to evacuate the land, and indeed said that they had come to induce the Aztecs to exchange their shameful idolatry for the worship of the one true God, the native dignitaries withdrew and broke off all intercourse with the foreigners. At the same time the natives received a command to cease providing the strangers with food.

At this opportune moment, the explorer whom Cortes had despatched returned with the information that they had found a spot farther to the north much better suited for an encampment. Thither Cortes determined to remove, but he first prevailed upon the army to constitute itself a colony and to appoint its own magistrates. Before these Cortes appeared with every mark of respect and solemnly renounced the powers which he had received from Velasquez. As was to be foreseen these new magistrates begged him to retain the offices of Captain and Justicia Mayor, and to govern the colony that was to be founded in the name of the King of Spain. By this prearranged comedy Cortes made himself completely independent of the Governor of Cuba, and henceforth derived his power from the choice of the colonists. Nothing was wanting but the ratification of the King to make him equal with Velasquez. The Spaniards now left the desert in which they had hitherto been encamped and marched northwards through a garden-like region, while the fleet sailed along the coast. On the way Cortes and his army paid their promised visit to Cempoalla, the cacique of the capital of. Totonakis. They found a flourishing well-built town of some 20,000 inhabitants, and in it met with a friendly reception. Very soon the sharp eye of Cortes discovered that the Totonakis, recently subdued by the Aztecs, were discontented with their government, and might become valuable allies in the struggle that lay before him. In answer to his inquiries, after some reserve, the cacique broke out into violent complaints of the oppression of Montezuma, and was evidently pleased at his promise to protect him from all injustice. He accompanied the Spaniards to a town but a few miles distant, named Chiahuitzla, close to which lay the ground for the new settlement, which received the name of Villa Rica de la Vera Cruz. Suddenly there appeared five Aztec nobles to demand the usual tribute from the Totonakis. The presence of the Spaniards and the friendly terms on which they were with the natives excited their anger and they threatened them with severe punishment. Then there arose a disturbance, probably at Cortes's instigation, and the ambassadors were made prisoners and given up to the Spaniards. Thus a thorough breach was made with the Aztecs, and the Totonakis found themselves dependent on the protection of the Spaniards. Exceedingly pleased at this event, Cortes sought now to ward off the danger on the other side. He treated the captive Aztecs with peculiar gentleness, and allowed them secretly to escape. The clever though double policy of Cortes was perfectly successful. Montezuma, who at the first news of the insurrection had given way to the wildest anger, was appeased by the report of the ambassadors.

There soon appeared in the Spanish camp a new embassy with costly presents, as thanks for the mild treatment of the captives. At the same time Montezuma announced that, out of respect to Cortes, he would defer the severe punishment of the rebellious Totonakis until after his departure, which must now soon take place. Cortes received the presents with thanks, and answered that the visit which he intended to pay to the Emperor in Tenochtitlan would no doubt remove all misunderstanding between them—an answer which evidently caused annoyance to the Aztec ambassadors.

Meanwhile the new town grew and promised to form a useful point whence to look for support in all future undertakings.   The people in authority were active, and the garrison that was to remain behind, under the command of the trustworthy Juan de Escalante, was soon chosen.   But before he started, Cortes wished to have done everything possible to give his power weight.   He therefore sent a ship under the conduct of Alaminos to Spain, in order to petition King Charles to approve of all that he had already done and to ratify his appointment to the office of governor.   In order to secure a favourable hearing, Cortes added his own share to the royal fifth of the spoil, and as at his instigation every one did the same, the whole treasure that had been collected was shipped off for the royal treasury.   Certainly a most striking proof of the influence which he exercised over the minds of his soldiers.

Drawing together the army for the march to Cempoalla he gave the celebrated order to destroy the fleet that lay before Vera Cruz.   The unsuitableness of the ships was merely an excuse, Cortes really wished by this measure to take away every hope of returning to Cuba in case of mishaps, and of compelling his followers to place their trust entirely in their own bravery and the wisdom of their leader. At first indeed there was a threatening of mutiny, but when Cortes appeared among the conspirators and placed before them his reasons, they all cheered him and demanded to be led to Mexico.   After the Totonakis had been induced by means both of constraint and persuasion to give up the bloody service of their gods and come over to Christianity in masses, nothing in the interior could stand against them.

Cortes set out on the 16th of August, 1519.   His army consisted of 400 infantry, 15 horse-soldiers and pieces of artillery, and he was accompanied by 1300 Totonakis and 1000 burden-bearers.   He also took with him forty of the principal persons from Cempoalla as hostages and guides.   Their way led them through the woods of the Tierra Caliente.   After a gentle ascent they reached on the second day the town Xalapa, and then saw before them the rugged range of mountains, with its snowy peaks, which yet remained to be climbed. With difficulty the army wound its way up the passes, suffering much from the alteration in climate, which changed from unbearable heat to cold rain and snow. When the height of 7000 feet was reached the scenery became more agreeable. Hills and low ranges of mountains alternated with green woody valleys and well-cultivated plains. The climate was refreshing.

Passing through several towns, which received them more or less hospitably—none, however, opposing them—the army approached the borders of the little state of Tlascala, which for several hundred years had successfully defended its liberty against the encroachments of the Aztecs, by whom it was surrounded. Almost overcome by numbers, cut off from all the necessaries of life—for half a century they had been deprived of cocoa, cotton, and salt—they still obstinately refused to submit to their mighty neighbours, against whom they entertained an invincible hatred. They were a stalwart agricultural people, earning their bread by the sweat of their brow from the soil of their little fatherland, and unceasing wars had rendered them remarkable for their power of self-control. Their speech and manners resembled those of the Aztecs, but were ruder and less developed. Their little state was not a monarchy, but was divided into four orders, dependent upon one another. The unity of the whole was maintained by means of a great council which decided all the most important matters, and in which the heads of the four orders played the chief part.

To this council Cortes sent forward some Totonakis to ask liberty to march through the country, and to invite the people to join him in his attack against their old enemy the Aztecs. But contrary to all expectation, in the council a feeling of mistrust prevailed with regard to the strangers, who were reproached with having cast down the gods of the people, and it was decided to oppose them. The young general Xicotencatl was accordingly instructed to open the war with the Spaniards, who had already passed the great wall which formed the east border of Tlascala. Thereupon began a struggle more obstinate than the Spaniards had hitherto experienced in America.

It was only after the utmost exertions and considerable loss that they succeeded in forcing their way through a rocky pass. Then the enemy yielded to the cavalry and formidable artillery, and retreated in perfect order. Cortes established himself cautiously at the mouth of the pass, and after some days accepted a second battle offered him in the open field by the great army of the Tlascalans, numbering full 50,000 men. The shock of these masses was fearful, and had it not been for the destructive effect of the artillery upon the thick ranks of the enemy the little handful of Spaniards would certainly have been overwhelmed. The struggle lasted for four hours, and only after repeated assaults did the enemy beat a retreat, in which Cortes left them unmolested. He returned to his secure position, and awaited the result of a second embassy which he despatched to the council.

But it was not until after the failure of a night attack that the overtures of the Spanish general were accepted. At last peace was brought about. On September 23rd followed the public entry into the town. The strangers were received as welcome guests, and by a warm response endeavoured to show that all hostility was banished from their minds. Tlascala acknowledged the supremacy of the Spanish King, and promised to support Cortes in his march against Tenochtitlan. Cortes, at the advice of the sagacious Father Bartolomé de Olmedo, desisted from his endeavour to introduce Christianity, fearing to shake a friendship of such recent date.

During their stay at Tlascala a new embassy appeared from Montezuma. He had at first witnessed with pleasure the march of Cortes against Tlascala, hoping that the sturdy mountaineers, who had so gallantly resisted the Aztecs, would overcome the strangers. But the news of the victories of the Spaniards and their alliance with the Tlascalans had changed this joy into dismay, and this time the messengers brought a very warm invitation to Tenochtitlan. This sudden change of mind, with the earnest request to come by Cholula, together with the warnings of the rough Tlascalans, excited Cortes's suspicions. But he contrived to conceal them, and in spite of all the counsels of the Tlascalans, who sent with him 6000 soldiers, began his march to Cholula.

This town in the eyes of all the inhabitants of Anahuac was peculiarly sacred; there Quetzalcoatl had reigned beneficently; there stood his famous sanctuary, the most gigantic teocalli of the whole land; there, in over 200 temples, were more than 6000 men yearly offered up to the bloody Aztec gods. The inhabitants of the town, numbering about 150,000, had the reputation of being very highly educated, wanting in courage, but not, as the Tlascalans asserted, in cunning and deceit.

The Spaniards, who were very warmly received, were astonished at the order and cleanliness of the streets, in which the traffic was very great. They were quartered in the court-yard of a large temple and abundantly supplied, while their Tlascalan allies, not to arouse any hostile feeling, had formed a camp outside the town.

But after a few days the conduct of the Cholulans changed and manifested coldness and dislike. Suspicion again awoke in Cortes's mind, but all inquiries were vain, until Marina, who had insinuated herself into the confidence of a cacique's wife, solved the riddle. She discovered a fearful conspiracy against the Spaniards, who on their departure were to be attacked and cut off in the streets. Already all kinds of missiles had been collected on the flat roofs, the side streets had been stopped by ditches and stakes, and an army of 20,000 Aztecs had been drawn together before the town, who were to advance at the first signal. Such were the orders of Montezuma.

Cortes, who at first was utterly perplexed at so great a danger, soon recovered his presence of mind, and determined to forestall the treacherous act by a fearful blow. Under the pretext of immediate departure he collected several thousand of the bravest Cholulans in the court of the temple in which he was living, and had them all cut down at a given sign. Then began a desperate attack of the people on the Spaniards, who made sorties and drove back the raging crowd. When the Tlascalans, according to agreement, forced their way into the town and fell upon the enemy in the rear, the victory was decided. Slaughter and rapine swept the beautiful city ; some of the streets and the most important temples, in which the Cholulans desperately defended themselves, were set on fire, and it seemed likely that the whole city would be destroyed, when Cortes caused the battle to cease and offered the vanquished mercy. Order was soon restored, but Cholula had for ever lost its splendour.

This bloody act spread far and wide terror and superstitious fear of the strangers, who were not only invincible in battle, but could be injured by no treacherous deceit. Montezuma trembled on his throne. He sent again an embassy to the Spanish camp with rich presents, and he asserted his innocence of the treachery : the troops had been only assembled to suppress an insurrection ; and as for the treacherous Cholulans, they had only got their deserts. Cortes appeared to believe in Montezuma's innocence and started for Tenochtitlan. The nearer they came to the seat of the Emperor the more carefully did they take every precautionary measure. They did not relax their caution for a moment, but marched in perfect readiness for battle.

At last the heights were reached from which opened upon them the beautiful view of the lakes of Mexico. With delighted astonishment the travellers saw at their feet the glittering sheets of waters, with innumerable white towns and villages lying on their shores, and in the centre the stately imperial city with its imposing palaces and pointed temples. Above it rose the lofty mountain of Chapoltepec with its strongly fortified castle. All around stretched wide plains of garden and arable land, interspersed with oak and cedar woods, which grew thicker away from the city up the beautiful slopes of the hills.

"And even now," says Prescott, "when so sad a change has come over the scene; when the stately forests have been laid low, and the soil, unsheltered from the fierce radiance of the tropic sun, is in many places abandoned to sterility; when the waters have retired, leaving a broad and ghastly margin white with incrustation of salts; while the cities and hamlets on their borders have mouldered into ruins,—even now that desolation broods over the landscape, so indestructible are the lines of beauty which nature has traced on its features, that no traveller, however cold, can gaze on them with any other emotions than those of astonishment and rapture."

The admiration, however, excited in the minds of the Spanish soldiers soon yielded to fear at the thought of the disproportion between their small force and the countless numbers of this brave and powerful people, whose beautiful home they had come in insolent confidence to conquer, and it needed all the forcible eloquence of their leader to reassure their fainting courage. With redoubled caution, by slow marches they descended into the populous plain, whose inhabitants, full of curiosity but in no hostile spirit, crowded to see the strangers. Once more came messengers from Montezuma, showing that the superstitious Emperor was at an end of all his resources, and begged them earnestly not to enter the capital, and promised in return for this concession to give the general and his captains enormous sums of gold, and to pay a yearly tribute to their King.

Thus, tortured by blind fear, did the Prince of a mighty empire humble himself before a handful of adventurers, not having yet tried the strength of the forces at his command. Truly the superstition and weakness of Montezuma were the best allies of the bold Spaniard, who without them had scarcely succeeded in his rash enterprise. Of course Cortes, with the unmoved composure which had already many times stood him in good stead, insisted upon entering, and Montezuma found himself obliged to consent. The Emperor's nephew, Cacama, King of Tezcuco, appeared to welcome the strangers, and when the Lake of Chalco was crossed by a great causeway, Cailkahua, Montezuma's brother, met them and conducted them to his royal city, Iztapalapa, in the palaces and far-famed gardens of which they found a splendid reception.

Iztapalapa lay on the shores of the lake, and at the mouth of the gigantic causeway leading across the lake to the capital, which appeared to float on the clear waters. From this point began on November 8th, 1519, the entry of the Spaniards. For hours the little army marched along the stupendous causeway, formed of gigantic blocks of stone and broad enough to allow ten men to ride abreast. Along each side lay hundreds of boats in which the curious Indians watched the strange procession. After a long ceremonious welcome from Aztec chieftains, the Spaniards passed by a wooden drawbridge into the town, at the entrance of which the Emperor himself met them. Surrounded by a crowd of the most illustrious of the land appeared the glittering litter borne by nobles. Over the head of the sacred person of the ruler four chiefs bore a canopy formed of brilliant feathers,

MEETING OF CORTES AND MONTEZUMA.

adorned with jewels and mounted in silver. Beneath it was Montezuma, a majestic man of about forty years of age, slight in figure, and with earnest dignified features.

On arriving near the royal litter Cortes dismounted and approached the Prince respectfully, who on his part, supported by his brother and nephew, rose and advanced some steps to meet the Spaniard. The strange interview, which one had tried as hard to avoid as the other had to procure, was short and formal. Montezuma bade the Spaniard welcome and promised him a friendly reception, and Cortes returned his thanks and hung round the Emperor's neck a chain of bright-coloured cut glass, which was esteemed of value in Mexico. He was about to embrace Montezuma but was prevented by those around him, who considered such an act a desecration of the imperial majesty. Then Montezuma returned to his litter over carpets spread by his retinue, that the feet of the ruler might not be defiled by the earth. All bent low in the presence of the monarch, and many in the excess of their reverence fell with their faces on the ground. Slowly the royal procession departed, while the Spaniards marched with flying colours and martial music into the town.

The great street along which the procession passed was broad and often crossed canals, by which the whole town was intersected, and upon which a very large traffic was carried on by means of flat boats. Thus the markets of the capital were provided from the surrounding country. The houses along the street were mostly built of a red stone found in the neighbourhood, and presented generally a very stately appearance. All had flat roofs, which were turned into fragrant gardens by the numerous flowers growing in pots. Among the houses of the citizens appeared the great palaces of the nobles, covering mostly a great space, and enclosing a a shady court with cooling fountains. Close by were gigantic temples with their strange pyramids, and from the open spaces

could be seen the snowy summits of the neighbouring mountains looking down upon the town. The splendid sight was
enlivened by the immense crowds of people surging through
the streets to enjoy the unwonted spectacle, few of whom had
any foreboding of the disastrous future in store for the Aztec
people through these iron-clad strangers. And as these
marched on in exulting pride, the brilliant variety of strange
sights which passed before their eyes made an ineffaceable
impression upon their rough minds.

A gigantic temple of the god of war was appointed for their
residence, and there Montezuma with exquisite courtesy again
appeared to bid them welcome. The prudence of Cortes
soon changed it into a fortress, the entrance of which was
covered by the cannon, and his soldiers being forbidden on
pain of death to leave the temple without permission, he
went himself the next morning with a slender retinue to
return the Emperor's visit. The palace to which he was conducted consisted of a great number of low stone buildings
spread over a very large space. In the courts played fountains of bright water brought in pipes from Mount Chapoltepec, the whole town being supplied by the same means.
The enormous rooms were lined with carved sweet-smelling
wood, the floors were covered with mats made of palm leaves,
tapestry of feather work adorned the walls. The air was
laden with choice scents, and the Spaniards half-intoxicated
were led from room to room until they found themselves in
the presence of the Emperor, who received them surrounded
by his chief nobles. The conversation which ensued, in
which Cortes immediately set forth the truths of the Christian
religion without making any impression on the mind of the
King, is chiefly important for the declaration of Montezuma
that he was ready to acknowledge the supremacy of the King
of Spain—a declaration of which Cortes soon made use
against the Prince. Overwhelmed with presents, the Spaniards

were graciously allowed to depart. The people were very
cordial to their Emperor's guests, letting them saunter unmolested through the streets and markets. Cortes in Montezuma's company even ascended the famous temple of the
god of slaughter, and enjoyed the wonderful view over the
whole valley of Mexico—a refreshing contrast to the blood-
stained ground, the hideous idols and the altar awaiting new
victims. With difficulty Cortes restrained his zeal for the
conversion of the people, knowing it to be in vain. The
Spanish soldiers were allowed to visit in troops the wonders
of the capital—the provisions supplied to them at Montezuma's expense were excellent. Yet in spite of all this
anxiety filled the hearts of all, and chiefly of the general.
How could they leave the great city ? By a secret departure
or in open day with the knowledge of the Emperor ? And
was it advisable to leave the city ? Would it not be giving
up the advantage they had gained, and destroying the prestige
which their success hitherto had won for them ?

To these considerations Cortes put an end by a decision which
accorded with his daring nature. He chose the boldest way,
thus putting the finishing stroke to his hitherto uninterrupted
success. He determined to seize as hostage the sacred person
of his host, and thus through the Emperor himself impose
upon the land the Spanish rule. A pretext was soon found
in the conduct of an Aztec chieftain who had attacked the
Spanish garrison of Vera Cruz. Several Spaniards had fallen
in the battle — Escalante himself, the commander of the
fortress, had died of his wounds, and the victorious chief had
aroused the country far and wide against the strangers. For
this Montezuma was to be made responsible. Cortes at an
audience demanded the punishment of this chief, and when
Montezuma had consented to this, he requested further that
until the matter was settled the Emperor would remove his
residence to the palace inhabited by the Spaniards. This

demand excited the Prince to the utmost. "Has anybody ever heard such a thing," he cried, flaming with anger, "as a great Prince like me willingly leaving his palace to become a prisoner in the hands of strangers? And even were I to consent to such a humiliation, my subjects would never agree to it!" All persuasion, all remonstrances were in vain, and the utmost which Cortes could obtain was a promise from Montezuma to deliver to the Spaniards as hostage one of his children—a promise which did not satisfy him. Two hours passed in these fruitless negotiations, when the Knight Velasquez de Leon exclaimed in wild impatience, "Why do we waste words on these savages? We have gone too far to retreat now. Let us seize him, and if he resists cut him down with our swords."

When the meaning of these threats had been explained by Marina to the Emperor in answer to his anxious inquiry, all power of resistance seemed gone. He felt that an irresistible fate was opposed to him to which he must bend. Deadly pale he arose, and almost inaudibly declared himself ready to follow the Spaniards. His litter was immediately prepared, and all arrangements made for his removal. When the people saw their Prince in the midst of the strangers passing to their residence, a loud outcry arose, and attempts were made to stop the procession by violence. But Montezuma himself interposed. If the Spaniards knew his weakness, his people should not guess his shame, and so he found strength to quiet the people, and to assure them that he was going of his own free will to visit the Spaniards. The people immediately dispersed. This event itself proved how serviceable the instrument would be with which Cortes intended to subdue the land.

In the quarters of the Spaniards the unhappy Prince was received with an ostentatious show of honour. The best rooms were chosen for him, and furnished with the splendour to which he was accustomed. A numerous court attended him wherever he went, and in his manner of life there was no alteration. All affairs of government continued to be conducted in his name, and the etiquette by which his sacred person was protected was rigorously observed by the Spaniards. Montezuma submitted to his fate without murmuring. He watched with interest the military exercises of the Spaniards, spoke to them individually, and gave them all proofs of his goodwill and generosity. He took a special liking to some of the Spanish knights, playing at the national games with them, and by his friendly amiable behaviour won the affection of his gaolers. For that he was a prisoner he could not conceal from himself, though he sought carefully to hide it from his Aztecs. A strong Spanish guard was posted in his anteroom, and admission to his person could be obtained only through the general. In the meantime Cortes, by Montezuma's commission, examined the captive chieftain and condemned him to be burnt. The sentence was carried out on the unhappy man, forsaken by his own master, in the court of the palace, the imperial arsenals being plundered at Cortes's command to form the pile, that no weapons might be forthcoming in case of a rising. During the execution Cortes put the captive Emperor in fetters that he might in this way, he said, atone for his share in the attack made on the Spaniards.

This unexpected disgrace deprived the unfortunate man of speech. Bursting into tears he submitted without resistance, and it was touching to see how tenderly his attendants held his feet in their arms, trying by soft cloths to mitigate the pressure of the cold iron. After a short time the chains were removed, but the whole proceeding had broken the Emperor's proud heart. Cortes thought he had by this time sufficiently humbled his prisoner, and offered him a free return to his royal palace, but Montezuma sorrowfully refused. How

could he after such humiliation return to the throne of his
fathers? And how would he be received by the proud nobles who
esteemed before all the glory and greatness of their country?
He preferred to remain in captivity, which in future became
much milder.   He visited the principal temple to perform his
devotions ; in the ships built by the Spaniards he made trips on
the lake, and several times hunted in his parks. . Of course a
Spanish general always accompanied him, but he never made
any attempt to escape from his miserable position.   Indeed he
took the part of the Spaniards against the Aztecs in every
attempt made by them to shake off the foreign yoke.   Cortes
was warned by him of the rising planned by the chiefs of the
land, and he helped to bring the King of Tezcuco, the head of
the conspiracy, into the power of the Spaniards, by whom
he was kept in close confinement.   At last he determined
solemnly to take the oath of homage to the King of Spain.
The ceremony was performed before a great assembly of
nobles whom he desired to follow his example.   As sign of
their submission they brought gold and articles of value in
such quantities that the royal fifth, which was conscientiously
deducted, amounted to 32,400 ounces of gold—according to
the present value nearly £130,000.   But most earnestly
did Montezuma defend himself from the impatient desire of
the Spaniards that the chief temple should be cleared for the
public exercise of their religion, and he warned them plainly
of the unfavourable impression which such an insult to their
religious feelings would excite in the people.

But again and again the Spaniards repeated their demand,
and at last an agreement was come to by which one of the
towers of the Teocalli was given up to them for their worship.
They immediately took away the idols, cleansed the space of
the blood of the sacrifices, and erected an altar on which they
placed an image of the Virgin.   Their religious zeal was now
satisfied, and with pious devotion they saw the cross shine

in the highest place of the capital. But the truth of Montezuma's warnings immediately showed itself. The friendly intercourse between the people and the Spaniards was exchanged for a cold reserve, and by the Emperor's own mouth Cortes was informed that the whole land was preparing to revenge the injury done to the gods.

While he was engaged in preparing to meet this expected insurrection, bad news reached him from the coast. There a squadron of eighteen ships had arrived, sent by Velasquez from Cuba to chastise his rebellious general, and assert his rights to the rich land of Mexico. To the command of this fleet he had named a Castilian nobleman, Pamphilo de Narvaez, entrusting him with an army of 900 men, including eighty horsemen and eighty musketeers, with a good store of cannon.

Trusting in this powerful force, Narvaez, who had landed on April 23rd, 1520, at San Juan de Ulua, was full of rash confidence, which was not shaken by the news of the great successes gained by Cortes. But his soldiers were dazzled by the glamour which such heroic deeds had cast over the name of the great warrior, and by the news of the riches which had fallen to the share of Cortes's army.

Comparing the friendliness, generosity, and martial talents of Cortes with the arrogance, niggardliness, and blind self-confidence of Narvaez, a feeling of detestation arose in them towards their commander. Cortes took advantage of this feeling. He hastily determined to quit Tenochtitlan with only seventy men, leaving behind him a garrison of 140 under Pedro de Alvarado, whom, on account of his long fair hair and majestic mien, the Mexicans called Tonatink, that is, the sun. In Cholula Cortes met with reinforcements, and with a little army of 266 men he surprised his rival on a rainy night in Cempoalla. After a short conflict Narvaez was taken prisoner, and his troops joined Cortes, hoping under his standard to reap honour and gold. Thus the great danger was averted, and the Aztecs, who had hoped that the strangers would destroy one another, saw the hated Malinché—so they called Cortes—return to the capital at the head of an army that had been increased threefold.

Here meanwhile the threatened disturbances had broken out, and the brave but incautious Alvarado had hastened the outbreak by a useless slaughter in which the noblest of the people had fallen victims. He despatched messengers to summon Cortes, and inform him of the extreme danger threatening the weak garrison. By forced marches the latter reached the capital on the 24th of June, 1520. But the streets were utterly deserted, and a mysterious silence rested over the whole city. In order to avert a renewal of the strife, Cortes set Montezuma's brother, Cuitlahuatzin, at liberty; but in this courageous and able Prince he gave the insurgents exactly the leader whom they needed. Under his command all the flower of the Aztec race assembled, and after a few days began a desperate attack upon the Spanish camp. For several days the Spaniards had the greatest difficulty in preventing the enemy from forcing an entrance, and the thousands whom they struck down with their firearms and swords were immediately replaced by fresh battalions, who rushed upon the fortifications with the utmost contempt of death. Only at night had the besieged any rest, and the frightful struggle was renewed every morning. Many were soon disabled, and the complete blockade made a famine imminent.

In this distress Cortes turned to Montezuma, and begged his intercession. Although convinced of the utter uselessness of such a step, the Emperor allowed himself to be persuaded, and dressed in his most magnificent robes, ascended the tower of the Palace. The noise immediately ceased, the raised lances fell, and the Aztecs gazed with awe at their imprisoned Emperor. There was a silence as of death when Montezuma began to speak. But when he desired that they should allow his friends, as he called the detested foreigners, to depart in peace, a storm of displeasure overwhelmed the base cowardly ruler, who had stooped to become the slave of a foreign oppressor, to whom he was willing to surrender even his land and his people. Curses were hurled at him, and a hail of arrows and stones directed against the person of the Prince to whom but a short time before his subjects had offered almost divine honours. Hit by a stone on the forehead, the unhappy man sank down, and was borne back by the Spaniards into the Palace, while his subjects, horrified at their own deed, immediately dispersed.

In vain did Cortes strive to cheer the broken-hearted monarch. He lay utterly speechless, and refused to have his wound cared for. He was unwilling to survive the injury done to him by his own people. When the Spaniards saw that his end was near they tried to induce him to embrace Christianity, but in vain. Only once did he open his lips in order to beg Cortes to commend his children to the favour of the Spanish King. He died in the arms of a few faithful followers, who had remained with him, on the 30th of June, 1520, at the age of 41, after having reigned for eighteen years, and having been for three-quarters of a year the prisoner of the Spaniards.

His death was a great loss to the Spaniards; with him they lost all influence over the Aztec people, whose wrath now knew no bounds. Storm followed storm, and the wearied Spaniards saw the moment approaching when they must be overpowered by numbers. There could be no doubt of the fate that awaited them. "At last the gods have given you into our hands," was the cry of the Mexicans. "Huitzilopotchli has long been looking for his victims. The altar is ready, and the knife sharp. None of you can escape, for the bridges are broken down." Even the bravest among the

Spaniards began to feel fainthearted, and in the hopeless struggle Cortes saw himself obliged to strike some decisive blow.

In order to raise the courage of his men he ordered a great sally. It was of the utmost importance to obtain possession of the neighbouring temple, from the roof of which the enemy cast missiles upon the camp. A picked band of Aztec warriors defended the sacred place, and to a man fell before the Spanish arms. The fight was particularly fierce upon the flat summit of the building. Here Cortes was in the greatest danger. Two young men cast themselves upon him, and it was with the utmost difficulty that he escaped from their grasp.

The conquerors at once cast down the hated image of the god of slaughter, and set fire to the temple which had been the pride of the capital. This deed, which the Spaniards looked upon as well-pleasing to God, so raised their courage that Cortes determined to make use of the favourable moment and begin the perilous retreat. Knowing that all the bridges had been broken down, Cortes caused a portable wooden bridge to be prepared, and determined that the retreat should be directed in a westerly direction towards the town Tlacopan.

He appointed the night of the 1st of July for the attempt. The march began in the pre-arranged order about midnight, and the Spaniards succeeded in getting safely through the town, which was wrapped in sleep, until they came to the beginning of the causeway. Here they stumbled upon a band of Mexicans, who immediately gave the alarm. Soon there resounded from all sides the shrill noise of the war horns, while the beat of the monstrous drums rapidly brought up fresh bands of warriors. While the rearguard could only with the greatest loss keep back the raging onset of the Aztecs, hundreds of boats had come up on both sides of the causeway,

CORTES IN DANGER.

and from these was poured an unceasing hail of missiles upon the army as it strove to advance upon the narrow path. Then there was a stoppage. The first breach was reached, and it was necessary to lay down the pontoon. This delay was fatal to many. At last the onward march was resumed, but soon a second breach was reached. A still longer and equally destructive delay ensued, and soon it was known that it had been found impossible to take up the pontoon and bring it farther. All discipline was then at an end, and the one desire of every one was to save his own life. The rearguard pressed irresistibly upon those in the van, and drove them nearer and nearer to the edge of the abyss. Here the climax of misery seemed attained. Happy were those who found a watery grave or met with a speedy death from the Mexicans. Many were knocked down and stunned, and thus fell alive in the hands of their enemies, who kept them as long-desired victims for the bloody altars of their gods. At last the terrible gap was filled up by cannon, baggage, and the bodies of the slain, and over this awful bridge the fugitives made their way. There was a third breach to be crossed, but fortunately for the fugitives, their pursuers were by this time so occupied with the booty that lay scattered along the causeway that the difficulty was overcome without much additional loss. By the dawn of day the shore was reached, and the exhausted warriors halted in a temple near Tlacopan.

Much cast down, the General reviewed the shattered remnant of his proud army. What a melancholy sight ! All the cannon, the enormous booty, almost all the horses were lost, and 400 Spaniards and at least 4000 of the Indian allies had perished. This terrible retreat, which they called the Nochetriste, was for ever deeply engraved in the memories of the survivors.

And how would it be possible for them, in their exhausted condition, weaponless, and deeply cast down by their disaster,

to continue the conflict ?   How were they to make their way
to Tlascala, where alone they could feel at all secure, through a
hostile land, of which all the inhabitants were in arms.   But
the confident bearing of the General inspired the troops with
fresh courage, and gave them strength to ascend the heights
which enclose the valley of Mexico, though having continually
to skirmish with the enemy.   After some days' hard marching, they reached the tableland, and then prepared to advance into the friendly Tlascala, when suddenly, on the 8th of
July, they found themselves face to face with an enormous
army of the enemy, which filled the whole valley of Otompan,
or Otumba, and cut off their retreat.   According to the reports of the Spanish writers, it must have been an army of
200,000 men, who, in proud confidence, displayed the utmost
pomp.   As far as the eye could reach there were shields and
waving banners, curiously-shaped helmets, forests of glittering
spears; and the heart even of the bravest must have sunk
when he compared with it the small number of the Spaniards
and their allies, ill-armed and enfeebled.   But Cortes's heart
knew neither fear nor despondency.   Without delay he placed
his little army in order of battle, and encouraged it by a
spirited speech, in which he promised it the protection of God
and the saints, and painted the delights of rest and refreshment after this last desperate struggle.   Then he ordered an
immediate charge, and from the height the little band rushed
upon the enormous masses of the enemy.   The shock was so
great that the foremost ranks were broken, and a broad road
was opened for the Spaniards.   But in a moment the endless
masses closed upon them, and raged like a stormy sea
upon a little island which they threatened to swallow up.
Opposed to such overwhelming odds, the utmost exertions
must be powerless.   It seemed as if nothing short of a
miracle could save them.   Then Cortes's eagle eye caught
sight of the General commanding the Aztec army, who was

easily recognised by his splendid attire and by the sacred standard waving over him. Instantly he resolved what to do. At the head of twenty men, to which number his cavalry had dwindled down, he cut himself a path through the enemy until he stood before this man. With his own hand he stabbed him to the heart, while his companions fell upon the body-guard.

When the Aztecs saw their General fall and the sacred banner in the hands of the dreaded strangers, a cry of horror resounded over the whole battlefield, the huge army broke and fled in utter disorder, the pursuing Spaniards and Tlascalans cutting them down with horrible slaughter. Twenty thousand Aztecs must have fallen in this battle, and the spoil of golden and other ornaments found on the dead compensated in some measure for the lost treasures of the night.

After this wonderful victory the march to Tlascala met with no further hindrance. There the wearied men were met with open arms, and were able to refresh themselves after the incredible exertions of the past week. But a long rest was not to Cortes's taste, and he immediately set to work to repair the losses he had suffered. He succeeded by his eloquence in persuading his companions in arms, who at first desired to retreat to the coast and take ship for Cuba, to persevere in the glorious enterprise, and again to encounter the dangers from which they were but just escaped. With the Tlascalans for allies, he forced the countries for some distance round to acknowledge the King of Spain; and having thus again inspired them with fear of the Spanish arms, he obtained the necessary means by the tribute he imposed, and increased the number of Indian auxiliaries who were to accompany him against Mexico. He laboured so unremittingly to strengthen and equip the Spanish army that in a few months it was ready for war. He found himself again in command of 40 horsemen, 80 musketeers, and 500 infantry, armed with swords and long lances. A part of this force were fresh troops sent by Velasquez to the support of Narvaez, whom he supposed to be in possession of the command. They had not for a moment dreamt of joining the victorious standard of Cortes. In the same way he had come into possession of nine cannon, which accompanied the army. The number of Indian auxiliaries—exaggerated no doubt—is estimated at 100,000 men.

Before the expiration of the year 1520, the restless man was again on the shore of the lake of Mexico, and fixed his head-quarters in the old town of Tezcuco, over which he placed as King, Prince Ixtlilxochitl. He wisely abandoned the idea of at once beginning the siege of the capital, the white buildings of which were reflected in the clear lake; but spent months in isolating it, desolating the land around, and subduing its in-habitants. Generally he placed himself at the head of these raids, while the trusty Gonsalvo de Sandoval remained be-hind in Tezcuco, and superintended the building of the ships with which Cortes hoped to rule the lakes. These ships, thir-teen in number, were built in Tlascala under the direction of an experienced shipbuilder, Martin Lopez, and were then taken to pieces, and the separate parts, together with the necessary iron-work, sails, and rigging, carried on the backs of thousands of bearers to Tezcuco, a distance of almost twenty miles. Even this gigantic undertaking rewarded by its complete success the foresight and thought which had been expended on its execution.

At last the necessary preparations were complete. The whole region around the lakes was subject to the Spaniards, the Aztecs were confined within their island city, and the ships were launched at Tezcuco. At the end of May, 1521, Cortes thought it was time to begin the attack on the capital. He caused the town of Tlacopan to be occupied by a division of his men under the command of the Captains Alvarado and Olid, and broke down the aqueduct which ran from Chapoltepec to the island. The body of his army, under the command of the brave Sandoval, he sent out to take possession of Iztapalapa, the key to the southern causeway, and while both these movements were successfully accomplished, Cortes himself moved his fleet—which, to use his own expression, he considered the " key of the war "—out into the lake, and destroyed a great fleet of Indian boats, running down some and sinking others by a heavy fire of grapeshot. Then he took possession of the advanced work called Xoloc, erected in the centre of the southern causeway, and affording a strong position, which Cortes, by means of fortifications and cannons, strengthened still more.

The town had for a long time been armed for the conflict. In the place of Cuitlahuatzin, who had been carried off by the small-pox—a disease brought into the land by the Spaniards —Guatemozin, his nephew, had been chosen, a younger warrior, but one distinguished by his bravery and strength of character. He had taken up the sacred struggle for the defence of his country against the foreign conquerors with the greatest energy, and had inflicted heavy losses upon the Spaniards by sudden surprises and ceaseless attacks, at the same time rendering their conquest of the surrounding region extremely difficult. But he was not in a condition to prevent their advance, and was ever obliged to yield to their superior arms and to the overwhelming numbers of their Indian allies, fired by a desire to avenge themselves on their ancient conquerors and by the prospect of rich booty. Still nothing could break the spirit of the young Emperor. Without hesitation, he rejected every offer made him by Cortes, and prepared to continue the struggle to the death. After the third causeway, the one leading to the north was occupied; and Cortes began an attack upon the one by which he had first entered Mexico. The many gaps in this were defended by walls and strong bodies of men ; but the guns of the ships cleared a passage for the infantry. One breach after another was passed and then filled up with stones, until at last the entrance of the city was gained. The streets were found to be intersected by many ditches and walls, behind which the principal forces of the Aztecs were established, while a murderous hail of missiles fell upon the heads of the assailants from the roofs of the houses. It was not possible for the Spaniards to establish themselves in the city. They succeeded by desperate charges in penetrating to the great square in the middle of the city, but were continually forced to retreat again. For several days these vain attempts were repeated, and some palaces were set on fire. Even during the night the wearied combatants could have little rest, for they were obliged to be constantly on the watch against surprises on the part of Guatemozin.

At last Cortes was over-persuaded by his captains against his better judgment to order a general assault. At first, indeed, everything seemed to prosper, for the separate storming columns penetrated far into the town. But at a given signal they were attacked and compelled to retreat ; and in the retreat they suffered heavy loss, especially at the passages over the numerous canals which intersected the streets. Even Cortes was in extreme danger, and was only saved from the terrible fate of falling alive into the hands of the enemy by the self-sacrifice of some of his devoted adherents. The attack was drawn off on all sides, and while the Spaniards returned downcast into their quarters, the whole city echoed with sounds of festive joy. As the evening advanced the besiegers saw with horror all the temples lighted and prepared for the bloody human sacrifices. Indeed, the clearness of the air allowed them to see the torturing and the slaughter of the prisoners.

The priests now announced to the Aztecs that Huitzilopotchli, pleased with the rich offering that had been presented to him, would again have mercy upon his people, and within three days deliver all the strangers into their hands. This prophecy flew with the speed of lightning, and at one and the same time inspired the Aztecs with fresh courage, and filled the hearts of the superstitious allies of the Spaniards with dismay, and led them to creep away from the camp by thousands. It was not until the week had passed away without the prophesied destruction of the Spaniards that they returned ashamed.

Rendered wise by the unhappy issue of the attack, Cortes determined to attempt the conquest of the city in a surer though more tedious way. He caused the town to be closely blockaded by his ships and by numerous Indian boats, so that no supplies could be brought in. He reckoned that famine must soon ensue, and the strength of the opposition be overcome. The cold-bloodedness with which he thus devoted thousands to the most miserable death becomes more terrible when we consider the methodical manner in which he arranged the destruction of the town. Each day a certain part of the city was taken possession of and utterly destroyed. The ruins of the houses were made use of to fill up the canals, and thus a broad ever-increasing plain was procured, which gave the Spaniards plenty of room for their military operations, and offered the besieged no cover for their surprises. It was only after a bitter struggle that Cortes resolved upon this terrible plan, which devoted to destruction the beautiful city that would have been the crowning trophy of his conquest.

On reading the report sent to the Spanish King by Cortes, in which he describes the painful necessity for the destruction, and the fearful execution of the plan, one cannot but feel that it must have been written with tears in his eyes. But he saw no other way of overcoming the desperate resistance of the

Aztecs. Guatemozin had rejected all the terms of peace that Cortes had made to him, and, following the counsel of the priests, resolved to continue the struggle to the very last. With wild joy the Indian allies welcomed the new plans of attack on the capital, which gave promise of satisfying their thirst for revenge on their oppressor, and the charges that Cortes gave them to spare the wounded fell on deaf ears.

Through the whole month of July the fight was continued according to the new system. The Spaniards pressed upon the city on three sides, under Cortes, Alvarado, and Sandoval. The Spanish infantry went first with cannons and muskets and drove the Aztec warriors out of certain streets. Then they made a stand and defended themselves against the attacks of the enemy, while the Indian allies destroyed the captured houses. That accomplished, the Spaniards relinquished their position, which it would have been impossible to maintain on account of the stench from the dead bodies, and retreated to the camp. This method of fighting caused them but small loss, and they only suffered from the bad weather and want of rest. But fearful were the sufferings of the besieged. Famine and pestilence rapidly lessened their numbers, and their Indian foes mercilessly slaughtered every Aztec who fell into their hands. With every step that the Spaniards advanced, more terrible were the scenes of grief and misery that were displayed. They found the earth dug up in the search for roots and worms, the trees stripped of their young shoots, their foliage, and their bark. Crowds of half-starved Mexicans crept about like spectres in streets and market-places, which had once been lively and animated. Corpses lay unburied in heaps about the streets, making the air pestilential —a proof of the utmost distress, for the Aztecs considered it a sacred duty to bury the dead. More horrible still were the sights that presented themselves to the Spaniards on entering the dwellings. On the floor lay the miserable remains of the inmates, some still in the death struggle and others already decomposed; distracted mothers with their infants dying before their eyes of starvation; wounded men trying in vain to crawl away as their enemies entered. But they all disdained to ask for mercy, meeting the foe with the savage implacable stare of a wounded tiger tracked by the hunter to his last hiding-place. In vain were the repeated commands of the Spanish General to spare the poor defence-less wretches. His Indian allies made no distinction; with wild cries of victory they pulled down the burning buildings on the heads of the miserable people, and the flames con-sumed the living and dead in one common funeral pile.

Thus the beautiful city was laid in ashes, and its inhabitants died daily by thousands. The three divisions of the Spanish force met on the smoking ruins before the last quarter of the town into which the miserable remnant of the population had fled. New offers of peace were rejected by Guatemozin with the old constancy. So the struggle began again for this last refuge of the besieged, who defended themselves in vain with unequalled fury to the utmost of their power. On the 13th of August the Spaniards poured in like an irresistible torrent over the last bulwarks, their progress being marked by streams of blood and flames running from street to street. During the *mêlée* a crowd of boats were pushed from the shores and endeavoured to make their escape over the lake. But the Spanish ships were on the watch. Some of the largest boats were overtaken by the ship of the Captain Garcias Holguin, and while he was preparing to sink them the Indians gave him to understand that the Emperor was among them. At the same moment a young warrior in armour rose and shouted, "I am Guatemozin. Take me to Malinché, I am his prisoner, but do my wife and followers no harm." The prisoners were taken on board the Spanish ships, and the Emperor being asked to stop the battle by a command to his subjects, replied,

"It is not necessary : they will cease to fight when they see that their Prince is a prisoner." He was right, the Aztecs at this intelligence gave up the struggle and submitted to their fate. On shore Cortes came to meet the imperial prisoner, and saluted him with chivalrous courtesy. The captive answered with dignity : "I have done all I could to defend myself and my people. Now I am reduced to this condition. You, Malinché, will do with me as you please." Then laying his hand on the hilt of the dagger which Cortes wore in his girdle, he added with vehemence, "But I would you would strike me down with this dagger and deliver me from life." Cortes tried to soothe him. "Fear nothing," he said, "you shall be treated with every respect. You have defended your capital like a brave soldier, and a Spaniard knows how to value bravery even in an enemy." He sent him, together with his young wife, a daughter of Montezuma's, and the chief of his followers, under Sandoval's care, to a town on the neighbouring coast. The siege was at an end, the town was razed to the ground. The remains of the population, about 30,000 men, marched in a long sorrowful procession out of the city of their fathers. About 200,000 must have fallen victims to the sword, the flames, famine, and the pestilence during the course of the siege. The besiegers calculated their loss, by which their Indian allies mostly suffered, at 30,000 men. It was weeks before the scene of this terrible struggle was cleared of the dead bodies and the pestilential atmosphere sweetened by the fresh sea-breezes. In the meantime the victorious army was occupied in feasting, thanksgiving, and dividing the spoil. This was considerable, 130,000 ducats in value, but far from satisfying the exaggerated expectations which the Spaniards had cherished. The ill-temper of the troops vented itself in bitter language, and at last turned upon Cortes, whom they accused of dishonesty. They demanded that the imprisoned Emperor should be put to the torture, in the hopes of discovering from him the place where he had hidden his treasures. When Cortes refused, he was suspected of a secret understanding with the prisoner, and so in an evil hour he gave his consent to the torture. It was vain, as might have been expected, and Guatemozin bore it with the patient courage which distinguished the unfortunate man. When his companion in suffering, the King of Tlacopan, broke out into groans, he reproved him with the words : " Do you think, then, that I am lying on a bed of roses ?" The wretched proceeding was soon put an end to by Cortes, but it was too late to prevent the stain which had been inflicted on his honour.

The fall of the capital rendered the rule of the Spaniards over the whole land secure. Even princes who had not been tributary to the Aztec monarch submitted to the mighty stranger, and did homage to the King of Spain. Arms were laid aside, and Cortes devoted himself to the ordering of the conquered land, in which he showed the same skill and untiring energy as he had done in its subjection. The capital rose again out of its ashes, although with a very changed appearance. Many of the canals were filled up, the streets were widened, and a number of churches built, of which the most splendid was the great cathedral dedicated to St. Francis, which rose in the place of the principal temple, and the foundation of which was composed of the uncouth images of the fallen idols. Rows of stately stone buildings lined the streets in which the Spaniards dwelt who settled in the city, while Cortes built for himself a spacious palace in the neighbourhood of the cathedral. For the defence of the capital Cortes built a fortress and provided it with seventy guns, some of which he took from the dismantled ships at Vera Cruz, and some were cast in a foundry that he had established in the land. Only four years after the taking of the city it presented again a pleasant, almost splendid appearance, and was inhabited by 2000 Spanish and 30,000

Indian families. Cortes was not less zealous for the spiritual welfare of the people. At his invitation numbers of priests came from the West Indies, and threw themselves with such zeal into the work of conversion that within twenty years all the inhabitants of this extensive country belonged by name to the Christian Church, mingling, however, with their new faith much of their hereditary superstition.

Cortes took great pains to discover the natural sources of the wealth of the land, opened some silver mines, and introduced useful plants. In the most important places he founded new towns, among other Zacatula, for which he anticipated a great future. Here he caused a fleet to be built for exploration and conquest as far as Asia, while at the same time he sent out ships from Vera Cruz to try and discover the long-sought-for passage from one ocean to the other on the northern coast of the Mexican Gulf. By means of his generals, Alvarado and Olid, he took possession of the southern lands of Guatemala and Honduras, and here a flourishing colony soon sprang up.

The most serious difficulty which the great man had to contend with was the satisfying of his greedy countrymen who settled down in the most beautiful and fruitful neighbourhoods. Very unwillingly he saw himself obliged to consent to the introduction of the wretched system of repartimentos. He took care that the burden of servitude should fall only upon those races that had been guilty of treason and cruelty to the Spaniards, and he tried to protect the slaves by a number of laws intended to restrain the tyranny of the masters. In order to prevent the pillage which had been so injurious in the West Indian colonies, he made a number of enactments which were all calculated to chain the white settler to the land, and to lead him for the sake of his own interest to cultivate the soil. The allotments of land only became the property of the colonists when they had held them for eight years, and they had to prove that they were worthy of the gift by the care which they bestowed upon them during that period. Every married man was forced to bring his wife into the country on penalty of losing the land allotted to him, and every bachelor was compelled to marry within a certain period on the same penalty. It was owing to these enactments that the new state became much more quickly than the other colonies had done the home of a large number of Spanish families who settled on their possessions, instead of wishing to return to their old homes after a few years with their spoils. By other laws the settler was pledged to take into cultivation yearly a certain piece of land, and to reside in the town for a portion of every year.

Beneficial as these laws for the most part were to the development of the infant state, and high as is the opinion which they give of the sagacity of the conqueror, yet they created much displeasure in the minds of those whom they affected. The sensitive and suspicious disposition of the Spaniard showed itself in a very ugly light, and persons whom the great man had overwhelmed with benefits calumniated and accused him at the Spanish Court. There from the very beginning the question had been undecided how Cortes should be treated. Velasquez was indefatigable in his complaints, demanding to be invested with the government of Mexico, and he had a powerful supporter in Bishop Fonseca, the leader in Indian Affairs. Together they had succeeded in sending out a plenipotentiary, Christoval de Tapia, who was to call Cortes to account. The latter, however, by bribery had prevailed upon him to leave the country. He had also at court warm partisans, especially the Duke of Bejar and the Count of Aguilar.

But his wonderful exploits and the valuable services by which he had so greatly extended the Castilian power interceded still more strongly for him. And so the Emperor

Charles V. signed a decree at Valladolid, October 15th, 1522, by which Cortes was made Governor, Commander-General, and Supreme Judge of New Spain, as Mexico was then called, with a considerable salary. This decision so affected his chief opponents Velasquez and Fonseca that they fell sick and soon after died. In Mexico, on the contrary, it caused universal joy, and for a while all his calumniators were silenced. We hear nothing more of them until the long absence of Cortes between the years 1524 and 1526. At that time he undertook an expedition to Honduras to reduce to submission by force of arms its conqueror Olid. The march was through perfectly unknown regions, where the climate was pestilential and the hardships and sufferings were very great. On this expedition the unfortunate Guatemozin, whom Cortes for security had carried with him, came to a sad end. He was accused of having taken part in a conspiracy by which the Spaniards were to be destroyed in an almost inaccessible pass. Although he asserted his innocence, Cortes pronounced sentence of death upon him, not so much from a conviction of his guilt as from a desire to be rid of the burdensome charge of such an important prisoner, and immediately after the sentence the unfortunate Prince, with several companions, was hanged on a tree. He died with the greatest composure. " I knew," he said, " what it was to trust to your false promises, Malinché ; I knew that you had destined me to this fate. Would I had laid hands on myself when they led me prisoner to you ! Why do you kill me so unjustly ? God will call you to account for it." These words cut Cortes to the heart, and stings of conscience with regard to this unrighteous deed of blood tormented him to the end of his life.

As the army passed through the land, the birthplace of the interpreter Marina, Cortes parted from his faithful companion, whom he presented with valuable estates and married to one of the knights of his retinue. In Honduras the General found the insurrection already suppressed, and the faithless Olid executed. But sickness laid him low, and contrary winds long hindered his return. In the meantime the report of his death was spread in Mexico, and the royal officers sequesttrated his possessions. When in 1526 he returned, the whole country received him with extravagant joy. For even the natives whom he had subdued had learnt from the oppression of the Spanish officials doubly to prize his gentleness and love of justice. But with the officials themselves he was henceforward at constant feud. Soon after some high Spanish officers came to the country to investigate the mutual complaints, and one of these, Estrada by name, went to the absurd length of ordering the great conqueror to leave the capital, because he had interceded for an old comrade, who for some slight offence had been sentenced to lose his hand. Cortes obeyed, but determined to extricate himself from such an undignified position by going to the King himself, and so took ship for Spain.

In May, 1528, he landed in Palos after a prosperous voyage, and went to Toledo, where the Emperor at that time resided. He was received in the most distinguished manner, and cleared himself of all charges and calumnies. The Emperor, who personally showed him the greatest attention and loaded him with honours, made him Marquis del Valle d'Guaxaca, and bestowed upon him in that valley and in other parts of the land enormous possessions, in which there were more than twenty towns and villages, with 23,000 vassals.

But the Emperor resolutely refused to entrust him with the government of the country, for it was the policy of the Crown not to give the rule of a conquered land to the conqueror and discoverer, lest he should be too independent and self-important. This refusal was rendered less bitter to Cortes by the reason assigned, namely, that it was impossible to do without his services in the warlike undertakings yet remaining to be accomplished, and by his appointment as Commander-in-Chief for New Spain and the South Seas.

For two years Cortes remained in Spain, where the most distinguished grandees treated him as their equal, and the oldest families felt themselves honoured by his alliance. His first wife had died in Mexico in the year 1522, and he now contracted a second marriage with a daughter of the Count of Aguilar, and lived in great state. In the spring he returned to Mexico, where meanwhile the civil government had been established. But all kinds of disagreements between the two powers were perfectly unavoidable, and when, in order to put an end to this state of things, the Spanish Court forbade Cortes to come within ten miles of the capital, he retired deeply hurt to Tezcuco, and later to his own city of Cuernavaca, where he built himself a palace, and took up his permanent residence.

For the next few years his activity was devoted to the care of his extensive estates. He introduced the sugarcane from Cuba, and merino sheep from Spain, and planted whole hedges of mulberry-trees, in order to promote the production of silk. But such a quiet life was not suited to content the active soul of Cortes for any length of time.

Between the years 1532 and 1534 he fitted out in the harbour of Tehuantepec two squadrons, which he sent out on voyages of discovery towards the north-west. They discovered the peninsula of California, to which Cortes himself conducted a colony. But his good luck had forsaken him ; the colony could not prosper in that barren land, and when he himself set sail on a voyage of discovery, he was driven about by a storm in the Gulf of Mexico—which for a long time bore the name of Cortes Sea—and at length compelled to return.

In the year 1539 the indefatigable man sent out a new fleet, under the command of his captain Ulloa. This brave sailor discovered the north end of the Gulf of California, sailed round the narrow peninsula, and went along the west coast towards the north. At twenty-nine degrees north latitude he sent back one of his ships to carry news of the discovery to the Marquis; but he himself continued his voyage towards the north, and was lost with all his companions.

Cortes intended to go with a considerable body of followers into the newly-discovered lands to take possession of them for the Spanish Crown, and to found a new colony, but was disturbed in this design by the new Viceroy Mendoza, who claimed the right of founding the colony himself, an open infringement of the right granted by the Emperor to Cortes. The latter saw himself thus cheated of the reward of his pains, and felt that he had expended enormous sums and burdened his estates with debt all for nothing. In order to procure justice, he determined to go once more to Spain.

Accordingly in the autumn of 1540 we find him in Madrid, where he had dealings with the Royal Council for India, and the next year he accompanied the Emperor in his disastrous campaign against Algiers. He was always treated with the most honourable attention, but his wishes and his grievances were not attended to. Like Columbus he was obliged to remind his royal master of his incalculable services, but like Columbus he saw that they were forgotten. After having for some years waited in vain for an improvement in the state of affairs, he determined to turn his back upon his ungrateful country. Shortly before the time that he had fixed for his departure he was attacked by a sickness in Seville, which quickly exhausted his strength, and he died in the village Castilleja de la Cuesta, on the 2nd of December, 1547. He was sixty-two years old. His body was first buried at Seville, but in 1562 was taken by his son to the New World, and interred in Tezcuco. But even here it was not allowed to rest. In 1629 it was laid in the cathedral of Mexico, and since 1794 has been buried in the hospital founded by him in the capital.

Cortes left behind him from his second marriage—he had no children by his first wife—three daughters, who made brilliant marriages, and one son, Martin, who inherited his possessions and his title. But in the fourth generation the male branch of the family died out, and the inheritance passed by marriage into another family. At present the ducal family of Monteleone, which boasts of descent from the great-granddaughter of the great conqueror, is in possession of his title and lands.

CHAPTER VII.

FRANCISCO PIZARRO.

In South America is an elevated plain much resembling
the tableland of Anahuac, and like it at the time of the
Spanish discoveries, the seat of a civilised people and the
centre of a mighty empire, the conquest of which by a handful of Spaniards offers a worthy parallel to the exploits of the
lion-hearted Cortes.   Between twenty and twelve degrees
south latitude there stretches among the peaks of the Cor-
derillas an uninterrupted series of tablelands, at an elevation
of 12,000 feet.   Almost in the centre of these mountain plains
lies the great lake of Titicaca, surrounded by gigantic vol-
canoes.   The islands which lie scattered over it are said to
be the mysterious place in which a powerful state had its
origin.

About the year 1000 A.D., so said tradition, which was
looked upon almost as history, the rudeness and barbarity of
the inhabitants of these plains had reached such a point that
the Sun-god could no longer look upon it.   Out of compassion he then sent down two of his children, Manco Capac,
and his sister and wife, Mama Oello Huaco, to teach the de-
based people order, morality, and how to lead a happy life.
These children of the sun descended upon one of the islands
of Titicaca, and then, obedient to the commands of their
father, pursued their way towards the north, until the golden
reed which they stuck every evening in the earth disappeared.
This spot they chose for their dwelling-place, and called it

Cusco. They collected round them the rude inhabitants of the valley and imparted to them their divine message. The people willingly listened to them, and learned from them the arts of ploughing, spinning, and weaving, being persuaded to adopt a settled and industrious life.

Such was the mythical origin of Cusco. It became the seat of a long series of wise and powerful princes, who were said to have sprung from the divine pair, and bore the title of Incas or Princes. The blessings flowing from their beneficent and salutary administration were extended farther and farther, partly by the willing submission of the neighbouring tribes, and partly by force of arms, for the Incas were all warlike conquerors.

When the Spaniards entered the country they ruled over all the mountain region from twenty degrees south latitude to the equator, and over the coast lands from the river Maule in Chili (thirty-five degrees south latitude) to the Gulf of Guayaquil (two degrees south latitude). All this extensive territory was united in one state, the institutions of which, though manifesting much resemblance to those of the civilised states of Asia, yet bore the stamp of a unique and highly-interesting character.

The rule of the Incas was necessarily absolute, because they were held by their subjects to be descendants of the gods, and therefore divine beings themselves. The number of the Incas was very considerable, for under that name were embraced, not only the reigning Prince, but all who could trace back their pedigree in the male line to the divine pair, and since every King had many hundred wives, the number of Incas increased with every generation, until they formed a numerous aristocracy, ruling the whole country. The King, always the eldest son by the only legitimate marriage of his father with a sister, considered these noble families as his relations, who had a right to a share in the splendour as well as the burdens of government, but there was a great distance maintained between him, and the principal nobles, and none dared to venture into the presence of the Son of the Sun except barefoot and with a light burden on his shoulder, in token of subjection. He was at the head of the priests and had the chief seat at the most important religious feasts. He took the chief command in war, imposed taxes, gave laws, named his officers, who gave account to him. He was the source from which all power flowed, and which gave life to the whole state. His appearance was extremely magnificent, he wore long flowing robes of the finest stuff, shining with gold and the rarest jewels, and on his head a bright-coloured turban covered with scarlet net, in which were placed upright two feathers of a rare bird, which the King alone might use for his adornment.

His throne was surrounded by his relations the Incas, who were bound to him, not only by a common origin, but by their inclinations and interests. They were distinguished from the rest of the people by a special dress and peculiar language, and for their support the best parts of the public lands were appointed. They lived chiefly at court near the Prince, who had been brought up with them, but they held all the high offices in the provinces, and only from among them could the higher priestly offices be filled, being in virtue of their birth qualified for priestly functions. The whole race of the Incas, as the shape of their sculls shows even now, must have been far superior in mental capacity to the other races of the country.

A second and inferior order of nobility consisted of the Curacas, the caciques of subject races and their descendants. They were usually continued in their authority, but their sons were required to live at the capital as hostages for their fidelity. Their power seems usually to have been only local, and always subordinate to the authority of the governor of the provinces, who was chosen only from the Incas.

The whole state was divided into four large provinces, each ruled by a governor. Under him were the officials in charge of the districts, each of which contained 10,000 inhabitants, and was subdivided into smaller districts of 1000, 500, 100, 50, down to 10 persons respectively. Each of these had a functionary at its head, who was responsible for his subordinates. The graver offences were brought before the governor, lighter ones were punished by the courts of justice of the towns or districts, and every province was visited annually by commissioners to inquire into the administration of justice. The laws were few, but since their transgression was an offence against a divine law-giver, it was considered a blasphemy against God, and thus the smallest fault deserved death as much as heavier crimes.

But the most peculiar regulations were those connected with the political economy of the country. By them all land capable of cultivation was divided into three parts, one for the sun and his priests, a second for the Prince and his house, and the third for the people. The last portion was divided in equal parts among the subjects. As soon as any one at the age prescribed by the law took to himself a wife, a certain lot of land was granted to him, which was increased as his family grew. This division was revised every year, that it might be always accurate. The people were required by the law to cultivate their lands and also the portions belonging to the sun and to the Inca. At daybreak, men, women, and children were called to work by the sound of a horn, and appeared adorned as for a feast. They performed their work cheerfully, singing harmoniously the while. First they laboured for the sun, then for the old and sick, then they cultivated their own land, and lastly that of the Incas.

The most important of the domestic animals were the llamas ; they fed in great numbers on the plains and were the objects of the greatest care. They all belonged to the King, and their flesh might be used only at court feasts or for sacrifice, but they were very valuable as beasts of burden and for their wool. At a fixed time they were shorn and their wool brought into the store-houses. Then each family was allowed as much as they were considered to need, and the women made it up for the family's use, being required also to work for the Inca. There were special officers appointed to superintend, not only the division of the wool, but also the women's work and the collecting of the cloth.

The mines also, the chief riches of the country, were the exclusive possession of the King, and worked for his advantage. As few hands as possible, however, were drawn away from agriculture, which was considered the chief occupation of the people. It had been carried to a high point, the natural fruitfulness of the soil being increased by manuring with guano, which was brought from some little islands directly off the coast. A network of canals, which frequently had to be cut underground through the rocks, carried life in all directions, and changed deserts into arable land. These singular arrangements, in which an enlightened despotism was led by its benevolent intentions to establish a communist equality, perfectly accomplished its purpose. The subjects were trained in a spirit of patient obedience and quiet content, which in everything that concerned the government saw a proof of superhuman wisdom. But there was nothing like advance for the Peruvian. As he was born, so he must die, and all his strivings to attain a higher lot were in vain. Even his time was not his own. He paid his taxes by work. Therefore the government had a right to treat idleness as a crime that injured the state. But the useful side of these institutions was seen not only in the constant growth of the national revenues, but also in the complete absence of all the passions of envy, ambition, avarice, and love of change. As long as people could remember everything had run in the same groove, and the Spaniards unanimously agreed that no government was better suited to the disposition of the people, and that no people could have been more contented with its lot or more devoted to its government.

One of the proofs of the care of the government for the general welfare are the wonderful roads which intersected the whole land, and the remains of which still excite admiration. All the difficulties of the ground—and no land could present more or greater—were overcome, rocks were broken through, suspension-bridges thrown over wild mountain streams, and ravines filled up. Also, wherever it was possible, water was carried along both sides of the roads, and they were shaded by trees planted for the purpose. On these roads the King travelled about the land and satisfied himself of the condition of the provinces. On them the armies also could comfortably move about, and messengers carried the reports of the governors to the capital. Also, for the comfort of travellers, every here and there inns were erected.

The Peruvians were particularly skilful in masonry. They could work huge stones with very simple tools—iron was unknown to them—and they fitted them together so perfectly that it was impossible to pass the blade of a knife between them. In this way they built gigantic fortresses, palaces for their kings, and temples for their gods. But how to fit in windows and to make pointed roofs to the buildings they did not understand. Their houses were dark, with flat roofs made of beams tied together, or loosely thatched with straw, the rainless climate requiring only shelter from the rays of the sun. The houses of the people were built in the simplest manner of mud. Next to architecture the Peruvians distinguished themselves by their skill in polishing jewels and working gold. This precious metal was not sought for in mines, but was found in large masses on the surface, and was used for every kind of decoration or utensil connected with the temples and altars. The Spaniards saw with astonished admiration their skilful work, especially noticing the exceedingly faithful representation of animals and plants made by the native goldsmiths with their rude tools. The excellent cloth also, prepared from the fine wool of the vicuña, won strong approbation from the Spaniards.

The Peruvians, surpassing the Mexicans in many respects, were behind them in possessing no money and trade not being encouraged by their government. Still more, the picture writing in use in Mexico was unknown to them. They had a very imperfect substitute in the quipus, a cord two feet long, formed of closely-woven threads of bright colour, from which depended a number of little threads. By knotting these threads in different ways certain things were expressed, and by this quipus not only were the reports of the officials communicated, but also the great deeds of the Incas were handed down to posterity.

The Peruvians acknowledged one supreme invisible Being, the creator and preserver of the universe, whom they adored under the name of Pachacamac and Viracocha, and whose temple served as an oracle. But the divinity to whom they paid most honour was the sun-god, the ancestor of the Incas, who introduced his worship into all the lands conquered by them. The ceremonies were full of solemn magnificence, and his temples were covered with gold within and without. The oldest of these temples stood on an island in the Titicaca Lake, but the most splendid was the chief temple of Cusco, covering a large space, and the interior of which was literally a vault of gold. The number of priests and attendants attached to the service of the sun-god was enormous, and the chief priest was next in rank to the King himself. To their great surprise, the Spaniards found features of their own religious service repeated in the Peruvian worship of the sun : the incense in the temples, processions, pilgrimages, even convents with their inmates dedicated to the sun, who led at least as secluded a life as their western sisters. Although the Incas cherished an universal reverence for their divine ancestor the sun-god, they were liberal or politic enough not to forbid divine honour to be paid to the gods of the subject nations. Their temples remained standing side by side with the new sun temple, and their priests were provided from the ample income of the sun, but the images of the gods travelled to Cusco, and served there, like the chief's sons, as pledges of the fidelity of the new subjects. The Incas took great pains to further the melting together of the different races among their people. For this purpose they chose the musical language of Cusco, the Quichuan, for the official language, and appointed teachers of it in every district.

The first information which reached the ears of the Spaniards about this wonderful state was very indefinite, and naturally chiefly concerned the fabulous riches of the country. Balboa had already heard of it, and had formed plans for the conquest of this Eldorado, which at last appeared to have been found. His ignominious death put an end to these plans, and the Spanish Crown lost the man best adapted to carry out the gigantic enterprise. His murderer, Pedrarias de Avila, was commissioned to search for the wonderful land, and prepare for its conquest. With this object in view, he removed the capital of his province, Castilla del Oro, from the Atlantic coast across the isthmus to the shores of the great ocean where, after Balboa's discoveries, the town of Panama had arisen. Thence he sent out several times expeditions of discovery, but generally they took the direction towards the north, hoping to find the strait which was universally supposed to unite the Carribean Sea with the great ocean, and the discovery and conquest of Nicaragua which followed, turned the attention of Spanish settlers from the south. An expedition was made in 1522 by Pasual de Andagoya to the west coast of South

America, following in the track of Balboa, but he soon returned
without having effected anything.   At last the man appeared
who, overcoming all obstacles, was to realise the great plans of
the unhappy adventurer, and to lift the veil which had hitherto
protected the golden land from the conquest of the Spaniards.
Francisco Pizarro, born at Truxillo, a town in Estremadura,
passed a very obscure youth ; even the year of his birth cannot be settled with any certainty, but the year 1471 has been
named with some probability.   He was of illegitimate birth,
his father, Gonzalvo Pizarro, being a captain in the Castilian
army, and his mother in a humble position.   The boy grew up
much neglected, without the beneficial influence of family life,
without any instruction, and, as all accounts agree in stating,
in the occupation of a swineherd.   From this poor position he
escaped as he grew up, and was one of the first to emigrate to
the New World in order to seek his fortune.   But even there
he had to go through a rough schooling, and instead of the
success which he had expected, he met with dangers and a
hard lot, for so late as 1510 we find him taking part, in a
subordinate position, in the expedition of Alonso de Ojeda
which was planned for the colonisation of Uraba. When Ojeda
left the colony in order to procure support from Hispaniola, he
knew none among all his companions to whom he could
entrust the command of the hungry, sick, and unruly crew
except the fearless and determined Pizarro.   He, true to his
promise, held out in the fearful position in which he was
placed for fifty days, and even then delayed his departure
until death had so decreased his band that those who remained
could be brought away on the two ships that they possessed.
During a storm one of these sank, and the other, which bore
Pizarro, fell in with Enciso, and returned with him to the settlement they had just left, which, by Balboa's advice, was
removed to the river Darien.   Here, in Santa Maria del Antigua,
Pizarro became deeply involved in the quarrel which finally

ended with the nomination of the bold Balboa to the governor-ship. To him Pizarro closely attached himself. He was his instructor in the art of keeping a crowd of wild adventurers in willing obedience, and of showing to the natives now kindli-ness, and now an inflexible severity. He was among the brave men who first traversed the isthmus, and the wonderful story of an inexhaustible land of gold in the south sank deep into his soul.

Later he united himself to the new Governor Pedrarias, and after Balboa's death accompanied him to Panama. After almost thirty years' service in the New World he had gained nothing beyond a captaincy and an unhealthy piece of land which scarcely supported him. He was fifty years old and longed for something better, and therefore was easily persuaded to undertake the conduct of an expedition to the land of gold, for which a man of his military experience, intrepidity, and unscrupulosity was exactly fitted.

He was asked to take a share in the promising undertaking by the hot-blooded Diego de Almagro, a man about the same age as Pizarro, and one who, like him, had sprung from the lowest ranks, and was an uneducated soldier of fortune. The third in the league was Hernando de Luque, a dis-tinguished priest from Panama, a man of some influence and generally beloved. He it was who drew up the whole plan of the undertaking and who assigned to each their parts. In November, 1524, Pizarro sailed with two small ships prepared by Almagro, which carried about 100 men. But the voyage over the unknown sea was far more difficult than had been suspected. The adventurers did not succeed in getting farther than 7 degrees north latitude, and then, after months of terrible want and suffering, were glad to be able to return to Panama. Almagro, who followed with the third ship, succeeded in getting as far as 4 degrees north latitude, but also returned without having accomplished anything. But in the struggles with the natives, whose territories they plundered, a small quantity of gold was obtained, and this kept alive the avarice of the adventurers and inspirited them for fresh enterprises.

The disapproval of the Governor Pedrarias prevented the three allies from at once repeating their attempt, but when he was superseded by a new Governor, Don Pedro de los Rios, all difficulties were quickly removed, and the three men went to work with fresh courage. It was then on the 10th of March, 1526, that they concluded the celebrated agreement in which they divided among themselves the Peruvian kingdom with all its treasures. It was expressly arranged that Luque, who provided the necessary money, 20,000 ducats, should have a full third of the land repartimentos, gold, silver, and precious stones; and in case the two warriors who conducted the expedition should be faithless to the agreement, his right was acknowledged to claim the whole property. But Luque, a priest of only moderate wealth, represented the licenciate Espinosa, who employed the treasures of Miaraqua in this way. The treaty was drawn up in a religious tone, and the historian Robertson cannot help exclaiming, " In the name of the Prince of Peace they concluded a treaty which had for its object plunder and bloodshed."

It was very difficult to obtain the necessary crews, for expeditions to the south were in bad odour even with the well-inured Spaniards on account of the almost insupportable fatigues to be endured. At last the preparations were complete, and in the summer of 1526 the bold venture was made with two ships scantily manned. At the mouth of the little river San Juan, 4 degrees north latitude, the adventurers were so fortunate as to find in a little village a rich spoil of gold, and while Almagro carried this to Panama in the hope of alluring others to join in the enterprise, the daring Pizarro sent out the second ship to explore under the command of Ruiz, and established himself on the coast, where he remained with a small band tormented by hunger and mosquitos. Ruiz returned before Almagro, having crossed the equator on the west coast of America, and having gathered from the crew of a great Indian boat astonishing accounts of the riches and high civilisation of the kingdom of the Incas. Encouraged by this good news, Pizarro, when Almagro returned bringing new men, resumed the voyage. But the ships were overtaken by dreadful storms, and after being driven hither and thither the adventurers found themselves on the shores of a well-cultivated land, full of towns and villages, the numerous inhabitants of which streamed forth armed and showed a hostile disposition. The Spaniards saw that they were too weak to maintain a struggle with such a superior force; they therefore determined at once to return to Panama and procure greater numbers for the enterprise. But a part of the crew were to remain behind under Pizarro in order to remove any doubt about the determination of the others to carry out their plan.

For several months these men waited on the little island of Gallo, 2 degrees north latitude, for the arrival of the reinforcements. Half-naked and tortured with hunger, for they had nothing to eat but shellfish, they also suffered greatly from fearful storms of rain by which the whole island was flooded. At last a ship appeared to relieve their miserable condition, but it was not Almagro who commanded it, but Tafur. He had been sent by the Viceroy with the express command to bring the rest of the expedition back to Panama, where the second failure of the undertaking had excited great indignation against its foolhardy authors, and the great sacrifice of men which it demanded.

If Pizarro obeyed the command of the Governor, there was, he felt, no hope that a sufficient number of adventurers to accomplish his plans would ever again join him. He therefore set the command at nought, and by a short energetic speech succeeded in inducing thirteen of his companions to remain with him. Some provisions being left them, the bold men watched their countrymen sail away, and then, by means of a rude raft which they constructed, transferred their residence to an island called Gorgona, which lay somewhat more towards the north. There began again the same life of want and misery, which the settlers had to endure for seven long months before they descried a sail. This time it was the faithful Ruiz, who had importuned the Governor so long that at last he allowed him to set sail with a little ship manned only by sailors. But this permission was granted only on the condition that Pizarro's new expedition should not occupy more than six months.

Without delay he left the island where he had endured so much suffering, and a favourable wind carried him to the south. On the twentieth day after the departure from Gorgona, the ship rounded a cape, and the adventurers saw before them the glorious bay of Guayaquil (2 degrees south latitude). It was a magnificent sight. High in the background rose the snowy peak of the gigantic Chimborazo and Cotopaxi, and from their base down the crescent-shaped bay stretched broad forests and well-cultivated plains, while nearer the shore rose stately cities. The ship anchored before Tumbez, which lay on the south shore of the bay, and almost immediately the Curaca sent on board all kind of refreshments and some live llamas, an attention which Pizarro reciprocated by a present of swine and poultry, both unknown animals in that country. His messengers returned with a favourable report of the inhabitants, whom they described as friendly and cordial. They spoke also with admiration of the great buildings of the town, particularly of the Temple of the Sun, covered with plates of gold and silver, and full of astonishing treasures. But alluring as these reports sounded, their small number forbade the Spaniards to think of satisfying their hunger for gold, and Pizarro enjoined on all his companions to show the utmost friendship and forbearance in their intercourse with the natives. He continued his voyage to Santa (8 degrees south latitude) finding the coast everywhere studded with towns and villages inhabited by a gentle and industrious people. He was also able to satisfy himself sufficiently that he had reached the long-sought land of gold. Returning to Tumbez, where some of the crew settled, he left for the north, and in the spring of 1528 ran into the harbour of Panama after an absence of nearly two years.

The news he brought immediately reversed the unfavourable opinion that had been held with respect to the undertaking, and he found adventurers enough ready to join him. But his associates were of opinion that it would be best to obtain first distinct promises and a regular appointment from the Court; and with this object Pizarro was persuaded to go himself to Spain. He arrived in Seville in the summer of 1528, where, by the influence of Enciso, whom he had assisted in deposing, he was thrown into prison. But a royal command soon set him free; and at Toledo he maintained his claims so convincingly before Charles V., drawing such an animated picture of the riches of the land he had discovered, that the Indian Council received orders to arrange with him at once in the most favourable manner.

On the 26th of July 1529, a document was signed in which the rank and title of Governor, Commander-in-chief, Adelantado, and Supreme Judge was conferred upon Pizarro for the province of New Castile (the name given to the kingdom of the Incas), which he was to conquer. At the same time a revenue of 725,000 maravedis was conferred upon him, and significant figures were added to his coat of arms. But while he took such good care of himself, he only procured for Almagro the appointment of Governor of Tumbez, with a revenue of 200,000 maravedis, and for Luque the bishopric of Tumbez, with an income of

1000 ducats, although before his departure from Panama he had pledged himself to obtain for them honours equal to his own. By means of money advanced to him from many persons—among whom was Cortes, who happened to be just then in Spain—he was able to equip a little fleet, and, with 250 chosen men, set sail for the New World in January, 1530. Among his companions were his three brothers, Hernando, Gonzalo, and Juan, who forsook their humble employments in the little town of Truxillo, in the hope of ruling over great nations in Peru. In Panama the expedition was delayed by a vehement dispute between Pizarro and Almagro, who could not forgive the selfish conduct of his colleague, and would hardly be pacified.

It was not until January, 1531, that the three ships, having on board, besides the 200 soldiers, twenty-seven horses, proceeded on their way—a contemptible force to venture to overthrow the enormous and well-ordered kingdom of the Incas. But Pizarro's confidence had already endured many hard trials, and he doubted not of a favourable termination to the enterprise. His first spoil, worth 20,000 ducats, which he obtained by assaulting the town of Coaque, he sent back to Panama, that more men might be induced to follow under the leadership of Almagro. He himself proceeded along the coast, meeting with scarcely any opposition until he reached the island of Puna, in the Bay of Guayaquil. Here the warlike Indians met them in arms, and though after a violent struggle they received a serious overthrow, yet the Spaniards were left in a situation of great danger, until they were relieved by the arrival of a fresh force of 100 men under the gallant Hernando de Soto. The little army then proceeded to Tumbez. When Pizarro five years before first visited the kingdom of the Incas, it was under the rule of the powerful Huayna Capac, who in his youth had conquered Quito and incorporated the great state. But this powerful ruler had since died, and on his death-bed had made dispositions which produced very serious results. According to the unchange-able law of the empire, the crown passed to Prince Guascar, the eldest son of his queen. But by a princess of Quito he had a favourite son, named Atahualpa, who grew up near him and won his father's whole heart. From love to him he separated from the empire the newly-conquered kingdom of Quito, and gave it to his favourite as an independent govern-ment. For some years the brothers were very good friends ; but at length a war broke out between the two, and the whole army, with the best generals, took the side of Atahualpa, who had passed his youth in the army, and the rightful King was obliged to yield. Before the gates of his own capital, Guas-car, a prince of excellent qualities, was overcome and taken prisoner, while his fortunate rival obtained the crown, dis-gracing his conquest by a terrible slaughter of the Incas, his relatives.

These events had just occurred when the Spaniards landed in Tumbez, in 1532, and they had left behind traces not only in the land, but also in the tempers of the people. The Spaniards found Tumbez, which had been represented to them as so delightful, wasted, it was said, by the inhabitants of Puna. The colonists that had been left behind in the earlier expedition had vanished, and no certain information concerning their fate could be obtained. Pizarro therefore gave up his plan of making Tumbez the headquarters of the expedition, and led his army along the coast in a southerly direction, until he had found a suitable place. Here in a fruitful valley not far from the sea, into which a navigable river flowed, he founded the first Spanish colony, and gave it the name of San Miguel. He spent the whole summer of the year 1532 in fortifying the town, in forming a community out of those soldiers who were disposed to settle, and in appointing the authorities, while the ships returned to Panama with the spoil already collected. From the information that he collected here with regard to the condition of the country, he found that the deposed Guascar was languishing as a prisoner in the strong fortress Xaura, and that the victorious Atahualpa, with his army, was distant from San Miguel only some twelve days' journey in the town of Cassamarca, whither he had gone for the warm baths. There Pizarro determined to seek him out, and on the 21st of September, 1532, left San Miguel with 105 foot-soldiers and sixty-three horse.

Their way soon led the little band out of the glorious scenery of the coast into the wild region of the mountains whose summits appeared to touch the heavens. They were well received wherever they stopped, and an ambassador from the Inca met them, who brought presents to their general, and an invitation couched in the most friendly terms. Suspicious, however, of these assurances, Pizarro continued his march ready prepared for battle, the cavalry under his brother Hernando and the gallant de Soto going forward to explore the road and the heights. But they met with no hostile demonstration, and even the most difficult passes, which might have been made invincible by a small garrison, were found open and unguarded. Was the Inca in earnest in his assurances, or was he trying to entice the strangers into a trap? The Spaniards inclined to the latter supposition, which gave them the right to be stern and dictatorial. They still continued to ascend, and at last, by a difficult mule path, crossed the inhospitable ridge which was the boundary of Cassamarca. Then began to reappear beautiful watered meadows and cornfields, and at last was seen the town itself in a lovely green valley, whence arose a pillar of steam, betraying the far-famed hot springs. A mass of white tents rising in front of the town showed Pizarro that Atahualpa was protected by a considerable army.

But without sign of fear he led his little army down into the town, which he found deserted by its inhabitants. He chose for his quarters a three-cornered place at the end of the town, which was surrounded by spacious halls. Although the evening was far advanced, he sent a troop of cavalry to the neighbouring baths to greet the Inca and see how things stood. They found Atahualpa in an open court of the palace, surrounded by his dignitaries, but neither by the arrogant message of their general, nor by surprising feats of horsemanship, could they produce the least impression on the Prince, who remained quite impassive, and betrayed nothing of the astonishment which the unexpected appearances must have excited in him. But he listened courteously to their invitation to visit them in the town, and promised to come the next day.

What did Atahualpa purpose? Were his intentions as harmless as he asserted? It was hardly to be supposed that a prince who had given such proofs of courage and sagacity could be blind to the great danger that threatened his town. Or did he purpose to destroy these dangerous strangers, and had with this end in view enticed them into the lion's den? But then surely he would not have been rash enough to trust his own person to them. His conduct remains a riddle to this day, in spite of the assertion of Pizarro that he meant to kill most of the Spaniards, keeping the bravest in his service, and in spite of the fact that in Peru, as in Mexico, there was an old tradition of some divine beings who were one day to return, and that this old story no doubt came to the help of the daring invaders.

The report of the messengers of the dignified bearing of Atahualpa and the warlike masses by which he was surrounded put the courage of the Spaniards to a hard trial, but Pizarro assured them that all was going just as he wished, and that the next day would make them lords of Peru. He determined by a *coup de main* to make himself master of the person of the Prince, and make him play the same part that

Montezuma had played in the hands of Cortes, whom Pizarro followed as his model most faithfully.

On the next day, November 16th, 1532, he communicated his plans to his troops. He then caused the guns to be placed in a neighbouring fortress, and ordered his men to keep themselves concealed in the great halls and, at a given signal, to burst out and begin the slaughter. When all the preparations for the treacherous assault were complete, the priests who accompanied the Spanish army performed a solemn Mass, and called upon God to take under His almighty protection the warriors who were to fight for His holy cause, and for the extension of His kingdom. With pious ardour the soldiers joined in the prayers and hymns. " One might have supposed them," says Prescott, " a company of martyrs about to lay down their lives in defence of their faith, instead of a licentious band of adventurers meditating one of the most atrocious acts of perfidy on the record of history. But the Spaniards were not hypocrites : in their mistaken piety they were perfectly convinced that their designs would be pleasing to God, and, unfortunately, there is no want in history of examples to prove that the warmest religious enthusiasm may exist side by side with the most utter want of principle and the coarsest selfishness."

Meanwhile the unsuspecting victim was approaching. Before the town Atahualpa stopped and sent the desired message, that he should enter the town unarmed and with but few soldiers, and that he intended to pass the night there. It was near sunset when the head of the procession passed to their destruction through the gate of the city. First came a hundred servants to clear away every obstacle; then followed other companies of various ranks and variously clothed, but all with great magnificence. A particularly fine appearance was made by the body-guard and immediate servants of the Prince, dressed in sky-blue; and the chief members of the aristocracy excited much attention by their rich attire, and by the large golden balls which they wore in their ears. They all united in solemn songs, "which sounded in our ears," says one of the pious discoverers, "like songs of hell."

Last appeared the Inca borne on a litter, seated on a stool of solid gold, of inestimable value. The litter was adorned with bright-coloured feathers of tropical birds, and glittered with gold and silver plates. The dress of the Prince much surpassed in splendour that of his attendants. He wore a necklace of emeralds of unusual size and beauty. His short hair was ornamented, and round his brow was wound the royal turban, the Borla, the fringe of which hung down to his eyes. The Inca looked round him with dignity, and was astonished to see the place empty where he expected to meet the Spaniards.

Then Father Vincent de Valverde stepped forward to meet him. He was a gloomy Dominican, Pizarro's chaplain. He held in one hand a Bible, in the other a crucifix, and said he came at the General's command to call upon the King to accept Christianity. With the help of his interpreter, the cunning Felipillo, he explained the chief doctrines of the Christian Church, telling him that the vicars of Christ, the Popes of Rome, were lords of all lands, and therefore of Peru, and that they had charged the Spanish King to convert that country to Christianity. The summary, in itself rather indistinct, was not rendered more clear by passing through an interpreter. Only one thing did Atahualpa understand, the statement that in his land another than he possessed the supreme authority. He cried indignantly, "I am greater than any other Prince upon earth! Your Emperor may be a great Prince, I do not doubt it, since I see that he has sent his servants across the sea to me, and I am ready to consider him as a brother. As for what you said about the Pope, he must be mad if he thinks he can give away lands that do not belong to him." Then he asked Valverde on what he rested such foolish statements. The priest pointed to the Bible. Atahualpa took it, and being perfectly unacquainted with the crooked signs which covered the leaves, let the book drop carelessly on the ground. The monk hastily picked up the sacred book, ran to Pizarro and told him of the insult to the word of God. " Strike at once," he cried, " I will absolve you."

Pizarro lifted a white handkerchief and waved it, a cannon shot resounded, and at this given sign the Spaniards rushed from all sides upon their helpless victims. A cry of distress was raised, broken by the battle-cry of the assailants and the thunder of the artillery. The whole place was soon a scene of utter confusion, the alarmed Peruvians seeking in vain to escape from the swords of their relentless enemies. In desperation they succeeded in forcing an opening in the stone wall, by which some of them escaped. Pizarro's object from the beginning was to obtain possession of Atahualpa's person. But the faithful guards, who surrounded the Prince, threw themselves between him and the Spaniards, and, unarmed as they were, tried to make a defence for him of their own bodies. It was not until they were cut down to the last man that the assailants succeeded in seizing the King and carrying him safely into the neighbouring building.

Then the struggle ceased, but an enormous number of the noblest of the Peruvians—the accounts vary between 2000 and 10,000—lay dead on the scene of the conflict, while of the Spaniards not one was wounded. On the bodies of the fallen, who were buried the next day, a rich spoil was found, which was much increased by the plunder of the Inca's palace. Well satisfied, and with the consciousness of having performed a work well-pleasing to God, they lay down to sleep.

The unhappy Prince, bewildered by the treachery of the assault, and overwhelmed by the fearful scenes which he had witnessed, was entertained as a guest the same evening at the table of Pizarro, who behaved to him with soldierly courtesy and assured him of good treatment. A suite of rooms were appointed him, in which he settled himself with his wives and retinue. Intercourse with his subjects was allowed him, only of course under strict supervision. He reconciled himself to his altered situation with the *sang froid* characteristic of his people, and while towards his subjects he displayed, even as a prisoner, all the majesty of royalty, to his jailors he was friendly and sociable. From them he learned to play at dice and chess, and often gratified them with costly presents.

Pizarro chose Cassamarca for his headquarters. He employed himself first in erecting a Christian church, and then in making all the necessary arrangements for the maintenance of the troops. Through the captive Prince he summoned back the fugitive inhabitants, dismissed the Indian army and obtained possession of their leaders. At the same time he sent out companies to traverse the country, put down all opposition and plunder the temples and palaces. They soon collected important treasure, and Atahualpa had good reason to imagine that the Spaniards were impelled less by religious zeal and love of honour than by covetousness. He wished to please them that he might procure his liberty. So one day he offered to Pizarro, as ransom, sufficient gold to fill the room in which they were to the height that a man could reach with his arm. This offer surpassed so much the most brilliant expectations of the avaricious Spaniards that they doubted the possibility of its fulfilment. However, Pizarro consented, and drawing a red line along the wall, he made a notary draw up the conditions of the agreement. The room was about seventeen feet wide, twenty-two feet long, and the line on the wall was at a height of nine feet from the ground. This space was to be filled with gold, but it was agreed that the gold should not be melted into bars but should be left in the form in which it was found. A smaller neighbouring room Atahualpa offered to fill twice with gold, and for the fulfilment of the agreement a space of two months was allowed. His messengers went to all parts of the land and demanded from the priests and guardians of the palaces the golden furniture that they might bring it to Cassamarca. The news reached even the imprisoned Guascar, and in the hope of purchasing his freedom in the same way he offered the Spanish general still greater treasures than his brother, who, not being a native of Cusco, did not know the place where the treasures were to be found. But Atahualpa heard of this message, and, from a well-grounded fear that Pizarro would constitute himself arbitrator between the two rivals, gave orders that his unfortunate brother should be murdered. So Guascar died at the command of his brother, who, himself a prisoner, denied any complicity in the murder without being able to convince his jailor.

The wide extent of the kingdom delayed the execution of the promise that Atahualpa had given, but day after day great loads of royal treasures arrived and were put into safe custody. The impatience of the soldiers to obtain their share of the enormous booty was so great that at last Pizarro began the division. On a careful reckoning it was estimated that the gold collected was worth the enormous sum of 1,326,529 dollars, besides a mass of silver of the value of 51,610 marks. It was the greatest spoil that, since the memory of man, had fallen into the hands of a victorious army. Pizarro first separated the royal fifth, taking care that the most valuable and skilful work should be included in it that the Castilian Court might be made acquainted with the skill and taste of its new subjects. The royal portion was conveyed by Hernando Pizarro to Spain, and he was charged at the same time to seek for fresh honours for the conquerors and reinforcements. On the division Pizarro's share amounted to 57,222 dollars of gold and 2350 marks of silver, besides the Inca's stool of solid gold. The officers' prize was very great, and even of the common soldiers the horseman each received 8880 dollars of gold and 360 marks of silver, and the foot-soldiers 4440 dollars of gold and 180 marks of silver. Smaller sums were given to the garrison of San Miguel and to Almagro's troops, who had arrived meanwhile in Cassamarca with a force of 200 soldiers, of whom 50 were horsemen. The priest Luque, the third partner, had died shortly before, but Espinosa, who had advanced the money, appears to have been richly repaid.

The newly-arrived forces at last made it possible for Pizarro to think of marching to Cusco, but he felt that the captive Prince would be in his way. Since the division of the spoil he had loudly demanded his freedom, although the treasures had not entirely fulfilled his promise. Pizarro hesitated, but at last determined to prolong Atahualpa's captivity and to look for an opportunity of ridding himself of his troublesome prisoner. It came only too soon. Reports were spread of threatened risings among the natives aroused by the dethroned Inca against the strangers, and the soldiers, who saw before them all the hardships of camp-life, demanded the death of the conspirator. Pizarro was decided. He sent away from the camp the chivalrous Hernando de Soto, the warmest defender of the prisoner, and formed a court of justice to try the unhappy Prince. With heartless hypocrisy great pains were taken to give to the arbitrary act an appearance of justice. Pizarro and Almagro sat as judges, an advocate was given to the accused, and a public official prosecuted.

Twelve charges were brought against him, the most important being that he had usurped the Crown and murdered his brother, that after the conquest of the country by the Spaniards he had wasted the revenues of the empire to the injury of the Castilian crown, that he was guilty of idolatry and adultery, and that he had tried to excite a rebellion against the Spaniards. The unfortunate man was unanimously declared guilty, and the only question that was raised was the advisability of a capital sentence. This, however, was soon decided upon, and the pious Valverde gave the matter his blessing. When the sentence was communicated to the Inca he was much distressed, although he had long foreboded it. For a moment trouble unmanned him, and he cried with tears in his eyes, "What have I done to deserve so miserable a fate? And you condemn me to it," he said, turning to Pizarro, "you who have been treated by my people with kindness and hospitality, with whom I have shared my treasures, and who have received nothing but kindness from my hands?" He begged piteously for his life, but the heartless man was not to be moved. Then Atahualpa recovered his composure, and calmly allowed himself to be led in chains to the place of execution. He had constantly resisted all attempts of Valverde to convert him, but the fear of being burnt alive overcame him, and the promise being given him of sparing him this fearful form of death if he was baptised, he professed himself a Christian. He had hardly entered the Christian Church under the name of Juan de Atahualpa, when the executioner put an end to his troubles by strangling him. So died, August 29th, 1533, the last Inca who reigned independently over the great kingdom. He was a man of great and brilliant qualities, both of the heart and understanding, though there were not wanting dark shadows on his character. But these fall into insignificance when compared with the black deceit and cunning cruelty to which he fell a victim. His execution brought upon Pizarro much well-deserved reproach, and he sought in vain to throw the blame of the detestable crime upon the officers who had urged him to it.

The death of the Inca, the sun round which the whole state system of Peru revolved, necessarily brought confusion into the entire kingdom, and rebellion broke out in the distant provinces, while at the same time an Indian army assembled before Cusco to prevent the Spaniards from entering the holy city. Pizarro tried to smooth over this difficulty by setting upon the vacant throne first a brother of Atahualpa's, and after his speedy death a brother of Guascar's, the youthful and heroic Manco Capac, and causing the Peruvians solemnly to pay him homage. The march to Cusco was delayed by repeated skirmishes, and many a difficult pass could only be won by hard fighting. But at last all difficulties were overcome, and the Spaniards saw lying at their feet Cusco, the holy city of the Incas. On November 15th, 1533, they entered it, and were not less astonished at finding such a healthy climate at the height of 10,000 feet above the sea than at the extent of the population, which is reckoned then to have numbered 400,000, and also at the regular arrangement of the streets and numerous fine buildings. The town was divided into four quarters by four streets which led to the four pro-vinces of the great empire. In the spacious squares rose gigantic edifices, the castles of the Incas, the temple of the sun, etc., while at the east end upon a hill stood a fortress, built of enormous stones, commanding the whole town. In all these buildings was to be found excellent masonry, on many also tasteful sculpture. But what delighted the Spaniards more than anything was the prospect of rich spoil, in which they were not disappointed.

Although the chief wealth had previously been sur-rendered for Atahualpa's ransom, and Pizarro had strictly forbidden the plundering of private houses, yet a treasure was collected and divided among the adventurers which was estimated at 580,200 ducats in gold, and 215,000 marks of silver. The sudden flood of riches naturally produced a most pernicious effect upon those rude minds ; very few ultimately returned rich to their native land, most squandered their wealth in the most foolish manner. Many fell victims to the love for gambling which seems born in Spaniards, losing all their property in one day. Then all the worst passions of the human heart were aroused, and the unhappy Peruvians saw their property, their honour, their freedom, their life treated as toys by wild inhuman masters.

In Cusco, where many Spaniards settled, the civil government was soon arranged, and attempts were made to convert the natives. Pizarro founded settlements in different parts of the country, and by the lavish manner in which he bestowed repartimientos attracted many Spaniards into the land. From among these infant towns he selected Los Reyes (the city of the three kings), which he founded on January 6, 1535, for the capital of the kingdom, and took great pains with the building of it. It prospered and increased rapidly, and its name was soon changed to that of Lima, from the river Rimac, on the banks of which it was situated. In a short time rose on the coast Truxillo and Santa to the north, and Nasca and Arequipa to the south. The fruitfulness of the soil, and the natural resources of the country, especially the mines, promised the youthful settlement rapid prosperity, but a succession of terrible conflicts soon destroyed these hopes.

First there was a fearful rising of the natives which called for all the efforts of the conquerors. The young Inca Manco Capac succeeded in escaping from the captivity in which his white masters kept him, and called his people to arms. He appeared in 1536 with a huge army before Cusco, which was garrisoned by 200 Spaniards under Hernando and Juan, brothers of the Governor. The attack was made with unequalled fury, and repeated day after day. To this was added a great fire by which a large part of the town was laid in ashes, and famine also made its appearance among the besieged. But they endured with heroic courage all the sufferings of a five months' siege, constantly making sanguinary sorties until at last the army of the besiegers was dispersed. Juan Pizarro lost his life in the defence of the town.　After having escaped this extreme danger it was not hard for the Spaniards to drive the rebel Peruvians step by step out of the cultivated portion of the country into the impassable mountains.　There, however, Manco Capac held out for many years, frequently descending to destroy with fire and sword the land over which his father had reigned so prosperously, and which was now bleeding under the iron heel of the foreigner.　It was not until 1544 that he met his death at the hand of an assassin.

Still more disastrous for the country was the renewal of the old dispute between Pizarro and Almagro.　The arrival of Hernando Pizarro at the Spanish court had caused universal astonishment and surprise throughout Spain.　His story and the treasures that he brought surpassed so much all that had ever been seen before that every one was inclined to consider it a fairy tale, and nothing but the evidence of their senses could persuade them of the truth of these wonders.　Thousands offered themselves for the gold land, and Fernando set out on his return with a great fleet crowded with new settlers. He was also the bearer of fresh favours from the Emperor to the two leaders.　Pizarro's province, which began at the river San Juan, 4 degrees north latitude, and extended 70 Spanish miles to the south, received an addition of 270 more.　All the country south of that was given to Almagro as an independent government.　Very soon arose difficulties about the boundaries of the two provinces.　Cusco, even Lima itself, became disputed territory.　Almagro at first undertook an exploring and conquering expedition to the south.　He crossed the Cordilleras in one of the wildest parts, where afterwards the inexhaustible silver mines of Potosi were discovered, and traversed the land of Chili in spite of frequent conflicts with the natives.　But he was forced to return without founding a settlement or finishing the conquest of the country.　He climbed up through the inhospitable desert of

Atacama to the tableland of Titicaca, where he arrived just in time to assist in overthrowing Manco Capac, who was besieging Cusco. He then laid claim himself to the possession of the capital, and succeeded in making himself master of it by surprise, and capturing Hernando and Gonzalo, the two brothers of his rival. A division of the army which was sent against him he completely defeated at the river Abançay. Pizarro not being then in a position to make head against him tried to avert the threatened danger by negotiations, and brought Almagro to consent to a temporary agreement, according to which he released the brothers Pizarro and evacuated Cusco. Meanwhile the Governor hastily made preparations, procured reinforcements from Central America, and soon found himself at the head of a large army, which he sent, under the command of his brother Hernando, against his old companion-in-arms, remaining himself in Lima.

Terrified out of his false security, Almagro marched to Cusco, and there, oppressed by age and sickness, surrendered his command to his faithful officer Orgonez. On April 26th, 1538, ensued the decisive battle at Salinas, before the gates of Cusco. After a bloody conflict Pizarro remained the victor. Orgonez fell, his army dispersed, and Almagro was taken prisoner. Fernando Pizarro, after having given Cusco up to plunder, called a court-martial to decide the fate of the rebel. The pitiable farce to which Atahualpa had fallen victim was repeated. Condemned to death, Diego de Almagro was strangled in prison, his body beheaded in the public square, and then buried with great ceremony, Pizarro's brother following the bier as chief mourner. At the time of his miserable death Almagro was an old man of seventy. He was of equally low origin with Pizarro, and had passed through the same school of danger and adventure ; but he differed from him in his cheerful disposition and frank nature, and was totally wanting in the cautious circumspect character which distinguished Pizarro. Hernando Pizarro would scarcely have dared to commit such an act without being certain of his brother's consent, and both were to receive the due punishment of their crime. Hernando went to Spain in 1539, where the friends of the murdered man had accused him, trusting that the treasures he brought with him would be sufficient proofs of his innocence. But he was coldly received, and without a trial was sent to the fortress of Medina del Campo, where he languished a prisoner for twenty years. He did not obtain his freedom until 1560, when, unbroken by his long confinement, he had attained a great age.

Long before that had the Governor Francisco Pizarro met his end. He had treated the numerous adherents of Almagro with careless contempt, neither attempting to win them by kindness nor to keep them down by severity. These discontented men formed a dangerous party in the new state. For all the sufferings and dangers they had endured, especially the march to Chili, they had been rewarded only by poverty and neglect. They found a head in the natural son of their late leader, young Diego de Almagro, whom his father had named his heir, but whom Pizarro had robbed of his inheritance. Under the guidance of a discontented officer named Juan de Rada, Diego made preparations for an outbreak. On Sunday, June 26th, 1541, the conspirators, only twenty in number, left Almagro's house and hastened to the palace of the Governor, shouting, "Long live the King! Death to the tyrant!" The inhabitants of Lima, quiet in their houses during the midday heat, paid no attention to the uproar, and so the murderers passed unhindered through the open doors of the palace, cutting down all who came in their way. Pizarro had been warned some days before, but considered the report a mere invention. He had just been dining in company with his half-brother, Martin de Alcantara, the chief judge, and the new Bishop of Quito, and other friends, when the noise warned him

DEATH OF PIZARRO.

of the greatness of the danger. He preserved his presence of mind perfectly, and commanding an officer to shut the door which led into the court, he hastened to put on his armour. But the officer in confusion ran straight into the arms of the conspirators and was cut down. So before the Governor and his friends were armed the conspirators were upon them. Nevertheless they fought desperately, and several of the assailants were stretched mortally wounded on the ground. Alcantara and the other friends of the Governor fell, and he himself was attacked, but brought several to the ground by quick powerful blows, till at last he received a severe wound in the neck and fell. "Jesus," cried the wounded man, and making with his finger a cross on the bloody ground, he stooped to kiss it, when another blow ended his life.

So closed this strange career, so rich in adventure, in brilliant feats and in horrible crimés, begun in poverty and dirt and reaching the highest honours and riches. No one can deny his great qualities, his unwavering courage, his quick discernment, his rapid action, his perfect self-confidence ; and the stains on his character which disgust us are to be found on all those unprincipled adventurers, disfiguring also a Balboa and a Cortes. But in Pizarro were wanting the redeeming features which almost reconcile us to the others and make us judge them rather leniently and admire their heroism. Their nobility of mind and chivalrous disposition were ill replaced by the cold calculation and passionless character of Pizarro, and his image remains gloomy and hateful. Apparently he was about seventy years of age at the time of his death. His funeral was conducted the same evening in the greatest haste and secrecy. Some servants carried the body wrapped in a cloth to the church, where it was buried in one corner without chant or prayer. "There was none," says the historian Gomara, "to say 'God forgive him.'"

Immediately after Pizarro's death, the young Almagro was

proclaimed Governor, and acknowledged by all in authority. But even after this revolution the troubles of the young state were not over. Shortly after, the judge Vaca de Castro entered Peru, having been sent out by the Spanish Government some months before to investigate the troubles of the country and call Pizarro to account for his deeds of violence. Immediately after his arrival he made use of his authority and summoned Almagro to submit to him, while at the same time, by his wise, firm, and moderate conduct, he gained the hearts of the chief part of the Spanish settlers. But Almagro, fearing for his life, withdrew to Cusco and prepared for war. A battle was fought in the plains of Chupas on September 16, 1542, Almagro was defeated after a gallant struggle, taken prisoner, and executed in Cusco with forty of his adherents. Under the judicious management of Vaca de Castro the land enjoyed a short period of rest, but was again disturbed by the intelligence that a new code of laws had been prepared in Spain for Peru, which would infringe the rights of the conquerors, by declaring the Peruvians free and protecting them against their masters. To carry out these laws Blasco Nunez Vela was chosen, and named Viceroy of Peru. He arrived in the summer of 1544, and entered Lima with great pomp. But the object for which he was sent out made him hated by all the Spaniards, and his violent conduct augmented the embittered feeling until at last it broke out in open insurrection. It was headed by Gonzalo Pizarro, the only one left of the four brothers, who, as Governor of Quito, had spent a long time on a difficult expedition down the Amazon. During Vaca de Castro's rule he had been engaged in working his rich mines. He was a brilliant soldier, but possessed no force of character. The Spaniards flocked round him, and he was soon able to lead an army against Lima, where the Governor shut himself up. Utter confusion ensued. At last in a battle fought before the gates of Quito on January 18th, 1546, Blasco Nunez was defeated and fell.

The fortunate victor was proclaimed Governor, and saluted with the title of " Deliverer and Protector of the people." His authority seemed firmly established throughout the land, his fleet ruled the sea, and even Darien was dependent on him. In overweening security he adopted a princely style of magnificence, and probably intended to declare himself independent King of Peru. But the end of his glory soon came.

The opposition to Governor Nunez had excited great displeasure in Spain, and in the new governor, Pedro de la Gasca, the right man was found for a most difficult post. He had given indubitable proofs of ardent loyalty and great qualities, while he was a man of gentle manners and at the same time of resolute character. By the decision of Charles V. himself, he was invested with unlimited powers and almost royal privileges, and embarked for America on May 26th, 1546.

It was not until his arrival that he heard of the complete triumph of Pizarro and the death of the Viceroy, by which he was placed in a most difficult position. But by his moderation and perseverance he succeeded ultimately in awakening regret for their rebellion in the minds of most of Pizarro's companions and persuading them to come over to his side. After a war of several months Pizarro's army was disbanded just before the battle which was to decide the matter. He himself was captured, and in April, 1548, with several of his associates brought to execution.

Gasca was equally successful in reducing the land to order, and when in 1550 he embarked for Spain, he left Peru in perfect repose, the Spaniards in the enjoyment of their lands and the Indians reconciled to their lot. The monarch, for whom by his wise and energetic conduct he had saved the brightest jewel of his foreign possessions, rewarded him with the bishopric of Siguenza, which he held until his peaceful death in 1567.

CHAPTER VIII.

THE LAST DISCOVERIES OF THE SPANIARDS.

IT has been already remarked that the discoveries of the
Spaniards are closely connected with the finding of the precious metals. In the search for them they shrank from no
difficulties and no hardships. Countries where gold and silver
were to be found were soon covered with settlements, and gold-
seekers streamed in unceasingly from the mother country.
On the other hand, those countries that were poor in the precious metals soon lost all interest, and it was only under exceptionally favourable circumstances that, after a long period,
immigrants began to stream into them.

Such natural advantages, however, existed for the Antilles
and the Isthmus of Darien. Those islands were the natural
and most convenient station for Spanish ships going farther to
the west ; as the oldest possessions, they had attained a higher
degree of order, and the towns planted on them had grown
up so quickly that the inhabitants felt settled and at home,
while their harbours showed signs of active prosperity. The
isthmus having special importance as the highway for all the
trade of Peru, the town of Panama developed rapidly.

Of all the countries along the coast of the eastern sea,
Mexico, so rich in silver, was most attractive, and the overflow
of its settlers went to found new colonies in the neighbouring lands to the north, where new silver mines were constantly
being found. Chihuahua was taken possession of by Francisco
de Ibarra in 1564, and a few years later the outposts of the

Spanish settlers extended to the wild regions of New Mexico, and were the scene of unceasing conflicts with the wild Indians.

The north coast of the Mexican Gulf had been explored in a series of expeditions, and claimed as a Spanish possession; but after, by searching the coast narrowly, it had been proved that the passage to the west was not to be found there, no further interest was taken in the swampy lands which gave no promise of precious metals. Florida was the only exception, being the object of many voyages of discovery, in consequence of dazzling accounts of riches reported to be found in a land sparingly endowed by Nature.

The old romantic knight, Juan Ponce de Leon, the discoverer of the land, had been attracted by a spring which was to restore youth. The unfortunate experience of Ponce did not prevent numbers of enterprising men from following in his steps. Lucas Vasquez de Ayllon, in 1526, tried to establish a settlement on the banks of the river Sautee, in the part now called South Carolina; but in conflict with the natives, who were irritated by treacherous attacks, he lost the greater part of his men, and led the rest back to Hispaniola. Then Pamphilo de Narvaez, the unlucky opponent of the great Cortes, appeared on the scene. Supported by influential friends, he received permission to conquer Florida, and equipped a force of 400 men, among whom were forty-five horsemen. With this strong force he embarked on board a numerous fleet, and appeared on April 12th, 1528, off the west coast of Florida. Deaf to all advice, he immediately landed his troops, and marched with them into the interior of the country, commanding his fleet to go in search of a desirable harbour. In spite of indescribable difficulties from the swampy land, and continued contests with the warlike natives, the march was conducted to the heart of the peninsula; but none of the desired treasures were found, and the army was obliged to return to the coast. There they wandered about, looking

in vain for the fleet, which had been scattered by a storm.
At last they determined to build boats, and in them proceed
along the coast. These frail barks, however, were all swallowed up by the waves, Narvaez himself losing his life. Of
all these brave men, only two were ever again seen by their
countrymen—the paymaster, Alvaro Nunez, who, after being
kept in hard slavery for many years by the rude tribes, appeared in the autumn of 1536 on the north border of Mexico,
which he had succeeded in reaching after a journey on foot of
incredible difficulty; and a sailor, Juan Ortez, who was rescued
by the next expedition.

Unterrified by the miserable result of all the earlier expeditions, Hernando de Soto, the chivalrous companion of
Pizarro, accepted the government of Florida, and employed
the great treasures which he had won in Peru in equipping a
gallant army of 1000 men, with which he proceeded to his
government on May 12th, 1539. He founded a settlement
on the Bay of San Spirito, which was afterwards removed to
the Apalachie Gulf, and penetrated with his army [into the
interior, where he had to struggle with the same difficulties of
the swampy soil and savage inhabitants as his predecessor
had done. More fortunate than he had been, Soto overcame
all difficulties, passed the winter at a favourable part of the
peninsula, and then, by deceitful accounts of a land rich in
gold, allowed himself to be persuaded into undertaking a
great expedition in a north-westerly direction to the river
Mississippi. Crossing it the indefatigable general proceeded
as far as the Arkansas, but then was obliged to return and
establish himself at the junction of the two streams. There
he was attacked on May 25th, 1542, by a lingering fever, to
which his constitution, weakened by excessive exertion, at
last succumbed. His army, thus left without a general, attempted first to reach Mexico, but in the prairies of Texas
was forced to give up the plan and return to the Mississippi.

On seven frail ships which they built there, the survivors, 350 in number, embarked on the 2nd of July, 1543, and, after a tedious voyage along the coast, reached the Atlantic harbours of Mexico in a miserable condition.

The unfortunate result of this brilliant expedition taught the Spaniards a lesson, and from that time they forsook the dangerous coast. It was only very gradually that there arose round the best harbours of Florida little settlements, which in time became towns. St. Augustine, lying on the east coast, 30° north latitude, is the oldest of these towns.

More successful were the enterprises which had for their object the rich mountain lands between Darien and Mexico. As early as 1515 and 1516 armies under Gonsalo de Badajoz and that Gaspar de Espinosa who afterwards defrayed the expenses of the conquest of Peru, swept over the country now called Costa Rica, and carried away rich spoil. Later Gil Gonçalez Davila arrived, having started, in 1522, with four ships to explore the coast of Panama. He visited the Gulf of Nicoya, which Espinosa had already found, and during a march into the interior discovered the great fresh water lake, which, from a neighbouring chief, was called Nicaragua. Here they met with a highly-cultivated people, closely resembling the Aztecs in their manners. The squadron proceeded at once to the north, and discovered the Gulf of Papagayo and that beautiful inlet of the South Sea, which, in honour of the President, received the name of Fonseca Bay (13° north latitude). The newly-annexed lands soon received a large number of emigrants from Panama.

Penetrating farther to the north, the Spanish discoverers met some of their countrymen, who had entered the country from the opposite direction. They were commanded by Pedro de Alvarado, the bold companion of Cortes, whom the latter had commissioned to conquer the country of Guatemala. He performed his task with horrible cruelty in the year 1524. The people of this land were highly civilised, related to the Toltecs in Mexico and the Mayas in Yucatan, but incapable of resisting the arms which had overthrown the mighty kingdom of the Aztecs. Alvarado remained until his death, in 1541, Governor of Guatemala, which attained such importance that in 1540 it was separated from Mexico, to which it had hitherto belonged, and was made independent under its own Captain-general. At the same time the rest of the territories in Central America were added to it, and also Honduras, which Olid had conquered in 1523. The Captain-general resided in Old Guatemala, a town which soon became, next to Mexico, the most splendid of the whole of Spanish America.

The north coast of South America was not occupied by Spanish colonists until later, although it had been made known by Columbus and Ojeda. This was probably caused by fear of the Caribs, who had inflicted fearful damage on the first Spaniards who entered their country. The country of Uraba on the Gulf of Darien, too well known by the miserable expeditions of Ojeda, was colonised by Spaniards from the south. Sebastian de Belalcazar, an officer of Pizarro's, had conquered Quito in 1534, and going on northward into the valley of Popayan, in which the river Cauca had its source, took possession of a province for himself, holding it under the government of Lima. Penetrating still farther northward, Juan de Quesada occupied the highlands of the Cordilleras on both banks of the Magdalena, founding there, in 1538, the new capital of Santa-Fé de Bogota, at a great height above the sea, and opening a way along the stream to the Caribbean Sea.

About the same time the neighbouring coasts from the Gulf of Maracaybo to the mouth of the Orinoco were occupied. All these territories were given by Charles V., in 1525, to his privy councillor, the merchant, Bartholomäus

Welser, who, being born (1484) a scion of a famous commercial house in Augsburg, by successful speculation became one of the richest men in Europe, and counted the Emperor himself among his debtors. As payment for a debt of 11,000,000 gulden, a long strip of the coast was given him for twenty-eight years. It was named Venezuela (Little Venice), from the villages built on piles in the sea, which the discoverers had found on the coasts of the Gulf of Maracaybo. Welser, in 1527, sent his trusted friend—afterwards son-in-law—Ambrosius Dalfinger into the country. He took with him some Jesuit missionaries, twenty-four German miners, and a company of Spanish soldiers. Coro, lying at the mouth of the Maracaybo, was the starting-point of expeditions by which he gradually subdued the numerous tribes of the natives. Nicolaus Federmann, of Ulm, who joined him in 1530, with fresh forces, has given us a faithful description of these savages, and of the wars waged against them.

But after the death of the Governor, Dalfinger, in 1541, the administration of the colony, the produce of which the Welsers brought under their own flag to the European markets, fell into bad hands. Quarrels with the Governors of the neighbouring Spanish colonies, and the cruelties which the agents and soldiers had perpetrated upon the natives, turned the attention of the Spanish Government to the mal-administration. Following the advice of a commission sent to investigate the matter, Charles V. took away the government in 1555 from the Welsers, buying back their rights and taking possession of Venezuela for the Spanish crown. The new Governor took up his residence after 1566 in Caracas, where Columbus had already founded a settlement under the name of San Jago de Leon.

The attempts to explore the course of the gigantic Amazon claim a special interest on account of the fearful sufferings endured by the discoverers. Gonzalo Pizarro, the youngest of the brothers, had scarcely been appointed Governor of Quito when he collected a considerable army to subjugate the mysterious lands lying to the east, where they expected to find the most valuable spices, and of course plenty of gold and precious stones. With 350 well-armed Spaniards, 4000 Indians, many horses and dogs, he marched out of Quito in January, 1540.

But the passage over this almost inaccessible part of the Cordilleras was only accomplished with the greatest difficulty, and a fearful earthquake, splitting the rocks and swallowing up entire villages, increased the terror with which the stern face of nature impressed even these bold minds. When the descent on the east side of the mountains was effected, the warm damp climate generated severe sickness, and the journey through the uninhabited region of the primeval forests weakened even the most hardened constitutions. The Spaniards were soon reduced to the most loathsome food, and their garments worn to rags. But the dazzling pictures called up by their imagination gave them strength to persevere. They pursued their march along the banks of the Napo, a tributary of the Amazon. Their strength continuing to fail, they built a ship with indescribable difficulty, melting down the shoes of the slaughtered horses for nails, using the gum of trees for pitch, and their torn clothes for ropes. After hard labour for two months a rough boat was completed, strong and roomy enough to carry half the company.

The journey was thus rendered easier, but their sufferings from hunger increased, and still there appeared no signs of inhabited or cultivated land. In this extremity Pizarro sent forward the ship with fifty men, under the command of Francisco de Orellana of Truxillo, to forage for provisions and await the arrival of the others at the confluence of the Napo and the Amazon. Pizarro and those who remained with him reached this spot after a wearisome march of two months.

But, to their horror, the ship was nowhere to be seen, and they learned from Sanchez de Vargas, who had quitted it, that Orellana, thinking only of his own safety, had pursued his way down the larger stream, hoping to be able from its mouth to reach Spain.

In their despair the only stay of the Spaniards was the heroic courage of Gonzalo Pizarro. He pointed out to them that there was no hope of deliverance, except in at once returning to Quito. But the sufferings endured on the road were fearful, and only eighty Spaniards and 1000 Indians reached (June, 1542) the point whence the expedition had started: and they were naked, famished, scarred, and wounded, and many of them bearing in their bodies the seeds of incurable diseases.

Meanwhile Orellana, who excused the faithlessness with which he had left his companions a prey to hunger, by the impossibility of steering against the mighty stream, had successfully escaped all the dangers to which the ship was exposed from the rapidity of the stream, the rocks, and the floating islands. He seldom ventured to land, since his weak and famished crew were not a match for the warlike Indians. At last he reached the coast, and steering northward came to the little island of Cubagua, which lies off Paria, and was then much visited on account of its pearl fisheries. Here he found Spanish ships, which conveyed him and his companions home. He mixed up with his report of their unendurable sufferings fables of an Eldorado, and of a race of warlike women that inhabited the land, which doubtless gave rise to the name still borne by the mightiest stream on the earth. He received permission to conquer and colonise the lands that he had discovered, and collected for that purpose 500 adventurers. They, however, could not agree, and dispersed when they reached the Canary Islands, Orellana himself dying of vexation.

For more than 100 years the upper and middle streams of
the Amazon, thus explored by him, were not again visited by
any European, but the land near the estuary was quickly
taken possession of by the Portuguese Government and united
to Brazil, to the coasts of which a large body of emigrants
was sent.

After Hernando Jacques had built (1526) Pernambuco, the
oldest of all the Brazilian cities, Bahia and Rio Janeiro arose,
and the whole land was placed under Captain-generals, of
whom the first, Thomas de Souza, fixed his residence in
Bahia.   Still farther south Spain maintained the right which
the discoveries of the unfortunate Juan Diaz de Solis
(1515-16) and of Magalhaens (1519) had given her over the
Gulf of La Plata.

In 1525 Pedro de Mendoza offered Charles II. to undertake
at his own cost the exploration and conquest of that tract of
country, and the land between the river Paraguay and La
Plata was conferred upon him with the title of Adelantado.
In 1534 he set out with fourteen ships and 3000 men, explored
the lower course of the two great streams which empty themselves into the Rio de la Plata, and by a victorious conflict
with the natives assured the Spanish dominion.   On a favourable spot he laid the foundation, in 1535, of the town Buenos
Ayres, and died on his way to Spain, whence he was seeking
reinforcements.

In 1537 Juan de Ayolas went up the Paraguay, and somewhere about eighty degrees south latitude reached the highlands of Peru.   On his return, however, the natives, whom
he had treated in a cruel manner, fell upon him and
killed him with all his companions.   Twelve years later
Captain Dominigo Martinez de Yrala repeated the attempt
to unite the Spanish possessions on the shores of South
America.   The way which he chose was south of that taken
by Ayolas, and led through wild mountain regions ; but he

succeeded in reaching Peru, and in returning again to Paraguay. On the way laid open by him constant intercourse has since been established between the two Spanish provinces.

The narrow coast land of Chili was explored in 1525 by Almagro, to whom the Emperor had allotted it ; but he neglected to establish permanent colonies, being too much occupied in maintaining against Pizarro his claim to the southern part of Peru. After his defeat his successful rival added the land to his own territory, and commissioned the brave Pedro de Valdivia to conquer it. He began in 1538, and by hard fighting established himself in the land. The first town that he founded was Santiago, which is still the capital of the country, and in 1550 the celebrated harbour of Valparaiso was formed.

But previously to that time there had been dissensions in Peru, and Pedro de Valdivia had sided with the imperial governor, Pedro de la Gasca, contributing more almost than any one to the triumph of the latter over Gonzalo Pizarro. As a reward the government of Chili was conferred upon him, as an independent Captain-general. But he only enjoyed this new honour for a few years. In 1553 he fell into the hands of the wild Araucans, a people inhabiting the south of Chili, and not yet completely subdued, and by them was slain.

The communication of the rich colonies in the Pacific with the mother-country was maintained through Panama, for in spite of the delays and difficulties accompanying the lading and unlading on the two coasts of the peninsula, this way was always preferred on account of its safety and speed to the tedious and dangerous passage through the Straits of Magellan. It was not until the discovery of Cape Horn by the Dutch that a commercial highway round South America was established.

CHAPTER IX.

THE SPANISH RULE IN AMERICA.

THE false assumption with which the Spaniards entered the New World, that in consequence of the Pope's gift the whole land was the property of their King, and that their conflicts with the heathen inhabitants was a holy work, became the source of endless misery. If an adventurer took possession, with the proper formalities, of an island or a coast in the name of his King, resistance to the foreign power was looked upon and punished as rebellion. And if any unfortunate native ignorantly accepted baptism, the slightest relapse to the worship of his fathers was sufficient to condemn him to be burnt as a heretic. It was on this false reasoning too that the conquerors supported their right to impose the yoke of slavery on the Indians, and to give an appearance of justice and piety to their selfish plans and heartless cruelties.

Rebellion and heresy were the pretexts made use of by the Spanish governors for breaking down the power of the native princes and sweeping them from their paths. The fate of Guatemozin and Atahualpa was shared by hundreds of Indian chiefs on equally frivolous grounds. It was often considered unnecessary to go through the form of a trial, and the Spaniards recklessly violated the most solemn treaties. and committed acts of brutal violence. Such was the conduct of Nicolas de Ovando in 1503 towards Anacoana, the beautiful and sagacious Queen of Xaraqua, the most westerly district of Hispaniola. He announced his intention of paying her a visit, and set out with 200 infantry and seventy horsemen. Anacoana, who had always shown herself a faithful ally of the Spaniards, received him with considerate respect, and in his honour caused a great dramatic dance to be performed. But the gloomy Ovando was brooding over a bloody requital. He invited her and her chiefs to a military feast, and while she, with surprise and delight, was gazing at the new spectacle he gave the preconcerted signal by laying his hand on his order. Instantly the soldiers turned their arms against their unsuspecting guests and a fearful slaughter began. Neither sex nor age found pity or compassion. Anacoana was taken alive, but only to be reserved for an ignominious death on the gallows. In order to escape from a threatened investigation of this crime, two years after her death Ovando instituted a trial of the unfortunate Queen and pronounced her justly condemned for an attempted rebellion. If those in authority were guilty of such fearful acts of violence against the princes, how could they successfully control the Spanish soldiers of fortune who came down like a troop of hungry wolves upon the natives. To have been born in Spain gave any one a claim to a piece of land and a number of Indians to cultivate it. These unfortunate beings possessed absolutely no rights, and a life of danger and a sudden accession to prosperity and fortune rendered their masters insensible to their sufferings. Besides the worst cases, unfortunately only too numerous, of perfectly inhuman cruelty and bloodthirstiness, there was also such a fearful amount of hardheartedness and indifference on the one side, and misery and despair on the other, that one can well understand the irritation that even contemporaneous writers display while narrating the gloomy history.

The Spanish Government did everything in its power to soften the lot of the Indians, partly from self-interest, for the unfortunate creatures were Spanish subjects and increased the national revenues, but also from compassion and humanity.

The pious Isabella tried to protect the Indians from the oppressions of the Spaniards, and after her death the Government continued the same efforts and drew up a number of laws by which they consented, indeed, that the Indians should be forced to execute a certain quantity of work, but endeavoured to secure to them their freedom and a humane treatment. But these laws could not be carried out in the colonies; the officials were much too avaricious to resist the temptation of rapidly becoming rich; and all authority was powerless against the resolution with which the colonists stood upon their supposed rights.

At the sight of such terrible events, the clergy did not forget their sacred duty as the protectors of the oppressed. The monks of the Dominican Order especially raised their voices loudly, and condemned from the pulpit the inhumanity of the Spaniards. They continued their heroic struggle against the tyranny of the colonists, in spite of the persecution which they had to endure from them, and although they were not supported as they ought to have been by the court, where the opposite party employed both influence and gold against them.

The noble Bartholomé de las Casas was the most indefatigable champion of the Indians. Born at Seville in 1474, he laboured as a priest in Hispaniola from 1504, and after that in Cuba. He relinquished his post there in order to plead the cause of the remains of the native population. After an attempt to found a model colony on the coast of Paria, which in spite of his efforts proved unsuccessful, he joined the Dominican Order in 1523, and for many years laboured successfully as a preacher of the Gospel in Mexico, Nicaragua, and Guatemala, constantly endeavouring to restrain the violence of the Christian conquerors, and beloved as a father by the poor heathens to whom he devoted himself. During this time he was often in Spain, where he did his utmost to make the court lay to heart the grievances of its brown subjects. In order to increase the effect of their complaints he drew up a detailed description of the cruelties of which the Spaniards had been guilty, calling it "A Short Account of the Destruction of India." In the most unsparing manner he accused both those in authority and also private people of arbitrary cruelty, and painted a horrible picture of the oppression to which the poor Indians were exposed. It is a terrible history of suffering, every line written in blood, and we can only hope that the benevolent man, in order to produce a more striking effect, lent a willing ear to many unauthenticated accounts of robbery and violence, and in righteous indignation exaggerated the cruelty. The book excited the greatest attention, the court was shaken out of its indifference, and drew up a number of beneficial laws. Las Casas was rewarded for his zeal by the offer of the rich bishopric of Cusco. He refused it, but afterwards was persuaded to accept the bishopric of the Mexican province of Chiapa. But after some years he relinquished his dignity and returned to Spain, where he withdrew into the convent of Atocha in Madrid, and occupied himself until his death with the completion of his great work, "The Universal History of India." Of this work, which according to his directions was not to be printed until forty years after his death, only a small portion was published, but it has served as an important source of information to all historians of the age of discovery. Las Casas died at a great age in the year 1566.

The interference of the Government came too late for a great part of the New World ; blooming provinces had become barren wildernesses, whole nations had died out in a few years, and the small remnant were not to be saved from the fate that awaited them. Besides the countless victims that fell before the swords of the Spaniards, thousands were mown down by the diseases introduced into the land by the strangers, and thousands more languished and died under the burden of the hard labour to which their masters had subjected them. The gold mines of Hispaniola and the fisheries of Cubagua constantly required fresh labourers, and new relays were forced to take the place of those that died.

The gentle inhabitants of the Antilles, unsuited to a life of such hard work and fearful suffering, had no other means of freeing themselves than self-murder, to which they had recourse in their despair. Whole companies killed themselves by inhaling the vapours of some poisonous herb which they kindled near their hammocks ; and it was not uncommon for the whole native establishment of a settler to hang themselves together, delighting in the thought that they were thus reducing their tormentor to beggary. These wholesale suicides of the Indians quickly depopulated the Antilles of their aboriginal inhabitants. As early as 1508 the number of the natives of Hispaniola had dwindled down to 60,000 ; in 1512 there were only 20,000, and in 1514 only 14,000. Somewhat different is the account of Federmann, who, in 1530, on a journey to Venezuela, stayed some time in Hispaniola. He says : " The Indians are completely subject to the Christians, and serve them—as many, indeed, of them as remain—but their number is comparatively small ; for, as we understand, of the 500,000 Indians in the land when the Christians first discovered it, not more than 20,000 are now to be found. Numbers have perished from a disease called smallpox, some have fallen in war, and many have died from the hard work in the gold mines to which the Christians have forced them : for they are a gentle people, and unfitted for such toil."

But even if the numbers given by Federmann are too high, they still confirm the striking decrease of the population, which continued from year to year. In Hispaniola the native race died out immediately after the arrival of the Spaniards ; in Cuba it was completely extinct in the year 1548.

But on the mainland the energetic interference of Government was just in time to save the principal part of the aborigines from such a miserable fate. True, even here there were whole provinces utterly depopulated, such as Darien and Veragua, previously thickly inhabited; and under the leadership of hard-hearted men, such as Pizarro, Dalsinger, and particularly Pedro de Alvarado, the most terrible cruelties were perpetrated. Yet in the highlands of Mexico and Peru there still lived millions of the aborigines, whose lives and possessions were at length protected from the bloodthirstiness and avarice of their oppressors.

But the most stubborn resistance was offered by the Spanish settlers to the humane laws procured by Las Casas. In Peru it amounted in 1546 to open rebellion against the new Governor, Blasco Nunez Vila, which could only be pacified by Pedro de la Gasca. Also in Mexico there was a continual resistance on the part of the Spanish settlers, who felt their stolen rights infringed by being thus deprived of their property. Only by the stern interference of the Viceroy could the rebels be kept down; and as late as 1567 the descendants of the great Cortes were subjected to great persecution on the charge of having stirred up the discontented Spaniards to rebellion.

One inevitable consequence of the dying out of the native population was the introduction of the African negroes into the Antilles. Unfortunately the noble Las Casas himself recommended this shameful human traffic in his great zeal for the protection of the Indians committed to his charge. He bitterly repented when he discovered, as he himself says, that one law held good for the natives and the negroes.

The introduction of negroes was begun in the year 1520, and only two years later we hear of the first negro rising. The extension of the growth of the sugar-cane, and the decrease of native labour, made the number of slaves brought in in succeeding years much larger. In 1560 there were 30,000 black slaves on Hispaniola; and an Italian traveller even then foresaw that the island must some day fall into the hands of the Africans. The rest of the Antilles kept pace with Cuba ; but the mainland, in which there was still a native labouring class, was almost completely spared the plague.

Unfortunately the monstrous territory, with its inexhaustible resources, was ruled in the same narrow-hearted and small-minded way that had been shown in its discovery. From fear of the expense, the Government had relinquished the undertaking, and left the task of the discovery and conquest of the New World to upstart audacious adventurers, and then watched them most suspiciously, and brought charges against them until the power that had been promised them reverted to the crown. Nor did the government of the newly-conquered territories bear that stamp of a superior policy which it is impossible to deny to the rule of the Portuguese in India, in spite of the very different adversaries with whom they had to contend.

The discovery of a New World was valued like a rich mine, according to its produce in silver and gold ; and if the silver fleets came in safely and punctually, all was attained that was looked for. At the same time the spirit of monopoly continually increased. As the crown reserved to itself the trade in the precious metals, so it would have preferred to limit to the Castilians the advantages to be drawn from the rich lands. And though it was found impossible to exclude the other Spanish subjects, the New World was closed to Jews and Arabs, and the trade with it was confined to Seville and a few other favoured harbours.

This exclusiveness, which has nothing in common with the true work of a healthy colonial policy, went hand in hand with a systematic repression of the colonies. All independent action was suspiciously watched and suppressed. Even those born in the land, the Creoles, who were the largest landed proprietors, and constituted the upper classes in the towns, were excluded from every position of influence. The higher offices were conferred upon trueborn Spaniards, and even they were only left in office for a few years. No attempt was made to procure for the glorious lands a higher culture and a richer development; on the contrary, every advance was checked and all cultivation limited, in order not in the smallest degree to overstep the requirements of the mother country, and so bring down the prices.

The Indians felt themselves well off under the despotic government, which towards them took a patriarchal form, and the clergy served as a support. In a few years they had baptised all the natives ; and the people of the time were so convinced of the importance of the work, that even a Las Casas was of opinion that the benefit of baptism quite made up for the curse of slavery, and that the Indians had no right to be angry at a revolution which had brought them so great a blessing. But what kind of Christianity was it with which the Indians were inoculated ? At the present day many travellers testify that they belong to the Christian Church without any inward conviction, that they do not understand its doctrines, and have adopted nothing beyond the external rites, under which are concealed many links with the heathenism of their ancestors. Also the well-intentioned care which the clergy— especially the Jesuits—exercised over the converts had not a beneficial effect. The characteristics of the Indian nature— dependence, carelessness about the future, indifference with regard to a poor way of living, an utter want of ambition and emulation—all these weaknesses of the natives were strengthened by the guardianship of the law, by their being deprived of property, and by the training of the clergy ; while their tendency to idleness was fostered by the many saints' days. The fact that the nation considered it advantageous to fan the hatred between the Creoles and Indians had the same tendency.

Therefore it can excite no wonder that, after hundreds of years, when the colonies separated from Spain, the Indians were in the same, if not a lower, condition than that occupied by their ancestors at the time the foreign yoke was imposed upon them. But even the mother country has reaped no benefit from the possession of the richest provinces on the earth. The enormous influx of gold and silver into Spain, especially after the conquest of Mexico and Peru, at one and the same time crippled the trade and agriculture of the country, and raised the price of all the necessaries of life. While emigration into the great provinces on the other side of the sea almost depopulated the country, the people were poor amidst their treasures.

In the hands of its princes, especially of the gloomy Philip the Second, this was a powerful aid in their infatuated attempt to stop the wheel of time and gain new conquests for the exploded ideas of the Middle Ages. The result of the conflict is well known. Vanquished Spain was shut out from the rapid advance of the next few centuries; and when at length she could no longer resist the general stream, her transatlantic provinces, the sources of her wealth, broke loose. Cuba and Porto Rico alone could be saved from the general wreck, and their possession has been retained only by incessant sacrifices. And Spain herself, to whom is wanting all the training and development which the last few centuries has brought to other nations, is now struggling, amidst terrible convulsions and internal conflicts, to attain a new constitution and to shake off the inheritance which the great century of her discoveries has left to her. By her own fault, that has become to her a curse which might have been an inexhaustible source of blessing.

THE END.

BILLING AND SONS, PRINTERS, GUILDFORD, SURREY.